# THE REMBRANDT DECISION

## A PIA SABEL MYSTERY

### SABEL SECURITY #12

# SEELEY JAMES

Published by
Machined Media
12402 N 68th St
Scottsdale, AZ 85254

THE REMBRANDT DECISION: A Pia Sabel Mystery
First Edition, released January 18th, 2022
Print ISBN: 978-1-7373223-4-4
ePub ISBN: 978-1-7373223-3-7
Distribution Print ISBN: 978-1-7373223-5-1
Sabel Security #12 version 3.40

Formatting: BB eBooks
Cover Design: Jeroen ten Berge

# SEE THE SEELEY JAMES COLLECTION

International intrigue, neo-Nazis, corruption, and justice for the underdogs. Join the millions of fans who think of Pia Sabel and Jacob Stearne as old friends and give the series a full five stars.

## VISIT SEELEYJAMES.COM/BOOKS

### FOR COUPONS, PRIZES, MUGS, T-SHIRTS!

*This book is dedicated to all the adopted families in the world, and in particular the three-year-old girl who adopted me when I was nineteen:*

Nicole Marie

For more information on our adoption story, visit
seeleyjames.com/adopted

# CHAPTER 1

## PHIL, THE DEAD MAN'S STORY

FROM A FEW YARDS AWAY, my assassin waits for me to die. The finality of this situation is terrifying. I'm taking my last few breaths of life lonely and afraid, and there's nothing I can do about it. I've already been through four of the five stages of grief: denial, anger, bargaining, and depression. Now I've reached acceptance.

Five years ago, a guardian angel pulled me from the wreckage after I crashed into a bridge abutment. Last year, a quick-thinking nurse helped me survive a massive heart attack. None of that's going to happen this time. No one can save me. I'm really going to cross over. Alone.

My body is stuck in an awkward pose, half falling over on the bench. My right shoulder is hooked on something keeping me from falling on the ground. My gaze is stuck on the spot ten yards in front of me where the harbor waters lap against the park's edge. I want to scream but I can't. A hollow panic zaps through me like lightning.

My murderer leans over sideways at the waist, trying to catch my gaze, searching for my last flicker of life. A phone splashes light in my pupils. The light comes closer. Cold, narrow eyes dart around my face.

I try to say, *Not gonna take the murder weapon, are ya? Nah, someone might see you with it. Or are you scared of touching me? Ya coward.*

Summer air dances and eddies around my neck like an angel of death toying with me. I'll miss these earthly sensations when I'm gone. Maybe they have new ones where I'm going. Yeah. I'll learn to like the snap and sizzle of burning flames.

Damn it. Why kill me? Why not talk to me or threaten me or beat me up or chase me out of town? Why this?

The fingers of my left hand squeeze the bottle, a loving reflex, not an intentional command from my brain. The bottle. The signs were there from the beginning. No one in this town would ever willingly drink with me. When someone offers a fine bottle like this … I should've known. But I couldn't pass up a chance like that, could I? No. Not Phil Jacobsen. When the finest tequila in the world is available, I gotta have a taste. Fell for it in a second. And it was definitely the best.

Until that last slug.

My lungs take in air by the spoonful. My heartbeat is slowing now. Slower and slower and slower. My mind slides back into a dark pit of fear. What's next? Is there a reckoning in the afterlife? Is that why I'm so scared?

What was that thing Kitty said at the party last week? She stood on my coffee table posing like the Statue of Liberty, crowing like an actress on stage: *Alas, how terrible knowing the truth can be when there is no help in the truth.*

I laughed then. I get it now.

I know a truth that is indeed terrible. One little truth could destroy so many lives. It's not my fault I found out. I try to look at my executioner, but my eyes still won't move.

I changed my mind, decided not to tell anyone. The assassin doesn't know that. Didn't ask. Damn. I'll take this truth to the grave—a lot earlier than planned. Why? Because no one trusts me.

Sure, I have a few drinks now and then and wind up saying the wrong thing. So what? Who doesn't do that? Sometimes the truth needs to be told, and the sooner the better. Other times, it's been hidden so long, you can't let it out. This is one of those things that can't be let loose. I get that now. No one needs to know. I took care of it. I made sure no one would find out.

In my head, I scream at my murderer, *I helped you! Ya just don't know it yet!*

Story of my life. Hauled to the altar and needlessly sacrificed for the greater good. No appeals. No chance for mercy.

The storm passed by earlier. Rain washed the park, the bench, the sidewalk, the whole Town Harbor. The gales have calmed to a warm and humid breeze, heavy with salt and the ever-present scent of the sea. Helluva time to realize how beautiful our little town is. I guess there are worse places to die.

Beyond this little bench, invisible in the black of night, waves crest and burst over the wind-whipped granite breakwater like the slow beat of the Grim Reaper. Tons of water burst into the air with a boom before crashing back to the rock. It slurps back to the sea, where it silently gathers momentum for the next assault. Boom, crash, slurp, silence. The same boom and crash the secret will make when this town discovers the truth.

Poseidon alone knows what I left beneath those dark and surging waters.

I think my lungs have stopped working altogether now. How much longer do I have?

My poisoner gets closer still. A sharp tongue slithers out to wet the edges of that tight little mouth, then retreats like a snake into a lair. That brain, thinking, calculating, figuring the odds. With a turn toward the harbor, the killer straightens up and stretches. I hear a sigh. We both know it won't be long.

My vision dims. I feel dizzy. My mind tries again to speak. *I was gonna protect you—and this is how you treat me? You won't get away with it.*

That's a lie. I'm powerless. What can I do now?

A gust snaps the fabric of our clothes, the living and the nearly-dead. This is it. I muster all my faculties in one final effort. My last chance to say something. My last chance to even think something. I want to hurl the bottle. I want to scream. I want revenge. I don't want to die in vain. Fear hits me again with a harder fist, banging away at my conscious life. I feel as if I'm rising from my body, soaring into this dreadful night. I must try one more time. Try to leave a clue.

My right hand twitches in response to my mind's call for resources. My index finger is the last soldier willing to answer.

The oil of my finger will leave a water-resistant contrast on the wet bench, right? Like on a fog-wet window? At least, if they dust for fingerprints, they'll see it, right? I try to rub out a few words before my murderer faces me for the last time. I get one word scrawled out, *secret*. That won't tell the tale. I need more. I focus hard.

My last heartbeat thumps in my chest. The Grim Reaper's bony fingers squeeze me hard, letting me know I'm his.

I've been dispatched into the great unknown by a misunderstanding.

I must leave a better clue. I focus harder and get four letters. And that's it. My finger stops responding. I'm done.

Is it enough to be visible? Will someone see it? Will it make sense?

A big wave thunders across the rocky breakwater. A sign from the gods: time to go. My body remains on the bench while my soul slips under that retreating wave. I feel my consciousness disappear into the sea, down to the depths where I've hidden Uncle Vinny's treasure box, leaving behind all my worldly cares. I intended to keep the secret. But if murder was my reward, I've left half a clue. I hope someone will figure it out and unearth the sordid story. The truth always comes out.

# CHAPTER 2

## CHRISTINE, THE BAKER'S STORY

THERE IT IS AGAIN, THE rapping on the glass out front. More insistent this time. It isn't the wind after all. Someone is out there. At four in the morning? I shake the flour from my hands and grab a towel and push through the swinging door. I elbow the light switches as I pass them, illuminating the retail floor. Over the top of the cases, across the dining area, outside the front door, I see a tall young woman in stretchy athletic wear peering expectantly around the "Closed" sign.

Pointing to the earbuds jammed in her ears, she makes it clear she's on the phone. She gestures for me to let her in.

"We don't open 'til seven," I say.

"The police chief sent me," she says through the glass. "He told me to wait at Mom's Bakery until he can take my statement."

She steps back to double check the sign overhead.

I frown and think through how smart it is to let a stranger inside. If Scotty thought the woman was dangerous, he'd have kept her with him. Wherever he is. I see no squad car on the narrow street outside, so I guess I should let her in. Because Scotty said so. As if I have nothing else to do.

There is something familiar about the woman. Like I might know her somehow. I know everyone in our little village, but not her. Still, I recognize something about her. Twisting between the display cases, I make my way to the front. Before I wrench open the sticky deadbolt, I look up and down the street. The shops opposite mine are as dark and silent as tombstones.

"I'm alone," she says. Her gray-green eyes pierce me.

She's tall, that's for sure. Fit and strong as well. I snap the bolt back and let her in, shutting it quickly after she slips through. Her dark-blonde ponytail swishes past my face. Walking with the silky confidence of a tiger, she reaches the room's center and stops, concentrating on her call. Beat up running shoes cover her feet. Below her trim waist a fanny pack rides her hips, patterned leggings stretch to her ankles, and a purple racerback tank top doubles as a sports bra. Her outfit reveals every inch of her toned body without leaving room for interpretation.

I never wore anything more revealing than sweats in my prime. Couldn't give the men an excuse to get grabby. But nowadays young women will wear just about anything. My gaze reaches her face, where her eyes watch me as if she's reading my mind.

She holds up a finger, demanding my patience. Really? These millennials. Expecting us to wait on them hand and foot all the time. She says something to whoever is on the phone. You'd think she could take a moment to introduce herself or something.

Her voice is a bit strained and frustrated. She's in the middle of saying, "… and if that's the case, Madam President." She listens intently for a moment. "Is that a German expression? I'm not exactly fluent." She listens again. "Ah, *Die Daumen drücken*, to press the thumbs. I like that one. We say, *keeping our fingers crossed*. Well, as I said, something's come up and my people will call to reschedule later today. Please extend my apologies to the entire EU Council for me. I've got to go. Bye."

As I'm catching up with what kind of call that was, she pulls the earbuds out and shoves them and her phone in a thigh pocket. Her glass-smooth skin is taut over the muscles and bones of her face. Ah, to be young again.

I want to hate her until she flashes a warm smile full of white teeth. She leans forward, her eyes greedy for personal connection, and extends her hand. "Pia Sabel. Sorry for the intrusion, ma'am. I'm sure—"

Holy shit!

That's why she looks familiar. And why she's so fit. Her pictures don't begin to capture her presence. She was a soccer star before she inherited Sabel Industries. Now that I know who she is, I'm gaping up at her like a speechless, open-mouthed moron. But she's a day early. And it's four in the morning. And she's dripping sweat on my nice clean floor. Why the hell is Pia Sabel standing in my little bakery dripping sweat an hour before dawn? She's still talking.

"—and please, don't let me interrupt your day. Carry on with—"

"Why did Scotty send you over here?" I croak when my voice comes back. My neck hurts from looking up at her while she answers. I'm still reeling in shock when her words reach my brain. A murder. A body on the park bench by the harbor. She found him on her morning run. She called the police. Scotty came and took over the scene. Told her to wait in my humble bakery, the only place he knew would be open and dry at this hour.

Why would he do that to his poor mother? Why wouldn't he call me first? Let me know Pia-fucking-Sabel is here—AND SHE DISCOVERED A DEAD BODY! This is not good. Not good at all. We were supposed to impress her, not let her find a dead body.

She stops talking.

I fill the awkward gap. "That was an important call you were on. Do you need to get back to whoever that was?"

I'm dying to know who *Madam President* is, and it was the only thing I could think of to pry it out of her.

"That can wait." She sighs. "I was rescheduling, and it didn't go well. You know, my competitive nature ends up pissing people off and I spend most of my time smoothing rumpled feathers and soothing scorched egos."

"If it's any consolation," I tell her, "a bakery isn't about yeast and flour, it's about smoothing feathers and soothing egos."

We share a polite laugh. Sweat is pouring off her.

"Would you like a towel?" I ask.

Her eyes fall to the floor as if she just noticed the puddle around her shoes. "Oh, I'm terribly sorry. Starting to cool down here. Yes, please, that would be great."

I consider giving her the one in my hand, but it's covered in flour which would turn to paste on her skin. Trotting into the back, I grab a clean towel along with my phone. There's a text on it from Scotty. I reach for my glasses, get flour on them, and put them on anyway. It says he's sending Pia Sabel over to wait for him. *Try to show her some respect, Mom.* Nice. Text me too late and tell me how to behave. That's what I get for not spanking the kids when they were little. I drop the phone in my apron pocket.

I hand Sabel the towel and the first thing she does is squat to wipe the floor.

I say, "Oh, don't bother with that. I'll get it—"

"My mess," she smiles up at me. "If you have a mop, I'll finish up."

She rises and wipes her face, elbows, and other points where sweat runs off her.

Retrieving the mop and bucket, I bring it out of the back. She takes it from me without a word and mops as if she's done this before. How could that be? Who taught her to mop floors? But she does it as well as a union maid: first drenching the affected area with soapy water, scrubbing several times, before shoving the head into the wringer. Muscles pop out of her arms and shoulders as she shoves the handle down with force. She extracts a desert-dry mop and uses it to soak up the dirty water from the floor.

I've spent countless hours trying to teach that simple task to the help. They just snap their gum and roll their eyes.

"Sorry," she says. "I didn't mean to be rude when I came in, but I was in the middle of a call with Brussels. It's nine over there."

"No problem. I'll get this. Go on back to your call."

She waits until I meet her gaze, then says, "You're more important right now."

She turns back and scrubs some more, extending her work all the way back to the front door where she first tracked in. She leaves a clean swath on my floor that makes the rest of the space look less so. Pulling her phone out of the thigh pocket, she pushes the mop and bucket back toward me on its squeaky wheels, eyeing her phone the whole time. She wipes her face and neck again and tosses the towel on the wringer.

And there she is. The real Pia Sabel. Here's the billionaire I expected to see. She's dismissing me like a servant. Privileged and aloof, treating the rest of us like we're hired help. Cleans up after herself to feel good about it, then hurls the dirty stuff back at me to deal with.

I reach for the mop handle but her hand flies out and grabs it in front of my nose. She's thumbing something on her phone and holding the mop firmly with her other hand.

She finishes her text, pockets the phone, then gives me another smile. "Sorry, just had to tell my VP where I am. I'll be overdue in a few and I don't want her alarmed. Where is the sink? In back?"

I nod and gesture meekly, but she's already gone.

She pushes her way through the swinging door. With one hand she swings five gallons of mop water over the lip of the sink and empties it. Sensing the laundry bag in her peripheral vision, she tosses the wadded towel into the hamper like a basketball star. She rinses the bucket and rolls it back in the corner.

I lean my hip against my pride and joy: my solid maple butcherblock kneading table. My large and spotless, flour coated workspace. The heart of my operation.

As Sabel turns around, her eyes absorb everything in my kitchen and storeroom like a spy. I took over an oddly shaped space that used to be a speakeasy, giving me an expansive kitchen. Her gaze takes in everything as if she's committing it to memory. When she glances up at my secret ingredients shelf, I feel a little defensive. I keep the labels turned away to foil prying eyes. Can she see anything up there? I get the impression she has X-ray vision. Does that sound crazy paranoid? Yes.

Sabel catches me watching her and continues her sweep of my back room until she stops on Scotty's high school hobby: a framed insect collection. He gave up on it by tenth grade, so I had it framed and put it where I could see it and remember the inquisitive boy who grew up to be our Police Chief. Nosing in, she examines it as if she were a collector. She looks up with a smile.

Next, she turns to my little shrine to Sara tucked in the corner of my tiny desk. She examines the picture in the center. It's surrounded by paper flowers and hearts. It's the two of us taken too many years ago to count. We're grinning with the confidence of teenagers before the world hits you in the face with a baseball bat. And—I just now notice—we're wearing incredibly short cut-offs and skimpy halter-tops. Lots of skin showing. Lots.

"That's you?" she asks, pointing while turning to me.

"And Sara Vitelli." There's a moment of silence.

"I have a tribute like this to my mother," Sabel says. "Sara was someone special?"

"Best friend back in the day. I was going to be her campaign manager, make her mayor, then governor." I stop talking so I won't choke up.

Sabel touches my shoulder with caring fingertips. My first reaction is to shrug her off. I don't like sympathy. It pisses me off. But I don't do anything. It's a nice sensation to have someone care about you for a moment. Even if she is a stranger.

"Lost her to leukemia senior year in high school," I say. I have no idea why I'm telling her this. "Everybody loved her."

I take a deep breath. Sara's memorial has become background scenery over the years. I haven't really looked at it in a long time. I'm not keeping her alive. Truth be told, I don't want to think about her anymore. Too many things in this town went to hell after she died.

Sabel says, "I feel like I've added some stress to your morning. Can I help with the brioche?"

Somehow, the way she says brioche reminds me of our family trip to Boston's Little Italy when the kids were young. Scotty couldn't get enough of the Sicilian buns, so I learned to make them. It was the same trip where he took up bug-catching. I crane over my shoulder toward the balls of unfinished buns on the kneading table.

Sabel's eyes had been on the secret ingredients shelf when she asked. Why was that? Am I being crazy paranoid again? I need to calm down. Just because this young lady can make or break the future of this town shouldn't make me nervous.

Suddenly I remember the croissants are done and the buns should've gone in five minutes ago. I grab a pair of mitts, fling open the top oven, pull the first tray out, and toss it on the kneading table. They're dark. Not burned. The second and third trays are in the same shape.

"Thanks," I say as I work. "I've got this. Go on up front and wait for Scotty."

Grabbing the milk and egg wash, I slather it on the brioche.

Sabel hesitates a moment, as if considering challenging me. Baking is therapeutic. She gets that. Satisfied, she leaves. When I hear her scrape back a chair in the retail space, I peer through the glass in the swinging door. Facing the street, she twists in earbuds and makes a call.

I have an important call of my own to make.

I dial the mayor. He doesn't pick up. I click off and dial again. He picks up this time, groggy and pissed. I don't care. I say, "Rick, we've got a huge problem."

# CHAPTER 3

## CHRISTINE, THE BAKER

THE BRIOCHE GOES IN THE oven, the croissants move to the cooling racks, the sourdough rises on the kneading table, and then—finally—Mayor Rick Tara knocks lightly on the back door.

I open it. On the other side of the building, the sun rises over the Atlantic. The thick morning fog holds the sky to a dim blue-gray.

"Did you talk to her?" Rick says without coming inside. His stick-figure frame is always in motion, stiff and jerky like a flipbook animation.

"A little." I rest a shoulder on the door frame. The man doesn't have the guts to come in and talk to her himself. I can't blame him. Bedhead, unshaven, wearing a Patriots sweatshirt, he looks like he rolled out of bed for an emergency. Which he did.

"What did she say?" he asks. "Why is she here?"

"I didn't ask that. I asked if she wanted coffee. She did. Drank half a pot, black. No sugar."

"Why didn't you? That's what we need to know. You keep talking about how much we've got riding on this—"

"Well, I'm not going to just pop that question out, am I? Besides, I figured it out. She's here to see what Deeping, Maine looks like before the mayor and the Chamber of Commerce give her a choreographed dog-and-pony show."

Rick takes a step back as if I'd thrown hot coals at him. He presses his long fingers to his lips and shakes his head. "Did she see the Plant?"

"I don't know. But don't worry, Scotty chased the junkies out of there two days ago. Anyway, she said she was out on her morning run. Went to York and back on Shore Road."

Rick looks sick. "That's … more than twelve miles. At this hour?"

"If you'd read the briefing I sent you, you'd know she's an insomniac."

"I read it. I read it. It's just that … didn't figure on that kind of intensity, is all."

"Uh huh. Well, smoking weed, playing video games, and saying 'fuck it' all day might qualify you for small-town mayor, but if you want to be voted MVP in a World Cup and run a major international corporation, you're going to be extra-intense."

Rick shrugs.

I check him out. His hair looks like Boris Johnson's, going every which way at once, only jet black. Too black for a man in his late forties. Shoe polish, no doubt. It sure doesn't look professional. "Run home, shower, shave, and get back here. Walk in the front when we open and recognize her. Act like it's a pleasant surprise. Be a politician for once. Lick her boots and kiss her ass. We need those jobs, Rick. A thousand jobs. Engineering jobs that pay—"

"Yes, yes, I'm well aware, but … but I don't know how—"

As he speaks, I sense my son crossing the kitchen to me. I twist over my shoulder to find him in full uniform. I'm glad I made him get fitted shirts; they show off his muscular chest and thick shoulders. With any luck, Sabel will notice. But a uniform at this hour means he worked the night shift. Why? Because our town can't pay the going rate for good cops to stick around. Scotty peeks around my shoulder to see who I'm talking to. I push the door open so the light catches enough of our illustrious mayor to make him recognizable.

"Mom, could I have a word?" he says quietly.

"We don't have any secrets." I nose over at Rick.

Scotty sighs sadly, hooks one thumb in his cop-belt, the other hand reaches for my shoulder. "It's Uncle Phil."

"What'd he do this time?"

"No." Scotty looks at the floor. "Ms. Sabel found him in the park. Mom. Your brother's dead."

"Oh." I stagger back a step and feel all the air leave my lungs. He's dead. Really dead this time. He beat the odds so many times before, I felt like his luck would hold forever, but his lifestyle finally caught up with him. The reality of it hits me like a ton of bricks. My knees begin to give out. I draw a deep breath and steady on Scotty's arm.

I can't breakdown in front of them. They need my guidance at this crucial time. I'll grieve later, after we've landed the Sabel Research Center.

"So the day has finally come," I say with a quiet sigh. I pause to think and find my mind wandering. "I've been expecting just this kind of news for years, now it's here. Hell. It really happened."

"Mom," Scotty sounds surprised.

"What?" I ask. Then I get it. "Well, when your brother's a hopeless drunk, you have to protect yourself emotionally."

From his expression, Scotty doesn't understand that. I need to say more but I'm at a loss for words. Neither of us speak for a long stretch. I take in a long, deep breath. It leaves me with a whoosh.

Then I break the silence. "Guess it was inescapable. What was it, alcohol poisoning?"

Scotty's mouth falls open as he stares. "He was murdered."

"Wha … No. Nobody would want to kill him. Why do you think that?"

"Ms. Sabel found him. She said she smelled cyanide in the bottle he was holding. The county is sending a crime scene guy, there'll be tests, but she's right. He was holding a bottle of tequila that smelled like almonds. Tequila's not supposed to smell like almonds."

"How would she know what—"

"Mom." Scotty grips my arm and stares into my eyes. "Uncle Phil was murdered. This is my job. I'll handle it. Let's focus on you and the loss of your brother."

I turn to Mayor Rick, who's looking at me with big, sad puppy eyes. I resist the urge to slap him. There's work to be done. If we want to win the Sabel deal, we have to look like a town that can handle emergencies without falling apart. Then I realize he's just relieved he doesn't have to talk to the Sabel woman. Lazy bum.

A timer goes off in the kitchen. I push past Scotty, grab some mitts, and start pulling racks out of the ovens. Rick follows me inside, where he and Scotty stare at me.

"Mom," Scotty says, "you don't have to do all that now. I called Amy; she's got LeeAnn Pratt coming early to watch the kids. She'll be down here in fifteen minutes to open the shop. Just take a seat and breathe a minute."

"Don't bother her." I toss another tray of blueberry muffins on the counter to cool. "A woman who just left her husband needs her sleep. I don't need any help. I can run this shop just fine."

"He was your brother."

"And I've prepared myself for this moment since we were teenagers. If it wasn't one thing, it was bound to be another." Then I realize what's bothering him. I pull the gloves off and squeeze his arm. "All those fishing trips he took you on—you don't know how much I worried about getting you back in one piece. When he crashed into that bridge a few years back, I didn't worry about him—I thanked God he was alone."

"Mom." Scotty looks shocked. "He was murdered."

"Well, you'll find out who did it." I pull the gloves back on and go back to the oven. "Because you have to. And you have to do it fast, because we can't have Sabel thinking we don't have crime under control around here. The town's counting on you, Scotty."

He looks sick for a moment, then turns to Rick for help.

A quick peek in the oven shows me the popovers need another five. I slam the door shut and lean against the wall. "You know, Mike Tenenbaum and Joanne Ranzell saw him fighting with Crazy Kitty yesterday afternoon. He called me, drunk-babbling about something. I didn't have time for him. Then Crazy Kitty came over, but who knows what she's saying half the time, going on in Old English or whatever. Think that's important?"

Scotty shakes his head in disbelief, still in shock that I'm not broken up. Well, I'm not. More like I'm relieved. When the inevitable happens, it's a weight off your shoulders.

I nod at Scotty and say, "Did you interview her?"

"She took me through the crime scene. She knows her stuff. But I've yet to take her statement."

"Well, get to it then. I've got work to do. Say, when does Hartley's Mortuary open?"

He's still shaking his head. "There's going to be an autopsy first, and then—"

"I'll take care of that. We'll hold the funeral tomorrow. We should bury him and get this over with quick. We still have to show off the Plant to Sabel."

I hear Rick inhale with shock. When I turn to him, he says, "Surely, we'll cancel and reschedule."

"We're not rescheduling. When do you think you're going to see an opportunity like this one again? The Plant's been empty since Scotty was in high school. Besides, she's a big city girl. You think they don't have murders in DC? Hell, if you'd read my briefing, you'd know she survived a bombing in St. Petersburg and a shootout in Mumbai. She's not some babe for you to drool over, she's the rock that holds up Sabel Industries. We'll never get her back here, Rick. Keep to the schedule. Show her one little crime won't freeze our whole town."

You'd think I was chopping up babies with a meat cleaver the way the two of them are staring at me with bulging eyes and open mouths.

"An autopsy takes days," Scotty says.

"They only take a couple hours," I say. "I'll call Cheryl. She does them same day for the Jews, she can do as much for me."

"Who's Cheryl?" Rick asks.

"Cheryl Walton, the county coroner." I give him a dirty look. "Make an effort, Rick. Our county doesn't have the population of a Boston suburb—you can learn the names of the local officials. Now go get cleaned up."

He rolls his eyes and puts up his palms in surrender. He backs up a step before turning for the back door. Never should've trusted him with the job.

I turn to Scotty, "You need to do your part for this town. Solve this murder fast. And I mean fast. We can't have her thinking we can't keep crime under control. Shouldn't you be taking somebody's statement or something?"

# CHAPTER 4

## SCOTT, THE POLICE CHIEF'S STORY

MOM'S BAKERY HAS A FEW tables in the retail space. Ms. Sabel sits at the two-top by the window with her back to the wall. She shows no hint of fear or uncertainty.

When she sees me approach, she signs off her call and puts her phone away. I hang my official police jacket over the ladderback chair facing her, take out my pen and notepad, sit, and gather my thoughts.

My stomach's been tied in knots since I first realized the dead man was Uncle Phil. Now Mom's reaction has me twisted up even more. That was a shock. I guess Uncle Phil has been a lifelong disappointment to her, but he was always nice to me. This project she's working on—landing the SRC—has her wound up pretty tight. And she never lets anyone see a second of weakness. But still, she could take a few minutes for grief.

Ms. Sabel's eyes stare into mine as I have an odd thought: If something happened to me, would Amy get upset? Sure she would. We've always been as tight as any other siblings. But then, I'm not drunk before dinner every night.

Behind me is a sound I've heard all my life: Mom sliding baked goods into the glass display cases. Not for the first time, it feels suspiciously like she's eavesdropping. Something she did so often when I was in high school that I was forced to meet my friends at Danny's Diner out by the freeway.

"Thank you for waiting," I say. Sabel's gray-green eyes feel like ray guns pointed at me. "I know you're busy and have a lot of important—"

"Losing your uncle is hard," she says and lays a hand on my wrist. "Anything I can do to help is important."

It's the first nice thing I've heard someone say this morning. I feel a bit of stress leave me through her touch, like taking off the ballistic vest at the end of a long shift. I take a deep breath and try to remember what I was doing. My brain isn't working quickly enough.

I say, "Thank you for not saying anything to Mom before I could break it to her."

"Your mom … is she pressuring you?" she asks.

Her question takes me by surprise. Was Ms. Sabel listening to our conversation? No. When I came through from the back room, she was staring out the window and talking on her phone. As much as I try to hide my shock, I know I've failed by her knowing nod.

I hear Mom slam a display case shut and scurry into the back.

"You chewed your pen," she says nosing at my ballpoint. "The ink is halfway used up, meaning you've had it a while, but the teeth marks are fresh and there are very few of them, which means your angst is new, so I figured you're under some pressure to solve this crime quickly."

Right on all counts. Normally, I don't chew pens, but I've munched bite marks into this one. What she doesn't say is Mom is the only one who could've applied pressure since we last spoke.

"She's upset, said a few things." I take another deep breath. "Understandable. Everyone handles grief differently."

I look around the room. The store is hours from opening. No one on the street. I don't see Mom's shadow behind the swinging door. Finally, I can do my job.

When my gaze comes back to her, Sabel says, "Your mom doesn't approve of your new girlfriend?"

Once again, my expression gives away my surprise. I glance over my shoulder to make sure Mom's not in earshot, then say, "What makes you ask that?"

"A tiny smudge of lipstick on your collar that lines up with the trace on your neck when you turn to your left, which you did a minute ago. Your mom saw it and turned a shade darker."

My eyes squeeze shut at the thought of my next conversation with

Mom. "What makes you think she's a new girlfriend?"

"She wouldn't be marking her territory like that if she had confidence in the relationship. But then, maybe it's your mother who's making her feel territorial."

"It's none of anyone's business." I sniff and feel my jaw clench. "I'm a grown man and can date anyone I want."

"Well, we have something in common," she says and bites her lip as if she regrets bringing it up. "I'm having dating problems too. I bought the company where my boyfriend was CEO and now he's my direct report. Which you're not supposed to do in the corporate world. But when you work hundred-hour weeks, where the hell are you supposed to meet men? No one's figured that out yet." She blushes faintly. "Yeah, um, probably not the same."

I appreciate her attempt to connect by giving her a perfunctory smile.

I stretch my arms and adjust the notepad. "Tell me again about the footprints."

In silence, she pulls her phone out, leans it against the napkin holder, clicks on the video. She's recording us. She says, "I'll send you a copy. It'll protect us both against the swirling quirks of memory. Why don't I start at the beginning, is that OK?"

She's right. Standard procedure is to have the witness tell the whole story in their own words, then circle back. I don't know why I asked about the footprints first. I'm definitely a bit scattered. I nod.

Ms. Sabel faces the camera, states her name, the place, the time, the date, the topic we're discussing, and introduces me. I wave at the camera with a little embarrassment. I should've been the one to say all that. Too late now. With the formalities over, she explains how she mapped out a running route down to York and back. She was half a mile short of finishing her twelve-mile run when she got to Town Harbor. There she saw a man slumped on the park bench in the periphery of a streetlight's illuminated cone.

"He was in an odd position," she says. "One that indicated severe stress. The only thing keeping him upright was his shoulder twisted against the back of the bench. I was behind him and called out to ask if he was OK. There was no movement. Nothing. So, I walked up behind him and right away, I knew he was dead."

I hold up a hand to stop her. "How did you know he was dead?"

"Skin color. He had that unnatural gray in his neck and right cheek." She watches me and realizes I don't understand the gray part. "Without your heart pumping, gravity pulls your blood to the lowest level. In this case, that would be his feet. And his eyes were open, unblinking."

"You've seen dead bodies before?" As soon as the question leaves my lips, I regret it. The briefing Mom sent out had several paragraphs about the murder of Ms. Sabel's parents and later the shooting of her adopted father. Both incidents happened directly in front of her. I wince.

"Too many," she says quickly. "I touched his neck about here to check his pulse." She presses two fingers to her neck near the jugular vein. "There was no pulse. His skin was not yet as cold as the bench but not as warm as a living human. Rigor was setting in on his face, but not the rest of his body. So, I guessed he'd been dead a couple hours."

That's when she called 9-1-1. While she waited, she took pictures of the footprints, the tequila bottle, and the writing on the bench. She shows me the pictures again. I can make out what might be a few letters written in rainwater, but they're subject to more interpretation than abstract art. The footprints she refers to look like smudges in the grass. Some blades of grass have raindrops clinging to them and others appear to be clean. An inconclusive result. By the time the crime scene guy arrived, a paramedic and two officers had already obliterated any traces. She texts the pictures to me.

"Thank you," I say. "Now, what was it you said about the tequila?"

"Del Porto Extra Añejo, very rare. Twelve years old, aged differently from most *añejos*, in port wine barrels instead of oak. It gives them a rich flavor. And each bottle is hand-painted by an Italian artist. They're unique."

Once again, she stuns me. She doesn't look like an alcoholic, yet her grasp of this brand is suspiciously detailed. It was a unique bottle with a long slender neck, a fat, round bottom, and psychedelic art painted on the lower half. It looked like a genie might pop out of it. Before I can ask, she's read my mind.

"It's a personal favorite of mine," she says with a fleeting, apologetic smile. "I don't drink much, but when I do, I prefer *añejos* over whiskey or vodka." She anticipates my next question with equal clairvoyance. "*Añejo* is Spanish for aged. Silver and gold tequilas are the kind that make you sick in college. They're distilled and aged for a week or two. Gold is just food coloring. *Reposado* is Spanish for rested, representing the first step up in quality and flavor. They've been rested for a few months to a year. The *añejos* are around three years old. Anything older is labeled as extra or ultra *añejo*."

"And this brand is special?"

"One of the finest and most expensive. Your uncle had great taste."

"How expensive?"

"I don't stock my bar personally, so I can't be certain, but I think they're around two thousand a bottle."

My jaw drops. If Uncle Phil had two thousand dollars, he would've bought a hundred bottles of Old Crow. I stare at the picture. "You said the bottles are unique? Could we trace where this came from?"

"I don't know if they're traceable. The bottle shape is the same, but they're hand decorated. You could check with a local distributor."

"The same shape." I scratch my chin in thought. "Eady's has a bottle this shape."

"Eady's?" she asks.

"Bar up the street." I nod outside. "Kubari Eady had a big fight with Uncle Phil last summer and chucked him out. Accused him of stealing money out of the till and called me in. Things got ugly."

Come to think of it, that's something I need to investigate. Kubari had motive and access to plenty of liquor to entice Uncle Phil to Harbor Park. I definitely need to get on that angle. But first, I have one more question. "Why did you suspect cyanide? I mean, you told me about the smell of almonds, but how do you know cyanide smells like almonds?"

"It smells of almonds, not exactly like almonds. It has a distinct smell." For the first time in our conversation, she looks away. Her gaze crosses the street, checks her fingernails, then comes back to me. "There was an attempt on my life. A couple times."

"Did they catch the culprits?" I ask.

"There may have been some government involvement." She blows out a breath, reaches for the phone, pauses the recording. "I traced a money laundering problem back to Laos. Not everyone was a fan. Listen, this is a distraction, Chief Jacobsen." She presses record again. "The lab will tell us more than my speculation. Let's keep focused on the man in the park."

We talk a bit more until I can't think of anything else to ask her, so I conclude her statement, thank her for the recording, give her a card so she can keep in touch. I gather up my notepad and start to rise.

She puts a hand on my wrist.

"Follow the facts," she says. "Don't let other people pressure you into getting ahead of yourself."

It feels a like a jab at my professionalism and my anger flares. I try to keep the bitterness out of my voice. "I'll keep my own counsel, thank you."

"Should you be investigating the murder of a close relative?"

The correct answer is no, and we both know it. I grit my teeth. "Small town, small budget. I'm chief; I have seven officers, and one of those I picked up when he was fired from McDonalds."

She understands with a nod.

"I'm here through tomorrow afternoon," she says. "If I can assist in anyway, let me know."

"Thanks. I'll handle it."

# CHAPTER 5

## ISAIAH, THE BODYGUARD'S STORY

I SIT BOLT UPRIGHT IN bed, firmly grasping the wrist of the hand that just touched me. Only a few months out of the service, my battlefield experience still keeps me hyper-vigilant. I'm waking as I assess my immediate environment for threats: floor, ceiling, window, person. The person the wrist belongs to is Tania Cooper, Pia Sabel's best friend and head of personal security. Also my boss.

She rolls her eyes, tosses a bushel of her wild hair over her shoulder, and impatiently says, "Stand down, Marine."

"Yes, ma'am." I let go of her wrist.

"None of this 'ma'am' stuff." She hooks her bra together and slithers into a T-shirt. She turns back to me and twirls her finger at the rumpled sheets. "This … never happened."

I'm hurt. I thought we had something going on last night. We did have something going on last night. Maybe I hoped it would last longer. My mistake.

"It was my fault," she says. "Won't deny it. But it's never happening again."

"Hold on now, never say—"

"I am saying. Ain't no arguing about it." She stands to tug her pants up and cinches the belt. "I need you up and dressed in five. Pia's on her way back here. She'll shower and be ready for her day before you know it."

I blink and run a hand over my face, then steal a glance at my watch. "I only closed my eyes an hour ago."

"Two. Things changed since then."

I take a deep breath and wonder what I got myself into. It has only been two months since the feds inserted me as a mole into Sabel Security to spy on the company. Jacob Stearne, Pia Sabel's other best friend and head of special operations, uncovered my role as an informant, freed me from the fed's grip, forgave me, and—instead of tossing me out of a jet at 50,000 feet—inducted me into the inner circle.

Suddenly, I'm on my first tour with the company owner, Pia Sabel, and I'm still not sure if they trust me. I feel like I've been sent to the principal's office, but I don't know if it's a good thing or a bad thing. With Tania's moves last night, I was feeling included. Now, I'm not so sure. This could be one big joke and I'm about to be left naked on the side of the road for my treachery.

"What changed?" I ask as I pull last night's clothes off the floor. Tania doesn't look away.

"A man was murdered," she says.

"Did she do it?" I step into my skivvies. In the short time I've been with the company, nothing would surprise me about Pia Sabel.

"She found the body."

We hear the downstairs door open. Ms. Sabel announces herself and crosses the ground floor to the master bedroom.

Tania continues, "Pia's going to need you alert all day until Miguel can fly up here from DC. I told Emma—she's the special operations manager—that you're on point, so she'll get you anything you need."

"Wait a second. Where are you going?"

"Across the pond. Something came up in the UK."

That means she's leaving me alone with the owner of Sabel Industries. I met Ms. Sabel on an operation last week. Yesterday, Jacob sent me to Boston Harbor, where I joined Tania and Ms. Sabel on her yacht, the *Numina*. Yacht's the wrong word—more like *personal ocean liner*. It comes with its own submarine. Ms. Sabel and I have never really interacted. It's nice to get time to shine in the company's solar system, but without a clear sense of how things work, flying this close to the sun can melt your wings. I expected to have Tania's expertise to rely on for a week at least.

Hell, I haven't decided if I want to stay at Sabel. I'm overqualified for being a bodyguard. Is there a career path for me?

I pull my pants on and buckle up.

Tania watches and makes like she's not impressed. That doesn't stop her from talking. "I'm heading out. Like I said, you're in charge, white-boy."

She shoulders a backpack and turns for the door.

"I told you that's not funny." I tug her arm. "I get it. I grew up real cushy, but that's no reason for disrespect."

She's not intimidated. But a hint of regret falls like a shadow over her eyes. "You ever have to deal with any real shit?"

She's talking about overt racism. Tania climbed out of the bad side of Brooklyn, went to West Point, and rose to captain in the Army. A feat engendering nothing but admiration from me. I'm sure she's heard the N-word hurled in hate, and no doubt a lot worse. I didn't have it tough, and she knows it.

"Yeah, I had it nice," I tell her as I pull the sheets on the bed straight. "I lived in a rarified environment, son of a neurosurgeon, and yes, they make bank. I went to private school, hung out at Dad's country club, and never heard a white man toss an epithet. But then, rich people never disrespect you to your face. Once, a club member asked me to bring him some fries. I laughed."

I square the corners and tuck them tight. Once a marine, always a marine.

"I had my share of covert or subliminal racism," I continue. "Micro-aggressions, bad manners, whatever you want to call it. There were parties where I was the only kid in school not invited. Senior year in high school, a teacher asked me where I was going in the fall. When I told him Dartmouth, he asked, 'The college?' I wanted to say, *No, the gas station.* But I let it go. Just one of the many slights and minor indignities I'm sure you've endured. Another time, a cop pulled me over for driving while Black in our manicured suburb. His official reason was my taillight was out. It wasn't. I put my phone in my shirt pocket, camera lens out, and told him he was on Instagram Live. His attitude changed, he let me off as if he were doing me a favor."

I smooth the blankets.

Tania crosses her arms and leans against the wall. "Dartmouth, huh? Not exactly top of the HBCU list."

She's calling me white again, making it like I'm beneath her for not having suffered enough.

"We come from places with different expectations," I say. "In your world, *Dartmouth* means I done good; where I'm from, it means I'm showing promise. Not that it was all that hard. The minute I landed in rural New Hampshire, I had lots of friends. Every time someone pulled a camera out, white people I'd never met would call me over, 'Hey, Isaiah, get in this picture with us.'"

Tania laughs. "I got that shit from the admissions office at West Point. 'We're doing a shoot tomorrow, be there.' Like all six blacks, both Latinos, and our three Asians would show up and they'd pull in a couple rando white kids passing by."

We share a laugh.

"I saw some racism at arm's length in the Marines." I plump my pillows and lay them flat. "You know how the grunts come from all walks of life, all parts of the country, thinking they're hot shit but unprepared for a diverse environment. I'm sure it was the same for you in the Army. As an officer, you have to break up rapidly escalating situations and reinforce military discipline. How often did you have to explain to some snot-nosed high school kid why proudly displaying the flag of our nation's enemies—like the Confederate battle flag—was an insult to those of us who swore to serve the United States of America?"

"I was in the MPs, so I did that ten times more than you." She unburdens her backpack, fishes around in it, and comes up with a quarter. She flips it in the air.

We watch as it tumbles in an arc toward the bed. It lands without a bounce. Tania shakes her head sadly.

I'm not giving her the satisfaction since we both know bouncing a quarter off the bed ends after bootcamp. If the sheets are that tight, you can't get in.

When she realizes I'm not falling for it, she asks, "What about your service?"

"I was a Recon Marine, special forces." As an MP, she wouldn't be as familiar with the shooting end of the military. I explain, "In combat, you tend to care less about the color of a man's skin and more about the quality of his eyesight. One day you might find him in a position to save your life with a single trigger-pull. The last thing you want while he's taking aim is for him to remember an insult or a slur."

"Ever lose anyone?" she asks.

"One," I reply. "Jamil, the only other Black kid in my school, went to Penn. Junior year, he drove out to the suburbs to have dinner with his girlfriend and her parents. He never made it. The cop who shot him claimed he'd made a threatening move. I knew Jamil. He was a skinny nerd of the highest order. He could recite *Lord of the Rings* chapter and verse. He knew every line from every Black Panther comic book, movie, and TV show. The only threat he ever made was if you touched his action figures. The cop never gave a reason for the traffic stop. His body camera had stopped working earlier that night. He was not charged, nor disciplined."

"Never are," she says sadly.

I see it in Tania's eyes. She's known more Jamils than I. A lot more.

Wanting to end on a positive note, I wrap up my biography by saying, "Worst thing happened to me was when my frat brothers left me naked on the side of the road. But they did the same to all the pledges."

I don't laugh or smile.

She reads my face and shifts the weight of her backpack. "I hear ya, brotha. You might be as white as Pepperidge Farm cookies, but Ima let it go."

"Hey now. Don't be throwing shade on my Mint Milanos."

She laughs and play-punches my shoulder. We have reached an understanding.

I pull on my Henley. "Where did you say you're going?"

"Manchester."

"England," Ms. Sabel adds as she steps around Tania.

I never heard the boss come up the stairs. I've been warned about her rapid-deployment lifestyle. I get it now. Her hair's dripping wet, and she hasn't put on any makeup, but she's squeaky clean, wearing another skin-tight athleisure outfit from her endless collection, and she's ready to get moving.

Tania waves and heads out.

Ms. Sabel gives me a once-over, assessing my readiness. By way of explanation, she juts her chin towards Tania and says, "She's having long-distance romance problems." She raises her voice for Tania's benefit. "She's flying over there to propose to Detective Benton."

"Am not!" Tania rounds on the stairs and salutes Ms. Sabel with a raised middle finger. She shoots me an embarrassed glance before disappearing down the steps.

I choke on that one. Tania has a boyfriend in England? Where the hell does that leave me? Feeling used and abused, to be honest. Now I get why, *This ... never happened.*

Ms. Sabel laughs off Tania and turns back to me. "Grab your shoes. There's something I want to check out."

She stops mid-turn. Her eyes drop and focus on something under my bed. Sweeping a foot beneath the frame, she toes out Tania's panties. She looks at me.

I haven't been an employee long enough to know what is and isn't allowed at Sabel Industries. I don't care what happens to me. All I know is a ladies' honor is at stake. I swallow hard and say, "You would think this Airbnb's owner would pick up better than that before renting it out to us."

She eyes me like a drill sergeant before saying, "Uh huh."

# CHAPTER 6

## CHRISTINE, THE BAKER

WE GET A BREAK IN the crowd after ten. Amy's still talking to Michael Arnold, her old history teacher. The girl talks to everyone like she has all the time in the world. Naturally, I keep the coffee and muffins flowing out the door. How long should I give her before I start cracking the whip? She came home in tears two days ago with kids in tow, no job, no savings, and nothing nice to say about Mr. Perfect, expecting me to drop everything and coddle her. Well, I did that. I'm done now. Isn't it time to move on? I have things I've got to get done. Today.

"Mom, what's with everyone?" she asks after Michael leaves. "Didn't anyone like Uncle Phil?"

"Did you?" I wipe down the display cases.

People get so horny for my muffins and brioche, they want to squeeze them through the glass, leaving greasy fingerprints everywhere. I toss Amy an extra towel so she can help.

She slaps it over her shoulder and leans her elbow on the case. She says, "I loved him. He was tons of fun. Well. I know some people thought he was creepy, but he never did anything really bad."

"Thank God for small favors. What did Michael have to say?"

"Oh, he just asked about Gary and if we were getting back together."

"Are you?" I ask while wiping the glass all the way to the floor where the toddlers drool over the cinnamon rolls.

"Mom!"

"Well, it's always possible. A little forgiveness goes a long way, ya know."

"I'm not taking marital advice from you," she snarls.

"That was different." I'm wiping harder now, making squeaking noises. "He left us. Nothing I could …"

I let it go. I'm not getting drawn into that fight again. She always wants to blame me, make it all my fault, drag up her unhappy childhood, blah blah blah. I noticed she didn't go running to my ex's tiny two-bedroom in Boston when she left Gary.

Her phone, lying on the counter in front of me, buzzes with a text. It's from Al Devino and reads, "We need to hook up again. We had us some good times, Ames." Amy's hand reaches in front of my eyes and snatches the phone away. I sure hope her second cousin means to hook up as in meeting to talk or have drinks, not something else. She reads and replies to the text with her back to me.

"Oh! Mom!" Amy says with bright excitement. "Did you see Pia Sabel's bodyguard?"

"Yes!" I nearly squeal with girlish glee remembering the hunk. In unison we say, "He looks just like—"

Amy finishes with, "Michael B. Jordan."

And I say, "Denzel Washington."

We look at each other in disbelief and again speak in unison, "Who is that?"

The doorbell dings as someone comes in. Amy turns and says, "Oh, hey there, Mr. Peabody."

I have calls to make. I push through to the kitchen and pick up my phone. Damn thing is covered in flour. Like always. After wiping it off, I call Cheryl. This time it doesn't go to voicemail.

"County Coroner's office, Dr. Walton speaking."

"Hey, Cheryl," I start, but she cuts me off.

"Oh, Christine, I'm so sorry. He was such a nice man—"

"If he was such a nice man, how come I had to pay for your garage after he plowed through it at two in the morning?"

"That was a long time ago. They put up a guard rail on that curve since then, and—"

"Are you busy?"

"Not for you, Christine. What is it? Anything you need, I'm here for you."

"I need a Jewish autopsy."

"A what?"

"Whatever you call it. Same day. I want to get him cremated and planted tomorrow. Hartley's has an opening at eleven."

"First of all, no one would ever call it a Jewish autopsy. Don't ever say that …" She leaves a long silence that ends with a huff. "And I, I, well, I can't just drop everything and do it on a moment's—"

"You said you weren't busy and at Lyn's birthday you said you could do an autopsy in two hours." I hold the *anything you need* quote in reserve.

She says, "After a few drinks with the girls, I might've bragged a little more than—"

"Listen, Scotty thinks Phil was poisoned and—"

"What?"

"—and I'd like to know sooner rather than later. That Sabel woman is in town, and it sure would look great if he could solve this case while she's here giving us the once-over."

"First of all, Maine has a law prohibiting cremation in less than forty-eight hours of death. Second, if Phil was murdered, I'll need to do a lot more complicated toxicology—"

"But you can still get it done today, right?"

Cheryl leaves a long silence this time. Long enough for me to check my phone, make sure we're still connected. Then she makes the right decision. "Sure thing, Christine. It's important that you find out what happened to your brother. And I'd be happy to help Scott's investigation."

"Thank you, I appreciate it."

"One question, though." She hesitates before adding, "What's she like?"

"Who?"

"Pia Sabel."

"She's a real bitch. I can't put my finger on it, but she was too nice. Dropped a call with important people in Europe to talk to me. Did the same for Scotty. Since when do rich people do that? And she notices everything, you know? She sees things everybody else misses. Too many things. It makes me suspicious."

"What do you mean, she sees things?"

"She could tell Scotty's been seeing Boo-Boo Vitelli again and keeping it from me."

"Oh, Christine. Scott's a grown man. So what if he's seeing an older woman? Besides, Boo-Boo's a hottie."

"You know about her troubled—"

"No one's going to be good enough for Prince Scott in your eyes. Let it go. Anyway, I don't see what makes Pia Sabel suspicious."

"Well … she's the one who found Phil."

We argue that one for a few minutes before I point out that she'll need to get the crime scene guy to release the body. Which means she needs to get to work. We click off.

I tap the phone against my chin while I consider the funeral arrangements. If I take Hartley's opening at eleven, I'll need Phil's remains. But we won't have him cremated for two more days. Damn. Maybe I could borrow a casket from them. No way. Stacy Hartley would make me buy it—or charge me an outrageous rental fee. Undertakers are worse than car dealers.

Wait a second: I never had my mother's urn engraved. I could just use that and tell everyone it was Phil. Who would argue with me?

Amy, that's who. She'd notice it missing from the kitchen counter and tell everyone.

Since I'll need to buy an urn anyway, I'll just buy one and leave it empty. Yeah. That'll work.

I hear Scotty out front, talking to Amy. I'm sure they're talking about me and how cold I am about Phil. There are more important things than Phil going on right now. They don't realize how this town might fold without the Sabel Research Center. We don't want to end up like Detroit and lose 30 percent of the population in twenty years. We need to work hard at winning the SRC so we can add a quick 30 percent instead. People who make more in a month than the average Deeping resident makes in a year.

Lyn Avery comes in the back door without knocking. She runs to me and hugs me.

"I just heard," she says. "I'm so sorry. Phil was such a sweet, sweet—"

"Who are you talking about?" I bump her out of the hug. "The same Phil who cornered you at Eady's and demanded you show him your tits?"

"Oh, Christine, he was drunk, and that was a long time ago. It's all water under the river."

Ignoring her malaphor, I ask, "How come we let men off with 'he was drunk' but we get called sluts whether we show 'em our tits or not?"

"You're right," she says, "he could be a bastard after a drink or two. Which was … a lot."

"You got my message?" I ask.

"Yes."

"Did you call everyone to see if they read it?"

"All anyone wants to talk about is Phil."

I want to scream. I push her back to the door. "Lyn, everyone needs to know their talking points. They need to actually read them and say them back to you. You need to hear them say the words. Push them a little. Test them. You chair the Chamber of Commerce, for Christ's sake, you need to make sure they don't act like flower shop owners who never drove farther south than the New Hampshire border."

"But they are flower—"

I push her out the door.

Movement behind her gets my attention. At the end of the alley, Pia Sabel is standing inside the dumpster tossing things around as if she were one of our bag ladies, scrounging for clothes or food. What the hell is a billionaire doing in a dumpster?

Lyn doesn't notice. Instead, she takes two steps, turns and says, "Don't you worry, Christine. I'm on it like rice on white."

When I turn around and head back inside, Scotty's in front of me. "How are you holding up, Mom?"

"I'm holding up just fine. But I'm worried about the Plant. You and Rick are giving Sabel a tour tomorrow afternoon and Phil was supposed to have it cleaned up. Have you checked to make sure it's ready?"

"Mom, I'm in the middle of a murder investigation."

"I know." I leave my mouth open to emphasize the last syllable. "Rick still has to give the tour and it has to be clean. If it isn't, we need to get the Larson kid over there to start sweeping up needles and spoons."

"I'm in the middle of *Uncle Phil's* murder investigation."

I exhale my exasperation while I sort through options for getting things done. I could point out that Phil will still be dead after Sabel leaves town. I could tell him to round up someone like Crazy Kitty and charge her with the crime. If she didn't do it, he can let her go—after Sabel leaves.

That's when I get it. I know what'll work. I say, "Phil was supposed to clean the place up yesterday. There might be clues in there."

# CHAPTER 7

## SCOTT, THE POLICE CHIEF

WHEN I ARRIVE, I FIND my newest recruit, Kathy Butler, examining the rusty playground equipment at the top of Harbor Park. I hail her from a few yards away. She waves. When I get close enough, I ask, "Find something?"

"Oh, no." She waves a hand at the seesaw. "I was waiting for you. Didn't want to mess up the crime scene and this looked like a safe place. Doesn't look like anyone's used it in twenty years."

A flash of nostalgia grips me for a second. "Mom's first foray into politics. When Amy and I were toddlers, there were no playgrounds in town, so she went to the city council and beat on them until they installed all this. Doesn't look like anyone's cared about it since we aged out."

She nods and looks away.

Harbor Park is a grassy couple of acres sandwiched between two thin brooks that trickle into the marina. If Amy stays longer than a week, Mom will make the council refresh the playground for her grandkids.

I wave toward the bench where Uncle Phil was found, and we start down the gentle slope. Puffy white clouds drift overhead, the air cleansed by the rains. The afternoon sun is warm on our skin.

"I'm curious," Kathy says in a hesitant voice. "I've only been with the department for a few weeks, and this is a murder investigation. The other guys have a lot more seniority. Why did you ask me here?"

"You graduated from the Providence Police Academy," I tell her.

She pops a quick look at me. "Didn't any of the other guys—"

"Nope."

She laughs. "The academy taught basic investigation skills but nothing like what we need here. So, really, why me?"

I look into her eyes and sense some anxiety. She's a good-looking woman. Young, trim, and fit, with olive skin and dark eyes. It takes a minute to figure out what she's worried about. "I never asked you why you were so quick to move from the big city to our little village for half the pay. Sounds like you had problems with superiors making unwanted advances. Maybe something worse. Only time will prove my words, but I promise you, Kathy, I look at my officers as family. You're safe with me. If anyone steps out of line, tell me. If you can't tell me, you can talk to my mother or Lyn Avery."

"OK," she says in a less-than-convinced voice.

"And," I add, "I have a girlfriend who'd kill me for flirting."

"C'mon, I've met Boo-Boo," she says sheepishly. "She's really nice. And she thinks you're pure sunshine."

Kathy's smart enough not to mention the age difference. I appreciate that. We stop a few yards short of the bench where Uncle Phil was found.

She asks, "They made you chief because you're the only one of us who went to college?"

"Yep." I let out a little laugh.

"You said, 'time will prove my words.' Kinda odd phrase for a small-town chief. Does that mean you were an English major?"

That makes me really laugh. "English Lit, to be precise. I always wanted to be a cop, but thought I'd write a few novels and get famous first. And since I'm here in uniform …"

It's Kathy's turn to laugh.

We look over the bench and grass. Everything's been disturbed by the crime scene guy.

"Why do they call it Deeping?" Kathy asks.

"That wall of polished granite out there." I point two hundred yards out to sea where the last ice age left a chunk of rock half a mile long and fifty to a hundred yards wide. "It's a perfect natural breakwater. When Europeans arrived four hundred years ago, it formed a harbor. Deeping became a prosperous fishing village. As time went on, and civilization powered into the Industrial Revolution, ships' drafts got deeper. Our big rock trapped silt and sand behind it, making it a liability. Portland and Boston had better ports and became favorites for the Steam Age. So they called it Deeping for marketing purposes."

"False advertising?" she asks.

"Keep an eye on the breakwater though," I warn her. "At low tide, the surface is high and dry. Fishermen go out and cast from there. But at high tide the waves slosh over the top. In stormy weather, the slow-to-leave have been carried out to sea."

To the west of us, the Deeping River runs a crooked path into town. Main Street follows the river until it reaches the revitalized Town Harbor where Kathy's gaze has landed.

"Classy harbor, right?" I ask her. "After the Great Recession, when Mom was mayor, she snagged some of those federal rebuilding dollars and got the streets paved in brick, the sidewalks trimmed with that fancy cement, and those reproductions of nineteenth century gas lamps."

"She did well. No wonder everyone speaks so highly of her."

People do speak highly of her—to her face. Her pushiness is the usual topic behind her back. But it's nice of Kathy to butter me up.

"Well," I say, "it's certainly a step up from the swampy, algae-choked harbor of my youth. It was supposed to make our town as attractive as Kennebunkport for summer tourists and wealthy yacht owners."

"How's that going?"

"The Plant killed any cachet we might've otherwise earned. Colossus of Rhodes it is not."

We turn to face the ugly pile of dark, slimed bricks leaning over the harbor entrance like a leering drunk.

"A few big yachts stopped by over the years," I continue. "Aside from those anomalies, Deeping is the summer destination for Maine's dirty-collar class: the school janitors, bus drivers, and garbage men who can't afford the expensive hotels and beaches in the prettier beach cities."

I don't give her the full picture. There were some who prospered and others who didn't. Mom's Bakery became a landmark. Same for Eleanor Andersen's trove of one-dollar knickknacks at the Sand Dollar. Olivia Benton's Fine Art struggles—even with velvets.

"Why is it called 'the Plant?'" she asks.

"Guess it was a manufacturing plant at some point. It was a recycling center when I was a teenager. It's been empty for nearly twenty years. The town council offered it up for free in their proposal to Sabel Industries for the SRC."

"Is she going for it?" Kathy turns her hopeful face to me. "Sabel, that is. I hear she's really something."

"What do you mean?"

Kathy leans in with a conspiratorial whisper. "They say she killed that Russian spy. Shot him nine times."

She sways back with deep admiration in her gaze.

"I don't know if that's ever been proven," I say. When Kathy looks disappointed, I add, "But she did kill those active shooters in front of the White House. That was on video."

"Well, yeah, obviously. That was necessary though."

I do a doubletake. Her answer has me wondering if Kathy is the right person to lean on as my top lieutenant.

"So." I take a deep breath to signal the change to work mode. "We're here to think through what happened to Phil. I figured two heads are better than one. How did he wind up in the park?"

We look around the area, both of us thinking for a moment.

"From his house," I offer, "Phil would've walked past the Plant, crossed the footbridge over the creek, and stopped here. Why the park? Was he on his way somewhere else? Was this where his killer asked to meet? Or was this where their paths crossed incidentally?"

Kathy twists one way then the other. "I saw him up at Eady's a few times. He always ducked out early though."

"He's been going back to Eady's?" I'm surprised. "I thought he'd been banned from there."

She shrugs.

Kubari definitely had means and motive. I'll make interrogating him a priority.

"Liquor store is in the opposite direction, though," she adds.

"He had that fancy tequila. Didn't need a store."

"Oh, right."

"Someone lured him here," I say. "He was a sucker for top-shelf liquor."

"Someone who knew him that well?"

"Everyone knew him that well. It's a small town."

"Did you find the keys?" Mayor Rick's voice calls to me from the Plant.

I hold them up and wave them at him, indicating I'll join him shortly. I turn back to Kathy, "That's why I asked you here. Fresh eyes on the town and the people. I need to follow up over at Eady's. Go see if the crime scene guy is done with that bottle. I'm going to need it."

# CHAPTER 8

## SCOTT, THE POLICE CHIEF

I MARCH UP THE PARK'S rise toward the stone footbridge, a hundred yards away in the foxtails. Halfway there, I lose my patience and jump the narrow streambed instead of walking the extra fifty yards. My leading foot lands in mud. I suck the shoe out and keep going, wiping the excess on the weeds until I come out near the Plant's parking lot.

Somewhere during the day, Rick changed into black slacks and a collared shirt with the sleeves rolled up. Business shoes adorn his feet. Mom must've given him a talking to about fashion now that Ms. Sabel is loose in town. He joins me mid-stride and asks, "You're dropping everything to clean this place up?"

"No. I'm investigating my uncle's murder. Right now, I'm going to check it out and see if I need to close it as part of the crime scene or release it to you to clean up for tomorrow's VIP tour."

"What, I'm the janitor now?" he asks with attitude.

I stop to unlock the door and take the opportunity to face him. "Unless you're qualified to take over the murder investigation." I wait for him to sink a notch. "But Mom says you can hire the Larson boy. He's got a girlfriend and needs gas money."

"OK, I'll figure it out." Mayor Rick nods his acceptance of Mom's terms.

I open the door and find Pia Sabel standing next to a young USMC veteran. I can tell Marines by the ramrod-straight backbone and superior air in their laser-guided gaze. This guy is taller than average, with thick, solid shoulders, and a trim physique. The pair stand in front of a heap of discarded industrial items, the leftovers from the last tenant. Rusty cans, broken shelves, opened and spilled containers of who-knows-what are scattered around an area where the junkies and vandals picked over them through the years.

"Uh, you can't be in here," I say.

"Why not?" she asks.

"What are you doing?" I ask.

She looks at Rick. "You're the mayor, I presume? Pia Sabel, and this is my advisor, Isaiah Reddick."

She paces toward us with a shiny smile and her hand extended. The Marine, her advisor, shadows her on the left.

Rick freezes with wide eyes. I elbow him.

He stirs like a man snapping awake. "Pleased to meet you, ma'am. I'm Mayor Rick. Well, that's what they call me these days. Actually, it's Rick Tara, but you can call me Rick. Or Mayor Rick. Whatever you want, really. I, um …"

He turns red.

She shakes his hand and turns him over to her advisor.

"It's a pleasure to meet you, Mr. Mayor, sir," he says.

Yep, he's a Marine, alright.

She faces me. "You came from the park. Did you find anything interesting?"

Too late, I react by moving my muddy shoe behind the clean one. I don't know why I'm doing it; she already figured out how it happened. But it puts emphasis on my question. Why is she in here?

In my experience, the rich sit on a secure perch looking down on the rest of us, amused by our daily struggle and rush. They get away with all kinds of things. It occurs to me that Ms. Sabel's attitude might be an act. How do I know they weren't her footprints in the park? But then, what motivation would she have to kill Uncle Phil? Maybe she did it to prove she could get away with it.

Maybe I'm grasping at suspects because I don't have any.

"I was surprised there wasn't any crime scene tape covering the hole in the wall." She gives me another smile, this time curt and perfunctory. She waves a finger in the direction of a hole in the bricks—big enough for a motorcycle to drive through—around the corner from the front door. Her gray-green eyes swing back to me with their unsettling intensity.

"Why would I need crime scene tape?" I ask.

"It might be the source of the cyanide."

"I'm sorry, why would there be any—"

"According to our site research, this was Duggins Computer Recycling until 2003, right?" She waits for my nod, then turns to the pile of junk. "Recyclers of that era often used industrial cyanide solutions to separate the gold used on circuit boards before illegally dumping the other parts in the ocean."

She's referring to why Duggins went out of business: they took shortcuts and got caught dumping computers on the other side of our granite breakwater. The state yanked their contract and sent the recycling to Malaysia where it was dumped in someone else's ocean. Duggins folded.

"Why did you research cyanide?" Rick looks pleased after asking his first relevant question of the day.

"We looked for a thousand other potentially hazardous waste problems as well," she answers. "We've no intention of getting involved in a location that could be held up for an EPA cleanup."

Rick and I share a glance. Neither of us had considered the EPA. Duggins removed the asbestos back in the day, so we figured that was it. I had no idea they were panning for gold in the old boards. Or that cyanide was involved.

She points to what used to be a blue steel drum, now half rusted-out. It has several things unartfully stenciled on the side: skull and crossbones, "Sodium Cyanide," "NaCN," and "Made in China." It's empty. But Ms. Sabel has a point. There could be more elsewhere.

Rick starts acting like the mayor. He says, "We'll have this all cleaned up before—"

"It doesn't matter. This place should be demolished."

Rick shakes his head. "This is a historic building. We can't demolish it."

"The fact that it's still standing is an accident of chance, not due to any structural or architectural significance. Its only historical value will come after its inevitable collapse on its unofficial residents." She points to the detritus of the junkies: a disgusting mattress, parts of sleeping bags, burned tinfoil, ash piles from small fires. "If the town's insurance carrier ever did an inspection, your rates would triple. Better to have it condemned and torn down."

"Oh," is all Rick can say.

A presence darkens the official doorway. The silhouette of our local bag lady stands at the threshold. She shouts, "Alas, how terrible knowing the truth can be when there is no help in the truth."

"Not now, Crazy Kitty," I call out.

Ms. Sabel gives me a sharp look, a visual rebuke. When she gets to know Kitty better, she'll understand why we call her crazy. Until then, I should mind my manners.

It occurs to me that Crazy Kitty was my uncle's favorite drinking buddy. I cross the open space toward her. "Kitty, come over here. Did you see Uncle Phil last night?"

"I shall go home," she says. "If thou wilt consent."

Four flannel shirts, torn men's trousers with a rope belt, and brand-new sandals cover her skinny frame. The sandals have Eleanor Andersen's Sand Dollar logo on the strap. Eleanor doesn't let her go barefoot. Her shoulder-length dark hair is so dirty it sticks out in places. She still hasn't gotten her front teeth replaced.

"Come here," I say. "I just want to ask you a couple questions."

She takes a few steps inside, stops, and points at me. "Most easily wilt thou bear thine own burden to the end, and I mine."

"Whatever. Where were you last night?"

"At my house."

It's nice to see she can speak regular English when she wants to. Rick and the others approach slowly as if Crazy Kitty were easily spooked. She is.

As is often the case with Kitty, I start losing my patience—my voice gives it away when I repeat my question. "Did you see Phil?"

"No, he's dead." She stares at me blankly. "Your mother told me. Sad day when the good are killed for being good."

"Did you see him last night? Answer me."

"Thou blamest my temper, but seest not that to which thou thyself art wedded." She backs up two steps, her usual prelude to running away.

I take a deep breath and think up a different approach. "Come on, Kitty. He was a friend of yours. I'm trying to figure out who killed him. Damn it, I need you to tell me if you saw him last night."

"I will pain neither myself nor thee. Why vainly ask these things? Thou wilt not learn them from me."

"You have to answer, Kitty! This is an official murder investigation. If you know something, you have to tell me. What is it?"

"Nay, I see that thou, on thy part, openest not thy lips in season: therefore I speak not, that neither may I have thy mishap."

From behind me, a man's voice says, "Sophocles."

Crazy Kitty cackles with her big toothless grin and points at Ms. Sabel's advisor. We turn to him in unison. As soon as I take my eyes off her, I hear her bolt.

"Jesus," I say as Kitty disappears across the parking lot and into the bramble by the brook.

"Go get her," Rick says.

"Be my guest." I wave an arm at the door. "She's quick and knows every culvert in the village."

Ms. Sabel's gone in a flash, running with speed I've never seen before. I know she was an athlete, but her acceleration is shocking. She catches up with Crazy Kitty in a few strides. She stops and says something, but they're too far away to hear what. Kitty tears off sideways. Sabel is on her again instantly. But as they run stride-for-stride, Kitty jumps in the air and lands both her feet on Sabel's ankle. Sabel falls. Crazy Kitty runs through the foxtails and gets away.

We rush to Ms. Sabel's aid. She gains her feet but immediately hops on one foot and says, "Fuck!"

I offer her a shoulder to lean on.

She says, "Thanks, I'll walk it off."

Gingerly, she takes a step and limps a few more. Everyone knows she was a world-class soccer star—one of those athletes who shake off injuries that would send the rest of us to bed for a week—but this looks worse to my untrained eye. I resign myself to trust her expertise. Her advisor shoves his shoulder under her arm, and they limp with us back to the Plant.

When we get inside, I ask the Marine, "What did you mean about Sophocles?"

"I think she was quoting the ancient Greeks. Sophocles or maybe Euripides, I forget which. It sounded like Tiresias refusing to divine the plague on Thebes. *Alas, how dreadful to have wisdom where it profits not the wise!* Or something like that, depending on the translation. It means, what she knows is more of a liability than an asset to her. That last thing she said means she knows the truth but if she tells you, it will be your problem."

All three of us are silent. Dumbfounded to be honest. Even Ms. Sabel looks surprised.

He shrugs. "I took a semester of Greek tragedies in college." When his boss's mouth falls open, he explains, "Great way to meet women." With a sheepish look at the floor, he adds, "They were a bit too Goth for me, though."

At our feet, a pack of matches lies next to a bent spoon. The matches have Eady's logo on them. Everything so far points to Eady's. I pull an evidence bag out of my pocket and, without gloves handy, gingerly coax the matches into the bag.

My phone rings, a call from Kathy Butler, my top officer. When I answer, she says, "The crime scene guy released the tequila bottle you wanted. He said the chemical analysis will take a few days, but he agrees: cyanide's a good bet."

"Bring it and meet me outside Eady's. Then go to the Plant with some gloves and evidence bags. Take Steve. I found an empty barrel of industrial cyanide here. I need you guys to go through the building and see if there are any other containers lying around. Bag it and send it to the lab for comparison."

"Yessir."

As I sign off, I notice it's nearly four. The bar should be open. It's time I paid Kubari Eady a visit and tell him I found his missing bottle of Del Porto.

I face Ms. Sabel and think up the most diplomatic way to say what I need to say next. "It was nice to see you again. In the future, should you have any ideas about where to look for evidence, I'd appreciate a call first."

"We have a consulting division that helps police departments convert to community policing." She tries to catch both Rick and me in her gaze while keeping her weight off the injured foot. "It's a method that's less confrontational, friendlier, lowers budgets, involves the community, and leads to lower crime rates."

A sales pitch. Great way to deflect that she's intruding on my investigation. She's clever, I have to give her that.

Rick starts to say we can't afford consultants, his usual answer to anything that costs money, so I cut him off. "That's interesting. Anything that stretches my budget sounds great. Where can I find out more?"

"I'll have my people call you."

I give her a polite goodbye-nod and stride for the door.

Rick has sense enough to try engaging her in conversation as I leave. But nothing stops Ms. Sabel. Limping badly, still leaning on her advisor, she leads Rick and his discussion in my direction. She's following me.

# CHAPTER 9

## ISAIAH, THE BODYGUARD & ADVISOR

MS. SABEL KEEPS A POLITE banter going with Mayor Rick while I help her limp a hundred yards behind Chief Jacobsen. He's walking a quick clip through the few blocks that make up the business district. It's almost like he's trying to lose her by taking advantage of her injury. The Chief glanced over his shoulder a couple times at the beginning but hasn't bothered since. He no longer cares that we're following him. He stops at a squad car parked in front of a restaurant. He takes a clear plastic evidence bag holding a funny-shaped bottle from his officer, then heads inside.

The squad car leaves the parking lot, rolling slowly toward us. Two officers have their eyes locked on me with a typical mixture of hostility and suspicion. When they see the mayor with me, their attitudes improve, they nod at him as they reach us, then accelerate after they pass.

Ms. Sabel scowls at them, turning to watch as they drive away. I almost say, *Welcome to my world*, but don't need to. Tania's been by her side for years. It's nice to know the company owner is aware some white people feel threatened by the presence of someone different.

Mayor Rick is reciting facts and figures about the town like an automaton as we approach the gray clapboard building with white trim. It looks like a large house, Nantucket modern. Six windows sit on either side of an oversized front door. Neon signs announce all three dialects are spoken here: Budweiser, Miller Light, and Pabst. EADY'S BAR AND GRILL is writ large across the front door's canopy. In smaller letters centered below, BBQ defines what kind of grill. The owners have carved out a niche in this neighborhood. Every other restaurant I've seen serves seafood.

The scent of roasting pork permeates the air—and suddenly, I'm starving.

Ms. Sabel limps ahead of me, opens the door, and, after a quick glance, hops aside to usher in Mayor Rick. As I follow, she leans in and says, "Take any initiative you see fit with Chief Jacobsen."

I look at her, a little confused. When my eyes adjust to the interior, I count seventeen midafternoon patrons scattered in a room big enough to squeeze thirty times that. There is evidence in the worn floorboards that it hits capacity every night. The three of us make it an even twenty. A country song by Willie Jones plays on unseen speakers. The next thing I see is a big, burly brother behind the bar. He's wearing a Howard University Bison T-shirt, has a towel over his shoulder, a neatly trimmed beard, and fiery eyes fixed on Chief Jacobsen.

Part of me senses a racist assumption in Ms. Sabel's order. As soon as she realized the bar owner was black she figured I should talk to him. The pragmatic part of me understands her concept. I'm in a unique position. Chief Jacobsen can't get mad at me because Ms. Sabel introduced me as her "advisor." Mr. Eady might listen to me because we share the ordeal of living in a predominantly white country. I'm not sure if I should react to the assumptive part or the pragmatic part. Then a different part of me swells with pride that she trusted me to take *any initiative* I see fit.

Ms. Sabel guides Mayor Rick to bar stools at the right end of the bar. Six empty stools separate her from Chief Jacobsen and Mr. Eady. Both men give her a glance before re-focusing on each other. Neither of them notice me standing alone.

I pick the middle between them and pick up a menu staged at an artistic angle. First thing I see is a list of the four main food groups in the world of pork ribs: Spare, St. Louis, Country, and Baby Back. They're offered with a secular array of sauces: Kansas City Sweet, Texas Spicy, Hickory, Maple, and Eady's Own. The mouthwatering smell drifts in from the kitchen accompanied by the smoke of mesquite charcoal. Now I'm really hungry. But I focus on the job.

Chief Jacobsen is saying, "… just asking where you went after you closed last night."

"Lawyer," Eady bellows. "Scott, I ain't talking to you about the weather without a lawyer. You got that?"

The funny-looking bottle in the plastic bag sits on the bar between them. Chief Jacobsen continues, "You're not a suspect. I'm not accusing you of anything. It's a simple formality. I'm trying to get a handle on where everyone in town was when he was killed."

"You were trying to get a handle on the same thing when you arrested me for letting your fucking uncle rob my cash register."

Chief Jacobsen holds his hands up. "I did not arrest you. I merely—"

"If slapping handcuffs on a man and breaking his wrist in his own place of business ain't arresting, I don't know what is."

I keep looking at the menu to avoid getting dragged into the fight before I know what's going down. That's when my eyes land on the drinks portion. Earlier, Ms. Sabel gave me a rundown on her discovery of the dead man and everything at the crime scene. Suddenly, the reason she told me to take the initiative comes into focus. Under "specialty drinks" is a list of rapidly rising prices for shots of exclusive liquors. The priciest one on the list is called Del Porto Extra Añejo and goes for $300 a shot.

I snap the menu edgewise on the counter to get his attention.

Both men stop talking and shift their gazes to me. Mr. Eady sees me for the first time. I can tell by his pleasantly surprised expression.

His reaction is not unlike the time I was lost in Hong Kong and finally heard someone speaking English. I'd felt a hint of hope at the familiar pentameter. Mr. Eady sees a similar hope in my presence. He's no longer outnumbered twenty to one. Now it's twenty to two and in our world, that's as good as it gets.

"Sir, could I get a shot of the Del Porto, please?" I point at the menu showing him I know how much it costs.

The big man looks me over, trying to decide if I'm a young man buying over my credit limit for show or a Wall Streeter with real money. If he thinks I'm showing off, he'll dissuade me. He can't decide, so he plants himself in front of me. "How you doing, sir?"

I smile big and point at his shirt. "I don't have to pray for the Bison to win a game this fall, so I'm doing fine."

"Oh, zat so?" He laughs. "Who you pulling for?"

"Big Green," I say and wait as his face contorts trying to figure out who that is. I help him out. "Dartmouth."

"Oh! Ivy, then." He laughs, slaps the bar, and says, "Brotha done good, huh?"

We give dap with smiles. My alma mater satisfies his concern about whether I can afford the good stuff. He turns to the wall of booze behind him and looks it over. He grabs a stool and steps up to reach the top shelf where he extracts a bottle with the exact same odd shape as Chief Jacobsen's—fat and round at the bottom, thin at the top, like a genie might pop out of it.

He brings it down with a big smile. "Ain't a fool in this town who can afford it, so you get to pop the cork."

He wipes dust off the top and neck with his towel and pushes it to me. I pick it up, read the label, admire the hand-painted artwork dabbled on it, then set it down. I take a long, slow look down the bar at the plastic evidence bag containing an identical bottle.

Chief Jacobsen lifts his elbow to clear my sight lines—and his. The dots connect for him. Instantly, he knows what I'm doing and flushes with embarrassment.

Mr. Eady follows my gaze, catches my drift, and steams up with rage.

"Izzat what you came here for, Scott?" His voice rises in volume with each syllable.

"No."

"Izzat the murder weapon? You fixin' to get my fingerprints on it?"

"Nothing like that, Kubari." Chief Jacobsen raises his hands in surrender.

No one in the room believes him. Even the casual observer knows he assumed the crime scene bottle belonged to Mr. Eady.

"You know what your word is worth around here, boy?" Mr. Eady slams his fist on the bar.

"Don't get an attitude with me—"

"You be up for planting evidence on me, muthafucka, and you don't think you deserve some attitude?"

"I was only going to ask you about it, that's all." Chief Jacobsen gets his back up and squares off with Mr. Eady. "I knew I'd seen this—"

"Get the fuck out of my place, goddammit!"

"Hey, now—"

"Sir?" Ms. Sabel's voice drifts into the mix from the far end. "Could I have a shot of that Del Porto too, please?"

Mr. Eady turns to her, rage in his eyes. He's ready to throw out anyone who's a shade lighter than Lupita Nyong'o and I don't blame him. Except that would be his entire clientele in his chosen state of Maine. And he knows it.

"She's with me," I say.

He cuts his glare to me, and I lose sixteen tons of his respect in the blink of an eye. With a snarl, he says, "Maybe you should—"

"Give us a chance," I say quietly. "We have a plan. Can you roll with me for half an hour?"

To tell the truth, I don't have a plan, but the last ten minutes have proven to me that Ms. Sabel has one and she's letting me in on it one step at a time. She knew we were headed here, she knew why, and she knew I was the right person to keep things from exploding. She and I are vibing on an intellectual plane.

Mr. Eady sizes me up and leans back, arms crossed. "You vouch for them?"

He nods over at Mayor Rick and Ms. Sabel, then tosses his eyes in the direction of Chief Jacobsen.

"Yes, I do." I lean across the bar.

He does a doubletake on Ms. Sabel who, even sitting down, is a head taller than the mayor. Without looking at me, he asks, "Is that—"

"Yes."

"—Pia Sabel?" His eyes slide to mine for a second. "Heard she was in town." He looks me up and down. "Say, you have done good. Real good." He puts two shot glasses on the bar and nods at the Del Porto. "Lady says she wants one too. You gonna unwrap that sucka or what?"

I pull off the plastic and pop the cap. The aroma of something strangely tart, richly sweet—and slightly dirty—wafts to my nose.

"If we can include the Chief," Ms. Sabel says, "I'd be happy to buy a round for the house."

Mr. Eady's eyebrows rise as he does the math. $6,000. That's a lot of money for a place like this. Then he frowns at me. I've half a mind to tell Ms. Sabel how deeply offensive her offer is—Chief Jacobsen likes to tell himself he's colorblind when he clearly is not—but I consider how she's a step ahead of everyone at the moment. I decide to trust her. This time.

"Dr. King would say yes," I say softly.

I can read Mr. Eady's mind. I know the feeling. I've felt the same way. *How come we always gotta make nice with them? How come they never offer us an olive branch?* Nazi-controlled countries made minimal reparations to Holocaust survivors, but four hundred years of slavery has been met with *deal with it*.

He reads my mind at the same time. This is one of those times we're going to be the ones who love our neighbors first. Sucks. But it's the only way life's going to work right now.

He slaps his hands on the bar and bellows to the room, "Hear that, folks? Chief Jacobsen's lady friend here is buying y'all a round of the finest tequila in the world."

Exuberant hoots and cheers follow.

After an ugly glance back at Chief, he racks up the shot glasses and pours.

Everyone crowds around Ms. Sabel, giving thanks, before swarming past me to get their glass. Ms. Sabel stands up, holding the chairback for balance, and tells them it's a sipping tequila. For several enthusiastic drinkers, it's too late. When I take a sip, I taste caramel cherries enveloped in agave syrup. It tastes more like candy than alcohol. Almost. The aftertaste is definitely alcohol.

I glance at Ms. Sabel and point at the menu. She nods her approval. She's hungry too—we skipped lunch. I ask Mr. Eady, "Can we get a whole mess of ribs to wash down the booze?"

He moves us, including Chief Jacobsen, to a table just off the dance floor. He brings a footstool and an icepack for Ms. Sabel's foot. She asks him to join us. After an awkward hesitation, he gets someone out of the back to cover the bar and pulls up a fifth chair. He sits with his arms crossed, frowns at the Chief, and smiles at Ms. Sabel.

"Kubari, I'm really sorry." Chief Jacobsen sounds genuinely repentant. "I did jump to a conclusion, well, an assumption anyway. It was wrong of me. If I'd stopped to think it through, I would've known you wouldn't buy two expensive bottles."

"Scott, I didn't buy the one." He centers the paper flower arrangement on the table. Anger still ripples through his muscles. "Remember that old rich guy came to town a couple summers ago? Couldn't get his gigantic yacht in the harbor so he rented Delaney's thirty-footer to come and go?"

"The resort king from Cancun? All the single ladies in town wanted to sit in his lap." Chief Jacobsen exhales a tinge of embarrassment. "Including Mom."

"That's the guy," Mr. Eady says. "Bill Koller was his name. He said my bar didn't have anything worth drinking in it. So, he ups and orders a ton of stuff online, has it shipped to me, no charge. Tells me I gotta pour his for free, but the rest I can charge whatever I want. Worked great for a couple weeks, exotic bottles coming in every day, he has some, the rest sells just fine. Well, then he gets tired of Deeping and sails off. This bottle—and just this one bottle—arrived the day after he left. Haven't heard a word from him since."

# CHAPTER 10

## SCOTT, THE POLICE CHIEF

THAT YOUNG MARINE IS LOOKING pretty pleased with himself. Smartass. It pisses me off. How did he know there was a bottle way up on the top shelf? I knew Kubari had one and I was ready to swear it was the same one Uncle Phil had his fingers wrapped around when we found him. So how did Sabel's *advisor* know? I need to get them to stop second guessing me. As well intentioned as they may be, this is my investigation.

The evidence bag and bottle stand in the table's center, a mute testimony to my ill-advised angle of inquiry. I consider setting it on the floor but moving it would only attract more attention.

Still unhappy, Kubari goes back to work in the kitchen.

Boo-Boo walks in the front door. Her beautiful silhouette impossible to ignore. She looks around but doesn't see me. There's nothing I'd rather do right now than jump up, wrap my arms around her, and get one of her soul-slaking hugs. But Mom would kill me if I walked away from Ms. Sabel. *Think of all the jobs!*

Boo-Boo sees me. I give her a nod. She sees the company I'm keeping, understands, smiles, waves, and leaves. She gets it right away. That's what I love about her.

The silence that descended on us when the food arrived lifts when we finish scarfing it down. Ms. Sabel empties the Del Porto into our glasses as we mop up the last of the ribs. I polish off mine and notice Sabel's not like other women. She can eat. Guess running twelve miles before breakfast keeps her lean.

"What do you think of our investigation, so far?" Rick asks Ms. Sabel.

I want to reach across the table and throttle him. What is he trying to do? When did this become *our investigation*? Technically, I report to the mayor, but he doesn't know shit about police work. He should stay in his lane and keep pushing all Mom's talking points to land the SRC.

"Chief's doing a great job," she says. Instead of giving me a smile, she flashes a look at her advisor. We all know what just happened with Kubari. Her vote of confidence rings hollow.

"I'm thinking we should call in some help from the county," Rick says. "The town shouldn't make him investigate a death in his own family—even if he is adopted."

Angry as it makes me, I ignore the reference to my family status because the first part of what he said makes me angrier. He never said anything about the county to me. He knows damn well I can't stand the pompous sheriff.

"We don't need county help," I say with too much venom.

"We can't afford another debacle, Scott."

"There was no debacle." I emphasize the last word out of spite. Is he trying to get back at me for putting him in charge of the Plant's cleanup?

"Killing a man is a number-one debacle." Rick has fire in his eyes. Sabel picks up on that fast and looks a question at Rick. He can't resist telling the story. "We had an officer-involved shooting three years ago. First fatality in town history." Then he looks at me. "I can't believe Boo-Boo Vitelli's running around with you now. You know how that looks?"

Put a little liquor in a man's belly and his hate and spite spew from his mouth like a filthy fountain. His anger at my family has been smoldering since Jill Williams left him years ago and married Uncle Phil. She left Phil too, though, so you'd think he'd get over it.

I must look ready to beat the crap out of him—which I am—because Ms. Sabel puts a hand on my forearm. I feel myself relax a little.

"Mike Davis was a known felon," I say, "aimed a pistol at me, and made threatening moves. I had no choice. And, as Rick knows, I was cleared by the district attorney."

I sense the Black guy to my right tensing up. I turn to him and add,

"He was white."

"Mike Davis was also one of Vinny Devino's mobsters," Rick snaps back. "And he was Boo-Boo's boyfriend on and off for many years. Defending the wrongful death suit cost this town plenty."

"Boo-Boo?" Sabel asks.

Rick faces her. "She was twelve years younger than her big sister, Sara."

Sabel's mouth forms the big O of understanding about where the nickname came from. She asks, "Is that the same Sara who was best friends with Christine Jacobsen of Mom's Bakery?"

Rick nods with a judgmental look my way.

It's none of their business who I date, damn it. She didn't belong with Davis anyway. He was a two-bit thug, a Mafia-wannabe. If I hadn't shot him, a real gangster would've done it. Everybody knows that.

"That's all over and done with years ago, Rick," I say. "And we won the wrongful death suit."

"We settled out of court," Rick says. He sounds more determined than usual. "And it cost your mom the Mayor's office."

"Your mom was mayor?" Ms. Sabel asks me.

"When Scott went off to college," Rick answers for me, "she wanted to make sure the town was attractive enough that her kids would want to come home. She didn't want them running off to Boston or New York like everyone else. She ran for office and snagged tons of federal money to spruce up the place. It worked. Just like when she joined the school board to make sure the schools were good enough for her kids." Rick tosses a jealous sneer my way—like it was my fault the schools are better off now. "Anyway, we're getting off-track. This isn't the first time he's assaulted Kubari."

Rick just had to throw that out there.

Ms. Sabel and her advisor stare at me. I feel compelled to explain. "OK. That one was definitely my fault. Uncle Phil was drunk and thought it'd be funny to steal all the money in the cash register. Kubari caught him in the act, wanted him arrested. It wasn't the first time Uncle Phil created a scene in here and … well, who can blame Kubari for wanting some justice? I should've taken him in for optics if nothing else.

But he's family. So, I got between them, tried to talk it out. Uncle Phil took advantage of my badge, got behind me, made some nasty remarks. Well, Kubari has a temper and started beating the crap out of him. I jumped in, not as an officer but … he's family. Was."

I toss my hands up, not knowing where to go with the rest of the story.

"Didn't arrest the thief? Broke the owner's wrist?" Sabel's advisor scoffs. "Is that how you spell white privilege in this town?"

He makes it sound bad.

But—I have to admit, given the way he puts it—he's right. Damn. I really screwed up.

Rick and Ms. Sabel share a glance that turns into some kind of nonverbal communication. And the advisor—what is his name?—is watching me like a hawk. I know what they're thinking. They're thinking my mistakes in the past mean I'm not qualified today. I'm not capable of handling my job. Well, they're wrong. I've got this. Just a misstep is all. No need to call in the county sheriff.

"You've had a lot of good ideas today," Rick says to Sabel. "Maybe you could help us out? We don't get a lot of murders here. None, if I recall correctly. A woman of your experience and resources could be a big help to us."

"I have to be in Brussels by tomorrow night," she says.

"Jim Brenner killed his wife back in '19," I say for no particularly good reason. "I solved that murder."

"He shot her right in front of you while you were climbing out of your car." Rick sees a need to add that detail. "Not a big whodunnit."

That leaves a silence at the table. Rick turns his pleading eyes to Ms. Sabel.

"Perfect people never accomplish much," she says. "If you're not making mistakes, you're not working very hard." She lets her words sink in for a beat. "Chief Jacobsen is doing a fine job."

I appreciate the vote of confidence and give her a nod of appreciation. I turn an icy glare at Rick. Maybe he'll stop second guessing me now.

# CHAPTER 11

## CHRISTINE, THE BAKER

HOW MUCH CHAOS GRANDCHILDREN CAN produce between dinner and bedtime never ceases to amaze me. I'm picking up after Amy's kids for the third time since I came home when there's an insistent knock on the door. I call Amy to get it, but she says she's about to take a bath. Great, that way I can juggle the kids and the guest.

As I head out of the kitchen for the front door, Teresa, six, chases four-year-old Thomas (not Tom) down the hall, crossing my path and nearly knocking me down. "Tere-omas, watch it!" I yell, mixing up the names. The kids stop to laugh at me. Why Amy had to name them virtually the same thing shows how much appreciation the young have for their elders' memory banks.

I push between them, into the foyer, and open the door to Mayor Rick. I ask him, "What now?"

"May I come in?"

"It may be nine o'clock to you, but you don't bake bread at 3:30 AM." I step back and land on someone's plush toy. It squeaks. "Make it quick."

Rick, whose nose is red and eyes are watery, marches in with a serious air and stands in the living room. I pick up the toy and follow him. "Well?"

"For twelve years, you were the best mayor this town could ask for." He has a speech prepared in his head and pauses to remember it. Nothing good comes from a start like that.

I say, "If it weren't for Kubari making a big stink about a little bruise,

I'd be nearing sixteen."

"Christine, his wrist was broken in three places. And it happened two weeks after George Floyd." He holds up his hands to stop me from saying anything while he recalls his little lecture. "Look, fair or not, that out-of-town lawyer took you down. I did what you asked. I stepped into the race for you, and I've taken your advice on everything since. But now, I need you to hear me out. If Scott were your real son, you'd—"

"He is my real son!" I shout so loud Rick nearly falls over.

"Sorry, I didn't mean … I, I don't know what I meant."

While his eyes wander around the floor, I regret my outburst. People don't know what they're saying when they say something that stupid. They don't understand the love that builds through the work involved, the hours spent, the bond you create from scratch. The older I get, the more it irritates me. I should let it go.

"You want a beer?" I point to the couch.

"Yeah, that'd be nice." He eases down and lets out a sigh.

"You look like you started early this evening," I call from the fridge.

"Pia bought the most expensive bottle of liquor Kubari had and gave us all a taste."

Oh, it's *Pia*, is it? Not Ms. Sabel? So now he's on a first-name basis with her? What is she doing, spinning a little web around everyone? Why would she do that?

She's getting everyone drunk so we'll cough up massive tax breaks for her. These big companies like Amazon and Walmart dangle their special projects out like meat over a den of starving wolves. Cities and counties jump and snap at it, dying for jobs and hoping no one will notice what this really is: socialism for the rich. We give up decades of tax revenue to them, while their workers choke our roads and schools. Their shitty health insurance forces our folks into medical bankruptcies and hospital closures. The windfall's for them, not our community. My plan is to win her project without paying her for the privilege.

I bring my stein and hand him a sixteen-ounce Dinner beer from Maine Brewing Company and a glass. He mutters his thanks.

I sit on the loveseat. "From the looks of you, she bought more than one round."

"That Del Porto was something else. Didn't taste like tequila at all. When we ran out, she bought a round of the second-best tequila. No comparison. None at all."

"Yeah, Rick. Now you're a connoisseur. Got it. So *Pia* got everyone drunk, and you came here because …"

"Oh. So …" He hesitates, sips his beer. "Christine, Scott's in over his head on this one. He needs help. If you'd been at the Plant today, you would've seen Pia spoon-feeding him clues about every aspect of this investigation. Frankly, it was embarrassing. Hey. Don't look at me like that. It's not his fault. As a town, we shouldn't be leaving him to investigate his own uncle's murder the very day the man died. Scott needs some time to grieve. Some time to let reality sink in. He'll be fine in a few days."

He stares at his beer, waiting for my response. I do my best to cool down. It's not easy having someone imply your boy's incompetent. Then I wrap my head around something he said. I shove his knee to get his attention. "Did you say Sabel was at the Plant?"

"Before we were. She was inside, looking at the—"

"You let her inside?" I can't keep my voice down. "Wasn't it locked?"

"Well, the door was, but you remember couple months back when Phil backed the rental truck into—"

"Didn't he patch that?"

"Uh, well, I don't know what he did, but it wasn't patched this afternoon."

"Oh, for fuck's sake!" As the f-bomb leaves my lips, I see the Teromas covering their mouths and pointing at me. The sight almost makes me repeat the phrase. I ignore them and turn to Rick. "How bad was the place?"

"Whether or not she moves forward, she recommends we have it condemned and demolished for safety's sake."

"Finally!" I shout. "Someone with some common sense. You need to get some engineers out there tomorrow and have them write a report. That'll shut up Madeline Benton and her little hysterical society. We'd still have outhouses—I mean, historic latrines—in our backyards if she had her way."

"Yes," he says before taking a good swig of beer. "It might solve that problem. But about Scott."

"You came here with a plan in mind. Out with it."

He looks me over and chugs some more beer. When he stops smacking his lips, he says, "I floated the idea of calling the county—"

"No way. The last thing we need is that pompous windbag getting in front of Pia Sabel. He'll get the county to throw money at her and put her new operation down in York. I put too much work into getting her to look at us to let that happen. And he'll find a way to get Scotty fired in the process. He's been wanting us to farm out police work to him for years."

"And those were my thoughts exactly."

I can't help sneering at Rick. "Then why did you float the idea, Rick?"

"For Pia's benefit." He faces me. "I wanted her to know how much the town and county are out of step. She picked up on that. Then I asked her to help."

"You did WHAT?" I can't help but slap him. Luckily, I had a pillow in my hand, so it didn't make a lot of noise. "What'd you do that for?"

When he sits back upright, he says, "Scott needs help. She owns a world-class security operation. Did you know her company starts up police departments in those new planned communities all over the country?"

"Yes, Rick, I do. Remember where you read that? In my briefing."

"Oh. Right. Anyway, they also consult for police departments of all sizes. I took a shot at getting a free sample of that, but—"

"C'mon, Rick. Tell me you didn't ask a lady billionaire for a freebie. You think she got rich by giving stuff away?"

"It was worth a shot."

"Now we look like a bunch of yahoos from Mississippi." I run my fingers through my hair to stop myself from screaming. "Was she nice about turning it down?"

My heartbeat ratchets up like a race car. I struggle to keep my breathing steady. As much as I don't want to see Scotty fail, the last thing we need is someone like Sabel coming in with a microscope and a horde of consultants. God only knows what she'd find under any rock she turns over in this town. Deeping has more twisted secrets than a Sandra Brown novel. A real investigation could spread out, cause some serious damage, drag out all kinds of things that are better left alone.

"She said Scott's doing a good job." Rick tops up his glass with the remainder of the bottle and attempts to control his burp at the same time. "And she's planning to leave tomorrow, come what may."

"You think she's already made up her mind?"

He gives me a sad look. "Hard to say, but if she were thrilled, she'd be planning to stick around for dinner tomorrow night, don't you think?"

I bite my knuckle while contemplating our options. I could have Scotty tell her he needs her to stay in town for questioning. He might even imply she's a suspect. What would she do? Oh, right. Lawyers. And that would kill the project. What else?

Rick says, "I figured involving her would get her to stay longer, get her to put some skin in the game, maybe give us a second chance."

"What? You thought she'd do the investigation herself? Rick, she has people who fold her underwear. She has people who sweep her driveway because leaf-blowers are bad for the environment. She won't get involved, she'll … just …"

An idea begins to form. Rick's not that bright, but he might be on to something here. Then it comes into focus. It's dangerous. It's risky. But what do we have to lose?

"Rick, I want you to go home. Turn off your phone. Don't just put it in privacy mode, turn it off. Get a good night's sleep. Don't answer the door. Stay down until the funeral at eleven, Hartley's."

"Funeral? For Phil? Tomorrow?" Rick watches me nodding in answer to his question. "Are you Jewish?"

"No. Cheryl informs me it's not just them. The Muslims do it in a day too. And the Hindus. In fact, Christians are about the only ones who let the body stew for a few days. Kinda gross when you think about it."

Rick nods thoughtfully. "Sells embalming services though."

"Don't just sit there, Rick. Get going and lay low until tomorrow."

He raises his brows and starts to speak. I cut him off, "Don't ask."

# CHAPTER 12

## ISAIAH, THE ADVISOR

I AWAKEN TO THE RHYTHMIC noise of clanking metal and look at my phone, 7 AM. That six hours of sleep just now was the longest stretch I've gotten in days. Working for a billionaire who sleeps three hours a night isn't as glamorous as I expected.

My phone has a text message from Dad. Apparently, the head of the neuroscience program at Johns Hopkins, his old med school, would love to meet me. That's nice. How do you tell your off-the-charts-smart father you'd wash out of the program? I did well at Dartmouth, but my GPA wouldn't get me into med school in Aruba. Besides, I discovered my calling in the wars: shooting people. Not exactly in line with the Hippocratic Oath—but so much more satisfying.

Which brings up the thoughts that've been plaguing me since I started at Sabel Security. They get into the occasional shootout, which piques my interest. But do I have a career here? Does Pia Sabel trust me, or does she think of me as a bodyguard? Taking the interview for med school could lead to a higher-paying career. Boring, tedious, monotony, but good money.

I toss the covers, throw on my basic wardrobe, and tread lightly downstairs. The banging grows louder as I descend. Miguel, the third in Ms. Sabel's triumvirate of inner-circle friends, is spotting her. He's a towering and powerfully built man who's gentle and peaceful until provoked. Judging by his sweat, he's been working out with her. He got in last night and took the late watch.

It occurs to me the free weights she's pumping weren't here when I turned in after midnight. Wealth has its privileges.

Miguel acknowledges my presence with a nod. Ms. Sabel has an icepack taped to her ankle. She should see a doctor.

A text pings my phone. Looking at it, I ask, "Who is Seeley James? Is he with us? He's texting me questions about—"

"Hell!" Ms. Sabel bangs the weights down hot. "Delete that. And then block him."

"Uh, OK. Who is he?"

"Claims he's my biographer. He's always nosing around trying to get someone to give him the inside story." She picks up the weights and starts pumping again, extra fast. "I should send out a company-wide memo—"

"That'll legitimize him," Miguel advises.

"You're right, ignore him. No one in their right mind would read his trash anyway."

The conversation leaves me feeling awkward and out of place. I want to feel like I'm included in the group. I want them to trust me with more responsibility. I want to show them I can handle a lot more than a bar owner. But I'm the new guy. I pat my thighs while thinking. Which leads me to ask, "Hungry?"

"Starving," Ms. Sabel says between heavy exhales. "When we finish, let's get some brioche at Mom's Bakery."

"That'll be another hour," Miguel says. "At least."

"How about I run down there and bring back an assortment?" I ask.

They like that idea. I head for the front door and stop at the mirror in the foyer.

My first order of business is situational awareness. My previous New England experience was a college town where I was popular—too popular. Well-intentioned kids who'd only read about people of color in books wanted to be best friends, but their lack of firsthand experience made for some embarrassing can-I-touch-your-hair type moments. And then there were the white women who wanted to find out if "it's true."

I'm not at Dartmouth, and I'm not protected by rank, so I need to be careful on my first outing alone. I firmly believe in the brotherhood of man, but this town has a trigger-happy chief and I've seen only one nonwhite person. For all I know, Deeping could be a hostile environment.

Statistics show a small percentage of the people I meet won't like me because of my skin. Another percentage won't like outsiders on principle. Four out of ten won't know what to think. And the last ten percent will be over-enthusiastically trying to fix racism in one shot. Which is nice—but uncomfortable. They will be who they are.

I do an inventory: I left my Sabel-issued pistol in my room. My hands are loose, my shirt form-fitting, my pants standard chinos. Nothing flashy, no triggering stereotypes, nothing controversial. Good; I'm not presenting a threatening profile. Then I deploy Mom's advice: always take a smile and a bowl full of prayer.

This walk isn't necessary. I need the space to meditate on my future. Dad thinks he can get me into Johns Hopkins, frat-boy GPA and all. That would be the smart path to follow. Maybe I don't cut it as a neurosurgeon and wind up only making half a million a year as an anesthesiologist. Not a glamorous job, not exciting or even fun. But it pays well, and it's respected. I'd be a fool to turn down that open door.

First problem I have with that path is being under Dad's thumb. He and Mom are terrific parents. Too terrific. They've been overinvolved in everything my sister and I have done since leaving the delivery room. I chose the Marine Corps because they couldn't intimidate my drill instructor. Now I'm finally on my own path, making my own choices. One of the things I discovered: I like a life of danger. I'm good at it.

That's why I like Sabel Security. Jacob brought me in, then left on special assignment. I felt adrift for a couple days before Ms. Sabel had me join her. I like her and the others. I like the high-profile missions they take on. After yesterday, I feel better about how Sabel Security works.

Ms. Sabel knew I'd pick up on her cues. It was like back in Recon when your platoon had trained together for so long, you'd work via telepathy. Everyone knew the plan and would improvise as needed to execute that plan. This feels like the same thing, only on a more intellectual level. And, as smart as Dad is, Ms. Sabel has something else going on. Where he's book-smart, she's people-smart. She may not know organic chemistry, but she hears things unsaid, sees things unseen, and predicts things unknown. There's much to learn being around her.

That reminds me: Jacob sent me a bunch of videos from her days as a soccer star. He said they reveal who she is and how she operates. I dial one up and pop in my headphones.

It's a post-World Cup interview. The host asks her why she played like a different person. He says, "It was like you changed every technique you ever used. Wasn't that risky? Why take the chance you might miss a pass or lose the ball?" Ms. Sabel answers, "Everyone studies game film. If I come to the finals with the same moves as the previous games, they'll know how to beat me." She turns to the camera as a sly smile grows across her face. She says, "To stay on top, you have to keep a few tricks up your sleeve."

That makes me laugh.

I watch a couple more of her public appearances and learn a few more things about her. Part of her success is deep research. When I was going to high school parties and playing X-Box, she was studying the life history of the opponents in her next soccer game. From coaches to stars to bench warmers, she knew everything about them: what they ate, who they read, what they did after practice, the name of their childhood dog. She knew them so well she could predict which way they would turn in a game. It occurs to me that she's doing that now, here in Deeping. She knew Chief Jacobsen's next move before he did and she positioned me, her best asset, for that scenario, where I could stop it from going bad. She relied on me. Trusted me.

I stop in my tracks. How could she trust me like that after working with me for only a matter of hours? Only one answer: she knows my life history. Holy shit. She studied me. Just like her old soccer rivals. That's what she does when the rest of us are sleeping. She gets ahead.

Am I up to that kind of scrutiny? If I worry about applying to med school, do I have what it takes to work for Pia Sabel? She probably knows my childhood dog was named Baldwin.

Suddenly, I feel a huge weight on my shoulders. What can I do to prove myself worthy? In a few hours, we'll be in Europe with a business agenda that may as well be in Russian for all I know about it. How am I going to get on her wavelength and join the working telepathy she has with Tania, Miguel, and Jacob?

I don't know. I do know I'm every bit as smart and capable as they are. They just don't know it yet. I feel a rising desire inside me to prove myself to Ms. Sabel.

As I reach the line outside Mom's Bakery, I'm pulled out of my introspection when I see a familiar face. A graceful lady steps out of the establishment, ignoring the crowd like a royal and looking hotter than Rihanna. I think I know who she is, but it's been a few years since we met. It could be her. I double check my assumption as she strides by me by saying, "Professor Zuma?"

# CHAPTER 13

## ISAIAH, THE ADVISOR

PROFESSOR ZUMA STOPS, SPOTS ME, tries to remember me, can't quite get there, and says with authority, "Remind me."

"Oh, you wouldn't remember me, ma'am. It was a few years back when you were a visiting professor at Dartmouth. You left a strong impression on me."

"Dartmouth." Her smile explodes with recognition. She points at me. "Reddick, right?" She snaps her fingers as her gaze goes up and down my frame. "Ishmael? No. Isaiah. If you graduated, which you damn well better have, you can call me Vanessa."

"Whoa. How did you remember—"

"When you look out over a field of silent snow and one enthusiastic raisin pops up and quotes Zora Neale Hurston, you remember him. *An envious heart makes a treacherous ear.* A beautiful phrase. What brings you to town?"

I'm impressed, just as I was in her class. "I'm here on business."

"You don't say." She looks puzzled. "What business is that?" She says this as if she's afraid I'm going to answer with some job punching below the promise of my degree.

"Sabel Security."

"What a coincidence—the owner of your company is in town. Wait a second ... I heard she brought a bodyguard." She says this with a frown of disappointment on her face. She expected more from me than *bodyguard.*

"They're not big on titles," I plead. "She introduced me to the mayor as her advisor. I've only been with them a few weeks. You know about her?"

"Do I? She took over a huge company at twenty-six when her father was murdered. Instead of floundering on her own, she took a gigantic risk and promoted a black woman over a thousand white men to run her company. Never asked anyone's advice, never checked with Wall Street, didn't care what the press said, she just did it. And it went damn well. Yes, I've followed Jonelle Jackson and, through her, Pia Sabel."

She looks at the white people sitting at the nearest sidewalk table, their napkins scrunched up for trash, clearly finished but still talking. She swirls her finger at them. "You're done."

It's not a question. It's a command. They look up, gather their things, and scurry away. Not even the military gave me that kind of confidence. Maybe it's the years of teaching. We take their still-warm seats.

"Are you still at Northwestern?" I ask. She has a decade on me and might not be interested in a younger man, but I've got to try. She's too fascinating to let go.

"Home for the summer," she says. "Mama died and left me the house. I added some real estate investments and find Deeping a great place to write between semesters."

I try to find something witty to say but come up empty.

She asks, "What's your career trajectory at Sabel, then?"

I stutter. It's worse than talking to Dad. I'm twenty-five, a former lieutenant, I don't need to analyze my career choices with strangers. But. Something about Professor Vanessa Zuma is engaging. I wanted to quote Hurston in her class because I knew it would impress her—while sending my classmates to Wikipedia.

"Biding my time until Jonelle Jackson retires," I laugh. "Seriously, I'm evaluating that very question now. I'm trying to add value and see how well it's received. Working directly with Ms. Sabel has been an eye-opener."

"Word is, she doesn't suffer fools lightly."

"So far, I've steered clear of that side."

We both laugh softly, the way the condemned might laugh at the executioner's ridiculous hood. Regardless of our mirth, the ax will inevitably fall.

My phone dings with a text from Ms. Sabel. When I steal a glance, Professor Zuma—Vanessa—gives me the go-ahead with a nod. Leaving the phone on the table, I open the message.

It reads, "We're not going to Brussels. We're staying here to solve the murder. I need your advice. I'll explain when you get back."

"The Phil Jacobsen murder?" Vanessa asks.

I'm surprised she read the message but realize my phone was as close to her as me. She shrugs without apologizing.

"Did you know him?" I ask.

"It's a small town. Everyone knows everyone."

"Any clues as to who wanted him dead?"

"Gossip, maybe. I'm not a big drinker and he … well, he partied like a freshman. Kitty Robinson could stand him. Ah, your expression tells me you've met the woman who has become Crazy Kitty. Don't kid yourself—she earned that nickname. She was a promising young woman not so long ago. No one knows if it's mental illness or substance abuse, but either way, it's a shame. Then there's Amy Jacobsen, his niece. Have you questioned her?"

"No." I lean in. "They didn't get along?"

Vanessa looks both ways and matches my conspiratorial posture. In a low voice, she says, "Almost ten years ago now, when I started teaching at Northwestern and Amy was in Bangor, the dean from her university called me for some advice. She and her uncle had started one of those college-girls-gone-wild type websites. All the participants were of legal age, but there were some questionable tactics involved in signing releases. The school got the site shut down but couldn't press charges against Phil. The dean called me because he knew me and knew I was from Amy's hometown. I advised him not to expel her. I mean, why take it out on the women?"

I lean back, thinking this over. If Phil kept some videos or photographs of young women in their wilder days, ten years later, when they're getting married and having children, they could be ripe for blackmail. A hundred other scenarios run through my head that might lead to murder: a jealous husband, revenge porn, an unhealed wound from signing releases while intoxicated, and so on.

"Did you tell Chief Jacobsen about this?" I ask.

"What do you know about him?"

"That he beat up Mr. Eady."

"Why volunteer information to someone like that if he didn't ask you?"

She watches me, taking measure of my stance on the police. Are they an enemy? Are they a well-intentioned institution with a few bad apples? I decide she believes we should deal with them the same way we deal with wild animals: cautiously, respectfully, and skeptically.

She says, "If it helps advance your career, go ahead and tell them. Just heed this one caveat: Don't dish it out gratuitously. Amy was young, and everyone does stupid shit in their youth. Remember, her reputation hangs in the balance here."

"Thank you, I'll respect your wishes and her honor."

She slips a card across the table to me. "If I can be of help to you, don't hesitate to call. Now you best get going. You don't want to keep Pia Sabel waiting when she needs your advice."

We part ways and I go inside to order food.

Soon I'm trudging back up the hill with a box full of delicious-smelling baked goods while considering how to respect Vanessa's caveat.

I open the door to find Miguel in the living room with a sympathetic yet resigned face listening to Ms. Sabel limping a circle around him and ranting. She's using an umbrella for a cane. He's retying his long, black mane into a traditional Navajo bun at the base of his neck with a strip of white cloth. They both break and look at me. Then they dive for Christine Jacobsen's down-home baking.

Miguel takes a cinnamon bun, Ms. Sabel takes a brioche. I'm partial to blueberry muffins. The one I crack open releases a cloud of steam carrying the scent of heaven. You don't get that at Starbucks.

Ms. Sabel wolfs down her bite, then points at the bag. "Did you ask for her phone number or did she volunteer it?"

My gaze follows her finger to find a flowery-feminine script under the top fold that reads, "Anytime" with a heart over the dotted I, followed by a ten-digit number. The young lady who served me at the counter had winked and smiled profusely. At the time, I missed those signals. My thoughts were stuck on Vanessa.

"Why are we staying in town?" I ask.

Miguel backs up as if waiting for Ms. Sabel to explode again.

Between bites, Ms. Sabel says, "The mayor's office put out a news release thanking me and accepting my offer to personally assist in the investigation into Phil Jacobsen's murder. His office auto-posted it on every social media platform at midnight."

It takes me a minute to understand the significance of the hour. She sleeps from midnight to three in the morning. I can almost predict what she's going to say next when she finishes her bite.

"By dawn, every small county and town in the country shared the story. Most of our fans piled on with support and positive responses. Our consulting department phoned after you left and told me I have to do this or they'll never get work again. They think we'll lose credibility. And if I solve the case, they'll be swamped with new business and get bonuses for years to come. I can't let down the two thousand people in that division. I'm trapped."

I notice Miguel makes no comment. Given the anger coming out of her, I defer to his expertise in handling the boss and take as big a bite of muffin as I can stuff in my mouth to cover my silence.

"I've got sixty thousand employees!" She throws her hands in the air and loses a chunk of brioche in the gesture. Miguel dives for it and rounds it to the trash can. "I know everyone thinks Jonelle runs the company—OK, she does—but my presence is an important role for high-level meetings. I was supposed to meet Ursula in three days. I'm due at Christine's in four."

Obviously not Christine of Mom's Bakery given the way she pronounced it. In Europe, the "e" on the end is pronounced Chris-teen-eh. Which is how she just said it. While Ms. Sabel inhales the rest of her brioche and grabs another, I picture the travel schedule in my head to remember who she's talking about. Ursula von der Leyen, President of the European Union. The next entry was Christine Legarde, President of the European Central Bank in Frankfurt.

I consider dropping Vanessa's gossip. While it would give my profile a huge boost, it would violate my promise. I consider my options and come up with another way to uncover that information without betraying the source.

After a pensive moment, Ms. Sabel lowers her gaze from the ceiling. "Not that I care that much about brown-nosing Ursula or Christine. I just don't like being manipulated. I really, really, really don't like being manipulated."

I want to add, *especially by persons unknown in a fishing village north of East Bumfuck.* But decide that wouldn't help. Instead, I say, "Then we should get going. Let's start with a look at Phil Jacobsen's house."

Miguel and Ms. Sabel snap glances my way. I think they like the idea. Maybe I've been too quiet.

"Did you pack a black suit?" she asks me. When I shake my head, she turns to Miguel, who also shakes his head. "Then we'll need to order some for the funeral. Call Emma in operations, she'll have them sent over. We'll go to Phil's before the funeral."

# CHAPTER 14

## SCOTT, THE POLICE CHIEF

PACING UNCLE PHIL'S FRONT PORCH with a roll of crime scene tape in my hand, a thousand thoughts roil in my mind. Thoughts like: Why did our genius mayor get Ms. Sabel involved? I don't need help. Not from some young jockette whose daddy left her billions. What does she know about police work? Last I heard, she was going to Europe. She should be a suspect, not my "special consultant."

I wonder if those conspiracy stories about her arranging her daddy's killing are true.

I try Rick's phone again. Straight to voicemail. Sleeping in past nine? That's not like him. Another reporter calls me. The sun is shining, the sky is clear, perfect tourism weather, but the news is all about our murder. No pressure.

Boo-Boo sends me a text about how she misses me already. She includes a picture of her lovely smile. Normally, I'd find that kind of thing annoying, but she knows I'm under a lot of stress and is trying to help. She always knows what to say or do. She's thoughtful like that.

Half a block uphill, Ms. Sabel and her advisor appear from beneath the rustling oaks. They're on foot and she's still limping. She's acquired a cane somewhere, one with a pearl handle, no less. They both wear lightweight jackets over athletic wear. Like yesterday, her clothes outline every muscle and curve. It's a little distracting.

She waves at me. I nod back. They stop at the weathered picket fence on the edge of Uncle Phil's lot and survey the scene. It's a large lot and a large house, especially for a single guy with no children. My dearly departed uncle bought this 1800-vintage two-story clapboard manse before it collapsed and tried to remodel it. He had big plans for a resurrected historic home. Thought he could sell tickets. He got a few rooms done before the hopelessness of it dragged him down.

I hail her as she approaches the stoop and open the front door for her. She responds kindly and hobbles inside.

"Morning, Chief Jacobsen," her advisor says. He stops in front of me and adds, "The name's Isaiah Reddick."

He goes in as well, leaving me to wonder how he knew I couldn't remember his name. I kick myself for ignoring him. After all, he saved me from making a big mistake yesterday. I owe him.

I walk in and close the door. Sabel's peering in the unfinished drawing room. Bare wires hang from where the light fixtures should be. Raw wood floors, wainscotting missing in places, paint peeling from the ceiling, and dirty windows don't leave a lot of room for clues. Across the hall, Isaiah's leaning into the parlor; its condition is not much different from the drawing room.

I aim to save them time. "The rooms he used were the kitchen at the back and a bedroom or two upstairs."

"When was the last time he worked on this room?" she asks.

"He was doing the work out of pocket, and the pocket's been empty for years."

"Then those would be someone else's boot prints?" She points to a fine layer of sawdust covered in distinct prints. Large boots, size 12 or 13. They look fresh and damp from last night's rain. Someone's been walking around in here in the last twenty-four hours.

"I was wondering about that myself," I lie. As long as I'm at it, I double down. "I texted Mom to see if he'd hired anyone lately. Or had someone looking at the house for something."

"Pest control?" she offers.

"One of my questions." Damn, but she's a step ahead of me. I gesture toward the back. "Want to check the places he spent most of his time?"

"What did he do for money?" Isaiah asks when he turns away from the parlor. I assume there were no footprints there.

"My grandfather left him something like a trust. Not much but enough to buy this house and have maybe twenty grand a year. He had a bunch of get-rich-quick schemes, but they never worked out."

"Cryptocurrency? Websites? Vitamins?" Isaiah offers.

"All the above."

Sabel mounts the stairs and stops after two steps. Gripping the banister, she limps her way up. Isaiah heads to the back. Divide and conquer?

I hear footsteps on the walkway outside. A quick glance out the side glass makes my heart stop. Al Devino. And he's in his full hipster-look: black hair in a gelled wave, too-tight shirt unbuttoned to the pecs, a sleek gray blazer, black jeans, and white sneakers without socks. I open the door, step outside, and pull it almost closed behind me.

Puffing up my chest and looking official, I say, "You can't come in here, Al."

Al comes up the steps and stands toe-to-toe with me. "He stole something from Uncle Vinny. A thing that don't belong to him. I need it back."

"This is a crime scene, Al. You can't take anything out of here."

From behind me, Ms. Sabel says, "What did it look like?"

"Who da fuck are you?" Al asks.

I twist to look over my shoulder. She's standing in the doorway, silent with a deadly look in her eye. Behind her, Isaiah assesses the situation and disappears down the hall.

"It's OK," I say. "He's my cousin. Second cousin, or once removed, however that works. He wanted to pick something up." I turn back to Al. "Not now. I'll let you know when we've processed the scene. You can come back then."

"Don't work for me, Scotty." He sneers and hooks his thumbs in his pants pockets, letting his jacket open a little to show off the Beretta in a shoulder holster.

"Like I said," Sabel says flatly, "tell us what we're looking for and we'll bring it to you if we find it."

He leans around me to eyeball her. "It's personal."

"So is murder," she snaps.

Al tightens his jaw and tries to stare me down. "Who da fuck is she,

Scotty?"

"Pia Sabel. The mayor asked her to consult on this case." I inch forward to force him back. "Don't force my hand here."

Isaiah appears around the side of the building. He has a large, black Glock tucked conspicuously in his belt. He says, "Everything good here, Chief Jacobsen?"

Al sees him, tries not to look surprised at being outflanked. His angry gaze comes back to me.

"Yeah, everything's fine," I answer without taking my eyes off Al. "This guy was just leaving. Weren't you, Al?"

He backs down the steps, his glare still locked on me. "Yeah, we're good here. When you gonna release the crime scene?"

"I'll call you."

Walking backward, he says, "You gotta come pay your respects, Scotty. We'll talk about it then."

He turns to his red Cadillac Blackwing, gets in, and burns a small patch of rubber on his exit.

Isaiah's gone already. I turn back to Sabel. "Sorry. Al watched too many Godfather movies. He's harmless."

"We're well acquainted with his kind." She's looking over my shoulder as if memorizing his license plate. "No one is harmless. Especially Al Devino."

"You know him?" I can't hide the surprise in my voice.

Her eyes come back to mine without an answer. I take that to mean he came up in the background research her people did on Deeping and Maine. Mom won't like hearing that. We don't need Ms. Sabel connecting us to the Devino crime family.

I should offer a thank-you for pitching in. There's no point in pretending Al wouldn't have forced his way in, compromised the scene, and taken whatever he wanted had I been alone.

She hobbles back to the stairs and grips the banister right away this time. I hear Isaiah back in the kitchen. I follow Sabel and find her in a bedroom facing the street. It's filled with junk: old suitcases, moth-eaten curtains and rugs, tools Phil bought at yard sales. A light coat of dust has settled on everything.

She turns those gray-green, ray-gun eyes on me. "I'm adopted too."

"I know." I hide my shock at her icebreaker as best I can. "I read up on you for the visit."

She looks around the room. Something catches her interest, and she leans down for a closer look, then dismisses it.

"How did you know about me?" I ask.

"Your ears are nothing like Christine's."

I've heard ear cartilage is as unique as fingerprints, but I never looked at familial resemblance in them. I wonder if she just made that up.

"Most adopted kids have great lives," she says. "No problems and are well-adjusted. Not me, though."

She peeks in an empty closet.

"Mine was a unique situation," she continues with a quick glance to see if I'm still listening. "It was just Dad and me. His mother and father never really got on board." She runs a finger through the dust, testing the depth. "They treated me like a phase he was going through and would give up on shortly. Now that he's gone and I'm paying their bills, they don't know what to do. Dad once told me that when a couple gets pregnant, the whole family, friends, and community get pregnant with them. But when you adopt, you adopt alone."

I'm not sure where she's going with this, so I stay quiet. Although she sure summed up my childhood. People always acted like Amy and I were different, outsiders. Mom overcompensated for it, sometimes making it worse by making it obvious.

Moving to the next room, she continues. "Potomac, Maryland has always been a transient neighborhood, lots of political appointees, diplomats, the like. Not a tight community like a small town. I never felt any more or less out of place than anyone else. But other adoptees have told me their communities excluded them in subtle ways. Deeping is a close-knit community. Everyone knows everyone and has since birth. How has it been for you?"

Pretty direct question for someone you hardly know. My back tingles like this is getting too personal and I'm pretty sure my face shows it.

Instead of answering, I ask, "You turned down helping me last night. What changed your mind?"

"The town posted a press release that cemented public opinion before I could get out of town. You and I are on the same page here. You don't think you need help. I don't think you need help. And I've got a thousand other things I need to be doing. Now we're stuck with each other."

She examines a spool of thick yellow marine rope, all but a few yards of it gone. She looks at the shredded end, then the label. It reads, "600 yards, ¾ inch nylon 8-strand, plaited, 17,000 lb." I consider telling her it could lift a Chevy Suburban, but she doesn't ask. She looks at the floor and I follow her gaze. At some point, a trail of water droplets splashed in the accumulated dust, leaving tiny craters. To me, it indicates the spool arrived here in the last day or two. She looks up at me to make sure I'm seeing it and is pleased that I have. I find it curious that Uncle Phil would have any use for it.

"How many actual murders have you solved?" I ask.

"A few," she says. "My parents, for one. But like your Brenner murder, I witnessed that. Then there were, let's see, twelve more. Including a high-profile case in England a few weeks ago involving the Morpheus Institute. Did you hear about it?" She waits for me to shake my head, then looks disappointed. "Any way you count it, not as many as a city detective, but a good deal more than you." She waits until I deflate. "Like I said, we're stuck with each other, Scott. We'll make the best of it for a couple days. If you and I can't figure it out, I'll bring in an army of professionals who'll solve every crime in this town going back to statehood. Deal?"

With a bright warm smile, she extends a hand. I stare at it. My first thought: is this another sales pitch?

Reading my mind, she says, "At my expense."

I feel a weight lifted and a truce of sorts in the offing. I shake her hand.

I tell her, "In grade school, Davy Jones had a dumb idea and I bought in. We got caught. He squealed and blamed me for thinking it up, totally turned the tables on me. Everyone took his word for it. The principal told my mom they didn't believe me 'because he's adopted.' I hated that. Still makes me mad. From then on, I heard that sentiment said in more subtle ways. I still hear and see it in people's actions from time to time. They make excuses for me and think they're helping."

"Like when Mayor Rick tried to undermine your capability?"

Something flashes inside my head. That hadn't occurred to me, but she's right. Rick was trying to make excuses in case I couldn't solve the case, blaming me—because I'm adopted. She knows the feeling, she's been there. A whole new appreciation for her forms in my head. I feel myself nodding.

We shuffle into the next room as Isaiah's footsteps come up the stairs. He catches us in the hallway.

"What's this about?" he asks as he holds up an old, dusty video camera. "There's a couple boxes of lights and microphones down there."

"He tried his hand as a videographer, doing weddings, bar mitzvahs, and the like. He made a little money up in Bangor for a while, but his Yelp reviews were all one star with comments like, 'Don't let this guy get near the bar.' And then, like everything else, he abandoned it a few months later."

# CHAPTER 15

## ISAIAH, THE ADVISOR

CHIEF JACOBSEN HAS TO HELP his mom at the funeral home, so we leave before we've finished our search of the dead man's house. We'll be back tomorrow, he promises. As we leave the property, Ms. Sabel decides we should walk to the Plant. When I ask why, she says, "Rope."

Her limp seems worse to me, her usually long strides are noticeably shorter. This is getting worse, not better.

"You should see a doctor," I say as we turn down the lane that leads to the Plant.

"I've walked off worse than this."

"Walking it off doesn't take twenty-four hours. We should find out if—"

"Not a big deal. Let it go."

"But it could be—"

"Let it go!"

OK, she's an adult and an international athlete who should know it's time to see the doctor. I consider asking Miguel to say something since he knows her better, but he's off on some errand for the boss.

My next concern is how to bring out the Amy Jacobsen story. There were no video tapes in the recorders, no SD cards or anything. I thought I'd find a computer but only found a place where a laptop had been. An officer had taken it to the station yesterday afternoon. Chief Jacobsen promised to give the Sabel Tech people a shot at it if his people couldn't guess the password. He didn't say how long that would take.

There's a squad car parked outside the Plant. The hole in the wall Ms.

Sabel and I ducked through yesterday has crime scene tape plastered over it in a crude attempt to obscure its existence. We walk through the wide-open office door to an overly eager greeting from the officer and a teenager as they sweep junk into a trash pile. The cop waves us through, telling us to make ourselves at home.

I look at the ceiling where sunshine pours in through fifteen holes, some the size of dinner plates. We make our way to the end nearest the water. A twenty-by-ten-foot stretch of floor has fallen into the basement. Harbor water slurps in and out through what might've once been basement windows. High tide left a ring several feet above the current level. Ms. Sabel limps to the edge and peers into the dark green goo sloshing gently in the cavity.

I ask Ms. Sabel, "If we're looking for something specific, does that mean you have a suspect?"

"We're looking for bright yellow nylon rope, the kind used on boats. Take a look down at that end. And no, I don't have any suspects yet. What about you?"

She keeps her gaze fixed in the water. I follow her lead, but I can't see more than a couple inches deep and I've no idea where the bottom is. She takes out her phone and clicks on the light. Copying the boss seems like a good idea, so I do the same. My company issued Sabel Satellite phone is bigger and bulkier than the latest models from other companies, but the reception is global, the security is airtight, and its flashlight is a whole lot stronger. So strong in fact, we get nothing but a reflection of the light. We both abandon that concept.

"Well, that mobster sure acted suspicious," I answer.

"I thought so too," she says. "He's Al Devino, heir to Vinny Devino's crime family, which itself is a remnant of the Gambinos. They're being overrun by cartels and their influence has been diminished. Still plenty dangerous, though. I'd expect them to be smarter than that kind of confrontation. Maybe it's intentional, maybe he's looking to intimidate Scott. He sure didn't expect you'd be there."

"Devino, Gambino?" Surprised, I turn to her. "You researched them?"

"It's in the court and newspaper records."

I process this. She couldn't go for her morning run with her messed-up ankle, so she did research from three until sunrise? Damn, that's dedication.

"No," she says, as if reading my mind. "I caught up with yesterday's emails and calls this morning. The local criminals were part of the site survey."

"How did you know what I was—"

"People aren't so hard to read if you pay attention. You looked impressed, which meant you thought I worked on it this morning."

She looks around the building, spots a broken broom and hobbles over to it. When she returns, she pushes it into the muck. It sinks about four feet, leaving only enough out of the water to keep her hand dry.

"How do you make that work for cases like Phil Jacobsen?" I ask.

She shrugs. "You can piece things together from bits of information. People are surprising, but mostly predictable. I learned that from reading about Auguste Dupin and Sherlock Holmes in my youth. They had the distinct advantage of working before the instant-information age—all their mistakes were edited out before their biographies were published. But their principles still apply. And research helps."

I laugh, thinking of my earlier assumption and decide to test it. I say, "You probably know my childhood dog's name."

"It's not so hard to figure out. You'll have to give me a hint, though. Did he have a person's name or a feature-name, like Spot or Socks?"

"Person."

"How old were you when you got him?"

"Sixth grade."

"You gave away the pronoun by not correcting me, so that helps. It was a male dog. OK. Let's see. You told me about studying Greek tragedies in college, so we can calculate you had that freedom because you studied all the white classics in high school: Austen, Dickens, Faulkner, Hemingway, Woolf, Steinbeck, Salinger. And we know your parents had high expectations for your academic career, which means in middle school they made you read Toni Morrison, Alice Walker, Malcom X, Langston Hughes." She stops cold. "You wouldn't name him Langston because there's only one. Your parents wouldn't allow Malcom

X, so you named him Baldwin, after James Baldwin."

"Holy …" I reel back a step in awe. "Why not Morrison or Walker?"

"A sixth-grade boy naming a male dog after a woman? No way."

I burst out laughing and clap my hands. "You nailed me. Let me try: you didn't have a childhood dog because you grew up traveling to soccer matches around the world. No time."

She puts her finger on her nose. "My biggest regret. I still want a dog. But I still travel, that's why we keep Jacob's dog at Sabel Gardens."

"So, using your method, I'm still stuck on why there were video cameras and no tapes or SD cards. What comes to mind is maybe Phil Jacobsen wasn't filming weddings. Or not exclusively weddings."

She cocks her head out of curiosity when she looks at me.

"He was into get-rich-quick schemes and wedding videos aren't on the road to riches." I pause. "Some kind of porn, I'd guess. Except he didn't have much money, so he didn't hire porn stars. He tried making amateur videos."

"You've got something there, Isaiah." She taps her chin while she thinks. "And that could lead to blackmail, bitterness, all kinds of terrible outcomes. That's why you wanted to know where Phil's laptop went." She gives me a light hug. "Nice work. I'm proud of you."

While I appreciate the compliment, I feel like I should credit Vanessa. But that would open a can of worms that would lead me to disclosing more than I should. I let it go.

She hobbles back and forth along the edge of the water. "We're going to need a diver or an underwater light."

"Why are we looking for a rope?"

"A guy who lives five blocks from the water and doesn't own a boat has a hundred feet of waterproof, heavy duty marine rope left over from a 600-yard spool, dripping wet in his home office. Where would the rest of that spool have gone?"

I look around the cavernous space. The only walls standing are for the offices at the far end. The officer and a kid are nearly finished sweeping up fifty yards away. There aren't many places we can't see from where we stand. "What about the office?"

"You don't need 600 yards to go from one end of the office to the other. No, that length takes you up the harbor to the dock or out to the breakwater. Maybe even out to the ocean."

"He could've tied something up somewhere out of town. Maybe on the state park up the road."

She nods. "Maybe. But he was lazy. And this was close by. At any rate, I'm not seeing anything yellow and ropey here. My thought was, he tied one end to a weight and dropped it in this pool. He would know where it is, and not worry about someone stumbling on it by accident."

"What's on the other end?"

"No earthly idea."

Her phone rings. After a brief conversation, she says, "We need to get back to the rental, get dressed. The funeral starts in half an hour."

When we make our way back, Miguel stands on the front porch, watching Ms. Sabel. He's wearing a perfectly tailored black blazer over a black T-shirt, dark slacks, and dress shoes. His long black locks, parted in the middle and tucked behind his ears, flow over his shoulders. I'm not sure which is more intimidating, in a bun or over the shoulders. Maybe it's not the hair that's intimidating.

Sabel Fashions, a division of Sabel Industries, delivered these outfits—with a shoulder holster built into the jacket—while we were out. They keep our sizes on file. Still blows me away.

Addressing the boss, Miguel says, "You should see a doctor."

She replies, "I've walked off worse than this."

"Walking it off doesn't take twenty-four hours."

"Not a big deal. Let it go."

Unlike me, Miguel lets it go. And doesn't get a snippy reply.

We troop inside to find a sun-dried, toothless woman in dark clothes brushing her wet hair in the great room. She stares at me blankly for a moment, then points the brush at me and cackles. It takes me a moment to recognize the cleaned-up version of Kitty Robinson. She says, "Tell Scott, 'Nay, thou art thine own plague.'"

She cackles again.

# CHAPTER 16

## CHRISTINE, THE BAKER

STACY HARTLEY IS GOING TO charge me for the sand she put in Phil's urn. Claimed the thing would fall over too easily without it. I should've said no and put a rock in it instead. God only knows what she'll ding me for five pounds of sand. Scott leads me to my seat. I don't need him fussing over me like I'm an old lady. I shoo him away to act as an usher.

I look around at the still-empty room. If Amy had any natural parenting skills, she would've had the Teromas dressed and ready on time so I didn't have to sit alone.

First to pay their respects, Mike and Nikki Larson. Naturally, their teenager, the town's odd-job boy, is the first one to the display. He takes the lid off the urn and looks inside—because that's what boys do. His mother smacks him, causing him to knock it over. All three scramble with too many hands at once, trying to put it back together and upright. They fail. Nikki slaps at it, knocking it into the boy's wrist, where it bounces off. Mike tries to grab the slick surface, misses, and sends it to the edge. It rolls slowly off the table while the three of them watch in horror as it clangs to the floor.

The sand is in a plastic bag which flops out sideways. The lid rolls on its edge under the first row of chairs. The boy darts like a minnow through three rows before proudly holding it up like the golden egg at Easter. Finally, Mike asserts the Dad Privilege, takes control, snatches the lid from the boy, and reassembles the pieces.

Nikki looks over her shoulder, sees me watching them, turns beet red, and covers her face with her hands. The incident is over in a minute, and, since no one else has arrived, I give her a shrug. She teeters over on her too-high-heels and apologizes profusely. I tell her to forget it. They go to the back row where they sit in shame and whisper rebukes at the boy.

Hartley watches from the side door. Whatever she was planning to charge for the sand just doubled. I can see it in her eyes.

Second to visit the urn is Pia Sabel with her advisor and a huge guy who must be an Indian, judging by his impossibly perfect cheekbones. They've got a new woman with them, and they're all dressed up in fitted black suits. I understand diversity, but her entourage looks more like a TV show than society in general. Not many Indians on TV though. She's got Hollywood beat there.

Then it occurs to me that Deeping must look pretty damn white to her. I'll have to adjust that somehow. I wonder if Vanessa Zuma is coming today. I'll have to find some way of engaging her in conversation. I'm sure Kubari won't show up. Who else do we have in terms of people of color? That doctor went back to Mumbai when Jose Orellana finished his residency and came home to Deeping. So that's one Latino and one black I can count on. Is that it?

This is a funeral, I remind myself. I've got to stop thinking of winning Sabel's project and start thinking about Phil. This town wants to see tears. They demand grief. Few of them know how many scrapes I've had to pull him through. No one knows how exhausting that crap gets after sixty years. I don't want to cry—I want to take a nap.

Sabel turns from the photos and flowers and approaches me, aided by a cane. There's a nylon ankle brace on her left foot that pushes her shoes wide. She doesn't say anything, only gestures to the open chair next to me. When I nod, she silently takes the seat, smooths her pants, slips her hand beneath mine, and puts the other on top. The shock of the assertive gesture is pacified by the warmth of her hands.

She whispers, "I'm alone now, too. I know how desolate it can feel."

She genuinely cares. That's unexpected. My mood changes gears. A pleasant and calming darkness envelops me. My eyes close. In the dark night of my mind, her words reach me. She lost her parents, and her adopted father. Never had siblings. She's alone in the world. As young as she is, she knows what I'm going through. Losing a parent is painful.

Losing a sibling, your last link to your youth, adds a lonesome sting to that pain.

Everyone I grew up with is gone now. I'm alone. Phil's death looms with more impact than I realized before. What was the last thing I said to him? I don't want to know. What was the last thing I did for him? I don't want to remember. Everything I did, I now regret. He's been nothing but a pain in my ass for years—but suddenly I remember the boy who loved to jump out of dark places to scare me when I least expected it. And there was that time Tim Dunn got friskier than I wanted. Phil came to my rescue. Got his butt kicked, but Tim Dunn never grabbed my ass again.

We used to build sandcastles on the beach. Even when we were older and back on break from college, we'd go out to Headland Beach, have a few beers, build a fortress, catch up on friends, and stay until the tide came in to wash it all away. There won't be any more sandcastles. No more complaining about our parents. No more talking him out of *running errands* for Vinny. Oh God, how he needed me. Frankly, I thought I was done, that I couldn't save him anymore. I should've tried harder. Overlooked his weaknesses. Trusted him more.

Too late.

There's not going to be a miraculous recovery, like when he plowed into the bridge abutment. He's not coming back from a heart attack this time. He's really dead. I feel the weight of the ocean fold over me. Salty tears fill my eyes. My chest heaves with a sob, then another. Sabel's hand crosses my shoulder, making circles on my back. She says nothing.

So many regrets. Things I should've done. Things I shouldn't have done. Now he's gone.

I hear someone crying and realize it's me. I can't show the town this kind of weakness. I have to show them nothing slows me down, I'm still here, doing my best for them. I'm their pillar, I'm their rock. I make the impossible happen. I solve the unsolvable problems. But I can't help it. My head fills with guilt and loss and regrets that spill into my heart. My face falls to Sabel's shoulder, her arm squeezes me, and all my grief rushes over me.

A flood of tears pours out for several minutes before I'm able to slow it down. I sense someone in front of me, offering sympathy. I don't want it. I want to dry my eyes and look at these people with a strong, reassuring gaze to let them know there's nothing wrong. I'm still as solid as our granite breakwater.

I reach for tissues and dab at my eyes.

When they clear a little, I see navy blue shoes with a gold buckle. Cheryl. You'd think a coroner would have black shoes in her closet, but in a small county, you take who you can get. She whispers, "I'll give you a minute, Christine."

Her shoes leave my visual range. My gaze remains stuck on the floor. Lyn Avery's sensible gray flats appear next—as if she were going to bingo night at Lobster Shack. She says, "I'm at a loss for your sorrows."

Apparently, she is.

Lynn follows Cheryl's lead and trots away. That leaves Rick. I've got to take him down to Boston and get him a pair of proper mayor's shoes. His scuffed and battered square-toed loafers were all the rage thirty years ago. He doesn't have Cheryl and Lyn's social graces. He stands there waiting for me to say something.

I sit up, wiping my eyes and blowing my nose. Sabel hands me a fresh tissue from a box on her lap that must've come from Hartley. I wonder what she's charging me for those.

When my eyes meet his, Rick recoils in shock. I imagine my red and swollen eyes and my smeared makeup is Halloween worthy. He's never seen me cry. He has no idea how to recover or what to say. This is the weakness I didn't want anyone to see. Now Rick's lost his confidence. He'll be off script before the preacher gets here. I tug his hand, "Thanks for coming, Rick. Take a seat. We'll talk later."

Rick darts away like a rat from a culvert in a spring runoff. Next to approach is Vanessa Zuma. She doesn't say anything, just looks into my eyes and pats my shoulder. As she walks away, I say quietly, "Let's talk later."

Vanessa doesn't hear me, but Sabel does. Perfect.

I need to remember what Vanessa does. Is she a schoolteacher? Somewhere in the Midwest, maybe?

Sabel leans over and for a moment, I hope she's going to compliment me on my diversity of friends. Instead, she tersely whispers, "I'm glad you forced me to stay. This case represents so many facets of our collective humanity. I assure you I'll find Phil's murderer."

She sits back and faces front. I'm not sure what her promise means. Her tone of voice made it feel more like a threat.

Amy hurries down the aisle, towing a kid with each hand. She stops in the aisle next to me, speechless that Sabel is sitting in her seat.

Sabel stands, clomps her bad ankle away from the chair, bows toward Amy because shaking hands won't work, and says, "You must be Amy. I hear he was a wonderful man with a great sense of humor." She leans down to the children. "Do you miss him?" When they nod, she touches her forehead as she says, "We keep the departed with us all the time."

The Teromas smile.

Sabel tracks around the three and takes a seat directly behind me.

For the first time, I notice the new woman sitting with her isn't a new woman at all. It's Crazy Kitty. I want to yell at her and get someone to throw her out, but she's clean and in a new pantsuit. Still toothless, though.

As I check Sabel and Kitty, I notice the whole room has filled to capacity while I was crying. Oh God. They all saw it.

# CHAPTER 17

## CHRISTINE, THE BAKER

HARTLEY APOLOGIZES PROFUSELY, THEN ANNOUNCES to the room that the preacher will be twenty minutes late. A collective sigh of resignation erupts. Then the parade of well-wishers offering sympathy starts and my skin crawls. Jana Siverling, hairstylist and gossip queen, leads the pack. She takes my hand, utters a cliché I don't hear, and adds, "I'm so glad you talked Phil into staying clear of Vinny."

I thank her and dismiss her by looking past her to Craig Balch, the tax preparer who filled the niche when the town's previous accountant was hauled off to jail. He says the usual *sorry for your loss*, and adds, "This may not be a good time to mention it, but—"

As he leaves that hanging, I let him twist in the wind a little. Then I say, "You know his financial situation better than I do. But when the estate is settled, if there's anything left, I'll be sure you get paid."

Next up is Mike Culpepper who insists he's a retired Army officer when everyone knows he was a spy. He looks around for Rick before saying, "You need to run for mayor again, Christine. You got rid of those damn meth dealers for us. They're back, you know."

"Meth dealers?" I'm shocked and pissed at the same time. "Where?"

"Yesterday, up on Elm. I sure don't want to see meth-mouth in our kids again."

"Did you talk to Rick about it?"

"I will. But what's he going to do? Now that Vinny's gone, someone has to deal with Al Devino."

I feel Sabel's eyes boring through the back of my head. I'm sure the woman has the hearing of a bat and didn't miss a word. Now I have to assure her there's no drug problem in this town. Well, thanks to Mike, that denial won't work. I'll tell her we have a plan to eradicate the problem. Yeah. I can sell that.

When he moves on, I see a line has formed. If we do this now, the reception will be much shorter. That works for me. Next is Julie Stafford, who runs a car dealership in Kennebunkport and is all business. "You are a model of patience, Christine. You did everything you could for that boy. I'd have shot him if he were my brother." She pats my hand, lets go, and moves on.

Mike Tenenbaum, the eco-terrorist from the wetlands research center up the coast, watches Julie's backside walk away before remembering he's standing in front of me. "Oh, uh, hi, Christine. Sorry for your loss." He scurries up the aisle after Julie. Men.

I look at the line. Joanne Ranzell, our Canadian transplant who won't let anyone forget their toque, is speaking, but I'm not hearing her because directly behind her is Boo-Boo Vitelli. Joanne follows my gaze, feels the tension, hurries through the requisites, and flees up the aisle.

Boo-Boo walks like an old skittish horse that's been spooked one too many times. Her face is covered in makeup and her eyeliner looks like charcoal. I wonder if she needs another vacation in rehab. I'm done paying for those. In fact, I'm done cleaning up her messes. Almost done. Boo-Boo stares at me with her mouth forming the words but none of them come out. I simply stare back. If I said anything it would be something I shouldn't say in public, like, *Keep your hands off Scotty.*

Finally, she says, "Phil was so nice to me when we were young. He was a remarkable man, Christine."

"Keep your hands off Scotty," I hiss as soft and low as I can.

She ignores me. "Sara always wanted to be the kind of big sister to me that you were for Phil. She was such a goddess and so much older. The three of you were my role models."

Here we go again, Boo-Boo blaming her addictions on being a six-year-old hanging around eighteen-year-olds. Sure, we drank whatever booze we could steal and smoked whatever weed we could afford, but at some point, maybe by your early twenties, you have to take responsibility for yourself. She hasn't yet, and her twenties are long gone. Most post-menopausal women figure out they don't need men anymore and truly blossom. Boo-Boo's not quite there yet.

We've stared at each other for a long awkward moment. The other people in line peel off, not wanting to witness the coming train wreck.

"Look," she fidgets her fingers. "I know you don't approve. I, I … there's a connection. It's special and, and … I can't explain it."

I can, but I won't. Not in polite company. Instead of making a scene, I say, "Find a chair and sit down, Boo-Boo."

She wants to say more, plead her case here in public where she knows I won't say mean things above a whisper. Instead, she looks up, sees something that makes her go pale, and rushes away.

Al Devino takes her place. Instead of standing in front of me, he stands half a step behind me, forcing me to turn in my chair to look up at him. In my peripheral vision, I see Sabel staring daggers at him. I also see the whole town watching as if they're in the suspenseful part of a horror movie.

Way at the back, Sabel's big Indian stands in the corner where his meaty shoulders touch both walls. A sentinel for protection, he recognizes a threat like Al and tears himself from his position to move slowly toward us. The man has the confidence of the biggest carnivore in the animal kingdom. Like a grizzly.

Al says, "We ain't talked since Vinny passed, Christine. You didn't show for his funeral. You shoulda come outta respect." Al tosses a glance around the room. "He had a bigger turnout than this. Lots bigger."

"You should leave," I say quietly. "You weren't invited."

"Hey, I liked Phil." Al spreads his arms wide, like a benevolent savior. "I tried to include him in the family. I invited him to Thanksgiving every year. Gave him opportunities. You always shot him down. Like you didn't want him improving his position. You didn't want him making good. Now I'm here, paying my respects, and you got nothing but rudeness?"

"Please leave, Al." My nerves are jumping like I've got my finger in an electrical socket. "We'll talk tomorrow."

The room is silent. No one is even breathing. I can't breathe either.

Sabel is breathing. She rises without her cane and faces Al. She's got a few inches on him and uses it to tower over him. Her fierce gray-green eyes stare into his as she leans forward, nearly nose-to-nose. She says, "There are many decisions in life, Al. Decisions that smart people take seriously. You have one of those decisions to make right now. You can leave here on your feet, as Ms. Jacobsen so nicely asked." She lowers her voice and growls. "Or you can leave here on your knees."

Al's eyes flash up the aisle where the grizzly stands with his hands dangling free at his sides. Al's jaw flexes as he thinks over her offer. "What did you say your name was, sweetie?"

"Chief Jacobsen told you once. Don't pretend you didn't look it up—sweetie."

His eyes narrow as he tilts up on his toes. "Your money don't mean shit to me. You can act all fancy, but you're not immune to accidents. And you won't stay in this town long."

"You're running out of time on that decision."

"I don't need to make no decisions. Those already been made. My answers will be delivered at the time and place of my choosing. It won't be here. It won't be now. But count on it landing soon as you leave town."

He sets out down the aisle. Every head turns to watch him go, including mine. I notice he wisely steps wide of the bear. I don't see Sabel's other guy.

Sabel takes her seat. I consider saying thank-you, but Al's point was easy to see: Sabel won't be here next week. I'll have to deal with Al somehow.

Crazy Kitty leans to my ear and says, "Thou art the accursed defiler of this land."

I face her, pissed as hell, and see a face scrunched up like the underside of an old tree that's been blown over, roots and knotted dirt converging on the center. I've never seen Crazy Kitty angry before. Usually, she's more like a jester. Sabel brushes her back with an arm. Crazy Kitty's eyes try to burn me alive.

I say, "What the hell is wrong with you?"

Crazy Kitty says, "I have escaped: in my truth is my strength."

Sabel glares at her. Then the old Crazy Kitty comes back. She cackles and pretends to zip her mouth closed. She's been getting worse for years. Maybe losing Phil sent her off the deep end. I face front and huff. Amy squeezes my hand, but that frees the Teromas and they take off up the aisle. Amy goes after them. The whole town sees me sitting alone because I can't keep my grandchildren under control.

My life is a living hell.

Diane McGar shows up wearing a clerical collar. It must be a side hustle from her cashier's job. Diane must be popular with the church crowd—they don't groan like they did when that Baptist guy showed up for Mom's.

Sabel leans to my shoulder and whispers, "What happened with Vinny?"

I twist to face her sideways. "He died last week of cancer. He was a smoker, so no surprise."

"I mean, what happened that allowed you to keep Vinny out of Deeping?"

That, I have no intention of telling her.

# CHAPTER 18

## ISAIAH, THE ADVISOR

WHEN I SEE AL DEVINO make a scene, I use the distraction to slip outside. I stand by the door, back to the wall, shoulder even with the jamb and listen. I hear him make his gangster threat and leave without giving Miguel a reason to shred him in public. But outside the door isn't public. I have more latitude to act. For a moment, the sound system screeches feedback. The noise covers my ankle extending across the threshold to trip Al-the-Big-Shot as he exits. The man tips forward, heading for a certain face-plant until I grab his elbow and pull him upright before he hits the ground.

At first, he's grateful, unaware I'm removing his pistol from its holster as I set him on his feet. It's a trick our instructor pulled on us in the barracks at Officer Candidate School. The unofficial exercise widened my peripheral vision by a factor of ten when moving through tight spaces. The Devino crime family didn't have such training. But Al isn't dumb and after a split second, he figures out he wasn't clumsy.

Quietly and calmly, I tell him, "Don't threaten my boss."

He doesn't respond as we face off. He's thin, not weak. While he's not bulging with muscle, he certainly has meanness. I've got a second-degree black belt in MCMAP—Marine Corps Martial Arts Program—and a height and weight advantage, not to mention the fact that I stole his Beretta. I'm perfectly willing to put the guy on the ground if he tries anything.

He backs up, spreads a smartass grin, and says, "Trying to provoke me, eh, ni…"

He cuts himself off. Not even gangsters can use the n-word anymore. I rejoice in the tiny, incremental improvement in American culture. At the same time, I know it doesn't mean he won't shoot me in the back.

He shakes his index finger at me as he backs across the front porch. "Nice try."

Spinning on his heel, he trots down the stairs and out to the Cadillac waiting in the street.

Suddenly, I realize Al is not dumb at all. There are two men waiting in that car. He chose to leave them outside, knowing his presence alone would create a scene. He didn't come in to make threats. He came in to count heads. Now he knows Scott, two officers, and the three Sabel people are occupied. He has calculated and confirmed that we left Phil's house lightly guarded.

I should ask permission but don't have time. I turn quickly into the funeral parlor, glide quietly to Miguel, and ask for the car keys in a whisper.

He doesn't look at me, just pulls them out and puts them in my hand. Either he knows where I'm going, or he trusts me to have a good reason for asking. I'm starting to click as one of the team.

I hurry outside and jump in the G-wagon Miguel brought to town. While adjusting the seat forward—I'm nowhere near as tall as Miguel—I notice new-car paperwork in the door pocket. A quick glance at the odometer tells me the car is brand-new. Damn. Why rent when you can buy?

I file that thought and hammer the gas.

On the drive, I call Emma in operations and ask her to text me everything we know about Al Devino. She promises a full report shortly.

It takes three minutes to roll up on a crime about to happen in front of Phil's house. Al and his two sidekicks form a triangle on one side of the street.

In front of them, a lone officer stands behind the gate to Phil Jacobsen's house, as if a battered, waist-high wooden gate will protect her. She's shaking her head "no." Fear streaks her face and her knees tremble.

I pull the G-wagon between them and park it. Hopping down, I announce myself. "Al, I distinctly heard Chief Jacobsen tell you he would call you when he released the scene. Why are you here?"

Al flexes his jaw as he weighs the situation. "Just checking to make sure nothing goes missing. Chief being all tied up today, you know."

"Not your concern."

"I got property in there. That's my concern."

"I give you my word: If you can describe it, and prove ownership, I will personally guarantee it's return."

"I don't gotta describe it. I know what it looks like."

"Does it look like a Beretta APX in gray?" I described his pistol, which, by now, I'm confident he knows is missing from his holster. And, until now, he thought he'd dropped in the car.

"Nah, much bigger," he says. "Solid polymer dry box about six feet by five feet, sealed. Sealed like a nun's virginity. Airtight, watertight, you get me? If I find it unsealed, there will be problems."

"That's a big box. Big as a bed. It would fill a room in there. I didn't see anything like that, Al. It's not there."

"It's thin," he says. "Maybe a foot thick. It could fit under a bed or up in an attic. You could put it behind a false wall or behind a curtain."

"I'll keep my eye out for it, then. If I find it, I'll call you. Now that you know the site is secure, and you have my guarantee, you can go home and get a good night's sleep. I wouldn't want any threatening moves to be misinterpreted and cause something regrettable—like what happened to Mike Davis."

I think that was the name of the guy Chief Jacobsen shot and killed.

Right away, I know I have it right. The two goons snap glances at the boss. He had a great bluff going until his boys lost their nerve. He clicks his fingers nervously, tosses a sneer at me. Then he gives me the same smile he gave me earlier. Like he has a joke going in his head. He backs to the car. "Don't you want my number?"

"Don't worry, I have it."

I pull out my phone, find the contact info Emma sent, and thumb out a text that reads, "You have my word." And send it.

When his phone beeps, he keeps his poker face and points at me again. "See you around. Say, what's your name?"

"T'Challa."

He looks confused, but his backup squad is already getting in the Cadillac. He gets in and drives away.

The officer behind me says, "Uh, thanks for helping out. But … did you just tell him you're the Black Panther?"

I face the woman. She's still trembling. "I figured he wouldn't know who Odysseus was, so I used a cultural reference that might better fit his milieu."

The officer's face scrunches up in confusion.

"Hand me your phone," I say. When she does, I enter a text to my phone number with one word, "Help" but I don't send it. I hand the phone back. "If you get nervous, even a tingling sensation that bugs you, press send—I'll be here in three minutes."

She nods. "You're that lady's advisor, right?"

"Isaiah Reddick at your service, ma'am."

She smiles with a sparkle in her eye. "I'm Kathy Butler. My shift ends at three."

"Good to know." I pat her shoulder and point at the G-wagon in the middle of the street. "Let him think I'm still here. Walk me through the front door, I'll go out the back, in case he's watching or swings by again."

We walk up the steps to the front door. As we step inside, we hear the Caddy cruise by on the street. I open the door and wave. It accelerates away.

It takes me three minutes to get back to Hartley's. This is the nice part about small towns: you can cross them on foot or in a car, no difference in time. I slip in the door and stand quietly against the wall.

The preacher is just finishing up her sermon. She says, "Would anyone like to say a few words about Phil Jacobsen?"

Pin-drop time in Deeping, Maine. Not a sound.

"Anyone?" she asks. "Anyone at all?"

Someone coughs.

"Just a thought, or a fond memory … maybe?" The preacher looks concerned. "Anything?"

# CHAPTER 19

## ISAIAH, THE ADVISOR

I FEEL LIKE SAYING SOMETHING about the dearly departed just to be polite. But it appears the town lives by the adage: *If you can't say anything nice, don't say anything at all.* The preacher gives up and dismisses the people with a disappointed sigh. I slip out to the porch before the crowd heads for the exit.

Ms. Sabel parks her back against the wall next to me and starts answering emails on her phone. Not wanting to break her concentration, I wait for a chance to tell her about my encounter. Before she looks up, Crazy Kitty barrels around a clot of people, jumps the stairs, and disappears into an alley.

I'm staring at the vacuum left in her wake when I hear Vanessa's voice closing in on me. "Such a bright future, that one. Terrible shame."

Ms. Sabel perks up and introduces herself. Vanessa tells her how she's followed Sabel Industries since Pia chose Jonelle Jackson and asks how extensive a search had been conducted. As they talk, I can't help but notice her easy eloquence in conversation and her beautiful profile. She defines class.

Ms. Sabel says, "No search at all. Jonelle was an obvious choice."

Vanessa looks doubly impressed. Ms. Sabel apologizes for working her phone but simply must make some schedule changes. She thumbs out replies, texts, and emails like a demon.

When Vanessa's attention returns to me, I ask, "What happened to Kitty?"

"Oh, she was one of the brightest kids in this town back in her day.

Graduated from Georgetown with honors." She sighs. "Fell into a bottle and never got out. Too far gone now."

"Did she always quote Greek tragedies?"

Vanessa gives me a curious look as Kubari Eady breaks out of the crowd, heading straight for me.

He beams and says, "Hey there, nig—"

He stops himself when his eyes cut to Vanessa Zuma. She watches us give dap wordlessly.

From her expression, I can tell Vanessa is old-school, like my parents, and doesn't hold with using the n-word in any context. To some it's not an epithet, it's a dehumanizing, blood-soaked symbol of hate with a gruesome history whether it's used in the lyrics of hip hop or chanted by a lynch mob. From an early age, my dad drilled into me that we Reddicks will not participate in our own degradation. A lesson that causes people like Kubari to see me as either out of touch, or white, or both. This time, I'm saved from dealing with the problem by Vanessa's scowl.

"I didn't expect to see you here," I tell Kubari.

"It's a village, brotha," he says with a laugh. "You don't pay your respects at a funeral, people don't pay their tab at your bar."

Vanessa laughs with him.

I ask, "What was Phil Jacobsen like?"

He chuckles and says, "The best worst customer you could ask for. I like people to have a good time, and Phil was life-of-the-party early in the evening. He'd show up about four but by dinner time, he moved straight to the drunk-jerk stage. That's when I stopped serving him. Sometimes he'd go home, and other times, he'd create a scene."

Kubari glances behind me, then mutters, "Damn, if it ain't that muthafuckin cop."

Chief Jacobsen joins our circle. Ms. Sabel gives him a nod before going back to her emails. Vanessa and Kubari exchange pleasantries with him as if he were a hungry polar bear. Kubari's understandable hostility makes me feel like I'm standing next to a simmering volcano. An awkward silence settles on us. There is something on Chief's mind he wants to say but has to work up how to say it. We let him.

Finally, he looks up at Kubari and says, "I already apologized for jumping to conclusions, Kubari. But I still feel bad about it. I don't understand why I was so quick to think badly of you. I'm not a racist. At least, I don't think I am, don't intend to be. I'm not sure if it's institutionalized racism or—"

"Do you know what institutionalized racism is?" Vanessa asks.

Kubari doesn't care, he's ready to deck the man. I catch his gaze and he eases off.

Chief Jacobsen shrugs before shaking his head. "Not enough to define it."

She looks him over before deciding he's genuinely interested. "Let's take a look at it outside your line of work so you won't be defensive. One example of institutionalized racism happened in banking when the government guaranteed mortgages from the 1920s through the 1960s for whites but not blacks. White people with the same income as their black neighbors could afford a move to the suburbs where the cost of living was lower. The whites then used their home equity to send their kids to college, and the kids got better paying jobs. That one program alone resulted in two generations of income and education disparity. Black people paid the same taxes as whites but didn't get the same benefits from the same institution."

Judging from the confused look on his face, Vanessa's explanation is too abstract for him. I bring it around to him by adding, "That economic disparity led to a quick solution for police and prosecutors facing an unsolvable crime: arrest a poor black man who can't afford a good lawyer. Keep him in jail until he makes a plea deal just to get out. Crime solved. After years of this, people see statistics leading them to believe blacks commit more crimes than whites. Contrast that against Bernie Madoff's $17 billion fraud conviction. One white man represented a greater economic impact than everyone else in jail combined regardless of race, yet people don't associate stealing with white people."

Chief's chin rises as his gaze goes to the ceiling. I think he's crossed the first bar of understanding. He chews the inside of his cheek while he processes racial disparity and realizes racism isn't confined to lynchings and segregated lunch counters.

As he begins to appreciate the enormity, he asks, "Where did I go wrong?"

"You singled out someone different from you instead of looking for the obvious," I tell him. "You assumed from years of skewed statistics that black people commit crimes. You were blind to other evidence."

"What other evidence?"

"For starters, Phil was involved to some degree in a local crime family. Who is more likely to commit murder, an established business owner or a criminal enterprise—made up of white people?"

"Yeah," he says and looks at the ground. "You're right. I gotta dig deeper into Devino. But. If Al killed Phil, why wouldn't he have gone to the house that night to take whatever it was he was looking for?"

"Looking to excuse the white suspect's behavior?" Ms. Sabel says over the top of her phone. "Plenty of dying men have given their killers bad information out of spite."

He meets her gaze. "Phil sent Al on a wild goose chase? Yeah. Possible."

"Don't think about it now," Ms. Sabel says. "Take today to grieve with your family. We can talk about the investigation when you're ready."

With a downcast nod, he turns away, then stops. He puts a hand on Kubari's arm. "I really am sorry, Kubari."

"Go mourn your uncle," Kubari says with remarkable restraint. "We'll settle up another time."

"Yeah." Chief Jacobsen crosses to his mother on the other end of the porch. They start out on foot for her house.

"You was asking about Phil," Kubari says. "He used to brag about his cousin Vinny Devino. Told everyone to be nice to him or he'd call Vinny. This one time, he was drunk, talking off his head, and claimed Vinny had something to do with the Gardner Museum robbery."

Ms. Sabel perks up with interest. "The heist of priceless works by Manet, Rembrandt, Vermeer and others?"

"Yeah, that one. Happened back in the '90s but they never found anything. And there's a $10 million reward."

"Murders have been committed for a lot less," she says.

"Paintings?" I ask. "Like, big ones?"

All three of my companions turn to me, curious about that question.

I explain my jaunt to Phil's house during the funeral and the encounter with Al Devino. Ms. Sabel watches me tell the story with a mix of admiration and concern.

She's concerned because I didn't tell Chief Jacobsen. By the time I'm done, her glances at Kubari tell me she figured out my people's tortured relationship with the police will sometimes lead us to withhold information. Just to make sure, I wrap up by saying, "I'm confident Ms. Butler, the officer on duty, will inform Chief Jacobsen of the incident at the end of her shift."

A nod tells me Ms. Sabel approves of this solution for reporting.

Then I ask about the Gardner Museum. To get the facts straight, Kubari looks it up on Wikipedia and relays the pertinent information. In the spring of 1990, two men dressed as police officers asked to be let in a secured door long after midnight. They tied up the two security guards and made off with thirteen works of art. In total, the police estimate the value at $500 million. The case has never been solved.

One of the stolen works, a painting by Vermeer, is considered the most valuable unrecovered painting in the world. But when we dig into it, it's less than three feet square. We check the sizes of the others and find one that stands out: Rembrandt's *The Storm on the Sea of Galilee* is listed at just over five feet by four feet. I'm guessing it might require a box with six inches of space on four sides, and maybe a foot deep.

A waterproof, airtight box.

# CHAPTER 20

## CHRISTINE, THE BAKER

WHAT I HATE MOST ABOUT Deeping funerals is how everyone feels the need to prepare excessive amounts of food. Scattered across every flat surface in my kitchen and dining room are caldrons of lobster bisque, cafeteria trays of lobster rolls, piles of corn, bowls of corned hake—we could feed the hungry children of Portland for a week. That's not counting cakes and pies. And now everyone's leaving. Of course, none of them ate a thing.

Jill Williams, Phil's once-upon-a-time wife, talks my ear off about what a wonderful man he was while a stream of people give me a hug and head out into the late afternoon. I'm tempted to ask her why she ran screaming from the house and slapped him with a restraining order if he was such a nice guy. But that's all behind us now and one day I'll end up in the old-folks' home she runs, so I have to keep on her good side.

Sabel says her goodbyes with her boys right behind her. Advisors. I kick myself for thinking in dismissive terms. When you're my age, every male under fifty is a boy, but Scotty told me we should be careful not to disrespect minorities. It's just good manners. You know you raised the kids right when they teach you to be a better person. *Advisors.* I have to remember that.

Sabel asks, "You have a good deal of leftovers. Would it be OK if we took some out to Kitty and her friends?"

"Kitty has friends?"

"Miguel counted nine in a lane on the edge of town. He took them tents and sleeping bags, but they could use a good meal."

"By all means."

As soon as I say the word, they load up everything they can carry. After avoiding me throughout the reception, Boo-Boo gives them a hand. Is she playing Sabel to get on my good side? Doesn't matter. Even if she cons Sabel into thinking she's a goddess, Boo-Boo cannot date Scotty. That's not negotiable.

While I wave goodbye to Sabel and her squad from my front door, the Teromas dart by me like a pair of cats, one on either side. Amy's hand reaches past me to grab one, while I instinctively grab the other by the collar. Decades of parenting and I've got the reflexes to prove it.

"Bath time?" I ask Amy.

"I'll be down in a minute," she says and hauls the kids upstairs, where I hear the bath running.

I stand still, enjoying the sudden peace and quiet of the almost-warm afternoon, wondering how many billionaires with sprained ankles hobble to the outskirts of town carrying bags full of lobster rolls. Then I consider seeing her in the dumpster. What was that about? Is it a new fad these millennials are doing? Maybe they want to draw attention to how wasteful we are as a society. Maybe she's one of those people keeping sharks safe from plastics. Or is it about me and what we throw out of the bakery every day? Mostly coffee filters and half-eaten muffins. She can cart those off to the homeless for all I care.

At least Rick's idea proved true. Sabel's here and she's taken an interest in the community.

Finally, I get around to thinking about where Scotty is with that investigation. I'll need to drag all the details out of him. If he'll talk to me. Halfway through the reception, he hissed his extreme displeasure about my tête-à-tête with Boo-Boo.

I listen to the house and hear faint hints of his friends and him in the basement rec room. As soon as his friends leave, I'll catch him.

After a few minutes of thinking, I notice a young woman coming up the walkway. Sneaking in, I should say. She reminds me of the zoo monkey that stole my apple. Stopping in front of me, she says, "You're Christine Jacobsen, right? Is Amy staying with you?"

"Who wants to know?"

"Nancy Shepherd." She gives me a summary curtsey and a smile. "She's here for the funeral, right?"

"Yeah, but who did—"

"I'm a process server." She slaps a thick stack of papers in my hand. "Be sure she reads this. Thank you."

"I thought you had to serve her personally."

"Nope. Next of kin, place of residence, done."

The woman turns and hurries away, scribbling in her notebook as she leaves.

I'm staring in disbelief when Amy reaches around me and yanks the papers out of my hand. I follow her as she backs into the living room wearing a look of shock and horror. Upstairs, I hear the Teromas laughing and splashing in the bath.

"What is it?" I ask.

"Goddammit!" She throws the papers on top of a three-gallon bowl of Caesar salad on the coffee table and stomps to the kitchen. "Where do you keep the bourbon?"

"Same place."

She's in the cabinet before I finish. I hear the clink of ice in a glass. "You want one?"

"Do I need one?"

She doesn't reply. I reach for the papers and stop. Not only are they soaking up salad dressing, but I can see from here it's a restraining order. I call out to Amy in the kitchen. "Yeah. I'll take a slug."

We meet at the dining room table. She slides a tumbler of ice and whiskey to me. "Don't ask."

"You're going to tell me," I say. "It's just a matter of time. Why not get it over with?"

She chugs her double shot, slams the glass down, and makes a pained face until the burn in her throat dissipates. A flush colors her as her gaze rises to meet mine.

"Why does Gary feel the need to file a restraining order?" I ask.

"He accused me of slashing his tires."

"Did you?"

She grabs the bottle and pours another. "He refused to take my calls.

What else was I supposed to do?"

"Well …" I don't know what to say. Instead, I point at her glass. "Don't go Uncle-Phil on me now."

"Just a couple drinks, Mom. No big deal."

"I can think of a bunch of ways to treat a cheater besides slashing his tires."

"He didn't cheat."

She sips this time, which makes me relax enough to have a sip with her. I give her a silent space to explain. She doesn't.

After a minute of quiet, I ask, "So why'd you leave him?"

A second big sip, not the whole thing but a lot of it, and another gasp before she's ready. "He threw me out."

I choke on my sip and take a moment to regain my composure. "He threw you and the kids out?"

"No, just me. Next day, I slashed his tires, picked them up early from summer camp, and came here."

Covering my shock with a long inhale, I let that one sit between us until she's ready to tell me more. After another sip of courage, she breaks down in tears. "He won't take my calls. He blocked my number. Emails are rejected. His office refuses to put me through. I don't know what to do, Mom."

Giving her a minute to calm down, I change seats to be near her. She drops her head to the table and sobs while I stroke her back.

Laughing as they come, Scotty and his friends pound their way up from the basement where they spent their teens. The lighthearted banter between them stops as each one reaches the kitchen and sees Amy in a heap. They give me their last condolences on their suddenly hasty trek to the door. Scotty sends them off, glancing nervously over his shoulder at his sister. He's a man, which means he'd rather go with his friends than find out what brought Amy to tears.

He does the right thing. He goes to the kitchen cabinet, finds a tumbler, clatters ice into it, and joins us at the table, picking a chair as far from us as possible. He doesn't ask what's eating Amy.

"Have you moved on those sparks with Pia Sabel?" I ask.

"What?" Scotty acts like she's not interested in him. "No. Jesus.

Mom. I'm not one of those guys, a, a … player. I'm not going to start pawing at her like some—"

"I've seen how she looks at you." I stroke Amy's back as her sobs continue. "You need to open your eyes, get a bigger world view. You're a handsome young man and she's a good-looking woman."

"And way out of my class, in case you hadn't—"

"Only if you think so," I tell him. "She doesn't. No one's in her class and that gets lonely fast. Did you hear the fight she had with her boyfriend on the phone twenty minutes ago? He's on the other side of the world and a little impatient about her not meeting him in that town, whatever it's called. The one in Europe."

"So what? She dates guys who're worth millions, not a small-town cop with a mortgage."

"Give it a try for—"

"Mom. Stop. I'm dating Boo-Boo whether you approve or not." He crosses his arms and scowls.

I have the perfect question to change the subject. "How's the investigation going, Scotty?"

"I can't talk about it, Mom. You know that."

"You can't tell me anything about who killed my brother?"

His scowl dates back to his middle school years when he first became cynical. It hasn't changed a bit. Pouring himself a double, he takes a sip.

Amy's sobbing slows to a rhythmic and promising tempo.

"It's great that Sabel's helping with the investigation," I say. "That doesn't mean you should let her take over. She's the kind who'll tear the town apart just to get some headlines. They'll track down every crime that's been committed since statehood. They'll do it to make you look bad, then come in here and sell the town on one of their services to replace you."

Something I said touched a spot that hurt. He winces. I was just talking, but he looks scared. Maybe she's already promised to solve all our crimes. He chugs some whiskey and does the gasp.

"Don't worry, Mom," he says. "I've got Ms. Sabel and her advisors on a short leash."

"Well, was it cyanide like she thought?" I ask.

"Labs don't get back to you next day," he says. "And I'm not talking about an active investigation. Drop it."

"Well, what did Sabel come up with? Anything or is she just a rich kid playing around?"

"She came up with a bunch of threads, the cyanide, of course. And something about a rope that I didn't get. But Isaiah found some video equipment. Didn't find any tapes or memory cards anywhere. Which is strange. All those weddings he did, you'd think he'd keep some of them. If for no other reason because he was too lazy to throw them out. We're going to have a look at his laptop tomorrow. Ms. Sabel has people who can crack his password if—"

Amy interrupts us with a loud howl, her face craning to the ceiling like a coyote. When she runs out of breath, she puts her head back between her elbows on the table and sobs louder and harder than before. Scotty and I exchange a concerned glance.

"What do they expect to find?" I ask.

He shakes his head to remind me he can't talk about the investigation.

To change the subject, he lays a hand on Amy's arm and asks, "Is it about Phil?"

She looks up for a split second to shake her head. Then it's back to deep sobs.

"It's the divorce," I answer. "Gary did something awful."

Scotty's face clouds red with anger. His fists clench on the table. "That son of a b—"

"I cheated on him, OK?" Amy's head comes up, then resolves into sobs again. Between them, she manages to explain, "I joined a lifestyle club. I didn't tell him. He doesn't go for that kind of thing."

I blow a mouthful of whiskey all over the table. I exchange a shocked glance with Scotty. I get up and grab the dishrag to mop up.

Over Amy's head, Scotty mouths the question, *lifestyle club?*

I shrug. I have no intention of telling him the other words that could replace *lifestyle* such as: swingers, sex, orgy. Instead, I want out of the room. There are certain things you don't need to know, no matter how much you think you do. Your children's sexual proclivities are something you don't need to know. It's one of those rooms you regret going into as soon as you arrive.

"The kids are done with the bath," I say when I finish wiping down the table. Scotty has a look on his face that says, *don't you dare leave me now*. I add, "I'll get them to bed. You two stay here and talk."

# CHAPTER 21

## SCOTT, THE POLICE CHIEF

IT'S JUST AFTER BREAKFAST WHEN I discover Ms. Sabel and Isaiah, like most of my visitors, have entered the police station from the wrong side. I forgot to mention we share the building with the Deeping Community Center, a place where old people have coffee and grouse about how much better the town was when they were running it. We're at the back, which reflects the council's priorities. I step out of my office and call her over.

She threads through the scattered chairs, still using a pearl-handled cane and favoring her braced ankle. Does that mean she hasn't been to a doctor yet? Either she's tough as nails or making a big mistake. Not that it's any of my business.

She's wearing a different athleisure outfit, this one in blue with gently swirling white lines running the length. I thought she looked pretty sharp in the black pantsuit at the funeral. Less distracting anyway. Isaiah wears business casual gray slacks with a Sabel Agent polo in royal blue.

When they make it to my side of the room, I lead the way to the windowless meeting room. My office is too small for three people, so I've set up the lunchroom. It's the only space that seats four. I've never hosted a billionaire before—suddenly my headquarters looks shabby.

I motion to the stackable chairs I picked up cheap when the local motel refurbed their banquet room. They surround a table I got at the same sale. Ms. Sabel takes the chair at the far side, facing the door. Isaiah positions another chair to have a complimentary field of fire.

I point to their arrangement and ask, "Is this Stearne's Law in action?" I'm referencing the adage of her famous employee, Jacob Stearne. Stearne's Law states: *Paranoia is the result of acute situational awareness.*

My rehearsed icebreaker works. They're visibly pleased that I'm aware of Sabel Security's most celebrated operator. Ms. Sabel answers with an amused smile, "In our world, Stearne's Law is a way of life."

My nerves settle down a notch as I move on to the next buttering-up item on my agenda. "Taking dinner out to Crazy Kitty was very nice of you."

"While we were there, we noticed some of the people thought Kitty knew something of value. Have you questioned her?"

"Have you? I don't mean that in a snarky way. I've talked to her many times over the years. Long ago she made sense, but these days I get nothing. She was Uncle Phil's drinking buddy. He let her sleep on his couch in winter so she wouldn't freeze to death. It's true though, Kitty might know something. I picked up a pack of matches at the Plant and it came back with her fingerprints. Trouble is, if she did see or hear something, I have no idea how to get it out of her."

"Last night she was still quoting Greek tragedies," Isaiah said. "It's like she's mixed up a bunch, so I couldn't tell you which one. She was adamant that I tell you, and I'm paraphrasing her words here, 'Tell Scott, he is the man he seeks.' Does that mean anything to you?"

Thinking it over for an extra moment doesn't clarify anything for me. Is she talking about the murderer of Uncle Phil? She knows damn well I was his second-best friend after her. I'd never hurt him. Maybe she means that as a man-up thing? Like I need to be the man who solves the case? No idea. After the silence of my thought process drags out too long, I let out an exasperated breath. "I know it's not kind, but there's a reason we call her Crazy Kitty."

They give me sympathetic looks.

This is a good time for a new subject. I ask, "Is your other advisor going to join us?"

"Miguel's handling some of my business matters for me. At the moment, he's taking flak for me from the EU Council of Ministers. A satellite deal they're upset about."

"Oh." It becomes apparent to me that her use of the term *advisor* is not a substitute for bodyguard. She relies on them. "I thought we'd go through the preliminary information, prioritize, and make a plan. Maybe split up some of the work."

"Will any of your officers be involved?"

I cringe and turn to Isaiah. "Kathy, my second-in-command, told me what you did out there during the funeral, Isaiah. I appreciate your help in that tense situation. But tell me straight up, how would you assess her analytical skills?"

He thinks for a moment then turns to his boss. "She didn't know what milieu meant."

I never thought of vocabulary as an IQ test. I say, "And she's my best."

"We've got this," Isaiah says and leans forward.

Ms. Sabel agrees with a nod.

Spreading my notes in front of me, I show them the photos the crime scene guy sent me. First is Ms. Sabel's picture of footprints in the park grass near Phil's feet. It's blown up to 8x10. "The area was too trampled by the time our photographer got there, but as you can see from your phone shots, we still don't have anything. There's nothing in it for scale and the smudges don't show tread or shoe design."

Her finger lands on a leaf in the photo as I'm about to put it back in the folder. "This leaf can be used for scale. Did you pick up the leaf?"

No way the CSI took a leaf. No one does that. They use tape measures, but they didn't think the smudges were footprints. For diplomacy, I say, "I'll check later."

"That's OK," she says. "I had my people extrapolate from the metadata. The print here is a man's size 12. In other words, we have Cinderella's slipper should we find a suspect."

She shows me an enhanced photo on her phone. With the contrast turned up, they are clearly footprints. She was right all along. Damn.

"OK," I try to hide my surprise. "That's good to know. Admissible in court?"

"It's not a strong piece of evidence without a tread."

Producing the next 8x10 from my folder, I slide it to her. "This is the writing on the bench. You were right. He did scrawl something. The fingerprint dust confirmed his prints and gave us enough contrast to see something."

Isaiah hovers over her shoulder to examine it. She says, "That's says *secret*, right?"

"I think so."

"And this other part, is it A-D-C-I? Lowercase d."

"The second letter looks like a sloppy plus sign to me," Isaiah says.

I add, "You get two letters out of the end? I thought it was an O with one side squared off."

"Like a backwards D," Isaiah says.

Ms. Sabel's gaze goes back and forth between us. "Funny, I see it clearly, A-D-C-I."

"If the second letter is a lowercase D, then couldn't the last letter be a lowercase L?" I ask.

Isaiah agrees. Ms. Sabel stares at me as if I said something wrong. She's used to getting her way, I can tell that much. No matter which letters they are, it doesn't say anything I understand. She gives me the distinct impression she knows what it means, or at least, thinks she does. Since she's not saying, I move on to the next topic.

"I got an email from the lab this morning," I say as I put a printed summary in front of them, "They confirmed the tequila was laced with a significant dose of potassium cyanide. They estimate the dosage was carefully calculated to kill after two or three swigs. It was most likely added when the victim got near the bottom to avoid the suspicious smell. That means the killer and victim were together quite a while."

"Premeditated," she notes. "Your people didn't find any at the Plant?"

"No."

"Makes sense." She shrugs. Her muscles flex with every movement she makes. Distracting. "Industrial applications mostly use sodium cyanide, which is difficult to get and expensive. Potassium cyanide is much easier to find and costs half as much. Entomologists, farmers, pest control people all use it. We'll want to check the local colleges to see if any has gone missing. Farmers will be hard to trace. We'll be looking for a blue-and-white bottle about the size of an off-the-shelf aspirin bottle.

There's an outside chance it was Nitropress, a medical derivative used for certain cardiac conditions. While it's administered via injection, it can be dissolved in liquid. But it has much less of the almond smell."

"Good to know." I find myself staring at her without anything to add. To fill the gap, I say, "The tequila bottle had Uncle Phil's prints on the neck, no one else's."

"Are you planning to make a list of people who you've cleared?" she asks.

"That was my project for this morning," I say quickly. At least the lunchroom has a whiteboard. I grab a marker and rise. "So, with my illustrious consultants to help me, I'd like to do that now. As we discussed at the funeral, we have the Devino crime family." I turn to the whiteboard and write Devino at the top left. "We have Al Devino looking for a 6x5 dry box."

"And 600 yards of marine rope," Ms. Sabel adds.

I write that down.

"I'm not big on dry boxes," Isaiah says, "but I couldn't find anything that size online. The biggest I could find were the size of a small suitcase."

"I've never seen anything that big either." I tap the pen to my chin and suddenly fear it's the marking end. I check and find it's the back end. I'm good. I don't know why I feel so nervous. "Dry boxes aren't made by do-it-yourselfers, so it had to be built to order. We could check with manufacturers to see if one was custom-built."

"I made a few calls this morning," Isaiah says. "The first question they asked was, 'When was it ordered?' From what I gathered, it could be anywhere between five and twenty-five years ago. They want a month and year."

"We heard a rumor," Ms. Sabel says, "that Vinny may have been involved in the Gardner Museum heist. The box would fit the stolen paintings. Is there any truth to that rumor?"

"I've heard that rumor too." I write *Gardner Heist* and put a big question mark next to it. "But that's all I've heard, the rumor. I doubt Al's going to confirm or deny anything."

"Let's talk about clearing the obvious suspects," Ms. Sabel says.

"You made a mistake with Kubari, but that doesn't put him in the clear."

I feel anxiety quicken my heartbeat as if a chasm to hell is suddenly opening beneath my feet. "The only thing pointing to him was the bottle, and he still has it."

"He said Bill Koller sent him one," Isaiah says. "We need to verify that. Don't worry, I'll handle Mr. Eady. I've already left messages for Mr. Koller, but he's sailing in the South Pacific this month. We expect to hear from him whenever his housekeeper can reach him. On a positive note: after the funeral, I noticed Kubari has smaller feet than mine and I wear an 11."

Which makes Kubari a size too small. Those aren't his footprints walking around the corpse. While it doesn't make him innocent, it does make him less likely.

"Thank you." My anxiety drops a notch. "Next, is our mayor. Rick Tara dated Jill Williams when she ran off and married Uncle Phil. That was a long time ago, though. And he's a nice guy—"

"A grudge can fester," Isaiah says. "Add him to the list."

"Then there's you," Ms. Sabel says. "Not to mention your mother and sister."

I'm confused for a moment. Then I get it. "You mean, any inheritance could be a motive. I'm not sure how much is left of his trust. I suppose—"

"I took the liberty of asking Craig Balch," she says, referring to the local accountant. "He estimated it at roughly half a million plus the house."

A whistle escapes me. "That is motive. But ... Mom? Amy? Mom got the same inheritance as Uncle Phil and used it to start the bakery. And that's always done well. She doesn't live extravagantly, but never wanted for anything. Then there's Amy. She came home suddenly—out of the blue—two days before he was murdered." I cringe when her tearful confession about Gary throwing her out rises like a bright sun in my brain. "But she loved Uncle Phil. She would never kill him. She wouldn't hurt anyone."

"The Medford Police has surveillance video of her slashing her husband's tires. That's a violent temper."

"Yeah. Heard about that last night. It's not like her, though. She was distraught."

Their eyes stay fixed on me as my words hang in the air for a whole minute. My brain is catching up to the events. They researched Amy? They've been working on this more than I realized. I've got to get my head in the game, or they'll get ahead of me.

"OK. You're right." I hang my head. "They're persons of interest until I can clear them. But I can't interview them—that wouldn't be right."

When my gaze rises from the table, they at least look sympathetic. That's when I realize why they brought up Kubari first: to make me glad for their help. They had this planned all along. They're taking over my investigation. Mom warned me about that.

"Can we get a look at the laptop now?" Isaiah asks.

Why does he want that? And why did Amy howl like a wounded animal last night at the mention of the laptop?

"Why are you so keen on it?" I ask. "The SD cards could be anywhere in that house. There are a hundred loose floorboards and—"

"An encrypted hard drive would be safer than a spot where someone might stumble on them or they could be damaged by weather, rodents, or a hundred other things."

Especially if Uncle Phil was going to blackmail someone. And, among his get-rich-quick schemes, blackmail would fit right in. Why else would the tapes be missing? Could Al have taken them?

I look at Isaiah and think up a delay as I speak. "One of my guys wants to have another crack at it. Uncle Phil wasn't all that clever and we're thinking we might have a few more passwords to try." Then something else strikes me. "You know something about this video business, Isaiah. It's written on your face. What do you think is on that laptop? Let me remind you, I'm investigating a murder here."

Isaiah grits his teeth in anger. His reaction surprises Ms. Sabel as much as me. I wait him out.

"I heard a rumor that involved a young woman. Since it was just a rumor, I won't repeat it."

"You have to," I say. "This is an active investigation. This is the law."

In my peripheral vision, it appears Ms. Sabel will back me up on this, but she wants to be more patient.

"A gentleman," he says with a determined voice, "would never cast doubt on a lady's honor. I ask you not to pursue this line of questioning until the laptop is opened and we can determine what, if anything, is on it."

Neither Ms. Sabel nor I are satisfied with that answer, but his Victorian pronouncement about a lady's honor has us both leashed and respectfully impressed. Part of me wants to cheer him for attempting to bring back decency and respect. Another part of me wants to throttle him for withholding information. And yet another part replays last night's drama, with Mom telling me not to let them solve all our crimes, and Amy … well, I don't want to think about what Amy might have gotten into.

"I don't like that answer," I say. "But we have plenty to do as it is, and I've come to trust you, Isaiah. I'll take you at your word for now. I'll start researching Al and his movements. I'd appreciate it if you investigated Uncle Phil's estate and then interviewed my family. To save you some time questioning me, I wear a bodycam and had it on for the whole night shift."

"We know." Ms. Sabel looks at me blankly. "Sorry, but I had my people check your office's cyber security. They ran your video and your officers' for the hours in question. You and your people are clean. Unfortunately, that proves your security is less than adequate. Emma, my special operations manager will have a new router with a stronger firewall delivered tomorrow. My gift to the department."

They hacked my official video system? I'm having trouble breathing with my anxiety spiking. I feel invaded, penetrated, robbed. She shrugs. After my screwup with Kubari, she wanted to know what kind of cop I am. I'm the good kind. At least, I try to be.

"If you knew I had a body camera, why did you record our interview?" I ask.

"Because your dead-battery light was on." She points at the camera snapped to my uniform. "The thing died just as you sat down."

I grip the table and say, "OK, I feel backstabbed, but I'll get over it."

"Good," she says as Isaiah pushes a thin stack of papers in front of me, the top of which reads, *Sabel Security Consulting Engagement Contract*. "If you don't mind signing these authorization documents, we can begin acting in an official capacity for you right away."

Mom was right: they're taking over. I turn to the back page and sign.

# CHAPTER 22

## SCOTT, THE POLICE CHIEF

PULLING OUT OF THE PARKING lot in my squad car, I see Ms. Sabel talking to Pat Armstrong and Bud Blaine through the windows of the senior center. She said she was going to interview Mom, but she hasn't even left the building. I can't imagine what the old timers are telling her. *Didn't have any crime in my day.* How many times have I heard that? One of them says it and then another of them will add, *Didn't need any police either.* Which is countered by, *Never had to lock our doors.* All of which is easily proven wrong by looking in the file cabinets. Pat Armstrong's file includes transcripts from bugs and phone taps—no warrants included—dating back to the seventies referencing the Symbionese Liberation Army, whoever they were. Bud Blaine and his wife were accused but never charged with burning their house down for the insurance money. When the insurance company reluctantly coughed up the cash, their replacement house was significantly more expensive than their income would allow. How did that happen? And I don't even want to think about Karen Smith. Her file from the early nineties takes up half a drawer. No convictions, though. Just a picture of a young Karen riding her Harley, flipping off whoever took the picture. Not all old people were as well behaved as they'd like me to think.

The drive to Vinny's house, now Al's apparently, is long and boring. I keep one eye on my phone, expecting Mom to call and complain about her interrogation. She hasn't yet, so that's good. Maybe.

There's a goon outside Al's front door wearing shades and a shiny suit. We don't speak when I ring the bell, which is one of those video camera things. It wasn't here when I paid my respects to Vinny two weeks ago. When I see it, I text a message to Kathy Butler telling her to look for doorbell video cameras around the park and Uncle Phil's house. Maybe someone caught something.

A different goon, same sunglasses, not-so-shiny suit, opens the door and tosses a chin inside, then leads the way. He takes me through the kitchen where a maple butcherblock table has replaced Vinny's dated tile kitchen island. It looks a lot like Mom's kneading table. Al copied Mom's Bakery. Nostalgia? Jealousy?

Al stands in Vinny's home office, a wood paneled room with a single always-shuttered window. Against the wall, three cardboard boxes filled with pictures and knickknacks wait to be taken out. A fourth sits empty, waiting for discards. The shelves retain a quarter of what was displayed there on my last visit.

*"Goombah! Mio amico!"* he says as if he speaks the language. He's as Italian as the Olive Garden. He steps out from behind the desk and greets me with a big hug that ends with a brotherhood handshake.

"I'm here to ask you a few questions." I start to pull back.

"Nah. You're here to get straight with me." He leans in close, still clenching my hand. "Ain't that right, Donny?"

A voice behind me laughs.

"This is an official visit, Al. I'm investigating Uncle Phil's murder."

"Sure, sure." Al lets go and backs up a step. "Ask anything. There's things we need to talk about too, me and you. You got a body camera going there, Scotty?"

He points at where I usually wear it as he rounds the desk and takes a seat.

"No. I figured you'd lawyer up if I had it on." I sit opposite him. "I left it in the car."

"Smart man. Didn't I tell you my cousin's a smart guy, Donny?"

I can feel the man behind me nodding.

"Go ahead, Scotty, ask your questions." He grins at me with his ever-present insolent expression.

"Where were you the night Uncle Phil was murdered?"

"I was here with Donny. Ain't that right, Donny?"

Another laugh.

"I'm serious, Al." I put my hands at my sides, my righthand unintentionally rests on the butt of my pistol. Not wanting to escalate things, I put my hands on the armrests. He watches me and I'm reminded that mobsters are critically aware of body language and how it relates to power dynamics. He's sizing me up and I'm squirming.

"We was talking about the business opportunities in Deeping—all night long." He chuckles. "Lots of money to be made now that Christine and Vinny got no deal going. You hearing me, Scotty-boy?"

"What size shoe do you wear?"

"Whoa now," he says as he leans back and puts his feet up, showing me the soles of his expensive loafers. "That sounds like an incriminating question. That sounds like a lawyer kinda question. Cuz it sounds like you're going to make shoe prints somewhere in my size so you can pin something on me. That ain't nice, Scotty. I tell you about business and you come back with shoe size? Maybe you ain't the right guy to be going into business with. Maybe you ain't so smart after all."

"Looks like an 11, maybe 12," I say pointing at his shoe. "What's in the 6x5 box you were looking for?"

"Got no idea. The box used to be under Vinny's bed, but after your boy Phil come round—it ain't here no more."

"Then why make a big scene in front of strangers?"

"Oh, dat's clever." Al leans forward, his secret-joke-face grinning wider while he shakes his index finger at me. "I get it. You're talking around the topic. Yeah, I get ya. I get ya. So the problem is the strangers in town. OK, we can deal with that, can't we, Donny?"

The voice of the goon behind me finally finds words. "Yeah, boss."

Keeping my eyes on Al, I ask, "What's in the box?"

"I'm serious, Scotty. Vinny never told me. All I know is he and Christine had one of those, whaddaya call 'em, mutually assured things?"

"Mutual assured destruction?"

"Yeah, that. My understanding is that box keeps Christine from doing anything stupid. You know what I'm saying? Without that box, I gotta think up new and interesting ways to make sure she don't do nothing stupid. *Capisce?*"

Is he threatening Mom? My heart sinks. "Mom … she's family, Al. That's what Vinny always told me."

"Yeah, sure, sure. She's family like my dad was family." Al's voice is tinged with anger. "They was brothers, Scotty. They was brothers and Dad thought he could say things to people he shouldna said. Dangerous things. Things might get Vinny in trouble. Dad thought he had some kinda special protection. Like nothing could touch him. Like Vinny wouldn't do nothing to him. You hearing me, Scotty? Now your mom's out there acting all big and tough, strutting around like she's in charge. Didn't come up here to pay her respects to me. That kinda thing hurts. It hurts deep. That kinda thing keeps me up nights worrying about who I gotta trust and who I gotta consider a enemy." He scowls at me and lowers his voice. "Who might be the kinda people who talk too much."

He's reminding me that Vinny killed his own brother, Al's dad. Family means nothing to these people—he's directly threatening Mom. Fear begins to empty my body. There's nothing in my chest but rats clawing desperately to get off the sinking ship. I inhale slowly to keep steady. "You don't have to worry about Mom."

"You see the way she treated me when I tried to show for Phil?"

"Yeah, Al. I spoke to her about that. She lost her brother. Her head wasn't in the right place."

"And she let that tiger-lady stand up to me. Who the fuck lets that happen, Scotty? As a matter of fact—where was you?"

"I was, uhm, chasing Amy's kids. I didn't catch what was going on."

"Yeah. OK. We're gonna let that slide because today you came to pay your respects to the new *capo dei capi*. That makes me feel good." Al rises and comes around the front of the desk. He leans his butt against it and stares down at me. "But don't forget about Mike Davis, Scotty. He was like family too, ya know. He was a friend. A good friend. And you killed him."

How the hell did I get this interview turned around on me? I've got to get this back under control.

"This box we're looking for," I ask while trying to mask my shaky voice, "could it hold some paintings?"

"Paintings? Whadda I look like, a art professor?"

"Was Vinny involved in the robbery of the Gardner Museum?"

Al appears genuinely stumped. "Why the fuck would anybody rob a museum? They sell tickets online, credit cards. There ain't no cash. What are you asking me, Scotty? Out with it."

"Back in 1990, some guys stole millions worth of paintings from the museum. They say the heist was worth $500 million."

He squints at me like I was crazy. He waves his hands around the room. "Uncle Vinny stole half a billion in art and leaves me this dump? Nah. He woulda been drinking Mai Tais in Malibu he had that kinda money. Besides, why would he keep them so long? Nah. Nah. I told you, it had something about your mom. Wait. You think your mom robbed the museum and gave him the goods cuz it was too hot to move? Nah. That don't make no sense neither, Scotty."

He's got a point. It's the right size, but why hold onto hot paintings if all they could do is send you to jail? There's something about this box story that just doesn't add up no matter how I look at it.

I ask, "So, what does the box look like?"

"Yellow. Bright yellow like you won't lose it if it goes overboard. Made to be buried underground, tossed into the sea, dropped from a airplane. Rock solid. Big thing like that, kinda hard to miss."

"We didn't find it. Are you sure Phil took it?"

"Phil was second to last seeing Vinny. I was last. Vinny told me he took it from under the bed. He was pissed, Scotty. Then he had a seizure and I got busy with the EMTs. Spent the next four days with him in hospice. With all that was going on, I didn't have no time to go looking for Phil. I had to get the family under control. You know what I'm saying?"

I know exactly what he's saying. To secure his position in the criminal world, he had to eliminate rivals en masse. In the near future, Lincoln County, Maine will find bodies washing ashore when the poorly poured cement around the feet of his rivals disintegrates. It takes all my willpower to keep from choking. I've got to get out of here.

"You OK, Scotty?" Al twists his face up, mocking me. "You don't look so good. You get a hold of a bad lobster roll or something?"

"Did you kill Uncle Phil?" My voice gives away my anxieties.

"Damn, Scotty, you got a lot a nerve asking a question like that. That's downright disrespectful, ain't it, Donny?"

The laugh from behind me ends in a cough.

"No," he says. He gives me a kind, soft face. "Poison ain't my kinda thing, you know? Potassium cyanide. Now, who does a thing like that? And ruins a first-class bottle of tequila while he's at it. Nah. C'mon, Scotty. Do some thinking here. When the press makes up all that stuff about the Devino family, they always talk about how we do it *lupara bianca*. You know what that means?" He checks my blank expression. "It means, white shotgun. White like virgin, as in, the shotgun was never fired. They claim we don't shoot people; we chop people up and feed 'em to the fishes. Crazy talk. You think I chop people up and feed 'em to the fishes, Scotty?"

"Uh. No, Al."

"These days, those CSI guys can get DNA out of a fish belly. Nah. Shooting people, that's too risky. Feed 'em to the fishes, that's for movies. What I hear? All the smart guys do stuff like dissolve 'em in acid. No traces. No DNA. Right? But me, acid? No way. I wouldn't do nothing like that. Can you imagine me doing a horrible thing like that, Scotty?"

Can I imagine the man who went to work for the mobster uncle who murdered his own father disintegrating people in acid? Yes, I can imagine that—vividly. I imagine he puts his victims in the acid while they're still alive and fully conscious. I take a moment to squeeze the crap out of the chair's arm rests and steady my breathing.

"You got any more questions for your little investigation, Scotty?" he asks.

"I'm, uhm … satisfied for now."

"Good." He pats my cheek like a child. "Because we got some business to take care of in Deeping. How long those strangers, the tiger-lady and her people going to be in town?"

"A couple days."

"Yeah, dat's good. I'm busy next coupla days anyway. You let me know when you find the yellow box. Then, after your strangers leave, me and you gonna sit down and discuss how this all works. It's kinda like, new hire orientation. You're gonna love it."

He excuses me, walks me to the door, slaps my back. I hurry down the steps to the driveway. In seconds, I'm aiming my car down the road.

Half a mile later, I fumble my phone, pick it up, dial Mom. Voicemail. I leave a message, "Mom, we have a problem."

# CHAPTER 23

## CHRISTINE, THE BAKER

TWO DAYS AGO, I SAW Sabel as a huge opportunity for the town. That was before she dragged me into a corner of my own store to interrogate me like a criminal. It makes her seem like a junkyard dog snapping at the locals who dared to think they could land a big project like her SRC. Is this her retribution for thinking we were worthy?

She came in here wearing a navy blue skirt suit and low pumps, not that spandex stuff she was wearing when I followed her to Scotty's office a couple hours ago. At some point after she left him, she decided to step up the professional look. Fashion as a power trip.

Her gray-green eyes are focused somewhere inside my head, like she's paying more attention to what I'm saying than I am. She makes my voice sound nervous.

We finish up the preliminaries: names, address, the reason for this interview—so it's on the recording. Then she announces that she called Phil's trust attorney asking him what they could've asked me. Phil and I coordinated our wills a few years back. My money and house go to Scotty, Phil's goes to Amy. Because Phil's house was then, and is now, worthless, Amy gets my business.

"And Amy is aware of the arrangement?" Sabel asks.

"She was at the time. They signed stuff so there wouldn't be any fighting over it. Didn't Scotty tell you this? Why'd you need to call the lawyer? He'll bill us for that you know."

"We asked if Phil had made any changes."

"Did he?" I ask.

"Did you stay in touch with Bill Koller?"

"Who is that?" I know damn well who he is, but I'm going to make her work for it since she didn't answer my question.

"Two or three summers ago," she says, "he had a yacht too big for the harbor and rented a smaller yacht to go back and forth. I understand he entertained people out there and was quite popular at Eady's. Your son said you liked him."

Well, that rat bastard. He never wanted me to have fun with anyone after his dad left us. It was my fault as far as Scotty was concerned. So naturally, he had to tell Sabel all about Bill Koller. "Oh, right, that guy. What does he have to do with this?"

"Do you happen to have his satellite phone number?"

"No. I didn't know he had one," I answer quickly. "What do you need it for?"

"Did Phil go to the park often? Was that his quiet place?"

"You mean like for relaxing or something?" I have to think about this for a moment. "No. We spent a lot of time at Headland Beach as kids. He still went there sometimes. Mostly after he was banned from Eady's, he'd go there to drink with Crazy Kitty and other folks. Why?"

"Before Vinny died, did Phil go to visit him?" she asks.

Yesterday, she was all nice and friendly. Today, the woman is all business—and ignoring my questions.

I answer, "I think so. Vinny was on the slow road to death, you know, throat cancer from all his smoking. He called in just about everybody. It was kind of creepy. He was making us pay our last respects before he died. Yeah, I went when I was called. I think Phil went a day or two later. Vinny gave me his family Bible. We were cousins on my mother's side. He wanted me to have it because Al didn't respect the Church. It's not like I ever went to church either, but I brought it home and put it on a shelf."

"Did he give Phil anything?"

"I wouldn't know," I say. She stares at me forever. I feel like I can hear a clock ticking in the next building over. Some odd feeling compels me to fill the silence. "I mean, I'm sure he did, but that was just a day or two before he was killed, so ..."

I feel myself choking up unexpectedly. Phil's dead. I don't know why it's hitting me now. Maybe because, now that I'm sure the Sabel project is lost and I don't have anything to focus on, I'm feeling guilty. Maybe I could've visited him more often. Talked to him about things. But I get up early, about the time he's passing out. Our schedules never lined up. Still, I should've tried harder. My baby brother—gone.

Sabel walks back from the counter with a glass of water and a box of tissues. I didn't notice her leave. I mutter thanks and dry my eyes as she sits back down.

Behind her, I see Amy looking pained about me crying. I have to stop. I have to be strong for her. Especially now, she needs me. Poor Amy. How will we get through all these problems? And the Teromas. Suddenly, it feels like my whole family is falling apart. I start crying again. I hate that.

The back door buzzes with a delivery. I have to take care of it. Amy has no idea how they constantly try to cheat me. If you don't watch every bag of flour, you'll get billed for twice as many as they left. I feel my breathing return to normal. I pat my eyes dry and blow my nose.

When I've got it under control, I look up at Sabel. Her gaze hasn't softened any. I tell her, "I have to get that delivery."

She pats my arm and says, "No problem. We'll keep talking while we work."

I'm not sure what she means until I head to the back and see she's brought the phone with her, still recording. She sets it on the secret ingredients shelf where it can see the whole room. Then she takes off her jacket and rolls up her fancy silk sleeves.

I sign the paperwork for the fifty-pound bags of flour lined up by the delivery truck's roll-up door. Sabel puts the first one over her shoulder like it was no more than a laundry bag and carries it to the back while leaning on her cane. After a quick glance around, she figures out my system, decides where it should go, and puts it there. No huffing, no noticeable exertion. The delivery guy and I watch her, awed by her casual strength. When she turns around. I look away.

"How did you manage to keep Vinny out of Deeping, Christine?" she asks as she approaches.

She has flour on her. You can't carry a teaspoon of flour more than two steps without getting some on you.

"Like I said, he was family. When he tried to move into York County, I told him to stay out of Deeping. He respected that."

"Fairly unusual arrangement. Don't people like that tell you to make room for them *because* you're family?"

"In the movies."

She picks up another bag. The delivery guy picks up a bag. He follows her into the back.

Sabel sets hers down and limps back to me. "I have considerable experience with conspirators. The only way a guy like that would stay out of your town is if you had leverage, like evidence stashed away. What did you have on him, Christine?"

Didn't take her long to latch onto some ugly truths about our little slice of heaven. I start thinking of ways to get rid of her. I reconsider my idea to have Scotty arrest Crazy Kitty for it. Why not? At least the woman would have a roof over her head and hot meals.

Grabbing another bag, Sabel—bad ankle and all—beats the delivery guy to the back while I think.

"You should go to the doctor," I call out.

"What do you have on him?" she answers from the far end of the room.

All business, no nonsense.

When she comes back, I say, "I've known him all my life. I knew things that could've put him away. We made a deal."

She stops in front of me. "And yet he let you live. How nice of him, considering he murdered his own brother to take control of the family."

Damn. How did she know that already? She's been talking to the detectives in Portland, I'll bet. That's why she took so long to get here after she left Scotty's office.

Once again, Sabel has a bag of flour and heads to the back. She's about to lap the delivery driver. He should be ashamed, losing to a lady billionaire with a busted ankle. I give him a look that says as much, but he's looking at it as less work for him.

When she comes back, her face is far from friendly. "What is Al looking for? Would it be the evidence you held over Vinny's head for years?"

"No."

She's gone with another bag before I can extrapolate. Then she's back and has definitely lapped the driver. She's letting me think about it. I've got news for her: I won't.

After her next loop, she asks, "What do you know about Phil's video business?"

This trip, I grab a five-pound bag of gluten-free flour. We used to need gluten-free in the big fifty-pounders, but that fad went away. Now we only need it for people who actually have celiac disease. I answer while I follow her. "You mean his attempt to take over from Steven Spielberg?"

"Any idea what happened to the tapes and SD cards from his cameras?" she asks as she sets the bag down.

"I didn't keep track of his harebrained ideas. There were too many."

"Did Phil work for Vinny?"

"They tried using him as a back door into Deeping." A few tense moments with Vinny come boiling up from the bottom of my memory. "I put a stop to that."

"How?"

"I pointed out Phil was a drunk and likely to brag or say the wrong thing. Vinny respected that."

Sabel gives me one of her looks again. The look that says she doesn't believe me. She takes the last big bag. I grab the baking soda and trot alongside. I'm worried and I don't know why. Maybe it's because God-only-knows what Phil had on those tapes. Given what Amy said last night, I have massive fears about what might be on them. She spent a lot of time at his house during her high school years. What would that mean? I don't want to know.

I sign the delivery papers and the guy takes off.

I face Sabel. "The day before he died, the neighbors were worried he was losing it. Did you follow up with them? Or Crazy Kitty? She came by here talking that gobbledygook."

Sabel meets me at my kneading table. She looks up at the shelf above.

"What are all those things?"

She still won't answer my questions.

I look up. "That's where I keep my secret ingredients with the labels facing away so nosy people won't start thinking about opening a competing bakery."

Her eyes scan the shelf as if she's taking an inventory. "Only ingredients? Nothing else?"

"My employees put things up there sometimes. I don't see anything out of the ordinary at the moment."

"Who worked the last three days?" Her gaze comes back to me.

Boy, if this is what she looks like when she's asking questions, I'd hate to have her mad at me. "Uhm, let's see. Jenni Cornell. Amy of course. The Larson boy runs errands for me now and then. I think Debra Freeto had a shift." I tap my chin and realize I just put a white dab of flour on it. I wipe it off.

Sabel watches me like a scientist watching an experiment.

Time to change the subject. I ask her, "Do you have a boyfriend?"

The question hits her like a bee sting. "Yes."

"Why isn't he with you?"

"It's complicated." She crosses her arms and sweeps the floor with the toe of her shoe. "I made a company-wide rule that bosses can't date direct reports. Then, I bought a company where Liam was CEO—and that makes him my employee. As fate would have it, I became the first person to violate my own rule. Albeit unintentionally. Uh, so, we have to resolve that. Somehow."

"I see. Either he leaves—or you stop dating."

"Yeah. It turns out to be a tough decision either way." She looks me over as if she understands why I'm asking. "Scott is not interested in me. He has Boo-Boo. She helped us feed the unhoused last night. She's nice. You should be proud."

"Oh, I didn't mean you and—"

"One last question: Why did you follow me to the police station this morning?"

"Oh. Was that you? I thought so. Small town coincidence. Uhm. I was going to the florists' to settle up. They're just up the street from there."

"They open at nine."

"Yeah," I say with a forced laugh. "I remembered that when I got there. I've been … a bit distracted lately."

# CHAPTER 24

## ISAIAH, THE ADVISOR

I'M STILL ON THE PHONE getting pointers from Chrisana Droigk, a Sabel Security interrogation specialist, when Miguel walks in carrying a dripping wetsuit, snorkel, and mask. He lets me know there's no yellow rope hidden anywhere in the harbor. I give him a thumbs up, trying not to break my concentration on what the former FBI lady is telling me. Ms. Sabel trusted me with an important part of the investigation. I've got to get information out of Amy Jacobsen.

Chrisana is saying, "Do you know what part of your body enlarges to eight times its normal size when excited?" She breaks into a laugh. "That's right—the pupil in your eye. That can be due to lying or due to loving the subject like a nerd. It's hard to tell but go with your instincts. You want to push them with uncomfortable questions, but gently. If you push too hard, they clam up and you get nothing. Remember: time is on your side. You can always come back later for follow-up questions."

"What do you mean about pushing too hard?" I ask. "How do I know what's too much?"

"It's a fine line. Takes years of experience to get it right, but they told me you're smart. Read the face. Maintain eye contact. You'll sense them pulling back at some point. Be sensitive to that and save the next question for later. Oh, and last tip: The guilty always throw shade on someone else. Like they're trying to distract you. It's one of those things, you'll know it when you see it. I'm happy to help. If you have any questions or need anything, call me any time."

I thank her, click off, and head for Mom's Bakery. Running my questions through my brain the way I test-prepped in college, I repeat the pertinent facts over and over. I'm basically talking to myself as I walk down the street. A quick glance around assures me no one is close enough to hear me. Maybe I'm overanxious to impress Ms. Sabel with my interrogator skills.

Pia. She insisted I call her Pia.

There are two customers in the bakery when I arrive. Mayor Rick and someone I have to replay the study-cards in my head to remember. Lyn Avery, the Chamber of Commerce lady. They're chatting with Amy about someone's dog when I approach. They draw me into the conversation. As we discuss pets—Rick's a dog lover, Lyn's a cat lover, and Amy likes both—I sense the closeness of a small town. A slower, easier pace with a more engaged community. Now I see why Kubari put his anger aside and sat down with Chief Jacobsen after the bottle incident. No matter how mad you get at someone, you'll run into him the next day, so you learn to cool down quickly.

Lyn pulls a bag of croissants off the counter and wiggles her fingers at Amy. "Well, it was nice for you to see me. Bye."

Mayor Rick turns to me, "Has Deeping been ruled out of the hunt?"

After spending the last twenty-four hours as an adjunct cop, it takes me a moment to realize he means the hunt for the Sabel Research Center. Pia did mention to me the town's above-average spending on education and the affordable housing. "I have no idea, sir. We haven't discussed the SRC since the funeral yesterday. Ms. Sabel … I mean, Pia hasn't said anything negative. I have the impression she likes the place."

Rick's face brightens noticeably. He shifts the loaf of sourdough in the crook of his arm, grabs another bag from the counter, and says goodbye, leaving Amy and me facing each other.

She lays her hand softly on my wrist. "Don't you love summer? The golden sunlight, the breeze panting on your neck, the cream of pollen in every blossom? And the bees buzzing to embrace the flowers with their love vibrations." She pauses and flutters her eyelashes. "I said you could call *anytime*."

"Uhm, right. Yeah. Let's keep this professional, shall we?" After sweeping the room with my gaze, I ask, "Is this a good time?"

Before she can answer, three men in their early thirties burst through the door dressed in hospital scrubs. They walk the display cases, noisily examining the muffins and pastries all the way down to the far end. Amy smiles and nods their way as if to say, *Give me a minute.*

Just then, Pia and Christine come through a swinging door and say goodbye to each other. Pia—splotches of flour on her skirt and jacket—slides between the display case flashing her long legs despite the limp. With a brief nod my way, she heads for the door.

The scrub with the thick, wavy hair says in a low growl he thinks only his friends can hear, "She can ride my Porsche's stick-shift any day."

Pia stops dead in her tracks and turns slowly to the voice behind her while everyone in the room braces for a small explosion. The guilty party blushes while his two friends back up a step, leaving him alone.

"What kind of Porsche?" Pia asks, adding the European -eh at the end.

Amy, Christine, and I exchange curious glances about her unexpected response.

The handsome guy with a scruffy face regains his composure and says with a touch of pride, "911 Targa."

"As metaphors go," Pia says in a firm voice, "yours was a terrible idea on three levels. First, the rear-engine monstrosity Porsche has been trying to get rid of for years demonstrates how little you know about cars. A mid-engine 718, or even one of the family SUVs might put you in a more favorable light."

His mouth falls open, but he recovers quickly. "Oh? And what kind of Kia do you drive?"

"Sometimes my Lamborghini Aventador," she says, "or my Ferrari Stradale. But my favorite is my McLaren Artura."

His mouth falls open again.

"Your second mistake," she continues, "is the bizarre assumption anyone would want to 'ride your stick-shift.' That expression demonstrates your complete lack of cognitive empathy. Why would anyone do that in your pornographic imagination? I've been around locker rooms and understand your desire to deliver a salacious quip for your friends' amusement, but c'mon. Is that all you've got?"

"Uh…"

"And third," she says, "is that scruffy beard. From that alone, it's obvious you can't keep a woman."

That announcement offends him. "I can keep a woman just fine."

"You haven't had a girlfriend for longer than a few months."

One of his friends pushes his shoulder before looking at Pia and asking, "How did you know that?"

"Easy if you look at him. For example, I can tell he's a doctor by his repetitively scrubbed knuckles. Just as easily, I can tell he's lousy with women by the scruff on his face."

The offender looks back at his companions, who also sport five-day-stubble. The three of them turn back to Pia and wait for an explanation.

"If you go down on a woman with stubble like that," she says, "you either chafe her or you don't get close enough to be effective. Either way, you're going to lose her. And if you don't go down on your girlfriend at all, you will definitely lose her. Your scruff is keeping you from having a long-term relationship. Grow up and shave—or grow a beard. This *Miami Vice* facial fashion is holding you back as much as your bad jokes and rear-engine Porsche."

A moment of shocked silence follows until Christine bursts out laughing. Amy joins her mother. I can't keep my professional-interrogator-face either and crack up.

Pia walks past me and leans in for a quiet word. "When he recovers, ask him if he keeps Nitropress at his clinic."

She walks out. They watch her through the windows.

"Well, Jose," Christine bellows, "now that you've been humiliated, what would you like me to get you?"

He grimaces his way into a wistful smile and starts his order.

I wait for Amy's gaze to come my way before resuming our conversation. As she looks at me, she crinkles her nose in disgust. My hand automatically rises to my unshaven cheek. "I only got a few hours sleep—no time to shave. Normally, I …"

My need to explain myself evaporates. I nose over my shoulder at the men who Pia leveled. "Who are they?"

She whispers, "Dr. Jose Orellana and his squad from the clinic on

Cottage and Shore."

"OK," I say, shifting gears. "I'm hoping you can clear up a few things about your uncle. I understand you spent a good deal of time with him after Scott left for college, is that right?"

"No." She wrings her hands on a towel. She's shifted from seduction to scared in a second. "I mean, yes. Back then. But that was a long time ago. I haven't spoken to him much since I got married."

"The old days are what I'm trying to piece together," I say. Her pupils open wide. "When I called the University of Maine about an incident involving him ten years ago, they said they weren't allowed to talk about it. You were in college there at the time. Do you know what—"

"No."

Her answer comes so quick and her face drains so fast, I fear I've crossed that line our interrogation expert told me not to. I thought it would be an uncomfortable question, but she looks like she's having a full-on panic attack.

"I mean," she says, "I, I, uh, don't remember. If anything bad happened, I'm sure I would remember and I don't remember, so I don't … I don't recall anything. Bad, that is."

"Did he visit you in Bangor?"

"Orono."

"Pardon me?"

"The university. It's in Orono, which is near Bangor; people get them mixed up."

I leave the long silence Chrisana told me would evoke an answer. Her face contorts, giving away her thoughts. She wants to answer, but she thinks through the next step which would lead her back to why Phil got kicked off campus. After a few twists of her mouth, she folds her hands on the display case and stares at me.

"So, he did visit you," I say. "And you don't want to talk about it. I'll respect that." I watch her eyes. She drops them to the counter and waits me out. After a few seconds, I say, "My next question is about his video business. Did you—"

"That was a long time ago too," she says quickly. Amy meets my gaze for a fleeting second before dropping it back to the counter. "I don't remember anything about that."

My tutor also mentioned that attorneys will caution clients to "forget" incriminating things, telling them to say, *I don't remember* or *that was so long ago*. Her reticence to help could be either guilt or shame.

"I have the feeling I'm making you uncomfortable," I say. "Before I go any further with questions about his laptop, would you prefer to have an attorney present?"

Her mouth closes like a string purse, her eyes flash, and her scowl adds ten years to her age. She yells, "Why aren't you guys talking to Crazy Kitty, huh? When I got here a couple days ago, they were having a shouting match in the street outside his house. Nobody wants to talk about that. Wanna know why? Because nobody wants to talk to the mentally ill. How is that my problem? Why are you asking me what happened ten years ago? You should be talking to Crazy Kitty. Jesus fucking Christ."

# CHAPTER 25

## CHRISTINE, THE BAKER

MY HANDPICKED MAYOR STANDS AT the back door with Lyn Avery by his side. I texted him to come alone, but Lyn doesn't always give people that option. I step out and leave my right foot in the jamb to keep it from locking me out.

"I saw your text, Rick," I put a hand on his shoulder. "Just because her advisor says she likes the place doesn't mean we won. You had a good idea, getting Sabel to join the investigation. It got her involved—just not like you expected. She's here, immersed in the community, and digging up all our dirt—instead of discovering what a great place this would be for her SRC. You need to get her off the investigation."

Lyn gets up on her toes. "Rome wasn't burned in a year, Christine. You need to give him time to put the moves on her."

I squeeze my eyes shut to keep from correcting everything she just said and reopen them to pin down Rick.

He shrugs. "She's thrown herself into the case and seems to be enjoying it a good deal."

"Sure is," Lyn says. "Yesterday, she got hold of the Attorney General's Investigations Division and got a whole briefing on the Devino crime family."

"Don't call them a crime family," I bark with too much heat. They both look at me like frightened children.

The Attorney General. The last thing we need is Sabel looking into my mother's family at that level. I have to make fixing the situation personal for Rick and Lyn. "Look, she's too good at this stuff. She's going to discover things the people of Deeping would rather forget. Don't act all innocent. I'm talking about your game warden problems, Rick. And your driving record, Lyn."

"What about my driving record?"

"Oh, I don't know. Why don't we start with: Which street signs haven't you plowed down? It's the shorter list."

"What do you have to bring that up for? You said it was all airbrushed under the carpet. Isn't that why we made Scott the chief?"

Rick snaps a look at Lyn that nearly breaks his neck.

I wave my hand between them to get their attention. Then something catches my eye. A fancy Mercedes SUV parked at the end of the alley. Sabel's big Indian is climbing in the dumpster. I can only imagine what they're looking for. I need them off this investigation and out of town. Or maybe not out of town. If Isaiah was right and she does like Deeping, then Rick's plan is working. We simply need to get her back on track with the SRC.

Rick and Lyn follow my gaze to the dumpster.

"One man's trash is another man fed for the day," Lyn says.

"You'd think a billionaire would treat her people better," I say.

Behind me the door opens and Scotty appears, looking ill. He says, "Did you get my message?"

"Sorry, we've been busy all morning. What is it?"

He looks at Rick and Lyn before nosing inside for a private conversation. I hold up a finger for him to wait while I give my team marching orders. "Come up with something. Get her focused on the town and get her off that investigation. We're never going to see another opportunity like this again. Remember, a thousand jobs."

I close the door on them and find Scotty pacing the length of the storeroom. He looks around me to make sure they didn't follow me in. He puts a hand on my shoulder. His eyes have an intensity I've never seen before. He says, "Mom. Al threatened us. What did you have on Vinny?"

"What are you talking about? Vinny was my cousin."

"Al claimed you had a 'mutual assured destruction' pact and that's over now."

"You sound like Sabel. Is that what she told you?"

"No, Mom. That's what Al told me. I just came from there. He reminded me that Vinny killed his dad for talking too much. Then he said he was pissed you hadn't paid him your respects."

In his excitement, Scotty's hand squeezes my shoulder too tight. Wincing, I pull out of his grip. He mutters, *sorry*.

Vinny was reasonable. Al is much more dangerous. He was a mean kid who grew up to be a cold-blooded killer. He would move on us without question. That could get ugly. All the guys I used to rely on to make a stand are sucking Metamucil milkshakes for breakfast these days. They're more interested in dinner than sex. You know a man's too old to answer the call when that happens.

"We have to stand up to him," I tell Scotty. "Who can we count on?"

"For what?"

"For a war, what else? We make an army, assign patrols and watches, we keep the Devino gang out of town."

Scotty's looking at me like I've died my hair purple. "Mom, is that what you did to get rid of Vinny?"

It's close enough to the truth to work. His dad and Phil organized what they thought was a citizen's army. They were armed with deer rifles and baseball bats. They didn't scare anyone until Karen Smith on her Harley and Pat Armstrong in her Pontiac GTO joined them. Girl power. Although the gunslinger's revolver Karen wore on her hip and the sawed-off shotgun Pat dangled out the driver's side window might have had some influence. But none of that kept Vinny out of Deeping.

I kept Vinny out of Deeping.

"That was the visible part," I say. "So, who do we have? Did you patch things up with Kubari? We're going to need him. And then there's Jose Orellana. Never mind. He just got his ass handed to him by Sabel. If he had any confidence, it's gone now."

"I haven't done right by Kubari—I can't ask him to stand up for the town that never stood up for him. And I'm not deputizing citizens, that's nuts. While we're on it, Dr. Orellana has always been the town's highest IQ—not our toughest badass. Now tell me the whole story. What was the not-visible part of keeping Vinny out?"

"That was so long ago. It just worked out, OK? I knew things back then, heard rumors, pieced together a bluff and ..." I trail off when he rolls his eyes and turns away. I hate lying to him. "Tell me what you guys talked about. What threat did he make?"

"He reminded me Vinny killed his dad because he couldn't trust his own brother. Then he mentioned you didn't call on him as the new *capo dei capi*. He considers that, and your dismissive behavior at the funeral, signs of disrespect. He wondered aloud if he could trust you not to talk too much. Then he metaphorically explained how he dissolves his enemies in acid and throws their remains in the sea." Scotty runs his fingers through his hair. "And, after Ms. Sabel leaves town, he's going to fill me in on how the new operations are going to work."

"Yeah, I heard he's got dealers working up on Elm."

"What? Oh no. He's not getting away with that. I'm sending Kathy up there, clean them out before they get started." He pulls his radio out and calls in.

Nice to see him being a man of action. It's the work of Sisyphus, though. Those guys will disperse at the sight of a squad car and return shortly after it turns the corner.

But he's right to worry about Al. When they get people hooked on meth, it takes years to get them clean. Took me decades to get Boo-Boo sober. She'd get off one drug and start another. I'll bet she never told Scotty anything about her many rehab holidays. Sara would never have let her get near that shit. A sigh escapes me as Scotty turns off his radio.

"Mom. How do we handle Al?"

"Well, you don't want to arm the citizens, and I've got nothing on him, so I guess you call him up and ask him what's your cut of the action."

He paces away with an anguished cry. He gets halfway to the ovens and turns around. "What if we ask Sabel for help?"

"No way. She's pissed at me for forcing her into the investigation—"

"You did that? It came from Rick's office."

I shake my head at his naïveté. "Rick never changed the passwords. If you see a press release, I wrote it. I researched her and figured out exactly what it would take to get her to stay a couple extra days. That's not important. Even if we asked her nicely and she said yes, how much longer could she stay? Deeping can't afford to pay you a decent salary, much less hire Sabel Security." I wait until he looks downcast again before I add, "Unless they pick Deeping for her SRC."

He looks up quickly, liking the idea before the odds of winning it sink in and his brow once again furrows into dark, gloomy lines. As he resumes his pacing he asks, "So whatever you had on Vinny won't work on Al?"

"Vinny and I grew up together. Our mothers were as close as any sisters could be, so I spent a lot of time in his backyard and he in mine. I watched him stomp on toads for fun. When he got older, he hunted the pets of neighbors who pissed him off. Al's dad, Lorenzo, was older and aloof. He saw Vinny as an embarrassment. He kept Al as far from Vinny as he could. Of course, by the time Al was a teenager, that had the opposite of the intended effect. Al was drawn to Vinny's life, the intrigue and danger, being bad and getting away with it. By the time you and Amy came along, I had nothing to do with Vinny and his mob. That's why I knew things about Vinny but don't know anything about Al."

"Then we're screwed."

It pains me to see him so distraught. He paces more, his fingers wiggling as if he's ready to shoot anything that spooks him. I want to reassure him. I tell him, "You don't have to worry about me. He won't—"

"Mom, he's proud of the fact that Vinny killed his dad. And, he has insiders in my department."

"No! Tell me it isn't true. Someone on the force is working for Al?"

"It's not like we pay enough to live on."

"What makes you think he's got a mole?"

"He knew Phil's cause of death," Scotty says. "He knew it was potassium cyanide in an expensive bottle of tequila."

"There's another way he could know that."

"Yeah. Maybe he did it, except ..."

The unfinished thought he doesn't want to voice is, *but what can we do about it if he did?*

# CHAPTER 26

## SCOTT, THE POLICE CHIEF

IT'S ODD MS. SABEL WANTS me to drive her fancy G-wagon Mercedes instead of taking my squad car. I won't complain about driving a car with forty-seven miles on it instead of my 200,000-mile squeaking-creaking cruiser. It's just that this is official business and should be conducted in an official vehicle. Maybe she doesn't want to be seen in a rust bucket. I buckle up, start the engine, and look around the driver's side. The whole dashboard is a flat panel. I feel like a hayseed gawking at it.

I am a hayseed gawking at it. It costs what I make in three years. At least it's comfy.

My mind wanders back to my biggest fear: If Al moves drugs in Deeping, what happens to Boo-Boo's sobriety? She's the best thing that's ever happened to me. I can't let Al lure her back into that living hell.

I should stay calm. The road to recovery is in the heart and should withstand temptation. It's not the availability I should worry about, it's her stress and anxiety. If I keep her world calm and centered, everything will work out.

When Ms. Sabel's seatbelt clicks into place, I head out for York County Community College. I'm glad to see she's wearing a business suit and skirt. That skintight outfit is inappropriate for police work. None of my men can get any work done when she shows up looking like she stepped out of a gym for singles. Her toned legs and firm abs will not be ignored. I return my gaze to the road.

Turning onto Route 1 for the five-mile drive, I ask, "You want to let me in on why we're going there?"

"They were vandalized two days ago. When we get there, ask questions and form your own conclusions about the incident. We'll discuss it after."

As odd as that feels, I settle in for a long, awkward ride. I know detectives like to compare notes after finding evidence to preserve perspective, but this takes it to a new level.

Right outside of town, we stop for an unexplained traffic jam.

"Has your mother always had a difficult relationship with Boo-Boo?" she asks.

This woman doesn't shy away from personal questions. I answer, "Sara was Mom's best friend and Boo-Boo was her little sister. After Sara died, Mom stepped in as Boo-Boo's big sister—with mixed results. Siblings always have rough spots, I suppose." Sometimes omitting pertinent facts is the same as lying. I add, "Well. Truth is, Boo-Boo had a drug problem and Mom was there to clean it up. Mom thinks once you're a junkie you're always a junkie."

We stay quiet for a long time after that. The silence gets uncomfortable.

"You never had siblings," I say. "Did you have friends who filled that big-sister role?"

"No," she says and takes a long, contemplative inhale followed by an equally long sigh.

There's a hitch in it that tells me I've cut through her uber-confidence to something raw and painful.

"I struggle with long-term relationships," she says. "Several therapists have told me it's my personality flaw. Being too competitive. But I disagree with that analysis. My competitive nature is what drove my inner champion. I know my aggressiveness bothers some people. I always have to win, be the first to cross the finish line, the one who hoists the trophy, she who destroys the other team. When people don't like that, I don't care. The therapists are wrong. What screws up my relationships is residual rejection problems. Twenty minutes ago, I totaled your local doctor for making a typical guy-comment. It was stupid of him, but equally stupid of me. I need that guy's help and I don't even know his name."

"Jose Orellana," I say. Mom mentioned the incident earlier. Now I wish I'd asked a few questions. "Mom had the town give him a full-ride scholarship through college and med school in exchange for him practicing here for the next fifteen years. Before you think he won it on a diversity thing, he didn't. He was obviously the smartest kid in school by a long shot. No one else even applied."

"No misogyny test, I take it." She laughs sardonically. "I should drop it. Women aren't so different in the locker room. We make extra-sure you can't hear us, though."

Traffic starts moving again. We pass a group of teenagers pushing a car into a gas station.

"Your relationship with Boo-Boo bothers her more than any other? Or is she a helicopter mom?" she asks.

"Both. I've never had a long-term relationship either. Self-sabotage in my case."

She nods nervously. Her index finger taps too fast on her knee. She says, "The adoption thing? What therapists call residual rejection? Abandonment, lost identity stuff?"

It hurts to admit it to myself, but she nailed it. I sigh like she just did, and say, "Yeah."

"Same."

Her answer shocks me, and I can't help myself. I glance over. She's got her face to the window where I can't see her expression. I ask, "You feel like that? But … your parents didn't abandon, or, uh …"

"Didn't put me up for adoption? Not exactly, but I grew up with parallel questions. What kind of people get murdered in a home invasion? Yes, I know the truth now, later in life. I didn't know when I was six. I didn't know when I was twelve. On top of that, my biological grandparents didn't adopt me; they left me to a stranger named Alan Sabel. I had some tough years, believe it or not. No amount of wealth can cover up that hole. I was angry all the time. People didn't like me. When they tried to get close, I'd drive them away. Wisely, Dad channeled my anger onto the soccer field from the beginning. I was lucky to have the resources … and I was damn lucky to have Alan."

We stop for traffic again. This time it's a stoplight that's out and no one knows what to do.

"Mom channeled my anger into the Boy Scouts and police work. I was damn lucky too."

When she faces me, her gray-green eyes are moist and swollen. They're no longer those intense ray guns. She turns to the side window again. She's reluctant to show any sign of weakness.

My first thought is: why? Why confide these deep, dark feelings in me? Surely there are therapists better suited to the task. She can afford them. Having been to a few, I know they aren't all adoptees. In fact, I never found one who was. They'd read the articles, they knew the right things to say, the right ways to get out of a funk, and they meant well. But it's not the same as sharing an experience with someone on the same road. Maybe she needs someone to talk to. Come to think of it, not *maybe*.

"Did your grandparents ever regret not taking you in?" I ask.

"I was illegitimate. They never believed I was their son's daughter. They thought it was some entrapment scheme by my mother—until I was sixteen and made headlines breaking the state record in the 100 meters. They reached out to Dad saying they wanted to reconnect. He asked me what I wanted. I said, 'Fuck 'em.' That was also the first year he was listed among the Forbes 400 richest people, so I never knew—or wanted to know—who they really wanted to connect with."

"Ouch." Traffic starts to figure out the process for getting through the broken light. We inch forward one car length.

"Yeah. Poor me." She sniffles and finds a tissue in the glovebox. After a quick wipe and nose blow, she turns to me. "Did you ever want to connect with your biologicals?"

"Yes," I say. "But I can't. The agency was broken into, and a lot of records were destroyed. Mine among them. Teenagers being jerks, they figured. There's a lot of minor vandalism in rural areas."

She looks hurt, as if it were her records that were lost. She asks, "They didn't digitize and store it in the cloud?"

"Immediately afterward, yes. Too late for me, though."

"Do you go through phases of feeling lonely, rejected, and …

something like grief? Real dark periods, lasting for months."

"Used to." My throat tightens, I feel a thickening in my eyes. "Especially in my teens—when I was mad at Mom."

In my peripheral vision, I sense her studying me.

"Same." She rubs her palms on her skirt. "More when I was younger. Years of therapy helped. Years."

We make it to the light, take our turn, and drive on. We don't get a quarter mile before workers hold us up for a broken tree limb. This is the worst I've ever seen this road and suddenly I'm in a hurry to get going. I don't want to express my innermost feelings in an impromptu therapy session with a billionaire who could make or break our town. It feels like my community's future suddenly rests on how much she and I share childhood pain. I don't want that pressure. But short of getting out and walking, I'll have to deal with it. Maybe I can turn it around.

"My childhood friends' parents were strange when dealing with me," I say. "What about you?"

"Very. I made a name for myself in soccer at an early age, and Dad had business successes all the time. We were both in the news quite a bit. That attracted moms who wanted their daughters on my team so they could spend time with Dad on the sidelines. Some wanted to trade up their husbands, others wanted him to hire them. Others wanted to be near success like it might rub off on them. Sooner or later, their kid would be jealous of my skill or pissed off about my mean streak. Then the claws came out. Say anything questionable to an extra-mom's kid, and her manners fly out the window. That's when I'd hear, 'because she's adopted' like it was a disease her daughter might catch."

"Same," I say. "The disease part, not the success."

She chuckles at that, then says, "You know what I hated the most? And I still hate it. When they'd say to Dad, 'If she was your real daughter, you'd understand.' Or something like that. Like, what the fuck? You're not real because you're adopted? It's dehumanizing."

"Yeah." This time I do choke up. I felt that deep in my chest. I want to add a thought or two, but I can't without blubbering. I clamp my jaw and feel my chin quivering on the verge of breaking down. She's bringing up stuff I've purposely not thought about for years.

The crew has the limb out of the road in record time. They wave us through. I hit the gas a little too hard and jerk us forward.

A mile later, I get my voice back and find a way to shift the subject. "You're right. It is dehumanizing."

"Like what some police officers do to citizens," she says.

Her words feel like a dagger jabbed in my ribs. Lots of people don't like the police but I didn't expect an attack from Pia Sabel.

"Hey," I say, "if you're referring to killing Mike Davis, I didn't have a choice. He pulled a gun, fired first, hit me in the ballistic vest, and … well, nothing I could do. But that was different. I wasn't dehumanizing him; he was very real and very human to me. I'd known him all my life. I knew he was capable of …" I let the sentence trail off.

She says nothing.

She knows he was a criminal. She's not talking about Mike Davis.

A few thoughts rattle through my head. She said *some* officers. "You mean cops who pull the trigger too quickly? You're talking about Eric Garner, Breonna Taylor, Freddie Gray, Michael Brown, and so many others? Too many. Yeah. I get it. One innocent death is too many. I've thought about that. George Floyd was killed over $20. Breonna Taylor died because they raided the wrong address. You're right, those cops dehumanized their citizens. They used deadly force when it was uncalled for. Those idiots weren't practicing law enforcement, they were brutalizing their own citizens. That's not what being a cop is all about. That stuff makes me sick. Wait, are you saying that's what I was doing to Kubari? Hey, I didn't accuse him of …" Again, I find myself unable to finish my sentence.

She says nothing.

"Yeah. OK. I hear you. That's what Black Lives Matter is all about, right? The statistics show the use of deadly force is overwhelmingly disproportionate against minorities. I've read about that. But that's not me. I don't do that. I don't let things get out of control."

She says nothing.

"Are you saying I would've let the confrontation with Kubari blow up? Cause I wouldn't have. I just want you to know that. I mean, sure, that one time with Phil, things got a little out of …"

She says nothing.

"Oh, you think I should invoke the Golden Rule? Is that it? Treat others the way I want to be treated? Is that why you brought up *dehumanizing*? So I could empathize or something? Because I know what it's like to be marginalized, compared to *real* kids as if other kids were somehow better than me?"

She still doesn't say anything.

"For what it's worth, I'm sick about what I did to Kubari," I continue. "That's not the law enforcement I want to practice. I want everyone to be equal under the law. I will be a better cop. Yeah. And. Well, I've got to make it up to him somehow."

I let out a compressed breath of relief when we pull into the YCCC parking lot. If I spend another minute in this car, she's going to have me spilling all my childhood trauma.

We climb out and head for the office.

She's still using the cane. Her limp is more pronounced. "You should see a doctor."

"I've pissed off a lot of people," she says as if I hadn't spoken. "Sometimes I was right, other times, spiteful or just angry. Take it from me, you can't 'make it up to him.' If Kubari's worth it, and you really care, spend time with him. Get to know him and his family. Humanize him. That's how you make a difference."

At the front desk she asks for a professor by name, Paul Thompson. He shows up as if stepping out of the college's marketing brochure: friendly, the far side of middle age, mostly bald with wire rim glasses, and a warm smile. He leads us to a classroom on the ground floor. It has big windows, one of which has two panes covered in plywood. He shows us around and describes how he found the room a couple days ago. A moth collection shattered on the floor, an ant farm scattered across the room, wall posters torn down.

While he talks, Ms. Sabel wanders away, looking at the shelves at the back. From ten yards, she calls out, "Professor Thompson, is this your kill jar?"

I'm reminded of my ninth-grade hobby of collecting fascinating bugs in kill jars. Mom helped me and handled the poisonous mixture. I mounted and labeled them. I think she still has it hanging in the bakery. It was one of those projects that brings you closer together as a family.

He answers her, "Why yes. Are you a collector?"

She asks, "What do you use?"

"Cyanide," he says.

# CHAPTER 27

## SCOTT THE POLICE CHIEF

WITH THAT ONE WORD, I understand why she brought me to the college and what she expected me to discover. Why didn't I put together a break-in at an entomology lab with cyanide? Because Mom handled the poison, I never knew what she used. Ms. Sabel let me discover the connection on my own. I feel an appreciative smile growing on my face. Ms. Sabel's a damn clever woman.

"Where do you keep it?" she asks.

"Right there," he points near her. "In the drawer."

"I looked but didn't see any. Maybe I don't know what it looks like. Would you mind showing me?"

Professor Thompson walks over to her. I stay where I am. I know the answer. He isn't going to find it. He rifles through some drawers becoming increasingly frantic in his search. He describes what he's looking for: a small, blue and white plastic bottle whose biggest feature is a poison warning.

I join them and ask the questions she expects of me. He answers: No, the sheriff's deputies didn't find fingerprints; they thought kids trashed the place for fun; they have no hope and little interest in finding the perpetrators.

With her eyes back in ray gun mode, Ms. Sabel watches me until I can't find anything more to ask. We thank him and leave.

Silence weighs between us as we cross the parking lot, where an un-forecasted nor'easter blackens a quarter of the horizon. We'll have a good summer storm before long. We climb in and buckle up.

Questions stream through my mind with winds as strong as the coming gale. I can't pick one, so I let one pop out. "Why didn't you just tell me what you knew? Why this expedition?"

"What did you find out?"

"Where the murder weapon came from."

"That's what I found out, too," she says. "Just now."

"Oh, come on. You knew what you were doing. You went straight for it."

"There are only four places where cyanide could come from in the surrounding area. You checked the Plant and didn't find any traces there. The kind Dr. Orellana keeps is not the same kind used to kill Phil. I checked, they come up differently on the tox screens. That leaves this place and a chemical supplier in Portland. The latter said they hadn't sold any in months. The YCCC had a break-in. When I called, they said nothing had gone missing."

I process this while driving way too fast down the road. A farmer pulls out of his driveway, causing me to do some hard braking. My knuckles turn white on the wheel as the tires chirp and shudder down to the speed limit. The farmer flips me off in his back window. Ms. Sabel doesn't flinch.

She's telling me she did hours of research on cyanide types and sources. Part of me is angry because she worked harder on my murder case than I did. Part of me remembers people don't like her because she's competitive. I just got a dose of that competitive streak. Still, I don't like that she didn't tell me.

I say, "If we're going to work together, you have to tell me what you're thinking."

"No, I don't."

"Well. Damn it. That doesn't work for me."

"Too bad."

"How about we just cancel the contract," I say with heat, "and you can go on to all your big fancy meetings in Europe."

"Do you want to know who killed Phil Jacobsen?"

"Of course."

"Then don't cancel the contract."

She twists in her seat, her shoulder against the window, and stares at me with those damned ray guns. We drive a mile like that with the farmer going extra slow just to piss me off.

I blurt out in anger, "WHAT? What do you want?"

Calmly, she answers, "Those periods of abandonment-rejection-grief-guilt we talked about—for me they always come when I'm under a lot of stress. When I feel like the world is closing in on me and the weight is too much. There's always something behind that weight. One big thing I can't deal with alone. You're in front of one of those periods and it's getting dark fast. Don't try to hide it, Scott, I can smell it. What is it? What's weighing on you?"

Then, like a fog lifting, I realize it's not the cyanide. We could've called and checked. This is why she insisted on driving together. She wants to know what makes me tick. She wants to check my pulse.

And worst of all, she's right. I'm stressed out.

Without a second thought, I tell her the whole story about the threats made against my town and mother by Al Devino.

# CHAPTER 28

## ISAIAH, THE ADVISOR

MIGUEL TOLD ME NOT TO take it personally, but how do you not? I'm a Dartmouth grad, a combat-tested Marine lieutenant, an ass-kicking fighter, and I've been assigned garbage detail. But. Orders. Grabbing the edge of the industrial dumpster, I climb in. A quick survey reveals a layer of black plastic bags atop an ugly mess of garbage. I'm supposed to open the new bags.

"What in the name of Pluto are you doing?" Christine's voice echoes down the alley.

I step on a cardboard box that implodes under my weight. It's full of airbladders for shipping. Thank god. "Looking for something."

"What?"

Peering over the chest-high edge, I confess, "I don't know. I'm supposed to know it when I see it."

She struggles to hand up a big black trash bag. "Here's twenty pounds of coffee grounds and dirty napkins. Knock yourself out."

She pauses after the hand-off. "I'm sorry Amy blew up at you earlier. She's been on edge because of her marriage and Phil, all that."

"It's OK," I say and toss the bag aside.

"You know, she's blown up a couple times already." A wistful look colors her face. "Smashed some dishes, beat the crap out of an old garbage can with a baseball bat. I said the wrong thing and she took a swing at me. Missed though."

"Has she always had trouble controlling her anger?"

Her gaze meets mine quickly as she realizes she's sharing intimate family problems with a stranger. Her eyes dart from side to side while she figures what to say next. She decides to say nothing and leaves.

I watch her walk away. Tossing the bag to one side, I start a rough inventory to create a method for my duties.

"What did you do?" Christine's voice comes from halfway down the alley. She points at the bin. "It's not a racism thing, is it?"

That elicits a laugh. I tell her, "No, it's a new-guy thing."

"Like a fraternity initiation?"

"Something like that." Only this time I get to keep my clothes on.

"Your buddy already checked this one—'bout an hour ago."

As she turns to leave, it occurs to me to ask, "Did Kitty get in a fight with Phil?"

"Constantly," she says over her shoulder without stopping.

"I mean the day before he was killed."

"That's what I heard." She disappears inside her bakery.

Black clouds fill the sky to the north and east. For a moment, I wonder if that is a nor'easter and then I wonder how bad they might be. I've heard they're like a hurricane going backwards, coming from Greenland instead of up the coast from the south. Might not be as big and wet as a hurricane, but colder and meaner.

Dad sends me another text about the joys of being a surgeon and how often opportunities like Johns Hopkins come around. In my head, I have answers like, *If I go to med school, it'll be somewhere you don't have any friends to keep an eye on me*. Which isn't nice. Maybe something with humor in it, *I'll put people in the hospital, you can patch them up and send them home*. I settle on reporting that I'm making a difference in the world working for Sabel Security. I leave out the part about rifling through garbage.

I get back to making my inspection plan. In truth, we're taking turns. Ms. Sabel—I mean, Pia—hit the dumpster behind Hannaford's Supermarket before dawn. Then she checked the one behind the drugstore. Miguel was here an hour ago, but Pia wanted it checked again. Mine is not to wonder why, mine is but to …

I get through five out of seven bags when I hear another voice say, "What the hell are you doing?"

Rising, I see Mayor Rick walking by.

"Looking for something," I answer. "Don't ask, I don't know. I'll know it when I see it."

"Oh. Must be art, then."

"Yeah. Hey, did Kitty get in a fight with Phil the day he died?"

"You'd have to ask Scott." He marches on, knocks on Christine's back door, gets let in, and disappears.

There were a lot of downsides to the military, but public humiliation wasn't one of them. Dumpster-diving just might outweigh the USMC's stifling bureaucracy, glacial pace of change, institutionalized toxic masculinity, triggering racism, and everything else.

If Dad pulls strings to get me into med school, would those same strings keep me from being tossed out later? As soon as I think it, I know the answer: No. I go back to work. I'll give this Sabel thing another week.

After the last bag, I decide either I didn't know it when I saw it—or it wasn't here.

I stand up in the dumpster and come face to face with Kitty Robinson. She's doing a pullup on the outside edge. Still wearing the funeral outfit, albeit streaked with soot and dirt, her hair looks like she rolled in the mud all night instead of the donated sleeping bag. Her eyes are a golden hazel and they're staring directly into mine with a disturbing intensity. Our noses nearly touch. The stench of her breath overwhelms the smells around me. I back up and stumble over garbage. Something slimy seeps into my shoe.

"Kitty, how are you?" I ask.

"Such am I—as thou thinkest—a fool."

Squinting at her doesn't help me translate her words. "Did you have a fight with Phil before he died?"

"Art thou most skilled to unravel dark speech?"

My jaw slides to the side and my mouth twists into a strange position while I think. She mimics my expression. But something's coming to me. She's trying to convey some meaning in the only vocabulary she can still access in her alcohol-addled cognitive state: the stuff she memorized in college. Then again, maybe they call her Crazy Kitty for a reason.

"Yes," I answer. "I unravel bits of dark speech. I'm a little rusty, so work with me. What happened with Phil?"

"Seized with madness in the night, our glorious Ajax hath been utterly undone," she says.

"Tiresias?" I ask her.

She cackles and shakes her head, no.

I vault out of the dumpster, landing next to her. Goo squishes out of my shoe. There's a streak of coffee grounds on my pantleg, a hand-sized smear of something mustard-colored on my shirt. She gives me space, but not much.

The Greek tragedy *Ajax* is about a man going on a killing spree when the military commanders denied him due respect. When he comes to his senses, he kills himself. I think.

Tiresias, the blind prophet, was chronicled by many ancient poets from Hesiod around 750 BCE to Pliny the Elder in the time of Christ. The largest surviving collections come from Aeschylus, Sophocles, and Euripides. Sophocles wrote *Ajax* but Tiresias didn't appear in it. There was a good-sized role for Tecmessa, a princess who hung out with Ajax. Again, that's what I think. I was only there to meet women. And that went badly. Crazy Kitty epitomizes the fate of those who major in the Greeks.

But she's trying to tell me something.

"What happened to Phil?" I ask. "He went nuts?"

She cackles again, the amber in her eyes sparkling. But she shakes her head, no.

"Did he hurt you?" I ask. "Did he fight with you?"

She looks offended and backs up. "It sways him no longer: the lightnings flash no more; like a gale, fierce in its onset, his rage abates; and now, in his right mind, he feels new pain. To look on self-wrought woes, when no other had a hand therein—this lays sharp pangs in the soul."

"You had a fight, he regretted what he said? He apologized?"

"No!" She stamps a foot. Her hands rise at her sides then drop against her legs in frustration.

"He went nuts, though."

She nods and cackles.

I search my brain for the plot of the play. Suddenly, I remember owning a small tool that can look up anything. I pull out my phone and check it: Ajax felt Agamemnon and Menelaus unfairly favored Odysseus by honoring him with the armor of Achilles. Ajax decided to kill them all. OK. Sounds like the kind of workplace grudges that still blow up today, only Ajax didn't have an AR-15 with a thirty-round magazine. Athena stepped in, drove Ajax crazy with fury, and had him kill the cattle and herdsmen instead of the Greek kings. Vaguely parallel to Christine's story about Amy taking out her rage on a garbage can. So what is Kitty telling me about Phil?

"He went nuts about something?" I ask Kitty. "He wasn't mad at you. Someone disrespected him the way Agamemnon disrespected Ajax and he went mad?"

"And which," she says with perfect clarity, "if the choice were given thee, wouldst thou choose—to pain thy friends, and have delights thyself, or to share the grief of friends who grieve?"

"I would share the grief of my friends."

She stretches up on her tiptoes as if speaking to the sky. Her hands stretch out to the sides as if beseeching the gods. In a theater voice, she says, "Alas, he darted forward through the door, and began ranting to some creature of his brain,—now against Devino, now against Vitelli, finally against Jacobsen—with many a mocking vaunt of all the despite that he had wreaked on them in his raid. Anon, he rushed back once more into the house; and then, by slow, painful steps, regained his reason."

That almost makes sense to me. He railed about the mobsters, not her. Then he calmed down. So now all I need to know is who or what pissed him off.

Of course, it might be as useful as the garbage I just searched.

A figure darts around the hood of the Mercedes. I see a capped head peek over the top, then disappear near the front left headlight. Kitty sees him too. He pops up again, grungy hair under a dirty watch cap with a silly grin. He holds up a bottle of Jack Daniel's, shakes it, giggles, then ducks down again.

When I turn back to Kitty to ask my next question, she's bolting up the alley quicker than a feral cat. She turns a corner and disappears.

Squishing more viscous liquids out of my shoe, I round the SUV to find the man in the cap gone as well.

From the crossing alley, which is nothing more than a footpath to Main Street, I hear Vanessa Zuma's voice calling to me. "Isaiah, what the hell happened to you?"

That's it. My humiliation is complete.

# CHAPTER 29

## CHRISTINE, THE BAKER

DEBRA FREETO AND JENNI CORNELL show up to work the same shift even though the schedule clearly shows Amy. I don't know what to do with these two. While I'm pushing Mayor Rick out the back door, Amy is taking off her apron and coming toward me with glistening eyes. I send Debra and Jenni out front to work the lunch crowd. They claim to have come in because they knew I'd need them.

As they pass through the swinging door, I hear Jenni say, "Dr. Orellana, you shaved! I like the new clean face. And your friends too! What happened, somebody lose a bet?"

Sabel has changed this town already.

From the look on Amy's face, this is going to be a long one. I pull my rolling chair from under the desk, brush off the top layer of flour, and crumple into it. As I rest my aching feet on a five-gallon bucket of sourdough starter, my eyes fall on Sara's shrine. Until two days ago, I'd forgotten it was there. Since Sabel asked about it, I can't miss it. In that same time frame, everything I worked so hard for is crashing down. I can't help but think if Sara had lived, we'd have Sabel announcing Deeping as the chosen site, Phil would be alive, and Boo-Boo would never have had drug problems. I don't know if Sara could've saved Amy's marriage, though.

She pulls up a stool at the corner of my desk, sets her phone down, parks her elbows on the top, puts her head in her hands. "I think I fucked up."

"Don't worry about it, sweetie. We'll find someone with a broader mind than Gary, that's—"

"No!" Tears fill her eyes. "I'm a whore just like my mother."

"Don't say that. Your mother was a princess in a faraway—"

"I'm not five anymore, Mom. Uncle Vinny told me about her." The tears flow. Between jags she blurts out, "That's not even what I'm talking about."

I stroke her back as I wait for the other shoe to drop. What could it possibly be? Something about the lifestyle club? No matter what, I'll support her.

Her phone buzzes with a text. She glances at it and clicks it off. I couldn't read the message, but the sender was Al Devino. My stomach tightens a notch. Nothing he could text her would be good.

"Why is Al texting you?" I ask.

She responds with a glare telling me to back off. I look away. She goes back to crying.

Finally, Amy's sobs weaken. I push the tissues to her. Taking one, she pulls it together slowly. She sits up, straightens her posture, brushes back her hair, clears her eyes and takes a deep, centering breath.

She says, "I never asked for my records, you know. You didn't want me to. I know, I know: You never said that. You were supportive, even encouraged me when I was pregnant, but you didn't want me to find my birth parents, not really—and I respected that. You're my real mom. You've always been there for me. So, I need you to tell me the truth. No more princess stories. What was she like?"

This question fills me with dread. Just knowing it would inevitably come up made me worry for years. The agency told me she would want to know one day. I always expected she would request her records in secret, which is her right. But I want to be her mom. Her only mom. It warms me that she called me her real mom. I'm the one she turns to in triumph or defeat. I don't want competition. I know that's selfish, but it's true.

I was glad Scotty's records were missing. It saved having that anxiety common to adoptive parents: what if he casts me aside when he meets them? Or worse: what if they reject him? I was there for all his important events, where were they? Silly things to think—but so human.

The counsellors told me not to worry. Many kids are disappointed when they find their birth parents. More often than not, the first meeting goes horribly wrong, they say. I never wanted Amy or Scotty to feel that pain.

"Vinny lied to you," I tell her. "I only met her once. She was young, in high school. Her mother was an Evangelical leader of some kind and wouldn't let her consider keeping you. Abortion wasn't even discussed. Her mother convinced her adoption was best for you."

"Really, Mom? Is that true?"

"That's what she told me."

"What about my dad?"

"No idea. She didn't mention him. I asked and she ignored the question."

"That's why I'm a whore. She was a preacher's kid."

"Stop slut-shaming yourself," I snap. "Vinny made that crap up to control you. You're not a … that. You're … you're an adventurer, that's all. A courageous explorer. As long as it's not whips and chains—"

"It's whips and chains. Restraints, denial, rewards, punish—"

"Oh, honey, don't ever let a man beat you under any circumstances."

"You don't understand, Mom. I hold the whip. I'm a dominant."

Damn. We're right back in that room of her sexuality where I really, really, really didn't want to go. But. She's a dom? My sweet girl is a dom? The only thing I know about that stuff is what I've read in a few romance novels. OK, a lot of romance novels. Maybe "romance" is being generous for the genre. Anyway. When in her childhood did she see someone modeling dominant behavior?

"Well, I was right, then," I say. "You're a courageous adventurer."

It was the only thing I could come up with on short notice. It appears to work. Amy leans forward, elbows on the desk again, but this time with her chin in her palm, more pensive. Her thoughts contort her face several times as she considers whether this is good news or bad. Amy asks, "Was she a criminal? A bad person?"

"What brought this up, honey?" I ask while hoping she'll say *forget it* and go back to work so I don't have to pay both Debra and Jenni.

"I fucked up." She's on the verge of tears again when she takes a deep breath and refuses to give in. Thank God. "On the night Uncle Phil died, I got blind drunk. I left the kids with you and drank a bottle of vodka. Somehow, I ended up down at Town Harbor."

I take her hand. "That's OK. Your marriage fell apart because Gary's a nineteenth century prude. You deserved a drink or two. That's no big deal."

She rises and starts pacing, agitated and angry. "It's not about Gary. He didn't want to get pegged anymore. So I joined a club, and that sent him over the edge."

This is one of those conversations I didn't want to have with my child. I don't know what that word about Gary meant, but given the context, I don't dare ask. I try to cover my shock by looking away for a second and taking a deep breath. When I turn back, I say, "Well, he should've accepted his place when he got married—"

"No! Mom!" she shouts. "It's not about Gary." She glares at me like a demon. "I killed Uncle Phil!"

Shock and horror fill me as I replay her words in my head. Did my baby just say she committed murder? I feel like I just had a door slammed on my fingers and the pain hasn't hit my brain yet … but I know damn well it's coming. I keep my head clear.

Since I wanted to be her only mom, it's up to me to fix this.

I look around quickly to make sure no one heard her. Debra and Jenni are talking to customers out front. We're alone. We're good.

Amy picks up the large earthenware jar of yeast and readies to smash it on the floor.

Jumping up, I grab it from her and say, "Don't ever say that again."

"But I did. I really did." In anguish, she pounds her fists hard and fast on the kneading table. "Argh! Damn it."

I don't know much, but I do know one thing: Never confess to something without a lawyer. Since I don't have one handy, I'll have to convince her she didn't do it. People are always lying to themselves until they truly believe whatever they want. I'll just gaslight her until she believes she couldn't have done it. I blurt out, "No. You couldn't have."

She stares at me like I'm missing a few gears. "You were asleep. You don't know."

Thinking fast, I add, "You couldn't have done it because—Al Devino did."

"You're just saying that."

"Am not," I say. "Al did it. Did you see how he acted at the funeral? And he's already trying to move into town. And he knew it was cyanide before Scotty did. I'm telling you, he did it. Scotty needs to find some evidence to make an arrest."

"No," she says. "I can't remember everything but I know I poisoned him."

"Just because you don't know what happened doesn't mean you did it."

I set the yeast on the counter.

She picks up a bread knife and brandishes it absentmindedly. I grab her wrist, pull the knife out of her hand, and return it to the table.

"I was mad at him, Mom," she says while waving her hands. "Really pissed. I saw him yelling at Crazy Kitty in the afternoon. I don't remember what he said, I was already drunk, and he was off the rails yelling nonsense like a madman. And now they can't find any of his videos. Mom. I think it was about that. We argued about the videos—and then I got mad and killed him."

I fall back in my chair. "What videos?"

"Mom, don't pretend you don't know. The whole town knows. He made videos of my friends."

"When you were in high school? Underage—"

"No. He wasn't like *that*. In college. It was my idea. I went to a party freshman year where … well, let's just say it was an eye-opener. I went to him with an idea. It took me a while to convince him it was OK. Then … well, he blackmailed the Allen girl. Remember her, Siobahn Allen? She got her big break in that vampire movie? He blackmailed her three days ago. She called me. I was so mad at him, I wanted to kill him. Then, when I came back to Deeping, he was harshing on Crazy Kitty. I thought he was going to hurt her. I left before he saw me. I know what I was thinking, Mom. I was thinking the world would be better off if he died."

She drops back to the stool, puts her head on the desk, and folds her arms over her head.

After a long silence, she mumbles from under her elbow, "I got drunk and went back and killed him. I killed my uncle."

I stroke her back again and let the moment drift by. I hear the wind picking up outside, whistling down the alley like a guilty conscience. I wonder if Isaiah is still digging through the trash. I'd like to take a walk with her, get her away from nosy people.

"Where did you get the poison?" I ask.

"I don't know. I can see it. From when I was drunk. I have one of those dim memories of it that's just a bubble in time. It had a label that was mostly a warning, but it was definitely cyanide."

"How big was it?" Now I'm scared. She knows details.

"What do you mean? It was a bottle."

I point to the secret ingredients shelf. "Some of those are gallon jars, others are aspirin bottles. How big was it?"

"Aspirin-sized, I guess. Blue and white."

"Where did you see it?"

"I don't remember. I was drunk. I can see it in my hand, clear as day. Somewhere with lights. Like indoors. Not at the park."

More details. It's like that first whiff of bread burning in the oven, something has gone horribly wrong and I have to fix it before it gets worse. My anxiety rises. So does my heartbeat. "Where was it? Where did you put it down?"

"I don't know. I can't remember."

"It doesn't matter, Amy. I don't believe you. I'm absolutely certain Al Devino is the killer. That's why he's texting you. He's making you think that."

"No, that's not what he—"

"He's feeding you these details to gaslight you."

"But that's not right, I did it. I should confess. I should tell the truth. You used to tell us the truth always comes out."

Damn my parenting. What was I thinking? I should've taught my kids how the world really works: whoever tells the biggest, most convincing lie—and sticks to their story—gets away with it. Everyone else gets screwed. I take her by the shoulders. "Who belongs in jail, Amy—you or

Al?"

She looks up at me, her face full of questions.

"Don't tell anyone what you just told me. Not yet. If you really did do it—and I don't believe that for a minute—you were forced to do it by Al Devino."

# CHAPTER 30

## CHRISTINE, THE BAKER

THE CLOUDS BUILDING OVER THE coast look ugly. The wind is picking up. It's going to be a bad one, yet the weather app on my phone says, "chance of rain." Even with all this modern technology, you never know what's going to hit you.

We arrive at Al's house after a long and boring drive. There's a goon outside wearing shades and a shiny suit. He doesn't speak when I ring the video camera thingy. A different goon opens the door and tosses a chin inside. He leads the way through the kitchen where I see Al has replaced the countertop with a replica of my kneading table. Imitation is flattery? Not when it's Al.

As planned, Amy and I both ask to use the bathroom because it was a long and boring drive. I go first. I run the water and check the medicine cabinet behind the mirror. Aspirin, band aids, Tums, and a couple other bottles, all of which have been there for ages. I flush and leave.

Amy goes in. If all goes according to plan, she'll be alone when she comes out and can wander the house looking for evidence.

I point the way and the goon follows me to Vinny's home office, where Al stands in front of nearly empty shelves.

"Nice of you to come," Al says and waves me to a chair. "But you're late and I don't like how you treated me at Phil's funeral."

"My brother died." I take my seat. "I wasn't in the best mood. Now I've come to pay my respects."

Al parks his butt on the edge of the desk, crosses his arms, and looks down on me. "Ah, that's nice, Christine. That's nice. Ain't that nice,

Donny?"

A man's voice near the door laughs.

Al brings his gaze back to me. "Late. But nice. Maybe too late."

"I don't think so," I say. "I understand you wanted to talk business with Scotty. He's not big on that kind of business."

"Oh, and what, you want to talk? Ain't that special, Donny?"

The goon laughs again.

Al leans down to intimidate me. "You ain't mayor no more, Christine. You ain't got no juice."

"Who do you think forced Sabel to stay?" I wait until he recoils after he puts the pieces together. "Nothing happens in Deeping without me."

"Nothing, huh?" He pushes off the desk. "When I tried to bring Phil some business, you shot it down. You went to Vinny and made me look stupid. That wasn't good business. That wasn't smart. And don't think I forgot about it neither, Christine. I gotta long memory."

"Then you remember how Phil would get drunk and brag about Vinny when he should've kept his mouth shut. I wasn't interfering with your business, Al. I was saving it."

Al's in the middle of cleaning house. He has real enemies vying for his territories. As much as he'd like to teach me a lesson, he has more pressing problems. I read his mood as open to negotiation if I offer something.

"Vinny and I had an understanding," I tell him. "Phil would've been a liability and Vinny knew that. Now Vinny and Phil are both gone, it's a different landscape. You're the *Capo* and I'm interested in new business opportunities. Lay it out for me. What will it look like? Just keep in mind, I've got big plans for Deeping: bigger, better, higher-paying jobs. We're going places, and the right business opportunity could go places with us—as long as it doesn't sink the town. You get me?"

He hooks a finger over his lips in thought and rounds the desk. He ends up standing behind the black leather executive chair, where he parks his forearms on the top and stares at me for a while. Then he says, "What'd you and Vinny have going?"

"He never told you?"

He leans over the chair. "I'm asking you, Christine."

"We knew things about each other."

"Things?" He smirks with a murderous look. "Like things about your kids?"

Suddenly, I can't breathe. I feel my heart pounding hard enough to make my blouse shake. I feel my face drain as that sneaky grin stretches across the bastard's face. He can threaten my town, but that son of a bitch better not touch my kids. Would Vinny have told him anything? I doubt it. As much of a sadistic fuck as Vinny was, he took care of family. Well. Except for his brother.

Al's always thinking, calculating, figuring the odds. But he's more mercurial than Vinny ever was. He's a temper tantrum away from murder. When he's under stress—and taking over a mob is a lot of stress—he's as dangerous as a two-year-old playing with a loaded gun.

"You asked what Vinny and I had on each other. Ever hear of a man named Bobby Donati?" I ask and wait until he shakes his head. "Bobby Donati robbed the Gardner Museum in 1990. He came to Vinny for help fencing the goods. Vinny took the stolen art, then killed Bobby, stuffed him in the trunk of his own car to make it look like he was the victim of a mob war."

I pause and check Al's reaction. There isn't one. As far as he's concerned, Vinny's treachery is simply how the game is played.

I go on. "A couple other people knew about Vinny's betrayal and came around looking for a piece of the action. Vinny took care of them one at a time until the rumors died down. But the blood of four murder victims got on the paintings. He couldn't sell them, he couldn't turn them in for the reward, he was stuck with them. They were evidence that could convict him."

Al nods and tracks around the desk to the front. He stands over me and looks down, like he did in the beginning. "So that's what's in the big box. And the stuff he had on you, he kept it in there with the paintings? You turn him in, what he had on you comes to light with it. That mutual assured destruction thing."

"I don't know what you're talking about, Al. What box?"

"Scotty didn't tell you nothing about this?"

"What box?"

"Phil stole a big 6x5 waterproof, airtight dry box from under Vinny's bed while my beloved uncle—your cousin—was dying. What kind of fucking monster does a thing like that?" He leans into my face. "Where's the fucking box, Christine?"

Again, my breathing stops, my heart stops, my brain goes into overdrive. In a flash, the last twelve hours of my brother's life become clear to me. His mad afternoon rant in the street that had Mike and Joanne thinking he was having a psychotic break. Disappearing after his rant and not surfacing again for hours. Crazy Kitty coming by the bakery and saying god-knows-what. It all makes complete sense now.

Phil thought he was going to be the hero who solved the Gardner Museum heist and win the $10 million reward. He was pissed I didn't tell him about that—and a few other things—years ago.

Al darkens his glare and gets his nose in my face. He's about to repeat his question when we hear someone running towards us. He looks up.

Amy bursts into the room. "Mom, we have to leave. I'm … I'm sick. I, I, I must be pregnant again, morning sickness."

Al looks up, then his face drains.

I turn around to face Amy. She's seen a ghost. Her pale white skin is clammy. Beads of sweat drip down her forehead. Her lipstick looks pink instead of red. I get up and cross to her. She's shaking.

"Sorry, Al," she says. Then she heaves with nothing coming out. She swallows and says, "I came to pay my … urp … gotta go."

She runs down the hall to the bathroom and spews into the toilet.

I look at Al and say, "I'd better get her home. I'll come back in a couple days."

"Yeah, yeah, get her the fuck outta here." Looking a little green himself, he waves at the door. "Take a day, and don't make it no longer. I got people wanna work Deeping, Christine."

The wind howls outside as I scurry down the hall. The goon doesn't follow me. I find her on her knees, arms wrapped around the porcelain like a college kid at a party. She heaves bile.

After making sure she isn't watching me, I re-check the medicine cabinet for those Tums. Pulling the bottle out, I freeze with the Tums extended toward her. I whisper, "Amy … Amy, look."

"What?" her pathetic voice answers.

I point at a small bottle on the shelf.

Amy grabs the Tums and pours out a handful. She looks over my shoulder. "What? What is it?"

She chews the tablets and splashes cold water on her face. Without waiting for me, she bolts for the car. I race after her.

Outside, the wind has turned bitter cold. Leaves and small twigs assault us as I get in, start up, and head out to the highway. She's silent, holding back the next wave of nausea. I've never seen her so white.

"Are you really pregnant?" I ask. She didn't have that ever-present pregnancy warmth last time I touched her.

Her head shakes back and forth violently.

I tap her knee. "He had cyanide in there. Did you see it?"

"WHAT?" Her screech shakes the car. Gasping like she just finished a marathon, her eyes remain on the road ahead while her fingernails dig into the dashboard. "No. No. No. You can't tell anyone. He'll kill you. Mom!" After digging in her purse for a second, she tosses a pamphlet in my lap. I'm driving, so I can't read it.

We're heading southwest, my rear window filling with roiling black clouds. I feel like Vinny's spirit is shrieking after me seeking retribution.

"I told you Al did it," I say. "It was in his medicine cabinet. That's what I was showing you in there. You're in the clear."

"I didn't see anything, Mom. Don't go telling people you did. He'll kill us. Oh, God ..." She drifts into silence, still pale and shaken.

After a mile, I ask, "You know anything about a box Al's looking for? Said he asked Scotty about it."

"Think about the kids. Who'll take care of the kids?" She says nothing else for several minutes.

"So, what's this?" I ask pulling up the pamphlet. A glance shows the easy-to-read-while-driving headline. Operations manual for a big machine. "What the hell is bio-cremation?"

"It's an automatic, liquid cremation machine!" Her shout can be heard inside the cars around us. "It's in his garage—and it's running!"

I drive for a while in silence, trying to piece together what she's saying. "Cremation is when you burn—"

"I know what cremation is," she spouts. "That's what it used to be. This thing melts people down into a liquid slurry that—according to the brochure—doubles as a fertilizer. That's what he's going to do to us if he thinks you spotted his cyanide."

I grab the booklet from her and stare at the cover again. Below the model name is a listing of the machine's features: 400 lb. capacity; 3-4 hour cycle time; Fully automated operation; 91% savings on fossil fuel usage; 100% elimination of air emissions. Below that is the marketing line: "… a powerful new technology that offers families an eco-friendly alternative to traditional flame-based cremation."

"And it's running?" I ask.

"YES!"

# CHAPTER 31

## ISAIAH, THE ADVISOR

DAD TEXTS ME TO SEE if I got his texts about med school. I respond about being busy.

Climbing into the G-wagon, I adjust the seat and mirrors. Leaves are flying through the air, the sky is dark, small trees are leaning to the southwest. Next to me, in the passenger's seat, Pia puts an icepack on her ankle, then stops and sniffs the air.

"Did you just get out of the shower?" she asks. Before I answer, she figures it out. "Dumpster diving is an artform. You'll get better at it in time."

I can't help but laugh at the woman who can rifle a dumpster and jump out as clean as when she jumped in. "How many women in your socio-economic strata have mastered that art?"

"Not enough, I can tell you that." She joins in my mirth. "If they did, there would be a lot less economic disparity."

I put the destination she gave me for the Second Chance Adoption Agency in the Mercedes map. It comes up with a route over forty miles north in Portland. I point at the screen. "Uhm, what is this about?"

"Fishing," she says. "Opportunity. I don't know, really. Remember the letters Phil Jacobsen wrote as he died? You thought it was *secret A+C* and I thought it was *AdCI*? Well, I have a feeling that relates to adoption, which could point to Amy or Scott, or someone else we don't know about yet. We're going to visit this agency to find out if it means anything."

Knowing her story, I can imagine her interest. Scott was cleared by his bodycam but Amy? She's a suspect I hadn't considered.

Before we leave Deeping, she says, "Tell me your life story, Isaiah."

I give her the short version: a privileged black kid in Glencoe, Illinois where Asians were the predominant minority at 2 percent. Where my identity was lost in the prevailing environment. And where inclusion was strained by racism on one side and the assumption I was their Magical Negro on the other.

"Magical what?" she asks.

"A term coined by Spike Lee twenty years ago about Hollywood casting black people in roles that only served to help white people. Like Whoopi Goldberg becoming a medium to help a white woman connect with her dead white boyfriend in the movie *Ghost*. Well-intentioned white people sometimes expect me to jump into their lives as their new best friend, make magic happen, and help them take on the world—as if I didn't have a life of my own with my own friends and my own problems."

"Ah."

I can tell she's reflecting on her friendship with Tania for a moment. Good.

Then she asks, "So what led you to the Marines?"

"After Glencoe and Dartmouth," I answer, "I was looking for a place a touch less white and parental. My parents meant well but got over-involved in my daily life. I knew they couldn't micromanage the USMC. Signing up let me escape and be me for once. But. Culture shock like you wouldn't believe. I was not ready for the Marines or the people I met there. The average soldier did not go to private school and the number of Ivy Leaguers I ran into was just short of zero. Yet for some strange reason, I loved it. My combat tour was like being on a drug. We had purpose, camaraderie, and tons of adrenaline."

"Yep, I struggle with an adrenaline addiction too," she laughs. "So why leave?"

"While I enjoyed being the smartest guy in the room, correcting a major's grammar gets old. And it doesn't help your career."

She laughs. After we exhaust those stories, we go quiet for a mile or two.

"You drive slow," she says.

Having heard she drives like Lewis Hamilton on amphetamines, I respond carefully. "The consequences for driving fast are different for you and me. When you get stopped, you get a ticket. When I get stopped, statistics show I have five times the chance of getting shot instead."

"Fair enough," she says quietly.

We hurtle down the freeway, both of us alone with our thoughts. The entire eastern sky is black and swirling. Even the big trees are swaying.

Eventually she gets down to business. "Word on the street is you encountered Kitty Robinson again."

"I believe she sought me out."

Pia turns in her seat to examine me. "Because you know something of Greek tragedies."

"That's all I can figure. She has something to say and no one else understands her."

"You didn't figure her message out or you would've led with that and skipped the small talk."

"True that," I say. "She quoted Sophocles again."

"My education didn't cover much on the Greeks. What was she talking about?"

"This time was clearer than last time. She quoted from *Ajax*, a play about the first disgruntled worker to go on a rampage. I looked it up and skimmed a bit. She keeps quoting from the Jebb translation of 1904 that uses Elizabethan English for dramatic effect with thee and thou. I can't quite grasp her meaning. When I asked her about her public fight with Phil Jacobsen the day he was killed, she gave me the impression it was not a fight, that he was raging like Ajax. The scene she focused on was when Athena made Ajax think the cattle and herdsmen were the Greek kings. He flies into a rage and slaughters them all. Kitty focused on one passage about Ajax raging, but she changed the subject of his anger from Agamemnon to Devino."

"In other words," she says, "hours before he died, Phil Jacobsen discovered something that drove him mad. Angry-mad? Sad-mad? Betrayed-mad?"

"In context," I say, "Ajax felt he'd been dissed. But what does that mean in regard to Phil? I don't know."

Outside, birds have given up struggling against the wind. The only thing flying are leaves and small objects. We're silent for another mile, thinking through different angles. Who would disrespect Phil Jacobsen and why is anyone's guess.

Eventually, Pia breaks the silence. "Thanks to you, we know Al Devino is looking for a dry box big enough to hold Rembrandt's *Sea of Galilee*, and that Al claims Phil stole the box. Kitty's telling us he was ranting about Devino. We have to assume she meant Vinny because Al claims not to know what's inside. If it is the Rembrandt, why would that upset Phil? He could have claimed the reward. What pushed Phil over the edge? What did he rant about that made someone angry enough to kill him?"

"Maybe the missing videos?" I offer. "What if Vinny stole them from Phil and put them in the box with the Rembrandt? Amy was cagey when I asked about the laptop. She did exactly what our Sabel Agent in Omaha said guilty people do: she threw shade on Kitty."

"If the videos were in the box," she says, "Phil wouldn't be upset, he'd be happy."

"True." I contemplate that problem for a mile more. "If they weren't in the box, he stole the box for nothing and still had to go back for the videos. Maybe that's why he was upset. Did he know about the painting? If it's in there, and he wasn't expecting it, he would realize he just stole something that Al would kill to get back."

"You're right," she says. "That means Phil's laptop might hold some answers. I'm texting Scott to let us look at it."

She thumbs out her message.

Rolling things over in my mind, I come to a sudden realization. Pia hasn't told me anything about the dumpster diving, the search for the yellow rope, the hunt for cyanide, or anything else. What's up with that? Sure, I'm the new guy she doesn't know that well, but don't I deserve a little more information? I glance her way and see she's catching up on emails on her phone.

To see her working calmly, something occurs to me. I say, "You know who did it."

"Yes." She takes her eyes off her screen for a second, checks the highway in front of us, then glances at me before going back to her phone.

"Well?" I ask.

"You know as much as I," she says with a tinge of frustration. "You can figure it out too."

I have no idea what she's talking about. What do I know that I can figure out? As she thumbs through more emails, I'm reminded of the interview she gave after the World Cup. I remember her sly grin before she said, *To stay on top, you have to keep a few tricks up your sleeve.* She has a trick she hasn't shared.

She drops her phone in her lap and says, "What we don't know is: why? And what's worse, we don't have a shred of evidence."

"Wait a second." I'm not sure what to say next, so I blurt it out. "You're looking for evidence in completely different places from me. Why aren't we working together? Why not share information?"

"Why would we follow the same leads?" She looks me over. "Isn't it more efficient to have you following the videos and Kitty, while I look for the yellow rope?"

I regrip the steering wheel and try to figure out how to explain my feelings without sounding whiny: I'm being left out. I don't like that. It feels like racism even though I know it's not. I take a deep breath.

Keeping her gaze on me, she says, "I know a lot of executives who started big companies in internet, healthcare, aerospace, all kinds of things. Their biggest downfall is believing their success in one field gives them clairvoyance in everything. They surround themselves with yes-men who stoke the furnaces of their explosive egos. They become addicted to total control and dictate what people should eat, wear, and think. That's not me. I never rule out the possibility that I'm dead wrong—and you're on the right track. I've more experience, but you're every bit as smart."

"Thank you, but why not include each other on information?" I ask.

"You see something in this video thing that I don't see. And—don't think I didn't notice—you feel the need to withhold names. That's fine. I trust you to protect the innocent while running down that clue. You're also the only one who Kitty relates to; we need you to keep that dialogue going—if it goes anywhere. That's how we work best, each of us following the ideas we're most passionate about and have the skillset to develop."

She touches my forearm long enough to pull my gaze from the road. She says, "You're not a bodyguard. You're an advisor. I need your advice on Kitty, on the videos, and anything else you see fit. We present your role as bodyguard because that gives you anonymity to explore on your own. No one asks where Miguel went—because he's just an off-duty bodyguard."

That makes me feel better about my role. Proud in fact. With one exception: she knows who did it—and claims I do too. *I don't.*

I'm sure as hell not going to admit that. I'm going to figure it out.

I start running suspects through my mind: Amy because of the videos? Possible, but she seems so nice. I can't let *seems so nice* blind me. She's still on the list. Someone else who was in a video? Possible, but I'll need the video to figure that out.

Kubari? No. At least, I don't see it. Maybe I don't want to see it. Have we cleared him yet?

Kitty Robinson? Maybe the whole Ajax thing is meant to throw me off the scent. It could've been a drunken prank she didn't realize would turn deadly until too late.

Then there's Al Devino. Definitely involved in something. The search for the box could be his way of keeping tabs on the investigation. Don't criminals come back to the scene of the crime to check their work? Is that what he's doing? And that reminds me: How does the Rembrandt fit in?

The Mercedes instructs me to pull off the highway. I stop at a light and ask Pia, "You still haven't told me what this trip is about."

"I know."

# CHAPTER 32

## ISAIAH, THE ADVISOR

I PICK MY WAY THROUGH Portland neighborhoods to a street filled with grand Victorian houses that have been repurposed for offices. Signs in the manicured front lawns announce an array of lawyers, doctors, dentists, and CPAs cohabitating in the well-kept homes. I find our destination and pull in. Yellow brick with white stone trim, it stands out among its gray clapboard neighbors.

With the wind twirling her ponytail in her face, Pia rounds the front and smacks her foot on a cement parking block lurking by the front tire. After a quick, "Ow! Shit!" and a grimace, she joins me. Her limp is more pronounced.

Pointing at the number two tenant, I say, "We should drop in. I'm sure they'll see you without an appointment."

The boss follows my extended finger. Beneath our intended destination of Second Chance Adoption Agency, the sign reads, PORTLAND ANKLE AND FOOT SPECIALISTS. She gives me a withering look. "I'm fine."

She hobbles up the steps behind me, relying on her cane. If I knew her better, I'd drag her ass across the hall to the doctor. But I'm still the new guy.

A plump and harried receptionist adjusts her glasses to inspect us before clacking the rest of what must be her doctoral thesis on an ancient computer. Finally, she gives us a you're-wrecking-my-day glance before making her way through a narrow door to announce us. A pleasant fiftyish woman with short gray hair comes out with her hand extended.

"Mary Arnold, it's a pleasure to meet you … Ms. um …"

"Sabel," the boss answers and shakes hands. "Call me Pia. And this is my advisor, Isaiah Reddick."

Mary ushers us into a cramped office where two walls are pale blue and the other two are pale pink. She motions to two chairs facing her desk and starts talking while she's still rounding her chair. "Just to make sure we're on the same page here, we specialize in the adoption of older children. We don't handle the adoption of babies."

"I know. That's why I came." Pia pulls a large envelope of papers from her purse and drops them on the desk. Pointing out the window at our ride, she says, "This is your new Mercedes. You'll be selling raffle tickets for it over the next six months. I still need it for the next day or two. I'll text you when I'm done, and you can pick it up at the airport. To make the raffle worth my investment, you'll need to sell at least 3,000 tickets at $50 each. Next week, you'll get a call from the PAS Foundation. One of my case managers will coordinate your PR and marketing to support the fund raiser. When you meet that ticket minimum, my people will release matching funding."

Mary has barely landed in her seat and is still trying to balance the chair when she nearly falls out of it. Gripping the desk, her head swivels from the window to Pia and back three times. "What?"

Pia takes a chair. "A lot to process, I know. I was adopted at age four. When I travel, I look for agencies like yours that specialize in older children. Not many in this country. When I stumbled on your website, I got excited. Mary, you have my undying gratitude for the work you're doing."

"You're adopted?" Mary's jaw hangs open. Then her eyes drop to a daily planner on her desk. "Oh! You! You're … you're that girl. You're THAT Pia Sabel." Mary points a bony finger in Pia's face. "You're the girl in DC—the one counter-protesting our right-to-life protest."

Pia shakes her head with bewilderment. "Sorry, I don't—"

"Oh, you wouldn't remember me, one in a crowd. But I remember you. Outside the Supreme Court, I was protesting abortion. You were walking by with a school group; you might've been twelve or something. You stopped, listened to us, and asked us how many of the 500,000 unaborted children in foster care we were willing to adopt. My whole group went silent. You said, 'If you haven't adopted an older child, you're not against abortion, you just want to tell other people what to do. There are half a million children who weren't aborted who need your help—right now.' Then you walked away. Do you remember?"

"Uh," Pia looks a little embarrassed. "Sorry, I've given that speech many times. It's easy to 'save' the unborn; it's a whole lot harder to save the born. Ninety-nine times out of a hundred that's the end of the conversation."

A wind-driven bird smacks the window, making Mary jump. She looks at us a little embarrassed, then composes herself.

"Well, your words made an impression on me," Mary says. "The name didn't register until just now, but what you said changed my life. Back then, someone in our crowd who lived in DC knew who you were and told us your story. Three of us worked here at the time and we knew how rare it was for a four-year-old to get adopted. The whole way back home we talked about how there's a waiting list for babies, but no one wants older kids. And the biggest problem is that baby adoptions have fallen 75 percent in the last twenty years, while the number of older children in need of placement keeps growing. Lots of agencies closed because of the baby shortage. Others resort to exorbitant fees bordering on extortion. We discussed it and decided to change our agency's mission. We now focus on older children. It's a lot harder, and we had to transition from employees to volunteers, but it's much more rewarding."

An awkward moment of silence follows while Mary stares at Pia as if waiting for an accolade—or maybe knighthood.

"Yes, well," Pia says, "I'm glad to find someone who listened. Anyway, I've a busy schedule today and I wanted to meet you and give—"

"Oh, right!" Mary picks up the papers. "A car. And match the raffle sales? Wow. Oh. Wow. That's three times our annual budget. We'll rename the place, the Pia Sabel Adoption—"

"No!" Pia holds up a hand. "Thank you. We will keep this anonymous. Like I said, someone from my foundation will help you every step of the way. I'm doing this because through some form of luck or divine providence, my life was filled with opportunity, while the vast majority of children in foster care are destined to be wards of the state, shuffled from foster home to group home, until they get their eighteenth birthday present: an unceremonious dumping on a sidewalk. I'm confident you'll do fine."

"Thank you, thank you, thank you!" Mary rises and rushes around the desk, her eyes brimming with tears.

Pia rises to catch her as she barrels into a bear-hug. This doesn't appear to be Pia's first hug-of-gratitude-from-a-stranger. She leans into it, rocks Mary side to side, then grabs her shoulders, pushes her back half a step, and says, "You're welcome. Use it wisely. If things go well, there will be more grants in the future."

Mary claps her hands in prayer and looks up at her benefactor with the eyes of a worshipper.

Pia looks uncomfortable at the adoration. She says, "There is one thing …"

"Anything, name it."

"Thirty-two years ago, a baby was adopted from this agency. At some point years later, vandals broke in and destroyed a lot of paperwork. Is there anyone still around who worked here then? Someone who might remember a few facts about the burglary?"

"That was all a long time ago," Mary says. "Leslie Dingwall might know, but her memory is getting hazy. She's in a retirement home in Scarborough."

We leave Mary in tears. Pia ignores me when I point to the foot doctor and heads out to the Mercedes.

The trip to Scarborough is quick but I manage to get in a couple questions. "You prefer anonymous donations?"

"Yes."

"And the burglary question?"

"Scott told me his agency was vandalized. Seemed odd somehow, thought I'd ask."

We pull into the senior's building and ask to see Leslie Dingwall. We're led to an active living area where people—many staring intently into an inner world—are spending the day. We find Leslie with a book in her lap, talking nonstop to a blank-looking woman.

Pia introduces us. She engages Leslie in small talk, then gets down to her real question. "Did they ever catch the vandals who broke into the agency years ago?"

"Oh, honey, were your records lost in that fire way back in … when was that. Well, a long time ago anyway." Leslie gives Pia a sympathetic once-over.

"A friend of mine."

"Well, I'll tell you the same thing I told the police back then. It wasn't any vandals, it was the Devino crime family. They tried to make it look like teenagers on a prank, but it was professional. You could tell because the alarms, uhm, something about the alarms …"

"They disabled the alarm system?" Pia offers.

"Yeah, that's it. Trouble is, we couldn't prove they did it. But who else could it be?"

"Sorry? I don't follow you." Pia pulls up a small stool next to Leslie.

"I sat there and pieced together every scrap of unburned paper and every shred of ash still legible. It was a tough task, but I figured out which files had been destroyed, and which were stolen. I notified everyone who had even a scrap of paper. If we knew the record had been burned, we told them. But the ones that were stolen, we had no way of contacting them. Your friend was notified?"

"I suppose so," Pia says with a concerned look. "But why do you think Devino is responsible?"

"There was a Mafia war going on then," Leslie says with a look of delight that someone needs her expertise. "A war between Vinny Devino and … someone else … hmm. Gambino? Vitelli? Bonanno? I can't recall right now. It'll come to me. Whoever it was had been involved in an adoption and Vinny was trying to … he wanted to, uh, you know, I can't remember what he wanted. But I knew at the time. I was sure of it." Leslie punctuated her statement with a fierce glare. "And don't you forget it."

"I won't," Pia said.

We talked for a few more minutes with diminishing returns. Clearly a flagging memory hampered her recall on all except the details in which she was intimately involved, like piecing the records back together. We wished her well and left.

On the drive back to Deeping lightning struck in the distance. I contemplated ten ways to ask Pia what that was all about. For the first few miles, she was on a conference call. When she clicked off, she read my mind.

She said, "As I said when we started out, it was a fishing trip. If I knew what it meant, I'd tell you, but right now, you know everything I know."

"But you knew about Second Chance," I said. "You didn't just pick it out of a Google search."

"Scott Jacobsen told me his adoption records were destroyed by vandals." She twists in her seat to face my profile. "When he told me he'd never reached out to his biological parents because his records were lost, I thought, I should donate to his adoption agency. When I found out they'd changed to a cause right up my alley, I was hooked. At the same time, the vandalism story sounded off. I can't imagine teenage boys targeting an adoption agency. 'Hey, Billy, let's go tear up the adoption agency?' Am I right?"

"I can't say you're wrong."

"And now we've learned what Leslie said about suspecting Vinny Devino. Even more suspicious: some files were burned while others were missing."

"Was Scott's missing or burned?"

"I don't know. Nor do I know if it has anything to do with Phil's murder. But it's an interesting thread, isn't it?"

"Fascinating," I say.

At the same time, I realize why she wanted me to focus on the video. I had a firm grip on where those clues might lead and how to figure out what they meant. What she was chasing meant something to her, interested her, and drove her to the next step. I wouldn't know how to ask Chief Jacobsen if his files had been burned or stolen. That would be too tricky a conversation for me. Not for Pia Sabel, a kindred spirit in the adopted world.

For just a moment, I don't feel like the new guy.

# CHAPTER 33

## SCOTT, THE POLICE CHIEF

I DON'T KNOW WHAT TO tell Boo-Boo. She sits in my office on the verge of tears—again. Same topic as always: kids. My mind was on Al Devino when I came in. Then it turned to the approaching storm. There's a lot on my plate. Still, Boo-Boo is important. When she came over unannounced, I made time for her. I do my best to say the right thing. "I don't need children, honey. It's fine."

"But we'd make such beautiful babies," she says, and the waterworks flow. "It's my last chance. Damn your mother!"

Mom explained to me how women Boo-Boo's age are at risk for all kinds of problems in pregnancy. Down syndrome, premature birth, not to mention health risks for the mother like high blood pressure and preeclampsia.

I say, "Mom was just pointing out the difficulties because she cares—"

"It's not that. She just had to remind me I already had a stillborn child." She breaks down, slumping her folded arms on my desk with her head down. Her pink Danny's Diner uniform with white trim stretches tight across her back.

"Oh. You had a … when was this?"

"Eons ago." She speaks between sobs. "When I was using."

Mom failed to mention that. Another thing I have to look up: if you have one stillborn, are you likely to have another? I wonder how much Boo-Boo's chemical dependency contributed to the problem or if it's genetics. She's clean and sober now. Does that improve her chances? No. I'm not going to look up anything. Who wants to bring a child into this world when there's someone like Al Devino waiting to co-opt them? I'll get snipped and that'll end the whole debate.

Rain's rhythm taps out a constant beat on the roof. The wind moans around the building like an ancient ghost. Branches skitter across the walls and roof as if scraped by unseen phantoms. It feels like the past is becoming a revenant.

She reaches for the tissues without looking, her hand flopping on my desk. I push the box under her wandering hand. Her moaning softens as she brings it down to sniffles and sighs. Her head stays on the desk. I reach across and rub her shoulder. "We'll get through this, honey."

A soft-triple knock on the door precedes the entrance of Pia Sabel. Boo-Boo snaps her head up and their gazes meet.

"Sorry to interrupt," Ms. Sabel says. Her cane taps into the room, where she stops with one foot in and not enough space for the other. "It was so quiet, I thought you were alone. Hi, Boo-Boo, nice to see you again. Sorry, I've never heard your first name."

"Boo-Boo's fine." She squeezes from the chair with a red and swollen face, smiles, and shakes hands. "That's what everyone calls me. I, um, I—"

Their clumsy conversation is cut short by *Hail to the Chief* playing in Ms. Sabel's purse. She holds up a finger with an apologetic smile. "I have to take this."

She clumps into the hall for privacy. Our walls are so thin, we can't help but hear her side of the conversation, "Mr. President, what can I do for you?" Pause. "I updated Ursula on a video conference this morning. The EU will cooperate fully." Pause. "Yes, the EU Central Bank is standing by, ready to shut down any account we can positively identify in the laundering operation. But it has to be a solid ID." Pause. "No, that won't be a problem. I missed the meeting in Brussels, but I'll be in Monaco day after tomorrow. Right on schedule. No more interruptions." Pause. "I understand, it's a lot of stress for you, sir." Pause. "No, no, don't worry about it. Call any time, day or night. Listen, I've got to run. Take care."

Our faces must have still been in shock judging from the way she looks us over after rejoining us.

"Well," Boo-Boo says, "you two must have a lot to discuss between now and *the day after tomorrow*. I've got to get back to work. Bye."

She leans across the desk, gives me a peck on the lips, and flees the building.

I wish I could flee with her. With my jaw still on the floor, I search my brain for words. Ms. Sabel just told the President of the United States she has to run because she's meeting me? I have no idea what she's dealing with outside our little investigation, but it must be huge.

"As you've just heard, I've got a deadline on this project, Scott." Ms. Sabel takes the only chair in front of my desk. "We have a murder to solve and a mobster to stop. But first, I have to ask, and I know this is prying: is everything OK at home?"

"She wants to have children," I say involuntarily as my hands wave nervously in the direction of Boo-Boo's hasty exit. Ms. Sabel has a way of getting answers to spill out of me. Even when I don't want them to.

Ms. Sabel's eyes turn to the empty doorway and frown, as if gauging Boo-Boo's age. Her gaze comes back to me.

I say, "Yes, we could have serious problems."

"You could adopt." Her ray gun gaze doesn't leave room for a reply. "Second Chance has children—out of the diaper stage—available today."

"Yeah, that's true." I shrug.

She continues, "Were you notified your adoption records were burned?"

"Mom might've been. I was in grade school when it happened. I didn't find out until I tried to connect with my birth parents."

"Your mother didn't tell you at the time?" The shock in her voice surprises us both. She regroups before going on. "I visited Leslie Dingwall, who used to run the agency. Leslie thought Vinny Devino did it, not vandals. She said there was a mob war going on. Do you know who he would've been fighting with and if your file might be at the center of that battle?"

I search my memory for stories about Vinny. Deeping's old timers wax poetic when talking about Mom taking on Vinny and winning, but I don't recall anything about a mob war. Bringing my gaze back to her, I shake my head.

I want to change the subject. I want to tell her about Mom and Amy's frantic phone call from the road. I want to tell her how scared they were about the bio-cremation system and how she discovered cyanide in the bathroom. I've never seen or heard Mom scared before. It shook me to my marrow.

But Mom told me not to say anything to Ms. Sabel. She wants to get the research project back on track. She thinks she can take on Al the same way she took on Vinny.

Mom's wrong. Al is not Vinny. He's perched on a precarious cliff over a sea of dangerous people. To survive, he must prove himself by destroying anyone in his way. Doesn't matter if they're family. For the sake of all involved, I have to ignore Mom for once.

I tell Ms. Sabel all about Mom's trip to Al's house and finding the bio-cremation machine. I tell her about Mom finding the cyanide and how I sent the Lincoln County Sheriff to get a search warrant. I give her all the details Mom gave me about how sick and scared she and Amy have been since they left. When I finish, Ms. Sabel says nothing.

Instead of asking questions, she changes the subject.

"We need to look at the laptop," she says. "You've had enough time and have made no progress. My people can break the password in a few days at most."

"We found the cyanide," I remind her. "At Al's."

"There are many legitimate uses for cyanide," she responds. "If he was using it for murder, why would he keep it in the front powder room? Sounds like an odd place. Let's see what the sheriff turns up. In the meantime, I'd like a shot at the laptop."

I'm shocked and take a minute to process her casual dismissal of the poison. "The sheriff was excited. He's been trying to pin a host of things on Al for years. This could be—"

"If you were the killer and you hid the cyanide in a bathroom, what would you do after two relatives rummaged around in there, then ran out like they'd seen ghosts?"

I let out a frustrated sigh. "Yeah. I'd dump it down the toilet and melt the bottle."

"The laptop?"

Her text about it was softer, but after her call with the president, I see she's losing her patience. Stalling will make me look like an idiot. "OK. My guys will be disappointed but that's fine. They'll deal with it. What do you need?"

"Just the laptop." She pulls a phone and a USB cord out of her purse. "Where is it?"

I reach into the bottom drawer, pull it out, and hand it over with the power supply dangling from it. "The guys just brought it back."

Her eyes say *bullshit*, but she doesn't give it breath. We both know it's been in my desk since my guys gave it minimal effort yesterday. After plugging everything in, she explains the process. "This phone connects to a Sabel Satellite, giving us high-speed internet access. My people at Sabel Technologies will make an electronic image of this entire laptop—chips, drives, memory, and so on—and create a million virtual copies in our grid-computing system where we have deployed over 48 thousand servers connected in parallel for operations like this. Phil's laptop allows up to fifteen characters for a password, making roughly 1.7 nonillion possible combinations. If you're doing the math in your head, nonillion is a one followed by thirty zeros; as in billion, trillion, quadrillion, quint, sext, sept, oct, and nonillion. Our grid system will try all of those on the virtual machines at a combined rate of 4,100 teraflops. If he used a short password, it won't take long. If he used all fifteen characters, we should be done in no more than five days."

One minute she's telling the president she has to run, the next, she's explaining nonillion and teraflops. And Mom thinks she'd be interested in a small-town cop? Sure.

All I can say is, "Yeah, OK."

"That will help us with one aspect of the investigation," she says. "Isaiah's taking the lead on that. But solving the crime won't be any use if we lose the town to Al Devino."

"Where is Isaiah, anyway?"

"With the storm coming, he and Miguel decided to move Kitty and her friends to a motel." She changes the subject again. "Did your guys find anyone dealing drugs on Elm?"

"Actually, they did." Part of me gets excited about this. It's my first success story in days. "Of course, the dealers walked away when the squad car approached. Dealers on the street don't keep anything on their person, they hide it nearby. Well, Mike Culpepper kept an eye on them and reported where they hid the drugs. So our guys went straight to the overturned bushel basket and took the stash. We seized 250 grams of crystal meth, about $5,000 worth, all packaged for sale."

I smile and lean back.

The curled lip she gives me tells me she's familiar with how dealers work. I think she's a step ahead of me. Scratch that: I know she's a step ahead of me. A big step. My pride ebbs.

"Nice," she says. "So then. If your men confiscated the drugs, you are about to bring down the wrath of Al Devino on Deeping, Maine."

# CHAPTER 34

## CHRISTINE, THE BAKER

SCOTTY ACTS LIKE HE STILL lives here even though he has his own home. He walks in without knocking and holds the door for Sabel. She stumps in on an ankle that looks more swollen than the last time I saw her. Rain and leaves chase them into the foyer like infiltrators, sneaking around their legs to hide in corners and under couches. The pair hang their wet coats and join us in the dining room. Sabel's carrying a small box.

"I-95 is closed for a multicar pileup," Scotty announces. "And Route 1 has trees blocking it in three places between here and Portland. No one's going anywhere. Good thing we're all home for this storm."

Sabel drags a chair away from the table to an odd place between the windows. It takes me a minute to understand why. She's picked the only place a sniper can't see her from outside the house. It's instinct. Too many enemies for someone so young. Pulling a side chair over, she puts her foot on it.

I grab an icepack and toss it to her from the fridge, brushing back Scotty. They're making small talk with Amy, who has come back from the brink but still looks like she stared into the demon's mouth and saw Armageddon.

"Thank you for coming over right away," I say as I drop into a chair.

"No problem," Sabel says. Her gray-green eyes pierce me as she pushes the box across the table toward me. "We have much to discuss, so I brought you a hostess gift."

She gives the box an extra push with her cane. I stretch for it and reel it in. It's been opened and repacked. I reach into foam padding to find a hefty bottle inside. It's a unique shape with a gooseneck and a potbelly bottom. Carefully setting it on the table, I realize what it is. The label confirms it: Del Porto Extra Añejo. I try, but I can't hide my shock. I hear myself gasping. I feel the blood draining from my face.

Sabel keeps her eyes hard on mine.

"What the hell?" Scotty jumps to his feet, his angry glare aimed at Sabel. "How could you? This is why you wanted to stop by your house on the way here? This is the very—"

Without taking her eyes off me, Sabel holds her hand up, stopping him mid-syllable. "It's a test of the delivery system for the only distributor of this brand north of New York. It arrived at my rental in ten hours. I wanted to make sure they could deliver it quickly, weather notwithstanding. I also tried to get them to tell me where any other bottles of this might've been shipped in the last year. They insist on a warrant."

"We don't have cause for a warrant." Scotty shakes his head in disbelief. "I can't believe you. This is a cruel joke."

In a flash, I understand Sabel—she's lonely. No family; no friends, only employees; and a lover she can't keep. Like a shipwreck survivor dying of thirst in the ocean, she's surrounded by people yet utterly alone. She said as much at the funeral. I have my family, she has nothing. It makes her angry and cruel. Bringing a copy of the murder weapon as a hostess gift is exceptionally and inexcusably harsh. She warned Scotty she had a mean streak. And I warned him she would take over the investigation.

"Get some glasses," she says to Amy. "We'll toast to finding Phil Jacobsen's killer."

Like a zombie commanded by a sorceress, Amy rises, finds tumblers in the cupboard, and sets four of them in front of me. I glance around the table. Scott's eyes are glued to the bottle, reminding me he's tasted this before. He looks anxious for another snort. Amy stares at Sabel as if waiting for her next instruction.

Considering she called it a hostess gift and proposed a toast to my brother, I see no alternative but to pour.

I open it. It's an oddly shaped bottle with an awkward, almost unusable neck. I slide my fingers under the round bottom to stabilize it, pour generously, and pass out the shots.

Sabel hooks hers with the cane's pearl handle. She raises it to us, "For Phil—may we bring his killer to justice."

Repeating her words, we each take a nip. Scott, who never liked alcohol much, looks like an addict getting a fix. Amy takes a big gulp obediently after waiting for Sabel's gaze to fall on her. I take a sip.

I must admit, Del Porto stands alone.

"Does that really cost two grand?" Scotty asks.

"I talked them down as far as I could," Sabel says. "I got it cheap, only eighteen hundred."

I'm dumbfounded. My eyes nearly leave their sockets when I stare at the bottle. One bottle of moldy cactus juice costs more than my furniture? I nearly choke on that thought. Who in their right mind would spend that kind of money on booze? Then I realize I'm sitting right next to her. And there was Bill Koller, who sent bottles to his friends—but who knew it cost that much? I always thought Kubari set the price high enough to keep anyone from asking for it, ensuring he'd have it on the shelf in case Bill came back.

I take another sip and appreciate the smooth aftertaste.

Feeling the pressure of Al Devino breathing down my neck, I conclude it's time for business.

"We have bigger problems," I say. "I take it this visit is because Scotty told you about finding the cyanide?"

"Yes," Sabel replies, "and he told me how he declared war on Al by—"

"He did WHAT?" Amy screeches.

Scotty holds up his hands. "It wasn't like that …" All eyes turn to him. "Well, I didn't mean to start anything. My guys couldn't make an arrest, so they raided the stash and confiscated 250 grams of his product. Ms. Sabel pointed out how Al's going to see that, well … as an act of war."

"No, no, no," Amy says. "You have to give it back."

"That's not going to happen," Sabel says. "We have a plan."

From the surprised expression on Scotty's face, it would be more accurate to say she has a plan. But then, so do I.

"We arrest Al Devino for my brother's murder," I announce. "We know he did it, we found the evidence, it gets him off the streets, and we can make it stick."

Sabel suppresses a laugh. "If you think he's mad now, he'll be twice as angry after his five-minute arraignment where the DA drops the charges."

"We were there, in his house," I say. "We saw the poison."

Without missing a beat or even a hint of surprise, Sabel says, "What did it look like?"

"Blue and white bottle, small, warning label, and," I pause for dramatic effect, "the word cyanide in big letters."

She looks skeptical.

Scotty leans forward. "Uh, Ms. Sabel pointed out that Al would most likely dispose of it after you left."

"But we know it was there." I sound defeated even to myself.

"Did you snap a picture in situ?"

"No. Didn't think of that. We were in a rush."

Amy's anxious face turns to me hoping I can fix this.

"You're right," I admit. "It'll be floating across the Atlantic by now." And just like that, my hopes shatter on the floor like top-shelf stemware in an earthquake. I search for something else. "But Al knew the murder weapon was potassium cyanide before Scotty did."

"I'm not saying Al Devino is not the killer," Sabel says. "I'm saying we don't have enough hard evidence to keep a lawyer from poking holes in the story and getting him released. He shrugged off sixteen murder charges on technicalities before he took over from Vinny. What will he do if you accuse him, get him thrown in jail overnight, and then he makes bail in the morning?"

My kids and I know damn well what Al will do. He'll toss us in that machine and make his lawn greener with our bio-cremated remains.

"It's time to make a real plan," Sabel says. "There's no doubt Al Devino is an existential threat to Deeping's future. That means our first priority is securing the town and driving Al Devino out."

"What about bringing him to justice for killing Phil?" I ask despite being afraid of her answer. Amy sinks in her chair, pours herself another shot, keeps her head down.

"We have evidence piling up," Sabel answers. "As the killer becomes aware of the mounting proof, they'll step out of the shadows and confess."

With Sabel's gaze piercing me, I check on Amy. She better not burst out with her confession like a diva singing an aria. I'll find evidence against Devino if she keeps her mouth shut long enough. I always make things work. Amy's hair cascades around her face, shielding her from the rest of us. I pat her thigh under the table.

When I face Sabel again, she says, "We need to build a citizen's army."

"Hold on," Scotty says.

"Don't worry, they won't be armed or deputized." She turns to me. "I've made a list of your friends."

Sabel hands me a piece of paper.

The list reads: Mayor Rick, Dr. Orellana, Cheryl Walton, Mike Tenenbaum, Lyn and Norman Avery, Kubari Eady, Mike and Nikki Larson, Vanessa Zuma, Stacy Hartley, and Mike Culpepper. After reading it, my eyes rise to her.

"And anyone else you can think of," she says. "We want them ready when the storm lets up in the morning and the roads reopen. We'll meet at the bakery. I'll have full instructions ready for them."

"What if he attacks us tonight?" I ask.

She swipes at her screen, finds something, and turns it to me. Adjusting my reading glasses, I see Devino's house in the picture. In the corner is a watermark that reads *Sabel Technologies*. A tree limb sways in the right corner, struggling to stay attached in the wind, the porch light is on, the door-goon is inside.

"He's assembling his people," she says. "The search warrant and the sheriff will slow them down some. Add in the storm and we're sure they aren't going anywhere soon. This camera will give us a forty-five-minute warning when they leave."

Dropping her cane to the floor, she rises, wincing when her bad foot bears weight. She blows through the exit formalities, before she and Scotty head for the coat rack.

"Wait!" Amy is in a panic. "You can't leave us. Where are you going?"

"Until Devino shows up," Sabel says over her shoulder, "I'm going to collect evidence against your uncle's murderer."

# CHAPTER 35

## ISAIAH, THE ADVISOR

MIGUEL AND I ZIP OUR jackets tight and get out of the Mercedes in a downpour. Wind and rain limit our visibility. Eight identical pop-up camping tents are lined up and staked down tight. They're tiny, thin, and barely chest high. They won't last long.

Beats of music and the sound of laughter reach us, modulated by the wind. There's a light on in one of the tents; the others are all dark. Judging by the pointed objects that keep poking the tent fabric from inside and the flickering, gyrating shadows, people are dancing in there.

Miguel did a great job staking them down, but Mother Nature is a powerful force. Two are about to tear from the ground. We grab those first. The insides are mostly empty. The denizens of this encampment keep their personal effects in shopping carts and boxes parked under a nearby tree. We roll the sleeping bags and toss them in the back of the G-wagon. One of the tents comes loose as we approach for round two. A wire deer fence holds it long enough for Miguel to peel it back while I collect the stakes. Wrangling it in the wind and rain takes all our concentration. The next one goes back in the bag with less effort as we develop a method for dealing with the weather.

We finish up tent five when we become aware of people nearby. Three scraggly looking people stand in the rain getting incrementally cleaner. A fourth person stands apart. It's Boo-Boo Vitelli, who helped us bring dinner to the unhoused last night.

Miguel calls to them, "Anyone helping us gets to ride out the storm in a free room at the Seafarer Motel."

The onlookers hesitate. When Boo-Boo convinces them it's not a trick, they dive in and immediately make a mess of the next tent. It takes off like a giant bat winging its way out of hell, flapping and folding, strings and tiedowns flailing in all directions. Miguel's long arm reaches up from the tent he's working on and snatches it out of the air. With some effort, we wrestle it under control and stow it.

Our friends help us collect them all except the party tent. Whatever's going on in there continues unabated. When the last bags go in the truck, we pull out tarps and tie them over the shopping carts.

With the rain dripping off our helpers' faces, Miguel asks, "Where is Joy Cobb?"

The three point to each other like a precision drill team re-enacting the Three Stooges.

"No, I mean, where can I find Joy?" he asks. "I met her earlier when I set these up. It's OK. I just want to make sure she knows she can go to the Seafarer."

The three hesitate before raising pointed fingers in unison toward the last tent. They remind me of a Greek chorus.

"You took our tents," one of them says. "We got nowhere to sleep."

The one in the middle slaps his chest. "He said we could go to the motel for free, dummy."

"Did you mean it?" the third asks. "We can go there?"

"I mean it. Made a deal with the owner, the rooms are paid in advance. Ask for Ruth Jackson. She has soaps and toothbrushes and anything else you need. First one there gets to pick their room."

"I'll talk to Ruth for you," Boo-Boo says.

The three unhoused people look relieved, giving me the impression Ruth is not an easy person to deal with—if you're unwashed.

Boo-Boo turns to us. "OK if I get the others? They camped beneath the underpass."

Miguel answers, "I wondered where they went. Yeah, we got rooms for everyone."

Boo-Boo leads her charges away. The rain obscures them in seconds.

We walk over to the last tent, where the party is still going strong. Next to the door is an empty bottle of Seagram's Seven. A yard away is an empty Jack Daniel's.

Miguel knows the etiquette for unhoused encampments, so I let him lead. He swipes at the fabric a couple times, then shouts over the howling wind, "Knock, knock!"

The music stops, the entrance flap unzips a foot, the face of a woman—not Kitty—appears. "What do you want?"

Her alcohol-and-unbrushed-teeth-breath nearly knocks us over. Miguel leans away while I fan the air. He grabs my hand. I guess that's rude.

"Joy Cobb," Miguel says, "remember me? Miguel Rodriguez. I brought the sleeping bags and tents."

She eyes him suspiciously.

"How come you didn't invite me to the party?" he asks.

She looks him over again before saying, "You said you don't drink."

"I don't. That doesn't mean I can't party. May we come in?"

Joy is confused and disappears. The zipper closes. A hushed dialogue takes place inside that leads me to count four voices. None of them Kitty Robinson's. A man's voice says, "Tell him to go away."

"I'm not going away," Miguel says over the storm. "The weather's getting worse. We want to move you and the party to the Seafarer."

The zipper opens a notch and a man's face pops out. Grungy hair under a dirty watch cap with a silly grin, it's the guy who shook a bottle of booze at Kitty, ending my interview with her several hours ago. He looks me over, then Miguel. "We don't want any."

Several voices inside cackle hysterically as he starts to zipper the tent closed.

With all due respect to my learned colleague, I give Miguel an I-got-this glance—that he returns with a sly grin—and unzip the tent.

The man who zipped it up looks surprised. "Who are you?"

"Isaiah Reddick," I say and step in. There's no room. I'm pressing unknown parts of my body against unknown parts of unknown other people. And I'm bent at the waist like the others. "Who are you?"

"Tom Baird. Did you bring anything?" He cradles a nearly empty bottle of Wild Turkey. On the floor is an empty Canadian Club. Behind Tom stands the silent fifth partier, Kitty. "We ain't got enough for everybody."

"His coat has four inside pockets," Joy says. All five of them laugh.

It takes me a second to grasp the joke: he's been shoplifting booze. I respond, "We're going to move this party to the Seafarer."

"Par-TAY!" rings out from most of them. The combined stench of their breath nearly sends me back into the rain. The music restarts and they start gyrating again. I'd call it dancing but the cramped space allows no more than flapping forearms and wiggling knees.

Tom takes a big chug from the bottle while Joy tries to wrest it out of his hands. The wrestling match sends an elbow into my eye socket. Moving to protect myself, I twist away from the action. A knee lands in my balls. One of the unnamed-unhoused has fallen and is trying to flail his way back up. Before I can react, the fight for the bottle has gone full scale. I'm knocked flat on my chest and inadvertently trampled. I make it to my hands and knees only to have my fingers stepped on by several mucky shoes.

In all the classes I took at Dartmouth, in all the training sessions I had as an officer in the US Marine Corps, not once did I envision a future that would include dumpster diving and dancing with the unwashed in a single day.

A finger pokes my butt cheek three times. Looking back, I see Miguel smiling. He says, "Had enough fun yet?"

I back out into the rain. My eye hurts.

As soon as I'm clear of the doorway, Miguel sticks his head in and roars, "EVERYBODY OUT! We're moving it to the Seafarer. NOW. MOVE IT."

He backs out. Like clowns spilling from a clown-car, they stagger out, falling over each other, pushing, pulling, and jabbering unintelligible syllables.

Joy grabs my jacket. "You gotta get her stuff. Kitty's books are in there. They can't get wet."

"I'll get them," I answer.

Kitty comes last, clutching something under her outer-most jacket. She looks at me like I'm the enemy who broke up a perfectly good party. She says, "'Twas in the middle of the night my ruin came, in the hour when sleep steals sweetly o'er the eyes after the feast is done."

A dim memory surfaces and I respond, "Euripedes? *Electra?*"

Kitty points at me, cackles, and follows her tribe. Miguel herds them to the end of the lane where the motel's red neon is just visible through the torrential rains. He points and tells them to find Boo-Boo.

I step in the vacated tent. Kitty's sleeping bag has been trampled by muddy shoes. A boombox circa 1980 sits in the corner. One cracked-open speaker has been gingerly pieced back together. It won't survive the quarter-mile trip. Next to it is a rack of books, lovingly arranged on a 2x8 piece of wood with a shoe under each end, keeping everything off the wet ground. Somehow in the scrum, the books were never molested.

Dropping to my knees, I read the spines. They're stolen library books with their Dewey Decimal stickers still attached. Kitty is an academic gangster. The titles both surprise me and make sense: *The Complete Works of Aeschylus, The Complete Works of Euripides, The Complete Works of Sophocles.* Other volumes are by subject, *The Oedipus Cycle, The Oresteia,* and so on. Dry leaves and twigs stick up between the pages as place markers. I pull the volume of Euripides and flip through pages. A leaf marks the passage Kitty just delivered: *sleep steals sweetly o'er the eyes after the feast is done.*

Miguel tosses in a handful of garbage bags. I double wrap the books and carry them to the truck. We stow everything in back, then climb in for the drive.

"You've worked with these people," I say. "How do I reach Kitty? She's trying to tell me something but I'm not getting it."

"Show them respect and speak with authority, they'll do whatever you tell them. No matter what, don't ever promise them cash, booze, or drugs."

When we arrive at the Seafarer, there is a skirmish going on in the office. Miguel wades in, speaks to Boo-Boo and Ruth, the owner. Once he grasps the issue, he stands on a chair. "Listen up. I'm ordering pizza for anyone who's had a shower, washed their hair, cleaned their fingernails, and brushed their teeth. There are two to a room. If you take ten-minute showers each, you'll be back here in time to get a slice."

The lobby empties as the unhoused rush to their showers. Kitty stays behind, a frightened look on her face. She says, "Books, books, books."

I point to her room, "Shower. I'll bring them to your room."

Lacking any hint of trust, she waits for me while I retrieve them and follows me to her room. Miguel made sure she had a room of her own, hoping I could have some kind of conversation with her.

Opening the bags, I set the books up, spine out, on the table. She watches me as if I'm carelessly handling babies. When I finish, she reaches around me, grabs one, and opens it to a twig. Her dirty finger scratches an underlined passage on the page. I take the book, my finger marking her passage, and flip to the start of the play. This is from *The Libation Bearers* by Aeschylus. It reads: *Chorus. Wont hath been, and shall be ever, / That when purple gouts bedash / The guilty ground, then blood doth blood Demand, / And Blood For Blood Shall Flow.*

Damn her choice of these hundred-year-old translations. Couldn't she steal a modern version? I parse out the passage's meaning. People will always seek revenge, blood for blood.

Facing her, I ask, "Is this about Al Devino? Was Phil killed for revenge?"

She shakes her head violently and grabs another book. Turning to a leaf, she points to the passage. This time we're reading from *Hippolytus* by Euripides: *Ill-fated curse of my father! the crimes of bloody kinsmen, ancestors of old, now pass their boundaries and tarry not.*

It's not the roles of the subjects in the plays, or even the play. She's looking for words to express what she has in her head. Somehow, this makes sense to her. I re-read it. It isn't reaching me. Is she referring to her father? Or Phil as a father-figure? Is she referring to herself as a bloody kinsmen?

"I don't understand, Kitty. What are you trying to tell me?" I ask.

She shrugs, disappointed that I don't get it. Solemnly, like the condemned, she rises and goes in the bathroom, closes the door, and starts the shower.

I pick up a Sophocles compendium and turn to the marked pages. The things she's said in the past are marked. The first entry is the one she delivered to Mayor Rick and Chief Jacobsen: *most easily wilt thou bear thine own burden to the end, and I mine.* The next is confusing because I don't recall the context: *Nay, thou art thine own plague.* And then at the dumpster, she said, *Such am I—as thou thinkest—a fool.*

Is she trying to tell me she killed Phil Jacobsen?

# CHAPTER 36

## SCOTT, THE POLICE CHIEF

AFTER DROPPING MS. SABEL AT her place, the Lincoln County Sheriff calls. As soon as I answer, he starts with a snarl. "Nice set up, Jacobsen. There was nothing in the cabinet, nothing illegal in the house. All the guns they have, and there are quite a few, are legally registered weapons. The machine in the garage has a partially decomposed dog in it. They claim they're testing it for a veterinary clinic he owns. Now I look like an idiot and I'm on his radar—not in a good way. Thanks a lot, asshole."

I apologize to dead air. He hung up on me. Ms. Sabel saw this coming a mile away.

Pulling into the senior center, I park, and head inside through a driving rain. The police station is too quiet. I hear a hushed conversation in the squad room. Attempting to conceal a conversation has the same effect as announcing it with a bullhorn. In the squad room, three of my people huddle around a monitor. They look up and fall silent instantly.

"Better not be porn," I say.

"No, sir." Kathy Butler stands at attention. She glances at her companions, hoping one of them will speak. When they don't, she says, "Mayor Rick has one of those doorbell cameras. He found something interesting and sent it to us."

They make room for me as if I came to defuse a bomb. My gaze moves to the screen. Whoever has the mouse, backs it up to a time stamp, then clicks play. It's a dark view of Rick's porch and street. Nothing happens. The mouse scrubs along the timeline to 12:38 AM. A figure appears on the right, walking down the sidewalk. The person disappears in a dark gap between streetlamps, then reappears closer to Rick's driveway.

It's my mother.

She's carrying a grocery bag and has her head down. The camera isn't set up to capture people on the public sidewalk; it's aimed for people coming up his walkway, so we can't see her expression or make out what's in the bag. Her pace is normal, neither hurried nor slow. In ten steps she's in the dark again. In another ten, her silhouette leaves the left frame.

"Send that clip to my phone," I say.

"Maybe I should be the one to interview her about this," Kathy says.

"No, that's OK. I'm sure it's nothing." When I look up, they're all staring at me. They look away quickly.

The drive is normally short, but a fallen tree limb blocks the road in front of Mike Culpepper's house. I work the long way around over three blocks.

Mom is surprised to see me. Amy is playing with her kids in the living room. Rain splashes against the clapboarding and windows as if someone were spraying us with a hose. Thunder booms in the distance.

Ushering Mom to her office in the dining room, I sit with her. "I have a couple follow-up questions about the night Uncle Phil died. These are official questions pertaining to the investigation."

She eyes me warily. "OK."

"Take me through the evening before. When did you go to bed, when did you get up and go to work?"

"Well, I went to bed like always, about nine. And then I got up at 3:30 AM and went to the bakery. It was clear that day, right? So I would've walked."

Mom watches Amy's kids run through the kitchen, squealing with delight before disappearing around the corner.

I drum my fingers on the table before pulling out my phone. Then I hesitate. "Would you have gone by Rick Tara's house?"

"Why are you asking me these questions, Scotty?" She looks as if I'd stabbed her with a fork. "Why not ask that Sabel woman?"

"Mom, please. Answer the question."

"Rick's not on the way to the bakery."

I push play and show her the video. "Why were you walking down Rick's street?"

She turns white, then, a second later, turns red with anger the way she did when we were unruly kids. "What're you doing? Why are you after me? Why all these questions?"

Now I remember why Ms. Sabel interviewed Mom the first time. I shouldn't be here. It's impossible to question your mother; whether she's lying or telling the truth, it feels wrong. I should've sent Kathy. But I'm here. Time to follow through. "Mom, please answer the question."

There's a moment of silence. Whatever Amy was doing in the other room has stopped. She's listening. With all the attention on me, I'm reminded of how I leapt to conclusions about Kubari. This time, I'm not jumping to conclusions; I'm giving Mom more latitude to answer. That is bias. But I'll have to think about that later. Right now, I have to stay on task.

Mom's frown distorts her whole face. She draws her mouth closed tight and clenches her fists. She checks the video, then backs it up and plays it again. After a long, uncomfortable moment, she relaxes with a deep, tired sigh.

"If you think I'm lying, I'm not. You asked me what time I went to bed and what time I got up. I told you. This is different. This is the middle of the night."

I watch her closely. "What does that mean?"

"One day, Scotty," she says, dropping into teacher voice, "you'll learn. Getting old throws new challenges at you all the time. Sleeping is one of them. I go to sleep at nine, but I often wake up again between midnight and two. Lots of people over fifty do the same. Sometimes I read. Sometimes I go to the bakery and putter around. Sometimes I suddenly remember things I forgot to do—and go do them. All the nights run together, so I could be mistaken, but I think that's Jana Siverling's casserole dish in the bag. It'd been in my kitchen since Easter, kept forgetting to take it to her. I'm pretty sure I returned it that night and left it by her back door."

Mom is family, so I'm not an objective interrogator. Nonetheless, her story makes sense. I could ask Jana if she got her casserole back, but she'd tell everyone in town I'm investigating my mother for murder—I'd never hear the end of that. I didn't see Mom that night on my patrols. I think I was in the office around that hour. I back up the video and watch it again. Could be like she said. It still seems strange.

"Do you get up in the middle of the night and cross town very often?" I ask.

"No, not often. It wasn't the first time and won't be the last. See, when you're awake and your mind is churning with things you forgot to do, you just figure, why not just do it? When I'm done, my mind is at rest and I can sleep another hour or two." Her voice rises a notch in volume and pitch. "Why are you attacking me about this? I told you, Al Devino did this."

"I have to investigate anything and everything. Al Devino is a different problem."

"How come you never told me about that box he's looking for?" she asks. "Where is it?"

"I can't talk about an investigation."

Tree branches screech across the dining room windows. Wind howls down the long-forgotten fireplace chimney like a taunt from the devil: *You'll never convict Al Devino.*

Mom's face bunches up with anger. "Why aren't you asking Sabel these questions? She's out running ten or fifteen miles before dawn. She could've done it." Mom pauses a minute then pounds the table. "You know what? She might've killed him and cleaned up the crime scene before she called you."

"Oh, come on."

"She knew all about that Don Portal or whatever you call it, the tequila. Only one person in this town knew what it was." Mom snaps her fingers and points at me. "Oh! And! She mopped the floor like a pro."

"The tequila is a good point, but what are you saying about mopping?"

"When she came to the bakery that morning!" Mom gets exasperated that I don't follow her. "She came in dripping sweat—she said it was because she was cooling down from her run. Wouldn't she have cooled down when she talked to you?"

Thinking about that for a moment, I replay the scene in my head. "No, she was doing short sprints on the street when I got there about a minute after the call. She talked to me for thirty seconds, then I sent her to you. It's a block away and she ran to the bakery." Mom looks disappointed. I continue, "What did you mean about the mopping?"

"When I pointed out the sweat, she insisted on mopping the floor, which she did like an expert. Where does a billionaire learn to mop at all, much less do it better than Debra or Jenni?"

"I don't know, but what does that prove?" I ask.

"That she knows how to clean—and that means she could've cleaned the crime scene before she called you. Did you find any prints?"

Mom knows damn well there weren't any fingerprints. If there had been any, it would've been solved by now. I still don't follow her suspicion of Ms. Sabel. "Why would she kill some random stranger?"

"I don't know. That's what rich people do. All the time. For all you know, she could be like the Marquis de Sade."

"Mom, you're reaching."

"You know damn well the rich do horrible things. Remember the pandemic when they wanted the rest of us to keep working so the rich families who never worked a day in their lives could keep living off corporate dividends? And who gave a damn about working people getting sick and dying? No one. That's the kind of thing mega-rich people do. You should be looking into Sabel."

I lean back. "I thought you wanted her in this town."

"I want her money—I don't want her."

# CHAPTER 37

## SCOTT, THE POLICE CHIEF

A HUGE WALNUT TREE FALLS on Dr. Orellana's house just as I drive by. Slamming to a stop, I run to the scene to see if anyone's hurt. As I jog up the lawn, Jose pulls into his driveway twenty yards behind me. His garage is collapsed, and his mudroom devastated. But he's safe and his fancy car is undamaged. We exchange looks through the driving rain. We live or die by simple fate.

I yell above the wind, "If you'd gotten home a minute earlier, you'd be under that tree."

He crosses himself. I give him Mike and Nikki Larson's phone number. They have a chainsaw and know trees.

I make it to Ms. Sabel's rental, where Isaiah opens the door before I get to the top step. He and Mayor Rick are saying goodbye. They see me coming out of the rain and back into the foyer. Isaiah closes the door quickly when I get inside.

"I was just telling Isaiah," Rick says, "this storm is a bad one, but we have it under control. The power company already has a truck deployed in case of power outages."

"How did you manage that?" I ask. The utilities usually clean up Kennebunkport and York long before remembering we exist.

"I thought you did it," he says with some surprise.

The three of us turn together to peer through the foyer into the living room, where Ms. Sabel types away on a laptop.

We face each other again. She's the only one in town who has the ear of important people.

"Oh, hey," I say to Isaiah. "I looked up that stuff you were telling me about institutionalized racism. I didn't know the GI Bill was for whites only. That was … I'm shocked."

He looks pleased that I've done some research. "While some bad actors have been successfully convicted for abusing deadly force, the problem is far from over. Cops are still three to five times more likely kill a Black citizen than a white. You don't have to apologize for racism. Just stop participating in it."

What he doesn't say is obvious: stop allowing it in my police department. He makes me think about what Ms. Sabel said to me, too. I silently resolve to invite Kubari to dinner. That's not going to be easy, but it's the right thing to do.

"Hey," Isaiah says, "does Amy have a violent temper? Like, does she get mad and break things?"

"No. Wait. When she gets really mad, yeah, she destroyed my bike once. And she took a hammer to my Lego Star Wars set. Why?"

"Aw, nothing. She kinda blew up at me when I interviewed her. She didn't get violent or anything." He laughs. "But if I have more questions for her, I want to know if I should duck."

He excuses himself, and heads to the kitchen.

Anticipating my next question about why he's here, Rick says, "It's time we get ahead of your mother on a few things. This fight with the Devino crime family, for one."

"I have a plan to deal with crime in Deeping," I respond before he can expand on his topic.

"Well, that's what I want to discuss. I know her heart is in the right place. Everything she does is intended to make Deeping better, but your mother's plan for Devino is not good for the town."

Mom has often waxed poetic about her stand against Vinny. There were too many civilians with firearms in that scenario for my taste. My concern for re-enacting that confrontation has doubled since their aim couldn't have magically improved more than a quarter century later. Friendly fire incidents are the last thing we need. I tell Rick, "We won't be deploying Mom's plan."

He looks surprised. He inhales, puffs his chest up, and smiles. "Have you told her that?"

"Since you're technically my boss," I say, working my jaw a few times while thinking, "I'd appreciate it if you would keep your constituents updated on the city's plans."

A hint of fear crosses his face. Together, we peer through the foyer into the living room where Ms. Sabel still types away on a laptop. Wordlessly, we resolve to let Ms. Sabel take the fall for us. She's leaving town shortly and won't have to suffer the consequences.

Rick laughs and punches my shoulder. "Sweet. Then we're on the same page."

"If we survive the storm." I give him a play-punch back. Then something like a genuine feeling bubbles out of me. "I'm glad to see you growing into the job, Rick."

He nods. "Same, Scott."

With that, he lets in a blast of wind and rain, tightens his coat, lifts his shoulders, and trudges away into the dark.

Something's on fire in the kitchen. Walking past it, I see the big guy, Miguel, holding green branches the size of his hand over the burners on the stove. I step in and see the smoke alarm lying on the counter with the battery removed.

I have to ask, "What are you doing?"

He points to a pot of something on the back burner. "Making juniper ash for seasoning. Navajo green chili with fry bread in ten minutes. You better be hungry."

Isaiah grates cheese on a plate. He nods in the direction of Ms. Sabel.

She's still working on the laptop, her foot propped up on the coffee table, topped with a bag of ice. She doesn't look up as I approach.

"You should get that thing looked at," I say as I sit on the far end of the couch.

She doesn't take her eyes off her screen. "I've walked off worse."

No point in challenging her on the ankle. A woman who dismisses presidents won't listen to me. Although it does make me question her fallibility. I resolve to go home after this, jot down every decision I've made, all the evidence we've gathered, and check to make sure I'm doing what I think best. Ms. Sabel is smart and capable, but this town depends on the Police Chief to take full responsibility for justice being served.

Fingers flying across the keyboard, Ms. Sabel finishes an email, presses send, and slaps the lid down. She spins it across the coffee table and turns to me.

In a confident voice, I state, "I need to ask you a few questions about the murder of Phil Jacobsen. Officially."

This time I have the presence of mind to start recording the conversation. I do the preliminaries with names, date, time, and so on. I prop my phone up on books on the coffee table.

"I have some follow-up questions," I tell her.

"About time. Fire away."

Her eagerness distracts me as much as the athleisure outfit she's wearing. That thought makes me realize she wears the snug apparel every time she meets me. Yet she wears a business suit when she's meeting other women. Is she trying to distract me? Everything she does is calculated, evaluated, and planned. Is she trying to control the investigation by keeping me preoccupied? Or is Mom right, she's interested in me? No way. I'm not on her radar. Probably. Damn.

I have Boo-Boo. I'm not interested in Ms. Sabel.

My thought process leaves an uneasy silence.

"I get it." Ms. Sabel fills the gap. "You have no frame of reference for how much time I spent with the body. I could've poisoned Phil and called you minutes or even hours later."

"That's true, but—"

"For all you know, I could be one of those sadistic rich people killing for sport. Like the Spartans hunting the Helots or Frémont hunting natives."

"Uhm, who?" I ask.

"The Spartans were outnumbered by their feudal servants, the Helots, by seven to one. To keep them in check, Sparta's privileged few made hunting them part of the military training for young men. Before John Frémont became a US Senator and Governor of the Arizona Territory, he hunted native tribes in California, killing two hundred in one massacre alone and starting what's known as the California Genocide—which ultimately killed over 100,000 natives. Then there was the hunting of landless peasants by wealthy landowners during the Spanish Civil War in what they laughingly called *reforma agraria*."

Anticipating my next question, she continues, "I was a history major." She sighs. "For years I've been accused of comparable behavior by conspiracy theorists."

The storm seethes outside, the wooden walls groaning at how easily I lost my train of thought. Taking a moment to regroup, my eyes are drawn to her toned legs, ice packs notwithstanding.

"Yeah." I clear my throat. "Uhm, the tequila. There are thousands of brands out there. It's quite a coincidence you spotted that one."

It's not a question. I know I'm out of my league, but I should've framed it as a question to elicit some kind of testimony. I have to be more careful.

She helps me out. Waving her phone at my phone camera, she says, "I'm dialing my home manager, Melissa Krueger, who executes the role of a butler in bygone eras. I'm putting her on speaker phone." We hear a ringing sound, then a female voice answers. Ms. Sabel says, "Mel, quick question: how many brands of tequila do we keep in the bar at Sabel Gardens?"

"Hold on while I pull up the inventory," Melissa's voice responds. There is a moment of silence, some key taps. "Here we are. Tequila only? As in, tequilas made in Jalisco and not mescals made in other Mexican states?"

"Let's count anything that brands itself as tequila whether it's legitimate or not."

"Then there are four," Melissa reports.

"Out of how many distilled spirits altogether, not counting wines?"

"Let's see, two hundred and … sixteen."

Ms. Sabel looks at me expectantly. She's opening the floor to any question I may have.

I realize I do have a question. I lean toward the phone. "Hi, Melissa, Scott Jacobsen here. I have a question. Which brand of tequila is the most popular?"

"Oh that would be the Clase Azul at five bottles a month. A close second is Pia's favorite, the Del Porto Extra Añejo at three bottles."

What does that tell me? I've no idea. I collapse back on the couch as Ms. Sabel thanks her 'home manager' and clicks off.

I want a home manager. I don't know what she would manage, but I want one.

"A generous observer," she says, "would say that confirms the coincidence. I recognized the tequila because we serve a lot of it. On the other hand, a cynical observer would say I have access to plenty of that brand and could've brought one with me. If you'd like, I can have the inventory taken to see if there are any bottles missing." She waits a beat, then realizes I've a bigger question. She laughs, "Oh, I don't drink that much booze by myself. There are business dinners and fundraising events held at Sabel Gardens almost every night with twenty to a hundred people at each. We go through a lot more vodka than anything else. I think single malt Scotch is second and tequila third. I only drink tequila."

"That's fine," I say. "I mean, I don't need an inventory. You don't have any motive, and I'm not buying the rich-eat-the-poor story either."

"I could've planted the evidence."

"Why bother? If you were killing strangers for sport, why leave any trace at all? Why wait two hours from his time of death to report it? And you're far too casual about it. People who think they're getting away with something act superior. You act … determined. No, sorry, not buying it." One last question remains, as obtuse as it seems. I ask it anyway. "One other thing, though; Mom says you mopped the bakery floor better than her employees. It seems an odd skill for a wealthy athlete to have."

A flush of embarrassment crosses her face. "Yes. Well. Without a lot of friends growing up, I would follow the maids around Sabel Gardens. I learned a good number of homemaking skills like making beds, mopping floors, cleaning fireplaces, and even some gardening." She squints at me. "You think I cleaned the crime scene?"

"Just curiosity. Your footprints were consistent with your story. The dew formed where it should. Nothing was cleaned or staged."

"OK." She nods. "I'm cleared then?"

"Yes." I turn off the video recording and sit there thinking.

Not only is she cleared, so are many of my suspects. According to Isaiah, two people at Kubari's bar swore he was cleaning up and doing books while they had a couple drinks after closing, taking him past the time of Phil's death. Kitty? Maybe, but where would she get a bottle of anything like Del Porto? Mayor Rick was home alone, but his doorbell shows no one leaving his property all night.

And that leaves Al Devino. I don't want it to be him because he would be tough to arrest and convict. The consequences for failing on either count would be death. Yet he's the most likely. In all the mysteries I've read, it's never the most likely suspect. Yet, in real life, it always is.

Mom found cyanide at his house. It's gone now, but it was there. The stuff does have commercial uses as a pesticide and for fumigation. There are legitimate reasons he would have some in his home. Legitimate excuses, I should say. There's no real reason for Al Devino to have a bottle of cyanide. So how do I find it and make it stick? For that matter, how do I connect him to the bottle of Del Porto in Uncle Phil's dead hand?

I'm the Police Chief and I have nothing.

"Do you think that box Al is after is a motive for murder?" I ask her.

"Depends on what's in the box," she says. "If it is the Rembrandt, the statute of limitations has run out and there's a $10 million reward. That's motive. But wouldn't it make more sense for him to come in with two or three of his guys and beat your uncle until he revealed the hiding place? Would he kill him for stealing it?"

"Yes. Al's that kind of guy. Now that you mention it, I think he'd kill Phil after he beat the hell out of him and got the box back."

"Maybe there was something else in that box?"

Something about Ms. Sabel's determined attitude wiggles away in my brain. She is determined to follow a certain path, always knowing what she'll find along the way but never sharing her expectations. Frankly, it's annoying. "I sense you're keeping something from me. You know who did it, don't you?"

Behind me, Miguel calls out, "Come'n get it!"

Ms. Sabel smiles. "Saved by the bell."

Miguel has laid out what looks like a stack of puffy tortillas, a big pot of green stew that smells like the southwestern deserts, and a mound of grated cheese. The stew is made up of garbanzo beans, chunks of pork, lots of green chiles, diced tomato, and purple corn kernels. I smell the juniper wafting in the air like camping in the Southwest. Miguel spreads a little cheese on the fry bread, ladles half a cup of chili in the center, and hands me the plate. We sit at the breakfast bar and eat them like big tacos. A light spiciness zings without burning. I've never tasted anything like it. It's delicious.

"But you have a suspect in mind," I say to Ms. Sabel between bites. "You said the evidence would force the killer to confess."

Miguel rolls his eyes as if I asked the wrong question. Isaiah nods knowingly. They've been through this exercise, and she hasn't told them either.

She finishes a bite before answering. "If I tell you who I suspect, and you go off half-cocked like you did with Kubari, how would that affect the investigation? We all have ideas, but none of us have any hard evidence. Let's keep following the facts. Everything will fall into place."

We each go for seconds, then eat in silence for a bit.

Ms. Sabel finishes a bite. "I have a question for you, though. How close are you and Amy?"

# CHAPTER 38

## ISAIAH, THE ADVISOR

IN THE MIDDLE OF DINNER, Pia and Chief Jacobsen break into the same conversation I had with her earlier. At least I'm not alone in thinking she's withholding her primary suspect's name. It's also reassuring to know my concerns are shared by others, even if it doesn't solve the underlying problem: why won't she tell us who killed Phil Jacobsen?

I finish up the fry bread and chili while wondering if I could make this dish at home. It wasn't a complicated recipe, just complicated ingredients. Where would I find juniper branches in DC? And how do you set them on fire without burning down your condo?

Outside under the light over the back deck, the cover to the gas grill comes untethered and flies off like a dark ghost into the night. Rain slashes across the surfaces. I'm reminded of the unhoused and wonder what Kitty would have done if we'd not been in town.

Breaking into my observations, a text from Emma buzzes my phone. I notice one I missed from Dad that came earlier, among a mass from other people.

Ignoring everything else for now, I check Emma's. The people at Sabel Tech cracked Phil Jacobsen's password. As expected, they found videos on the laptop and uploaded them to a secure cloud drive. She sends me a link to share with whomever I deem appropriate. Now I must face my fears: are they some form of porn and, if so, is Amy Jacobsen in them?

I've been raised to watch what I say and how I act around white people. I've been taught, and I have learned, they easily feel threatened.

Watching a video that might have her in it might change my perception of her in a way I can't hide—which might lead her to feel vulnerable. And that's not me being squeamish; that's history. Emmett Till was pistol-whipped, shot in the head, and dumped in a river—a ceiling fan tied to his neck with barbed wire—for allegedly whistling at a white woman. Do I want to be the creepy black guy watching videos of unknown content in this all-white town?

Maybe I could get Pia to watch it. As one woman to another, the secret would be safer, right? Except, how does the new guy ask the boss to do that? *Excuse me, ma'am, would you mind watching some porn for me?* Not happening.

After dinner, Pia limps Chief Jacobsen to the door, where they talk about the storm and listen to the wailing wind.

I help Miguel clean up. At the sink, I say to him, "I need some advice, as one minority to another."

He gives me a suspicious look that turns thoughtful as I explain my problem. I finish with, "What do you think I should do?"

He taps a finger to his lips in thought for a moment, then says, "I found the yellow rope."

"You did?"

"Yep." He pours the remaining chili into a plastic container and shoves it in the fridge. "What looks like an oversized sewer cleanout cap was where the Duggins crew dumped the computer parts they were supposed to be recycling. It's a big ol' pipe, three feet in diameter, drilled through the granite breakwater and empties into the ocean on the other side."

"He put the rope through there?" I ask. Wetting a sponge, I clean the countertop. "Why?"

"Phil gave this project a lot of thought considering he had only an afternoon to figure it out. He came up with a clever solution." Miguel hoses down the cooking utensils in the sink. "He pushed the rope through the pipe with a remote-inflatable buoy on the end. When it came out on the ocean side, he inflated the buoy, tied off the rope, and sealed it with what looked like a sewer cap. Then he went out in a boat with the big waterproof box, tied it to the rope, weighted it, and sank it. That way, when the coast was clear, the rope would allow him to retrieve the box, but it wouldn't be hanging on a buoy where someone else might stumble on it."

"You found the big box then?"

"I found the rope. Don't know for sure about the box, but it's logical. The storm came in. Waves were lashing the barrier too hard. When the seas calm down, I'll go back and pull it up. But why else would he go to such lengths to obscure the rope?"

I nod my agreement. It makes sense.

"So, what about my problem?" I ask.

He slaps a big hand on my shoulder and smiles. "Dude, I found the rope, Pia found the cyanide. You decided to chase the laptop."

He laughs as if this is hysterical and walks away. He tells Pia my problem when she comes back from the front door. They glance my way and share a good laugh before he heads into the weather to quell a small riot among our guests at the Seafarer.

It's nice to know my problems keep everyone amused.

The list of questionable activities my job entails is growing: dumpster diving, moshing with the unbathed, and now porn watching. Maybe I should take Dad up on the Johns Hopkins interview. A stable, boring job under Dad's thumb for the rest of my life? What's so bad about that?

Grabbing the laptop, I take a chair at the dining table and get to work. The link Emma sent is front and center. The team put everything in folders and subfolders. At the top is a self-opening document that unfolds before me. In it, someone named Jesmyn Mobley describes the folder arrangements. White people get anxious when the spelling strays from the ancient Anglo-Saxon orthodoxy. One could spell it Peter—or Petyr, Pytar, Petar, or even Petir and it would sound exactly the same, but they won't do that because it could call someone's whiteness into question. Jesmyn is not a white name. Jesmyn could be Asian or even Middle Eastern. Somehow, I'm pretty sure this is written by a sister who understands my problem. Unlike Miguel, Jesmyn is looking out for me. That's nice.

She reports the videos have been sorted into weddings, funerals, family reunions, and the last category: "Salacious Content." Under that last one, there are sub-categories: Explicit, Preliminary, and Soft-core. She says the techs, who she doesn't name, checked the actors using facial recognition programs. None feature Phil or Amy Jacobsen's face. From those appearing in the Salacious Content videos, three people are now Instagram influencers; two have OnlyFans sites, which Jesmyn notes with an asterisk; and twelve have LinkedIn profiles listing themselves as actors. Another thirty have not yet been identified. The asterisk explains that OnlyFans is a site known for offering adult content via subscription. Jesmyn's last note states records were uncovered showing there was a website featuring some videos from the Salacious Content folder. The university got wind of it and convinced Phil to close it down after he grossed a whopping $182.37.

I do a quick sweep of the easy, non-salacious folders. The Yelp reviews for weddings and other events were right: the camera becomes increasingly unsteady within minutes of recording. Even at the funerals.

Moving on to the Salacious Content folder, the videos are already sorted by date. In a period of a couple months, hundreds of videos were produced. I start with the subfolder called Preliminary. I understand the title once I flip through the first short video. These are the model contracts being signed, IDs shown, the actors matched, and real names and stage names discussed. It's the legal stuff. Behind the camera is a man's voice. I presume it belongs to Phil. The conversations are simple, but the actors are clearly inebriated at the signings. That confirms my suspicion about potential bad blood. I scrub through five of them, all essentially the same.

Next, I try the Soft-core subfolder. It features what look like frat parties: a minimal theme, club lights, loud recorded music, and lots of drunk college-aged kids. My frat hosted similar parties at Dartmouth. With one big difference: In Phil's, the stage and sets look professional, not cobbled together by pledges. The lights are guided by a central system. The music was put together by a professional DJ. This party was beyond the financial reach of a fraternity. Someone spent money on this—and Phil didn't have any.

Rolling the video, someone shouts into a megaphone about wet T-shirts. I can't make out the voice because the audio is terrible. A grand prize of $20 is announced and cups of water are splashed on semi-willing participants. A couple of them have instant regrets. After a winner is declared, the stakes go up. This time, it's show-us-your-tits, the prize rising to $50. As I expected, when the announcer gives the go signal, half the guys in the crowd whip off their shirts. Hell, I would've. Everyone has a laugh before the announcer eggs the ladies on. I scrub ahead. I don't need to see this. Although, I must admit, the winner was an obvious choice.

The rest of the videos in this folder follow the same format with different ideas for getting women to take off their clothes. I'm about to shut it down and move to the harder stuff when the camera swings to the announcer for just one second.

Al Devino.

That explains who bankrolled the parties. But it raises more questions: do these videos give Devino motive to kill Phil? Why would a guy like Al care if the college told him to take it down? I'd expect him to leave it up. Unless it wasn't the college making demands. What if one of the victims of the sketchy contract signings was the scion of a prominent family?

A possible scenario. But, like Pia says, where's the evidence?

I mark the video showing Al and move on to the next folder: Explicit. My finger shakes as it hovers over the mouse button. Suddenly my mind recalls Professor Zuma striding by the alley in time to see me dripping dumpster goo from my shoes. That was bad. This could be worse. There's no way I can let anyone see me open a folder labeled *Explicit* during working hours. I look around to make sure I'm alone.

This folder is the motherlode. Hundreds of videos with numbers instead of names. I pick one at random. A naked woman stands between two naked men, holding them by their handles. A female voice off camera barks orders like a drill sergeant. "Kiss Jeremy. Harder. Now kiss Cameron." The instructions continue, increasing in vehemence and directing ever-increasing explicit acts. The actress in the scene hesitates and a whip comes from behind the camera, brushing the woman as a warning, not inflicting pain. The instructor says, "I told you what to do, Tiffany. Now DO IT!" With a cowering glance at the off-camera voice, the woman obeys her instructions.

I check several more videos. They're all different combinations of actors, two women with one man, two women and no men, three women, two men with no women, three men, and so on. They seem intent on bringing every erotic kama sculpture on the Konark Sun Temple to life. All with a dominating instructor off camera. In these videos, the camera never pans to the instructor. And they're all voiced by the same female voice, a voice that is hauntingly familiar, yet I can't place it. I let the next video roll on. I'm not watching as much as listening and thinking.

At this point, I'm not sure what to do next. I can confront Al Devino and ask him questions—which will lead him to giving me sarcastic answers. That would be a waste of time. I can go back to Amy and ask her what she knows about this. Is that her voice? I interviewed her in a noisy bakery with a tremendous echo effect. The tone of voice used in these videos is completely different, more assertive, more confident and commanding. In the interview, she sounded the exact opposite of that. Hell. It could be anyone. If it's not her, asking her about it could be the most awkward thing I've ever done. And if I blow it, there could be harassment repercussions for the company.

Obviously, asking the boss is the next logical step. It's her company, her call.

I sense someone standing behind me. The video is still running. I close my eyes in shame. The way my luck is running, it must be Pia. The slurping sound tells me she's just taken a bite out of a peach. She leans over me, watching my screen, her body heat just over my shoulder. She stops chewing for an instant. With her mouth still partially full, she says, "Holy shit! Is that Amy Jacobsen's voice?" She stands again and resumes eating her peach before saying, "Oh, you have to ask her about this."

I was wrong. *Now* my humiliation is complete.

# CHAPTER 39

## CHRISTINE, THE BAKER

AS SOON AS THE TEROMAS are bored, they hop down from their chairs and run wild. Hunger overcomes my desire for well-behaved toddlers, and I let them go while Amy and I finish eating. I always wanted to be a mother, despite Mother Nature insisting otherwise. Until Amy showed up unannounced at the bakery, I enjoyed being a grandmother. For the first day or two, my routine was a mess, my house was noisy, and I found bits of jam or banana smeared in the strangest places. The grandchildren pushed me out of my comfort zone. I'm coming to terms with it finally, more so now that Amy needs me again.

She fills me with purpose. A feeling of motherly love floods over me. I think of all the things I need to do for her.

First among them is to keep her from confessing to murder.

Lightning explodes brighter than daylight outside the windows. In the next room, the Teromas countdown to thunder. Before they can yell "two," the noise shakes the house. The oak scratches outside the dining room wall as if all the troubles in the world were trying to claw their way inside.

I finish my meatloaf—the only leftover from the funeral that didn't have lobster in it—and move on the Tater Tots. The best thing about having grandchildren in the house is the excuse to serve Tater Tots. I smother them in ketchup, then turn to Amy again.

Noticing my maternal gaze, Amy says, "What?"

"Sabel shot down my plans for Al," I tell her. "We've got to find where Al stashed the poison and get Sabel to find it. She's an unstoppable force when pointed in the right direction."

"Yeah." Amy's unfocused eyes drift to the ceiling. In a dreamy voice she says, "She's so confident. So … in charge. So commanding."

My understanding of my daughter has grown tremendously in one day, yet this is a side of her I never expected. She's in love. I watch her until her gaze comes back down to mine.

She cocks her head at me and once again says in her petulant voice, "What?"

"If you're gay," I say, "just say the word. I'll study up on being an ally—is that what you call it? Oh, honey, you know I'll do anything to support you. I will always love you, no matter what."

"MOM!" Her mouth hangs open like I'm the dumbest parent in the world. "I'm not gay. Jesus. Gender-targeted sexuality is SO last century."

She tosses her napkin on her plate in disgust and stomps into the other room. Gathering the Teromas, she herds them upstairs to the bath.

Did I hear that right? *Gender-targeted sexuality?* I've never heard the expression before and already it's been left behind? Since when did targeting a gender … what does that even mean? I was on the tail end of the free-love generation, and we thought that was radical. Becoming an ally was a huge step forward for me—and I don't know what an ally does. Apparently, whatever they do is over.

I stack several plates and carry them to the sink. I must keep Amy and her dreamy-eyed-thoughts about Pia Sabel from blubbering a confession.

Amy's phone, still at her place on the table, buzzes with a text. I'm about to yell up to her when I notice it's a text from Al Devino. With the screen locked, the text is obscured. I try her PIN from her college days and am surprised it still works. The text reads, "Why you ghosting me girl? After all I done for you?"

My heart stops. What the hell does that mean? Ghosting is good, right? She's not talking to him. But he wants to hear from her. I let the phone go blank again. Should I ask her about this? No. It was an invasion of privacy. I'll have to find some way of digging it out of her.

All the plates are scraped and the table's cleared. I start in on rinsing and loading the dishwasher.

Another bolt of lightning flashes outside. Upstairs, the Teromas shout their countdown, this time getting to a hasty three. The windows rattle and the oak scrubs the house. I feel like I'm under siege.

What about the dry box? I shouldn't have given Al the idea it holds a Rembrandt. Big mistake. The reward's a lot of money. It won't save me from Al's wrath, though. He didn't spill blood on the paintings, Vinny did. Al won't care if the blood implicates his late uncle in murders. He'll go straight for the reward money—and then turn Deeping into crystal meth central.

Wait a minute. Al was looking for it before I told him about the Gardner Museum heist.

Which can only mean one thing: Vinny kept something else in that damn box.

A glass shatters on the floor. Since I'm the only one in the kitchen, I must've dropped it. Picking up the big shards, I toss them in the trash. Then a realization hits me that makes me ill.

Vinny knew my secret. Al was with Vinny until the end. So, Vinny told Al how to blackmail me into letting him take over Deeping. Al owns me—and with the Rembrandt a threat against Vinny, not Al, I have no leverage. That's why Al's feeling so bold.

I wet a paper towel to sponge up the tiny bits of glass on the floor.

As soon as the skies clear, Al and his horde will descend on this town like they own the place. They'll toss Town Harbor looking for that box. When they find it, nothing Sabel has planned will help us. He'll shove her aside like crumbs off a plate. He knows I'll do anything to protect this town—and my family. I'll even let mobsters sell meth on Elm Street.

I return to rinsing dishes and thinking. My top priority is to protect Amy. The best way to do that is find the box. I can take what I need out of it, trade the rest to him for our lives, and let Al collect the reward. I need that box.

What did he say it was, six feet by five feet? That's big. No one found it yet because Phil, bless his attempted heroism, did a good job of hiding it where only he can find it.

And that would be Headland Beach. In a flash, a memory of Sabel asking questions about Phil comes to me. She asked if Harbor Park was Phil's quiet place. I told her no, he preferred Headland Beach.

I slam the dishwasher closed and fire it up. It chugs to life with a groan. I'm not the only thing getting old around here.

Without a second thought, I dial Jana Siverling. When she answers, I launch right in, "Did anyone see those Sabel people sniffing around Headland Beach yesterday or today?"

"Oh yes, that big Indian fella was flexing his six-pack up there this morning. Had scuba gear and went diving. Lyn saw the whole thing. She says he's built like that Greek god, whatshisname."

"Adonis."

"No, she said someone else."

"God only knows what Lyn actually said. What she meant was Adonis. It doesn't matter. Did he find what he was looking for?"

"Who?"

"The Indian, with the abs. He was diving and this isn't the Great Barrier Reef, so what did he find?"

"Oh, I don't know. All she told me was how chiseled the guy—"

"OK, thanks, Jana." I click off.

Did it ever occur to either of them that, no matter how well-built a guy is, diving off the murky, muddy coast of Maine is unusual? My conclusion: He was looking for the box but didn't find it. If he had, he would've dug it up—and the ladies would've added his shoulders and biceps to their observations. Headland Beach was a good guess, though.

And that means Sabel's searching for the box as well. I have to outsmart her and get to it before she does. She has a considerable advantage with two studs working for her. But I have the advantage of knowing Phil.

Lightning flashes bright enough to feel it like a sunburn. Thunder quakes the house before the flash dissolves. Then everything is dark. The electricity is off, not just my house, but everything outside the window, including the streetlights. Upstairs, the kids shriek with delight.

I have bigger problems. Where the hell would Phil Jacobsen hide a mattress-sized box with a Rembrandt in it?

# CHAPTER 40

## SCOTT, THE POLICE CHIEF

BEYOND THE EDGE OF THE storm, the sun has set, stealing what little light filtered through the clouds. My officers are burning up the radio trying to help citizens frightened by the power outage. People think the police can solve every problem including storms.

The office lights are on because the community center has a generator to fill in as our town's emergency shelter—not because of the police station at the back. I march inside and find the geriatric crowd filtering in. The old folks keep up on local news and know where they're supposed to go. Maybe they never went home.

I plow through the chairs, repeating the same cursory answer: "Don't know, I have the same weather app you have." My last full night's sleep happened a day before Uncle Phil died. My bones are tired and I'm getting punchy. I should watch what I say to the people I'm sworn to protect.

Everyone is busy answering phones in the squad room. Someone made a list of problems on a yellow pad but was soon overwhelmed and abandoned it. I skim it: Stacey Hartley's mortuary basement flooded and the caskets are floating; the roof at Jana Siverling's hair salon is leaking all over the wigs; Mike Culpepper wants to know if we need auxiliary cops (he was an MP once); Jenni Cornell's cat is in the attic and won't come down; Bud Blaine's wife says he went drinking with his buddies and she wants him to come home; Eleanor Andersen says the storm surge has the harbor flooding into Main Street; Madeline Benton wants to know what we're doing to preserve the historic buildings; and Ruth

Jackson has changed her mind about hosting the unhoused people at the Seafarer Motel. I toss the pad back where I found it.

It serves as a stark reminder that I need to prioritize my problems.

Kathy Butler tells me she has an open line to the electric company. That's never happened before. We compare notes and decide this is the first time we know of that the power company said anything nicer than *so what?* in response to our outages. They're re-tasking a crew from York but they won't have an assessment for twenty minutes. Most likely scenario: we'll have power in an hour or so.

I have her pad the time estimate and get the word out that we hope to have power in four hours.

Then I go to the lunchroom, where I met with Isaiah and Ms. Sabel twelve hours ago. We've done a lot since then. I wonder if Ms. Sabel's life runs at a breakneck pace like today all the time. It must. She doesn't seem the least concerned about any of this. I still can't believe she told the president, "I've got to run." And that's what she's been doing for the last three or four hours since then—running. With a bad ankle.

The whiteboard has unfinished notes about the dry box, a shoe size, and yellow rope. Not my best work. I grab the eraser and wipe everything clean. I'm taking it methodically this time. From the beginning. I make a headline: Crime Scene. I make a bulleted list under that.

- Phil Jacobsen poisoned with potassium cyanide in $2,000 bottle of tequila
- Lured to the scene
- Wrote letters on the bench, ADCI or A+CL or something
- Shoe prints, men's 12
- Body found by Pia Sabel, billionaire athlete and philanthropist.

Below that I put a new headline: The Plant. Under that I write:

- Crazy Kitty said strange things; Isaiah thought they were from Greek tragedies
- one quote from Kitty, "It's my problem. If I tell you, it'll be

yours."

There I stop, grab the eraser, and wipe off "Crazy." That's neither nice nor helpful. I continue with a new heading: Phil's house. Below that:

- Yellow rope missing; Boot print in front room dust from day of killing
- Isaiah interested in video camera with no tape or memory cards
- Al Devino shows up looking for a 6x5 dry box.

From there, the notes are more subject oriented than place. Laptop: Isaiah interested in video because a young lady was involved, refused to say who. Ms. Sabel discovered the YCCC was missing potassium cyanide. Doorbell video of Mom on the street after midnight. Al Devino wants to move drugs in Deeping, threatened Mom. Mom saw a bottle of cyanide on his shelf. Al knew the lab results of the poison at the same time I did. Mom and Amy scared to death of Al. Ms. Sabel anticipated Al making a move, knew my drug bust was an act of war.

I stand back to admire my work. I consider putting down another point: Ms. Sabel keeps talking about our experiences as adopted children. I decide not to write it. While those have been interesting—albeit uncomfortable—conversations, they're not relevant to the case.

The next thing I notice is the follow-up questions popping up in my mind. Why was Ms. Sabel so interested in what Phil wrote on the bench? We could barely see it before the fingerprint guys got there, and then it didn't make much sense, yet she insisted it said ADCI. Does that mean something to her? All I found from a quick Google search was *Association of Diving Contractors International.* I doubt Uncle Phil even snorkeled. What was Kitty talking about? If she tells me something, it becomes my problem instead of hers. What does that mean? Is she trying to protect me from something?

I make a mental note to call on Isaiah and ask him if he's figured anything from the Greek tragedies. That thought reminds me that I need to thank him for helping avoid a mistake with Kubari. I apologized to

Kubari but never thanked Isaiah for bailing me out. If it weren't for him, Kubari would've torn my arm off, wound up in jail for assaulting a police officer, and it would've been my fault.

I'm reminded of my conversation with Ms. Sabel on our drive to the YCCC. Without saying much, she made me reevaluate how I serve the community. I went after Kubari with only a hint of evidence. Probably motivated by a desire to rehabilitate myself from when I assaulted him. God, that was stupid.

Is that what's going on across the country between police and minorities? An officer looking for a suspect makes an unfounded but convenient accusation that would piss off anyone—which is what I did to Kubari. The falsely accused man reacts to the justice system descending on him like a knee on George Floyd's neck—which is what Kubari did. When the suspect resorts to the human instinct of self-preservation—he lands in jail.

In most cases, without intervention like Isaiah's, it's a self-perpetuating cycle turning on arrests, prosecutions of convenience, and coercive plea bargains. The problem rolls downhill, getting bigger and uglier every day. You can't let people assault police officers, even if the officer is behaving badly. At the same time, officers should never behave badly in the first place. Which is exactly what I did to Kubari last year when protecting Uncle Phil.

I'm part of the problem.

Isaiah told me not to apologize for it, just stop participating in it. I can do that. I'll make my officers aware of this. We should never be the cause of these problems. Well, at least, never again. We're the good guys. We have to be the good guys, or the criminal justice system doesn't work.

My gaze returns to the list. Isaiah was interested in the laptop. I gave it to Ms. Sabel; do they have answers yet? And what's that note about Isaiah protecting a young lady? Why did he do that? Who was it? Come to think of it, he asked me if Amy had a violent temper. That's one of the things we're supposed to look for in murder suspects. Why was he asking that? Why didn't I ask him more questions?

And then the answer comes to me: because I don't want it to be

Amy—yet I think it is. Come to think of it, Ms. Sabel asked me how close Amy and I are as siblings. I thought she was asking as adoptees, but she was really asking if I'm protecting Amy. Am I? From what? Isaiah and Ms. Sabel know something and aren't telling me.

That pisses me off. I appreciate the help, but this isn't right. I'm the Police Chief. I'm in charge here. I can't have them directing the investigation. What if they send it off track? That's why I did this exercise, to get level with them if not ahead.

My tired eyes scan the whiteboard again. Something that's not up there stands out: Pia Sabel is not concerned about Al Devino as a murder suspect. Instead, she said we have to make sure the town survives Al's assault. He's the suspect with the means and motive. Mom saw cyanide at Al's house. That tells me Ms. Sabel is prioritizing: first destroy him in the streets of Deeping, then take on a weakened Devino for the murder.

I look over the board again. Something else jumps out at me: Where is Miguel in this? There were scuba tanks in the mudroom, a wetsuit hanging in the shower. Is that why Phil wrote ADCI? Somehow diving is involved. Ms. Sabel must have had Miguel looking for the yellow rope while she ran me out to the college. Why? Because the yellow rope is tied to the dry box. The wetsuit means they think it's in the ocean. With a bad ankle, she wouldn't be out in the surf. She kept me busy while her man searched for it—why? Because she doesn't want me to find it. Al's looking for the box. Ms. Sabel's looking for the box. For all I know, half the town could be looking for the box. Does everyone know about the $10 million reward?

The answers are probably staring me in the face, but I'm too tired to see it. I should sleep on it.

Boo-Boo sends me a text: "I'm at your place. No electricity here either. My phone's almost dead. When will you be back?"

I should head straight there, but one thing still bothers me.

Ms. Sabel's been one step ahead of me from the beginning. I need to get ahead of her. She said our priority is keeping Devino out of town— because she wants me focused on a fight with Devino while she finds the box. What happens if I turn the tables on her? If she's ahead of me on what's in the box, what angle of this investigation will let me get ahead of her?

# CHAPTER 41

## CHRISTINE, THE BAKER

"READ THEM A STORY," I tell Amy while I wrestle my raincoat. "That always calmed you and Scotty down when you were little."

It's not the Teromas who are scared. Amy stands at the top of the stairs on the verge of tears, her angelic face framed in the camping lantern. What kind of dom can't handle a little thunder and lightning? Well, she did imply that the dom only comes out when the clothes come off. She still believes she killed Phil and it has her spooked.

I have to prove it was Al before she has a breakdown.

Thunder rattles the house. I shrug my coat on. She's still staring at me.

"I'll be back before it's time to tuck them in." I wave my battery-operated camp lantern. "I have my phone."

Those kids should've been in bed an hour ago. But she does things differently. And that's a fight I'm too tired to have right now. Those of us who get up to bake bread four hours before anyone takes a bite need to hit the sack early. But there's no time for that right now. I've got to find that box.

I give her a stern motherly glare and shake my finger. "No matter what, do not confess anything to anyone for any reason. Do you hear me?" When I get a nod, I say, "I'll prove it wasn't you, Amy. Trust me."

Amy nods again and disappears into the dark hallway. Her self-confidence, shattered by her guilty conscience and destroyed by the storm, put her on an anxiety-rocket to the moon.

I shove my regular shoes into the shrimper boots I use for galoshes.

Then I stop. Sabel hung her jacket here mid-afternoon. Did she see the shrimper boots? Lots of people double up in the wet, so what? I remind myself to keep focused on the box and stop worrying about Sabel. I stamp my feet to the bottom and head outside.

The rain hits me in the face right away. It's cold and heavier than I expected. They keep saying climate change is making our storms dump bigger loads and this looks like a good example. The storm drain at the corner has a tree branch stuck in it, forcing a small river down the street into Karen Smith's yard. I tug on the branch, but it's jammed up good.

Black husks of buildings loom over Main Street like sentinels of the damned. They watch me sneaking into Town Harbor with eyes of dark windows. The occasional lightning flash animates them. I pull my coat tighter.

My first stop is the odd-shaped storage space in the alley behind Eleanor Andersen's Sand Dollar. It's too narrow for anything commercially useful, so I had the town condemn it. Phil and I have used it for spare storage ever since. Working the padlock, I open the steel door and find two inches of water slurping across the floor.

Getting past my old furniture requires me to turn sideways and inch my way in. Losing weight would help, but it's been a losing battle lately. I feel pinned between the brick wall behind me and a mattress I should've tossed ten years ago. Raising my lantern gives me enough light to see the far end. A lightning bolt helps me for a second.

"The hell are you doing, Christine?" Eleanor's voice makes me shed a layer of skin quicker than a reptile. I clutch imaginary pearls.

When I get my breath back, I face her. "Thought I had a generator in here. A little one."

I lift my lantern and see she's holding a regular flashlight in one hand and a metal pipe in the other.

With a hint of embarrassment, she tosses the pipe behind her. It clanks in the alley. "Sorry, thought you were burglars taking advantage of the storm."

"Did you see Phil in here last week?" I ask.

"No, can't say I did."

"Scotty?"

"Nope." She shines her beam to the far end and lifts it. It's smaller but has a stronger spotlight than mine. "See what you're looking for?"

What I don't see is a large dry box with a Rembrandt in it. Just old boxes of junk Phil thought would magically become either useful or valuable if he held onto them long enough. How was he supposed to know "limited edition" doesn't mean the same at Walmart as it does at Tiffany's? There isn't enough room in the space for what I'm looking for. He didn't hide it here.

I start squeezing out of the confines while Eleanor judges me with a disdainful eye on my girth. Somehow, she managed to stay trim as she aged. I eat what I bake. No sense letting muffins go to waste at the end of the day. Thankfully, there is no cork-popping noise when I get back to the alley. I slam the door and hook the padlock.

"What are you doing here?" I ask Eleanor.

"Guarding my property. You never know who might show up at times like these."

"When was the last time you saw Phil?"

"Don't remember." She loops her arm in mine. Rain forms a waterfall pouring off our hats. "Come have a cup of tea with me."

"I'd like to, but the grandkids are back at the house. They've never been in the dark and they aren't buying *it's an adventure*."

"Oh, I see. Hey, you know what? I did see Phil the day he was killed. Not here though. At low tide he was out on the breakwater."

"Out on the rocks?" I ask. "Did he have anything with him?"

"Not a thing. I thought he was fishing like those other fools pushing their luck trying to catch something before the tide washes them out to sea, but he was just looking around."

I take my leave and head back. Eleanor picks up her weapon, slips in her store's back door, and clacks the lock.

Around the corner, out of Eleanor's sight, I knock on the back door of Olivia Benton's Fine Arts. She and Phil were friendly once or twice. He might've asked her to hold a giant box for him.

There's no answer. I try the aging wooden door. Locked. I turn my light off, look around to make sure I'm alone this time, then slip a screwdriver out of my purse. Jamming it into the latch, it slides the bolt back easily. The wind catches the door and slams it open against the wall. If Eleanor's hearing is as fit as her figure, she might've heard that. I take a long look toward her store until I'm sure she's not coming out. I pull the door closed behind me and barge inside.

First thing I see is a red flashing light and a keypad. Security. For the stuff Olivia sells? Holding the lamp up to the pad, I try her birth year. Nothing happens. I try her house number. The red dot dims. It should go green, right? What does dimming mean? On the LED readout, a sign appears, "BATT." Then the light goes out. No sirens. No alarms. She needs a new battery.

OK, that works.

With my lantern held high, I look through her tiny storeroom. There's nothing here, not even paintings. I crawl up the narrow ladder to the upstairs storage space. Nothing in there but rat droppings. Next, I go to her show room.

A brilliant painting the size of a window hangs in the most prominent space. It's a beautiful oil of the breakwater with fishermen standing on the slick granite. Black skies on one side, sunny on the other, and one of the fishermen is recognizable: Tim Dunn. Now that I look at it, I realize the other fishermen are heading back to shore. Tim has his fishing pole bent toward the sea, determined to haul in that last catch. He's standing his ground against the waves breaking all around him. He looks defiant, tempting fate to destroy him. It did.

I look at the signature: Nikki Larson. Well damn, she's immortalized the day Tim Dunn washed out with the tide, never to be seen again. Not that I'll miss the grabby bastard. It's a damn good painting though. I've seen her work before and … well, I never saw a reason to buy one. But this painting might change that.

Leaning close to the price tag, I squint to make sure I'm seeing this right. $5,000 for a Nikki Larson? Who is she kidding? Take two zeros off and I'll think about it. It is beautiful, though.

I head out the back door and shut it behind me. Walking out to Main Street, I wonder aloud, "Where the hell did you hide that dry box, Phil?"

The wind steals my words into the night.

Another lightning bolt sears the sky above Town Harbor. Boats bob in the water, crashing into the brick-topped pier. Storm surge splashes across the road and laps at Eleanor's front door. If it gets higher, the Sand Dollar's in trouble. As the flash leaves me in the dark, I catch one last glimpse of the Plant.

And that's when I know. Scotty might've searched the place, but Phil was no dummy. Well, he was a dummy, but when he tried hard, he could be clever. Somehow, he hid it in the Plant. I don't know how, but I know he did. I feel it. Wading toward it, I quickly realize I'll need to go the long way around. If I go through Town Harbor, I'll wind up singing in the choir invisible with Tim Dunn.

Even the footbridge crossing from Harbor Park to the Plant is several inches deep in rain and sea water. My use of shrimper boots as overshoes works like a dream. The office door is locked but the crime scene tape covering the hole Phil left in the wall flutters in the wind. I duck through.

Sheets of rain come through several holes in the roof high above. Lightning flashes outside those holes. I hold my lantern high. The room's been cleaned, broom marks scratch across a thick patch of oil and dirt, the trash heap is gone, and fresh caution tape flaps around the collapsed corner of the floor.

I walk the four corners as best I can. Structural oak beams, later reinforced with iron, obscure a few areas. Nothing lurks behind any of them. The office is a wreck of broken plaster and missing floorboards. The main room is a broad expanse of emptiness. Marks on the walls show where dividers and interior walls once stood. Now it's one large and utterly empty space.

Maybe I was wrong. Where would Phil hide a box that big? In the flooded basement? No, too easy to have the whole building collapse on it, burying it forever. He would've put it somewhere he could get to it but far enough away no one would stumble on it. Sabel was thinking the same thing. That's why she sent her man up to Headland Beach. He scoured the coast and came up empty. That tells me she didn't find it there. And that means, it must be here.

That's when I see it. On the back wall, an oversized sewer pipe. It's too big to be a sewer. You could toss a toaster oven down that pipe. I recall the Duggins man confessing to me that they dumped computer parts *down the tube*. This is what he meant. It empties into the Atlantic on the other side of the breakwater. But Phil didn't put a bed-sized box down that tube. He must have put a map, or a clue about where to go from there.

I move in closer and hold my lantern up high. It takes a very big wrench to open the cover. I don't see one lying around. Yet there are fresh tool marks on the head. It's been opened recently.

The Indian did this when Sabel had the rest of us distracted. Well, doesn't she think she's clever?

There must be a way to get this open. I'll need to figure it out and act fast if I'm going to beat Sabel to it. Do I have any wrenches at home? Not anything big enough. My home tool kit cost twenty bucks at Home Depot. Which means I need to go to Phil's house and steal something from his shed. That's another walk from here. I'm so tired, I consider letting it wait until morning.

Sensing something behind me in the cavernous space, I crane over my shoulder to see a strong flashlight held by a dark silhouette. The beam is pointing at the oil and dirt smudge in the middle of the space.

Pia Sabel calls out, "Judging from these tracks, your boots must have a terrific grip in the wet."

# CHAPTER 42

## ISAIAH, THE ADVISOR

AMY JACOBSEN TURNS GHOSTLY PALE when she opens the door to my smiling face. No doubt she's recalling the last question I asked her. She knows that's why I'm back, standing at her front door with rain dripping off my cape hat. Holding the doorknob tight enough to break it, she twists it back and forth while she searches for a polite reason to slam it on me.

Before she can act, I plead my case. "I'm new at my job, I don't know what I'm doing, I'm trying to impress the boss, and I'm messing everything up. Can you help me?"

I finish with my puppy dog eyes.

A crack in her façade appears. A hint of the woman who gave me her phone number and wrote *anytime* next to it appears. I think. It's dark and I'm purposely holding my flashlight to the floor behind her. Like the town, her entire house is dark. Two kids in onesie-pajamas squeal through the hallway behind her, oblivious to the storm and the stranger. Kids up this late seems odd, but what do I know about raising kids? Maybe the power outage is an adventure for them.

I gesture toward the foyer floor, a request to come inside just two feet.

She twists her back to the wall, giving me the space. When I enter, she closes the door behind me and presses her back to it as if she's caged prey and I'm a hungry tiger.

"I can't really help you," she says. "I don't know anything."

"It's not that," I say as softly as possible. "Let me tell you a short story about how this morning started for me. You'll see how you can help when I get to the end."

She appears to be on the verge of screaming in terror. Instead, she croaks, "OK."

"See, I'm not a professional investigator. I'm not a professional bodyguard. I'm an advisor. But this morning, Ms. Sabel asked me to conduct an interview with you—and I blew it." I wait for a reaction. There isn't one. "She set me up with some rushed, last-second training from a former FBI agent who now works in our Omaha office. Chrisana told me not to push a witness too hard or they'll feel attacked, and they withdraw. Two minutes into my interview with you, I blew it, and—just like she said—you didn't want to talk anymore. I came here to apologize. I'm sorry."

Amy relaxes her grip on the door. Again, she croaks, "OK."

I move my flashlight beam to the wall where it reflects off the white paint enough to see her better. I forge ahead. "I'm under a lot of pressure. I've only been with Sabel a few weeks and already they assigned me to work with the owner. She trusted me to do this interview on my second day with her."

I leave a silence.

"You didn't blow it," Amy says. "I got scared, that's all. It's not your fault."

"No, I made a mistake. I asked you about Phil's laptop when I shouldn't have." I wait for the fear to sink in again. It doesn't take long. "See, we finally cracked his password, and I got a look at his video recordings. Hold on now, don't take it like that, Amy. Amy. Don't freak on me. And don't worry, all the secrets are safe with me. I hold things like this in the strictest confidence. No one else needs to know. Take a deep breath. It's going to be fine."

It's not exactly fine. She's hyperventilating. Reaching out, I grip both her upper arms and look in her eyes.

"Amy, listen to me. Scott doesn't know. Your mom doesn't know. Your story doesn't need to go anywhere." I intentionally leave out the part about how the investigation will demand I explain it to someone if it isn't germane to the murder—and everyone if it is. I hate lying to her, but she could pass out if I don't. "Take deep, slow breaths. In. Out. In. Out.

Easy now. That's it. Let's not alarm the kids. Are you with me?"

She nods.

Letting go of her arms, I back up a step. "From my point of view, it's quite clear that a couple authority figures in your life abused their positions and taken advantage of you."

Her first expression tells me more than I wanted to know. The guilt in her eyes is there for the world to see, but she's not ready to talk yet.

When she calms a notch, I continue, "There are a few holes in the story I need to patch up so I can tell Scott and Pia to look elsewhere for evidence."

She gives me a totally blank face.

"There's something else the former FBI agent told me to look for," I tell her. "She told me when you get close to the truth, guilty people try to deflect suspicion on someone else. When I mentioned the laptop this morning, you immediately told me Phil and Kitty had an argument. You deflected. Why?"

She looks ill again. It was a tough tactic, but I think it's working. I press on. "I've since learned he wasn't yelling at Kitty. He was raging about something else altogether. Kitty was listening to him. Do you know what he was mad about? Was it about the videos?"

She shakes her head. "I don't know. I couldn't hear what they were saying."

"Well then, back to the videos. You know, when older relatives tell us to do something, we tend to do it." I wait until she nods her agreement. "I figured out Al Devino teamed up with Phil to make these videos and somewhere along the line, they roped you into it. What I don't understand is why they stopped—"

"No, no, no, no." She tromps past me into the living room and motions for me to follow. "I've got to tell someone. It's been eating me alive for years. You promise you won't tell anyone?"

I hang my dripping jacket and hat and trot to catch up. I move a Styrofoam airplane from the loveseat that's at a right angle to her and sit. "You can trust me."

"I started dating Al Devino my first week of college," she says. "He came to visit and wanted to make sure everyone respected his family. We hit it off. He was the bad boy, and I was in my lusting-after-bad-boys phase. Motorcycle, leather jacket, wads of cash from selling drugs, everything a stupid young girl could want. He made a joke about college girl porn, and it flipped a switch in my head. I'd seen lots of girls in the freshman dorm doing things they never dreamed of before—and would deny forever after. I knew we could make a mint with Uncle Phil's video business. It was my idea from the start. They both tried to talk me out of it until I snuck them into a frat party. Finally! The idiots saw the potential. We could've made a fortune."

It's dark, my flashlight sits on its back end, its beam reflecting off the ceiling, but I see tears form. She puts her head in her hands and sinks. I give her a minute.

"We had everything going on. Lots of footage, lots of fun, lots of parties—then dumb fucking Al goes and brags to Uncle Vinny about it."

The two kids stand in the opening between the living room and dining room, pointing at their mom and laughing at her F-bomb. She waves them off. They scurry into the dark.

"Vinny decided no woman in his family is going into that business. He told Phil and Al he'd use their body parts in lobster traps from the Canadian border down to New Hampshire. He gave me a lecture about bringing shame to the family name. And he told me my 'real' mother was a whore and if I showed any signs of following in her footsteps, he'd stash me in a brothel—and I'd never get out."

When she pauses, I say, "I find it ironic that Vinny Devino—drug dealer, pimp, and murderer—would've been concerned about you smudging the family name."

Amy stays quiet for a long time.

I guess it wasn't funny. I break the silence. "So you guys packed it up."

"Vinny made Phil give him all the tapes and SD cards."

"OK, so that's why Phil did that," I say. "He transferred everything to his hard drive before turning over the physical tapes. Vinny, being old school, didn't think about digitizing. Phil waited for the day Vinny died, then … what? He was going to build that website and start making money?"

"That part, I don't know exactly. He never said anything to me about his plans. But Siobahn Allen, the actress who played that sexy vampire a couple years ago? Yeah, her. He tried blackmailing her. She called me, mad as hell and threatening to sue. I'd just left my husband and I was angry at the world. I focused all my anger on Uncle Phil."

She's trembling now. Her whole body is shaking. I sense we're on the verge of a breakthrough moment. I hold my tongue.

"I got drunk that night." Her tears start flowing. "Blackout drunk. After he and Kitty argued—or whatever. I got so drunk I can only remember snippets here and there. Like walking to Town Harbor after midnight." The tears turn to sobs which go on a long time. I find a box of tissues and hand it to her before she can go on. After a lot of nose-blowing, she says, "I saw the poison. I don't know where. Some place with lots of bright light. It's one of those flash-memories you can remember through the haze, but you only get that fragment. I've tried, I just don't remember where it was, only that I was holding it in my hand."

That's a wrinkle I never expected. I'm stunned. After catching myself, I say, "Your mom saw it at Al's house. Did you drive up there?"

"She saw it two days later. I'm pretty sure—"

The front door opens and Christine walks in, shaking out of her wet things.

Amy holds a finger to her lips with a angry glare. She mouths the words, *Not a word to Mom.*

Chrisana's advice comes back to me: *Time is on your side.* The first time I pushed and lost. I've just regained my rapport with her and this time I'm not going to lose it. We can finish this later. I nod and gesture that my lips are sealed despite the tantalizing information about the poison.

Christine notices my jacket and hat while hanging hers. She spins around and sees me. "You Sabel people are everywhere. Your boss just walked me home. What the hell are you doing in my house?"

Amy starts to answer.

I beat her to it. "I had some follow-up questions about the argument she heard between Phil and Kitty."

"And you came out in a torrential downpour?"

"Beats sitting around wondering. And talking to Kitty isn't getting me anywhere."

"There's a reason we call her Crazy Kitty."

I rise and thank Amy for her time. "If you think of anything else, give me a call and I'll swing by."

Christine watches me suspiciously as I put on my rain gear, take my leave, and head into the gale.

My head spins with scenarios regarding the cyanide during the three-block trudge back to our rental house. All those scenarios are plausible but none feels certain. Where did Amy see the bottle if later it was at Al's house? She dated the guy a long time ago. But she just left her husband; did she hook up with him for old time's sake and Phil walked in on them? No. Al wouldn't bring cyanide to a hookup. Or would he? Maybe Amy was the target.

A hundred more combinations of Al, Phil, and Amy fighting over videos of Siobahn Allen swirl through my thoughts as I finish the walk.

Back at our rental, Vanessa Zuma stands at the front door, holding a bag from Target and looking as if she's about to knock. When I hail her from the walkway, she faces me. "What are you doing here?"

"I'm staying here," I answer.

"I rented it out to someone named Emma something."

"She's our operations manager, makes reservations and the like. You own this Airbnb?"

"Indeed, I do."

I open the door. "Care to come in out of the cold and damp?"

"Wait … is Pia Sabel staying here too?"

"That's right. She's out somewhere but she'll be back soon."

"Well, I'll be damned." Vanessa follows me in. "How do you guys have electricity when the whole town is dark?"

I close the door quickly before the rain floods the foyer. "Emma had one of those battery packs installed when the forecast changed. That's what ops managers do."

"You had a what?"

"One of those house-sized batteries for emergencies. They didn't have time for a generator."

"I didn't give anybody permission to install a battery."

"Well, I'm new around here, but my understanding is, Pia needs electricity 24x7 to run her empire."

"I came over with some battery-operated lamps." She holds up her bag. "But I guess you won't need them."

Behind us, a blast of cold air whirls in carrying a good deal of rain with it. Miguel rides the wave. Right behind him, Kitty Robinson.

Miguel says, "Guess who got kicked out of the Seafarer?"

Vanessa watches Kitty staggering in, then turns to me. "You're gonna need my help."

# CHAPTER 43

## SCOTT, THE POLICE CHIEF

ONE HOUSE ON THE STREET is lit up like an electric light parade. Naturally, it's the one rented by the richest woman in town. Life is like that for them. Nothing touches them. Not a power outage that blacks out the town, not a password-protected laptop—nothing gets in their way. I pull into the driveway, park my aging secondhand police cruiser, and watch through windshield wipers that need replacing as the rain beads perfectly off her shiny new Mercedes. While her wealth might give her many advantages, I need to get in front of her on this investigation. It's my responsibility.

Exhaustion slows my reactions. I feel like sneaking a quick nap before I go in. But there's work to do. I grab my hat and creak the door open. The wind howls it out of my grip, but a good slam gets it closed. I splash my way to the front door, where Miguel lets me in. When I ask for Isaiah, he points me to the living room where Isaiah's in a deep conversation with Vanessa Zuma and Kitty Robinson.

Isaiah looks up and joins me as if I'd summoned him. He appears to welcome the break. Knowing Crazy Kitty as well as I do, I can't blame him.

"What's up, Chief?" He all but salutes me. Still a Marine.

"I never thanked you for helping me with Kubari. This is a small town and making a mistake like that could ruin my department's relationship with the citizens." I read something in his face and understand where I went wrong. I made it all about me and my department. I add on, "And make our service to the minority community worse than it already is. You helped me see how to make the department serve our citizens better, including those I've left out in the past."

He relaxes and gives me a sympathetic nod. "You're welcome."

I offer a hand. He shakes it warmly and I extend the gift: a bottle of Allen's Coffee Flavored Brandy. I explain, "It's a Maine brand. Might take a bit of getting used to; but it's a staple in these parts."

He thanks me profusely but stops mid-word and cranes a glance at Kitty. Holding the bottle where she can't see it, he nods toward another room. We slide in, obscuring the booze. The room is filled with free weights, all new and shiny.

I drop the big question on him. "What did you find on Phil's laptop?"

It's an assumptive question, challenging him to deny his people cracked it. I phrased it that way because I don't believe a Dartmouth-educated Marine would lie to me.

Isaiah doesn't break eye contact. In fact, he says nothing for so long that he may as well have said *we found everything*. His silence is testament to the content being adult in nature. Against my better judgment, I throw my biggest fear in front of him. "Is Amy involved?"

His mouth twists as he thinks up a diplomatic response. Finally, he says, "She does not appear in any of the videos I've skimmed."

We stare at each other in silence. The fact that my sister does not play a starring role in porn is a great relief but a tiny victory. I deconstruct his fact-elusive statement. He skimmed rather than watched and hasn't skimmed everything. Why so specific about the term *appear*?

"Isaiah, thank you for protecting my sister's honor. I appreciate your chivalry. At the same time, this is a murder investigation. I need you to tell me what you found. Your candor will save me the spirit-crushing task of sorting through the videos myself."

He's a good man. Pointing to a weightlifting bench, he takes another facing me. We sit. In tasteful verbal sketches that avoid specifics, he takes me through his discovery process of identification and age-verification videos, the frat-boy parties and wet T-shirt contests, and comes to the discovery of Al Devino's involvement.

That stuns me. Mom had gone to great lengths to keep Uncle Phil away from anyone on the Devino side of the family. Mike Davis and Al both were off limits. Mom must not know about this, or she would've killed him.

We discuss Al for a moment. We speculate about Al funding Phil's adventure because the parties presented an additional avenue for drug sales.

Then, with great diplomacy and tact, he explains the hardcore videos with Amy's off-camera voice providing specific direction.

Gutted, I'm ready to leave. I want to go home, pull the covers over my head, and sleep until this nightmare comes to an end.

I start to stand when he puts out a hand, stopping me.

"There's something else." He takes a deep breath. With reluctance, I sit back down.

"I visited Amy to ask her about it," he says. "Luckily, your mom wasn't home which allowed her to open up. She told me she dated Al in college and—"

"She what?"

"You didn't know either? She kept it from your mom, too."

"Mom wouldn't let her date family, and neither would I. We're not royals."

I can see it on his face: he's about to say something about adopted kids not being blood-related, as if that made the relationship OK, but he's an intelligent man and wisely decides not to offer an opinion. He stammers a bit, then says, "There's more."

He explains that Vinny shut everything down. And that Phil decided to use Vinny's death as an invitation to blackmail Siobahn Allen. "That set Amy off. She got mad at Phil and went to confront him, but he was ranting at Kitty. When Amy saw Phil raging about something, she went and got drunk. Somewhere in her inebriated state—she doesn't know where—she found a bottle of cyanide. She was going to tell me more but stopped cold when your mother came home."

We stare at each other as that concept rolls around in my head. In an instant, I see the problem. She was drunk and can't remember one of the most crucial details of our investigation. Which implies she killed Phil. Or she knows who did. This is something she should've volunteered before the funeral. Either she can't or won't tell us; which is it? If she dated Al years ago; would she cover for him now? I feel my face tighten up as I begin rhythmically nodding my acceptance of the depressing situation.

"Scott," Isaiah says quietly, "everything I've just told you I swore to her I would not tell you. I'm violating her trust in me."

"I understand. Thank you." I get up on jellied legs and almost fall over.

Isaiah walks me to the door.

As we pass by the living room, Kitty calls out, "Did the king listen to Tiresias? Dost know thy lineage? Nay, thou know'st it not. And all unwitting art a double foe."

Her statement doesn't make sense aside from being a rude dig at my adoption. Isaiah and I look at each other.

"Don't worry about it," he says and opens the front door. "If there's any meaning in it, I'll figure it out and let you know."

Everything I've learned in the last ten minutes leaves me confused and shaken. Staggering to my car, I get in, start it up, and stare blankly where my headlights light up the Mercedes. I close my eyes for a few minutes to see if the world is still fucked up when I reopen them. Thoughts scream through my head at light speed. When I reopen my eyes, nothing has changed.

Amy never told me about dating Al. That hurts. We were close growing up, but when she started at Maine, I was a senior at the University of Vermont. I had my life opening ahead of me. She made her own path from then on. Maybe I should've taken time out and looked in on her. Maybe. But I didn't.

I back out of the driveway onto the street and see Ms. Sabel striding through the rain with her pearl-handled cane. She's on her phone, talking fast and gesturing wildly. As I roll close, I roll down the window to say something.

She's yelling at someone, "… fuck the rules, Liam! If we're going to make this relationship work, we have to figure out another way."

She mentioned dating someone who ended up working for her—which caused a workplace problem. It doesn't appear to be going well. I can relate. Mom doesn't want me dating Boo-Boo; Ms. Sabel's HR department doesn't want her dating Liam. Apparently, some things do touch the rich just like the rest of us. I decide she needs her privacy and drive on.

I go back to my main problem: not letting Ms. Sabel and company leave me in the dust. Thinking through what I've learned, I hope something will pop out at me. Amy was dating Al. They get a bright idea to make money in porn and bring in Phil. Vinny steps on the whole thing and forces Al to dump Amy. They wait until Vinny dies, then Phil is murdered, and suddenly Amy is terrified of Al.

Mom said they found the cyanide at Al's. Amy got drunk after seeing Phil the afternoon before he was murdered and saw the cyanide in that drunken state. Mom saw it at Al's house two days later. Did Al do it and Amy helped? Or did Amy do it and Al is covering for her? Are those two still in love? Amy would not be the first drunken lover to make a pathetic booty-call after midnight. If she did that, when did she become afraid of Al? And why?

I stop in the middle of the street and watch the rain stabbing through the yellow cones of my headlights. Amy has been less than honest with me about a murder. That's not something I can cover up. At a minimum, she's impeding my investigation.

I always wanted to be a policeman. I wanted to be the hero who uncovers the truth and brings justice. The truth just hit me like a ton of bricks. If Amy did it, why was the poison at Al's house? Did she plant it there to make him look guilty? If so, what do I do about it? If Al did it, how did Amy see the cyanide? Did she help him? Did he take advantage of her inebriation?

It's a tough choice: do I stand for truth and justice, or do I help my family? Family is the most important thing in my life. Amy is my "real" sister. Al is a distant relative. Amy is a good person. Al is far from it. Therefore: It must be Al.

Boo-Boo texts me. "Are you coming home?"

Shaking my head to clear it, I blow out a breath, blink several times, then step on the gas. Before I make any accusations, I need sleep.

# CHAPTER 44

## CHRISTINE, THE BAKER

I'M SITTING IN THE DINING room, repeating a mantra to Amy—"You didn't do it; do NOT confess anything"—when the lights come on, stinging my eyes. A quick glance out the window tells me the whole town has the power back. Amy's still pacing the living room, having an anxiety attack of epic proportions, unaware of what electricity means to the Teromas.

I bolt upstairs to switch off all the lights in their room just as they rub their eyes. If they wake up, there will be whining and crying. I whisper the goodnight song, watch them snuggle their pillows, and close the door. Crisis averted.

I'm too exhausted for grandchildren right now. What I need is to cross the hall to my room and dive between the sheets. It's long past bedtime for a baker. Since gaslighting Amy isn't working, I consider the many other things I need to accomplish. Find that box.

Back downstairs, I rummage through my toolbox. Just as I thought: two screwdrivers, a pair of pliers, and a roll of tape. There's nothing in here that'll get that cap off the pipe. I slam the plastic box shut and close the pantry door.

What the hell was Sabel doing at the Plant anyway? She must've followed me. Nice of her to walk me home, but doesn't she have an empire to run? I was an idiot for listening to Rick Tara. She would've packed up and left town yesterday if I'd left her alone. So what if we don't get her fancy SRC? Maybe I could get the historical society to shut up long enough for Home Depot to tear down those old farmhouses and open a regional store on our side of Route 1. Wouldn't pay the same, but I wouldn't be worried about airing all our secrets in front of strangers.

What am I thinking? Al Devino is my biggest problem, not Pia Sabel. We need those jobs. There's a lot more of them and they're full-time so we won't have to hand out food stamps. Still, she's a nosy bitch.

I sense Amy standing behind me. She's biting her nails.

I give her a hug. She leans into it and starts whimpering again. We stand there for a long time. She hasn't needed me like this in fifteen years. It feels good to hold her and help her through this. Although I do need to sit down. I'm drained.

"How about a drink, honey?" I pat her back and guide her to a chair.

That fancy tequila is right where Sabel left it, in the middle of the dining room table. I rummage around for proper shot glasses and find a couple with palm trees painted on them. Our one Florida vacation. I pull my chair close to Amy, put one arm around her shoulder, and pour. While I do, I consider the cost of this bottle. It's insane. Why would Bill Koller spend that much money on tequila? But then, why would Pia Sabel? And she just left it here, about $1,500 worth.

I do the math. "You, know honey, this is a $100 shot of tequila. Kubari charges $300. And it doesn't even need a slice of lime."

Trembling lips form a weak smile on her beautiful face. She takes her glass and taps mine. We both sip. *Mmm, mmm, mmm.* Smooth.

Amy stares off blankly.

Who would have a big-ass monkey wrench I could borrow without asking too many questions? Is that what I need? Or do I need a crescent wrench? Or a socket … thing? Men aren't good for much, but one thing they're handy with is pipes, wrenches, bolts and the like. Now that I think of it, Mike Larson has that kind of thing. Yeah, but he'd want to know what it's for so he can mansplain exactly how to use it properly. That would take a week.

Back to my plan to sneak into Phil's house. How does that happen without Sabel showing up unannounced? How did she happen to wind up in the Plant? I'm not buying that story about wandering around in the rain trying to figure out what to do about her boyfriend.

Amy starts gasping for air. Wide-eyed and staring at the tequila bottle, her hand reaches out, pointing at it.

"What is it, honey?" I ask and squeeze her tight.

"Tequila," she answers between gasps. "The tequila."

Her heart is pounding so hard, I can see her veins pulsing. If she were my age, she'd be having a heart attack right now. I make soothing, shushing sounds. "Take it easy, honey. Take a deep breath."

Her breathing becomes bigger versions of short, panicked breaths. Her finger still points to the bottle. Her chest heaves as she tries to deepen her breathing. But it doesn't work; the shallow painful gasping accelerates. I repeat my instruction for deep breathing. Instead, she holds her breath. She turns crimson.

I keep murmuring reassurances. "It's going to be fine, honey. Mom will take care of everything. Don't worry about it. It'll all get fixed by morning. You need some sleep. Let me handle this. It will all work out—"

"Mom." She turns to me with a jerk. "I saw the bottle."

Again, she breaks down in panic. My breathing picks up a notch, too. She's scaring me. "What do you mean, honey?"

Her hand flaps at the bottle as if trying to wave it away. "I saw that … that same thing. Brand. Painted bottle."

She buries her face in my chest, sobbing. I pat her back and hold her with both hands. She's never needed me this much. It feels good to have her need me. I want her to need me. Although, I'd rather go back to talking about her sex life. It feels like the lesser evil at the moment. Purring reassurances to her, I make big circles on her back like I did when she was little. She seems little now. More scared than ever.

"I, I, I saw it … with the poison." She sobs and squeezes tight to me. "Butcher block. Sitting on the … on the table."

"Of course you did, honey." More soothing circles. "It's OK. It'll be fine. Maybe your memory is a little hazy."

"No, I can see the butcher block. I see it." More sobs, more squeezes.

"You mean at Al's house?" I ask. "On his counter? Is that why he's been texting you?"

I begin to wonder how long she can keep this up. At the same time, a deep and foreign fear seizes me. Feeding off her panic, I feel my heartbeat rise. I can't let that happen. I have to be strong for her or we're all cooked. I take a deep, slow breath. Inhaling through my nose and exhaling through my mouth. *Keep it steady*, I tell myself. *Steady.*

"The poison and the bottle." She gulps. "In the bakery."

I pull away fast and look at her. "What? What were you doing in the bakery?"

"Maple butcher block. I can see it." Her eyes are red, swollen, and filled with tears. Her face is splotchy. "At the bakery. Yours is the only maple table in town. Oh, Mom, I can't believe I killed him."

She collapses back on my chest.

"You didn't kill anyone," I say. "Stop saying that. Al Devino has a maple butcher block counter, too. Your memories are jumbled, that's all. Why would you have been at the bakery?"

"I remember now. I had a headache."

I look at the bakery keys hanging on the hook by the back door. The front door key with a yellow rubber band and the back door key with black, so I can tell them apart in the dark. They're always there. I would've noticed if they were missing for a minute.

I tilt Amy upright and look into her eyes. "You didn't have a key."

"Mom, please." She makes a pained smile. "Scotty and I have been breaking in there since high school. You always went to bed early; we'd sneak out to the park and party. If it rained, we had a spare key we kept between the bricks. It's still there."

Her arms circle me as she falls on me again.

Damn those sneaky teenagers. But I guess that's what teenagers do.

Her guilt is mounting by the minute. She's like a flood-swollen reservoir about to burst through the dam.

"Did Al Devino know about this extra key?" I ask.

"Sure, everyone in town knows."

Great way to help your mother maintain security over the family livelihood. Jesus. But that's a minor problem compared to the big one. Amy could ruin this family. If she confesses now while Sabel's in town, she could bring down the whole deal. Years of work destroyed in a minute. I could kill her.

I need to find that damn box. But how?

The whole thing is teetering on the brink. The town, my family, the

SRC, the future. Everything hangs by a thread tonight. The pressure weighs on my chest. Suddenly, Amy's head feels like an elephant sitting on me. My breathing ramps up again. My heartrate explodes. For years, I've fixed everything. I stood in the gap and kept this town from falling apart.

I can't do it anymore. I need help.

"Mom, Mom! MOM!" Amy's voice bursts through my inner wail. "Don't pull your hair like that."

My hands let go as pain sears my scalp. I wipe my palms over my face. She needs me. I have to pull it together for her. She actually believes she did it. What really happened doesn't matter. I have to make her believe Al did it.

"You didn't kill anyone," I say. "You have to convince yourself of that. Get these thoughts out of your—"

"But I had the bottle and the poison in my hands, and I …"

"Your imagination is filling in the blanks from a drunken blur." I take her hands and squeeze them. "You would never hurt anyone. You know that. You must believe in yourself. Al has the same table and he's been texting you for days. Somehow, he's tricked you into thinking you did it. I'll figure it out. Don't worry. Right now, you're going to bed and going to sleep. You're not going to tell anyone anything about bottles of tequila, or killing Phil. I'm going to talk to Scotty. We know Al did it, all we need to do is find the proof and make sure it leads to him. I'll get it fixed."

Amy nods, her eyes downcast. I pull her chin up and smile at her.

"OK, Mom." She rises grudgingly, kisses me, downs the rest of her shot, and trudges away.

I listen to her clomp up the stairs and into the bathroom. The water runs, the gurgling sounds of brushed teeth follow. Light switches click, off in the bathroom and on in her room. The door closes.

I dial Scotty. Straight to voicemail. He's done for the night.

I can't do any more now. I'll rely on my one superpower: the baker's waking hour. I'll be up and on task while everyone else dreams of monsters in the wildflowers.

I pour myself a second shot to sip while I think. Fatigue pushes my eyelids down as a thousand things roll through my mind. I need to find that box. I need Scotty to find the evidence on Al. If we need to nudge a few facts, he'll do it for his mother who loves him. He'll do it for his sister. He'll do it for the town. And he'll do it because putting Al Devino behind bars is a good deed done.

# CHAPTER 45

## ISAIAH, THE ADVISOR

KITTY ROBINSON'S EYES ROLL AROUND in her head like lost marbles on a ship's deck. Drunk on cheap whiskey, she's not happy that Vanessa and I are pelting her with questions. We contemplated pouring coffee into her, but Miguel advised us against it. Since he saw a lot of what he calls manifest-genocide-induced alcoholism in the Navajo Nation, leading him to lead a sober life, we rely on his expertise.

Kitty is neither asleep nor awake. She's catatonic in an upright position in the corner of the L-shaped sectional sofa. Miguel had the foresight to bring Kitty's library along. Vanessa pages through a volume of Aeschylus, skimming the underlined passages. As bad an idea as it is, I'm still trying to talk to Kitty.

"Before the funeral, you told me to tell Chief Jacobsen, 'Nay, thou art thine own plague.' Why was that important, Kitty?"

Pia bursts through the front door, her cane pounding on the floor in anger. She's in the middle of closing a conversation that sounds equally irate. When she steps from the entryway to where we can see her, she looks embarrassed. Even Kitty is staring at her bug-eyed. We all look away at the same time. Pia pounds her way to her room and shuts the door with an uncharacteristic vehemence. Not quite slammed, not closed calmly either.

I glance at Miguel, who's working on a laptop. He shrugs and goes back to work. A few seconds later, something on his screen makes him smile. He crosses the room to Pia's door and says through it, "The *Numina* will be here in the morning. They'll stay at sea for safety and be ready to move when you give the word."

She replies with words I can't make out. The two of them are cooking up something involving her biggest yacht that appears to be on a need-to-know basis, and I don't need to know. Which means I'm still the new guy. I need a breakthrough to get myself included in the group. Otherwise, I may as well take Dad's offer.

A glance at Vanessa tells me she stayed for more reasons than being the only house in town with electricity. At first, I thought she was trying to reconnect with Kitty, who had once been such a promising young woman. Now I realize she stayed to help me solidify my position at Sabel Security. She wants to figure out what Kitty is trying to say—as much to help me as to find the killer. That she's taken an interest in my success makes me feel good about my chances. We share a smile for a moment.

In that smile, I see more than that. I think Professor Zuma wants what I want. Interesting. Maybe we'll get to know each other better.

A light shaking of Kitty's shoulder opens her eyes. I ask, "Kitty? Why is Chief Jacobsen his own plague?"

Her eyes roll up and she falls over onto the cushions.

Vanessa's gaze tracks Kitty's fall, then comes to me. She holds up the Sophocles book and passes it to me, open. I look at a leaf-marked page and see an underlined passage. It's a speech by Tecmessa in *Ajax*. After killing her father, Ajax took her as his lover—common dating practice in those days. She's reporting Ajax's errant behavior with an overtone of pity. It reads: *'Tis changed, his rage, like sudden blast, / Without the lightning gleam is past / And now that Reason's light returns, / New sorrow in his spirit burns.*

Which is a close translation to what Kitty said at the dumpster.

Vanessa says, "You told me she also quoted a nearby passage about making a choice. If you would benefit, would you make a choice that brings grief to your friends? How does that tie into Phil?"

"The obvious answer is no, you wouldn't hurt people," I answer. "That tells me Phil made some kind of choice that day."

Giving her another light shake, I ask her to look at the passage. "Is this about Phil? Is this what you're trying to tell me?"

She sits up and looks at the page with unfocused eyes. Her head lolls on her shoulders until she can bring her eyes to mine. She says nothing. I'm worried she might get sick.

Pointing at the book, I ask, "Was Phil upset about something, got mad, then calmed down?"

Kitty gives me an indecipherable shrug and falls back to her pillow.

"You might have something there," Vanessa says. "You told me he was raging in the street outside his house in the afternoon, right?"

"Yep."

"And Kitty was with him. So, if I'm reading the mythology right, Ajax got pissed off, then went and killed all the wrong people. But Phil was the one who got killed." She stares at me waiting for me to get it.

"Phil was the wrong person," I reply. "Phil is not Ajax here. The killer is Ajax, mad at Phil for the wrong reasons?"

Vanessa makes a *maybe* expression and opens another volume to another leaf.

"Kitty," I say softly. "Was Phil killed for the wrong reason?"

My intoxicated guest shoots upright and shouts, "Alas, how terrible knowing the truth can be when there is no help in the truth."

She falls back to the pillow.

"I'd take that as a yes," Vanessa says with a sad glance at Kitty.

I flip through the pages to the passage she's misquoting. "This translation uses wisdom where she says truth. She's altering these quotes."

Skimming through *Ajax* quickly, I find the other passage she quoted at the dumpster. In it, Tecmessa reveals that Ajax, railing his grievances to a voice in his head, cursed Atriedae and Odysseus. But when Kitty said it, she said the names of others.

I give her one more tug, hoping it's not the one that will spill her half-digested pizza on my shoes. I already wrecked one pair today. She sits up, her gaze wandering the room.

"Kitty, you said someone was ranting about Devino and Jacobsen. Do you mean Al Devino killed Phil?"

"No," she says. "Phil had Scott's birth certificate." She flops a hand on my shoulder and tries to look me in the eye with limited success. "It's best if you shoulder your burden and I shoulder mine. So fuck off."

"Hey, you spoke plain English," I say. "Tell me what these passages mean in plain English."

"If I do—I will die." Kitty pushes off me and tunnels under couch pillows until only her feet remain visible.

Vanessa and I share a confused look. She says, "Why would a birth certificate set him off?"

"Scott's records were thought to have been destroyed when his adoption agency was vandalized. If Phil had Scott's birth certificate, he probably had all the records."

"Someone killed him for that?"

"I can't see why." I press my fist to my lips while thinking.

"It makes perfect sense," Pia's voice comes from behind me. She limps around on her cane to where I can see her. "It's starting to come together, depending on what that birth certificate says. You cleared it up. Great work, you two. That's amazing. No one else could've gotten anything out of Kitty."

She starts to turn away.

I hop up and ask, "Since we know who did it, shouldn't we tell Chief Jacobsen?"

Pausing while half turned, she slowly faces me. "If we told him, he'd be in denial and then where would we be? In this situation, don't you think it best if we lay out all the clues and let him figure it out?"

She doesn't wait for an answer. She plants her cane, turns on it, and hobbles away.

"You should have a doctor look at that ankle," Vanessa calls to her.

Pia doesn't answer. She disappears into her room. I fall back on the couch somewhat dejected.

Vanessa looks at me. "Do you know who did it?"

"I have no idea." I toss my hands in the air. "But she thinks I do. Which is both the frustrating and intriguing parts of working with her. She figured it out and firmly believes I see it as well."

"Better not tell her otherwise until you know her better." Vanessa laughs.

"Exactly."

We stay silent for a moment, each thinking our own thoughts.

Miguel waves to me and points to his laptop screen. "Radar shows the storm clearing up in about six hours. That means I-95 and Route 1 will be passable not long after. It'll clear from north to south, giving Devino a head start. Get some sleep—we're going to be at war by dawn."

I acknowledge him, then turn to Vanessa. "Phil didn't have a birth certificate at his house that I saw. Scott could've found it and taken it with him. It's his, so it's not the kind of thing he would think to tell us about. At the same time, he's doing his best to be an ace cop, which means he wouldn't remove anything from a crime scene. So, that leads me to believe it wasn't there. Where is it and why was Phil going crazy over it? Or was Phil the one going crazy about it? Maybe our Ajax-person was the one flipping out."

"Well, you have the riddle of the sphinx to solve there," Vanessa says as she stands. "It's far past my bedtime, so I'll leave you to it. Thanks for letting me have a look inside your world."

"I had the distinct impression you wanted to see more of my world," I say as I rise to her. We stand toe-to-toe.

She smiles. "You know, I'm old enough to be—"

"A twelve-year difference doesn't make you old enough for anything more than a fine wine."

"Oh, you did the math?" She laughs. "Presumptuous."

"Hopeful."

"I like a man with a positive attitude." She tugs on my Henley and glances at the stairs. "Is it more positive the higher up you go?"

# CHAPTER 46

## CHRISTINE, THE BAKER

BAKERS AROUND THE WORLD RISE before dawn to get the ovens heated and the dough rising. There's plenty of work to be done every morning, but today it's double. I finish laying out the buns on the baking table to rise a moment before I hear Lyn Avery's knock on the back door.

"You're late," I tell her as she tracks mud into my pristine bakery.

"Good morning to you too, Christine." She makes a face, stomps her boots, and comes in. "You should be grateful I got up this damn early. A bird in the hand gets the worm, you know."

"Whatever. Just go through to the front." I lock the door behind her.

One last check: ovens are heating, dough is rising, back door is locked. I'll be back to get this finished in time. I head out front, where Lyn is wisely donning a rain poncho over her raincoat. We start off into the dark downpour, the wind angrily snapping our clothes.

This storm is working out to my advantage. Al is stuck up north at his house, while I can get a head start on finding the box. If I can get it and Sabel figures out how to stop him, then I win. If Al gets that box, whatever secrets it holds will bury me. If Sabel gets that box first, who knows what might happen.

We make our way through flooded alleys to Phil's shed. After positioning Lyn streetside, I go back and wait for a moment. That Sabel woman has a bad habit of turning up at the wrong time. I listen for Lyn's warning whistle. Nothing but wind and rain.

I lift the crime scene tape and yank the flimsy wooden door. It drags across the muddy gravel in a worn groove. The roof leaks in several places.

My flashlight brightens the ungodly mess. Phil never put anything away. When he had a job, it would go poorly, then he'd toss the tools in the shed in disgust. The only thing recognizable is the lawn mower. It's accessible because, after constant complaints from neighbors, he would drag it out and cut the weeds down to stubble and dirt, then let it go calf-high again. I push it aside and sweep left and right. After moving several dust- and grease-covered objects aside, I see the red iron handle of what I'm looking for and yank it. A clatter of junk crashes from the inverted pyramid it had held aloft just seconds ago. Everything jangles like a metal waterfall to the floor.

At least I have what I came for. I turn around to find Lyn peering at me.

"Are you OK?" she asks. "Sounded like a bomb went off."

"I'm fine, let's go."

Lyn's light scans the mess left and right. She tsks, "One man's trash is in the eye of the beholder."

"Yeah … c'mon."

I lead Lyn across the half-submerged footbridge to the Plant. Positioning her outside the hole in the wall, I give her instructions to whistle if someone's coming. I duck under the crime scene tape and make it two steps when Lyn gives the signal whistle. I freeze. My heart stops. Shit. We're caught. Already?

"What am I looking for?" she asks.

"Lyn!" I whisper-shout. "We went over this. I'm checking to make sure Scotty did his homework, OK? If I get caught in the act, people will lose confidence in him. Keep your eye out for anyone walking a dog or whatever."

"If you have to check on his work, doesn't that mean you don't have any confidence in him?"

"It means I'm his mother. Children can't survive without our help, you know that."

Lyn thinks about this a moment before going back to her assignment. She has kids. She knows.

I find the tube and cap and then look at the wrench. How the hell do these things work? I pull the top part and get nowhere. There's a middle section that twists. After twisting it a long time, the mouth widens. I keep on twisting until it's all the way open. It barely fits over the nut, but I get the teeth set and push the wrench.

Nothing.

I move the wrench to where the handle is hanging off the nut at three o'clock. This time, I put my weight into it.

Nothing.

I tug on it. I hang from it. I push it. I hit it. That hurts my hand.

"What're you doing?" Lyn's light blinds me.

"Turn that off. And give me a hand."

"How am I supposed to see where you want my hand?"

"OK, turn it on, but aim it at the floor."

I have her join me on the handle. It finally creaks a bit. We count to three, then jump up, shove it down, and it gives half an inch. We catch our breath, count off again, and give it another genuine jump with everything we have. Suddenly, it spins around like the second hand on a clock. We stand still like victims in a horror movie waiting for it to come around the top, knowing damn well it's going to hit one of us but unable to tear ourselves away.

Lyn is the unlucky one. It slams into her shoulder, falls off the cap and clangs on the ground. The echo is muffled by Lyn shouting, "Fffuuuuccccckk, that hurts."

She shrugs out of my reach when I try to help her. Pacing a circle, she holds her arm to support her shoulder and says, "I'll be fine. Stings, that's all."

I unscrew the cap and try to take it off. It's way too heavy for me to control. It slips through my fingers and bangs on the floor. The echo drowns out Lyn's swearing.

I look inside. A yellow marine rope tied to a wedge is lodged in the opening. I tug on it and discover it's heavy. Back when Scotty was refusing to tell me specifics of the active investigation, he mentioned Sabel was looking for a rope. Why? I look down the big tube and get it. Somehow, Phil figured out how to hide the big box in the ocean and this rope leads to it. But the box everyone is after would never fit down this tube. What was his plan to retrieve it?

Then I remember it was Phil. There was no plan to retrieve it.

Outside, I hear the surf pounding against our granite protector. Tons of water burst into the air with a boom and crash back to the rock. It slurps back to the sea, where it silently gathers momentum for the next assault. Boom and crash. I need to find that box or life in this town is going to boom and crash.

No one will get to it in this surf, though. Divers like it nice and calm, that much I know. I'll need to hire a diver and a boat, and then wait until the surf is down. Who's my best team? Mike Culpepper has a boat, but he'd ask too many questions. Spies are like that. Mike Tenenbaum dives in the Bahamas but that doesn't mean he owns the gear. Does Rick Tara have all that stuff? I'll have to make some calls. Somehow, I have to be out there before anyone else. Maybe I should book every boat in the harbor to keep everyone else on shore.

At any rate, my Rembrandt is safely hidden beneath the storm for now.

"C'mon, Lyn. We're done here." I put a hand on her shoulder to turn her toward the exit.

She shrieks in pain.

"Y'know," she says through gritted teeth, "I think it's broken."

We walk to her place, where she swears her worthless husband will drive her to the urgent care. Since I don't get along with her lesser half, I leave her to figure out a good story. As long as she doesn't tell anyone about the yellow rope, it'll all work out.

I make my way back to the bakery. It should be dawn, but thick clouds still squeeze out sheets of rain. I hurry my steps. There'll be hell to pay if the muffins aren't ready at seven.

When I get back to Main Street, the lights in Mom's Bakery blaze like there's a party going on. I unlock the front door, let myself in, and lock it behind me. Sneaking around the display cases, I peer into the kitchen.

Amy pulls boxes off the shelf, looks in them, puts them back.

"There's no poison here," I say.

She jumps and wheels around with a knife. "Oh, Mom. You scared me."

"Who's watching Teromas?"

"LeeAnn Pratt," she says as if I should've known.

"At this hour?"

"Where were you?"

"Lyn Avery broke her shoulder," I tell her. "I went to help, but, as you know, Mr. Avery—"

"Hates you. Yes, everyone in town—except Lyn—knows you two had an affair. What happened to her?"

"We did NOT. That was the problem. He got mad when I said no. Hell, it doesn't matter if you say yes or no to men. Either way, you wind up paying for it for twenty years."

She shakes her head. She doesn't believe me; she prefers to believe the lies people whisper.

"What happened to Mrs. Avery?" she asks.

"Didn't get the whole story. What are you doing?"

"I'm looking for the poison. It's eating me alive, Mom. I'm going to grab it and turn myself in."

"The hell you are." I put my fists on my hips and glare. "First of all, it's at Al's house, not here. He did this and by daybreak I'll prove it. Scotty will—"

There's a knock on the back door. We share a look. Neither of us are expecting anyone.

Crossing to the door, I say, "Who is it?"

"Pia Sabel."

Jesus, I can't turn around without that woman showing up. I open the door to find Sabel standing in Noah's flood as it sloshes through the alley. She nods toward my kitchen. I figure, I'm a step ahead of her now that I've found the rope. I have nothing to hide. Pulling the door fully open, I step aside with a welcoming gesture.

She says, "Have you called your people? Are they ready to defend the town?"

"You know, I haven't gotten around to that just yet. I'll make those calls as soon as I get the brioche started."

"It's fine," Mayor Rick follows Sabel inside. I hadn't seen him out there. He continues, "I called everyone. They'll be in front as soon as I send a group text."

"Why?" I ask. "What's the rush?"

Sabel says, "Ten minutes ago, Al Devino and ten others left his house."

# CHAPTER 47

## SCOTT, THE POLICE CHIEF

PEOPLE WALK INTO MOM'S BAKERY like zombies converging in the dark. I trudge along with them, Boo-Boo's arm looped through mine. The rain is lighter, the harbor's still swamped, and the clouds are still too thick to know if the sun has risen or not.

The coffee is free, which means Ms. Sabel paid for it in advance. Mom never gives things away. I take a cup and see Mayor Rick waving me over. He's talking to Ms. Sabel in front of the center display case. I leave Boo-Boo to mix in her cream and sugar and join them.

Everyone with an orbit in Mom's solar system is here.

"What's the plan?" I ask.

Rick looks at me and his mouth forms a word. Before he can say anything, Ms. Sabel puts two fingers in her mouth and makes an eardrum-piercing whistle. She says, "Good morning, people. Mayor Rick just reviewed his plan with me, and I have to tell you, I now understand why you voted for him."

Rick snaps around to look at Ms. Sabel, the shock on his face telling me whatever plan she's referring to was hers, not his. But he appreciates the accolade. Mom stands in the kitchen doorway with her arms crossed and a disapproving scowl on her face. Behind her, Amy wipes tears from her eyes with a tissue.

"He's going to tell you how it works," Ms. Sabel continues. "We don't have much time to get into position, so please listen close."

Isaiah appears at my elbow with a carboard box the size of a toaster. We exchange nods.

Rick straightens up and begins explaining his plan. While he talks, Ms. Sabel and Miguel hand out note cards and small stacks of paper to everyone. I look over Jill Williams' shoulder to read her card. It has two addresses on it and a phone number. Rick explains how it works. There are three roads into town off Route 1. People are assigned strategic intersections. When they finish their assignments, they fall back to the second address.

Rick says, "Police Chief Scott Jacobsen will give us the word when to fall back via group chat, so watch your phones."

I'm stunned. No one filled me in on the plan. I've no idea how this works. How am I supposed to give instructions?

Everyone in the room turns to me. I give them a smile and tip my hat to them. They look relieved to know I'm in charge. They all turn back to Mayor Rick when he continues explaining things.

"It's a good plan." Isaiah leans to my ear. "It's the Battle of Cowpens strategy in a modern setting." He looks at me as if I knew what he was talking about. "Morgan versus Tarleton, the Revolutionary War's only double envelopment and a brilliant way to use untrained people against a more experienced and deadly force. Three-quarters of Morgan's men were poorly trained sodbusters he expected to run at the first sound of cannon fire. He positioned them in the front lines and told them to shoot once and fall back behind the small number of veteran soldiers. He positioned the veterans in a semi-circle around the green recruits but out of sight. The British attacked, saw the soldiers shoot once and flee, and pursued them—right into Morgan's trap. You're the trap. You'll make the arrest."

He smiled at me. I don't feel like a good trap. And I'm not sure who I'm arresting except that Al is the obvious choice. I'm not sure how this will go down. The only time I've fired my weapon in the line of duty was when I killed Mike Davis—and then I pulled the trigger more because of a spasm of fear than an intent.

Sensing my uncertainty, Isaiah adds, "I'll be with you."

When I met Isaiah, I considered him an arrogant Marine. Now I'm on the verge of giving him a hug and thanking God for his presence. Instead, I nod my thanks.

I've missed hearing a good deal of Rick's plan. He wraps up and everyone seems to be excited. They swing by me and slap my shoulder, saying things like, *We couldn't be in better hands.* And, *Great that you're leading us.* As they walk by me, they take an odd-looking phone out of the box Isaiah's holding.

Ms. Sabel talks to Rick, her ray-gun gaze firing over his shoulder at me. She hasn't told me everything she knows. I can tell by the look in her eye.

All the phones are distributed. Isaiah hands the last one to me. It has a *Sabel Satellite Systems* logo on the back.

"It's set up for this operation," he says. "The only text you can send goes to everyone who just left. If it rings, it's someone in the operation calling you."

Isaiah starts to say something else, then stops, looks around, and takes a step closer. He says, "We think Phil had your birth certificate. Did you find it?"

"My records were ..." It hits me. Why Ms. Sabel is giving me that look. They found something. "What makes you think he had them?"

"We got something out of Kitty. She said that's what he was ranting about in the afternoon before he was killed. It took hours, and that's all we got."

He looks dead serious, so I decide not to question the reliability of his witness. "My records were destroyed."

"Several records were burned," he says gravely. "Yours weren't. According to Leslie Dingwall, who was there at the time, some were missing and some were burned. She figured out which were burned and notified those families. Christine told us she wasn't notified, which means your records were stolen."

My head is shaking involuntarily as I refuse to believe it. Yet he and Ms. Sabel have done the research on this and believe it's true. That leads me to consider discovering who was listed as my birth parents. Do I want to know? Not all reconnections go well. Some are joyful reunions. Others are sad disappointments, and still others are a reopening of old wounds.

Isaiah pats my back. "I shouldn't have dropped that on you until after we get Devino. My bad."

"That's OK. I'll compartmentalize for now." Which is easier said than done. "Let's go set up."

As Isaiah leads the way to the door, Mom tugs my elbow. I face her. She looks worried.

She glances over my shoulder and back at Ms. Sabel. Feeling safe from their ears, she whispers, "If I get a bottle of cyanide, will you plant it on Al?"

My eyes practically pop out of my head. I search her eyes and see nothing but a cold, hard stare. She's serious. My mind races through a hundred questions. I settle on the most important. "How will you get it?"

"Never mind that." Her eyes bounce from my left eye to my right eye and back. "Will you do it?"

What she's asking goes against everything I believe in. Is this the mother who taught me the difference between right and wrong? I weigh her request against the inference that Amy either did it or helped Al. She has a good point. Putting Al away would solve a lot of problems.

But I'm a lawman. I want to be the good guy here. I have to be. There's no point in having a police force if we're not honest. There's no way I'm planting evidence. There's no way I'm framing someone—even if he's as deserving as Al. It's just wrong.

"Why would we set him up, Mom?"

"We're not setting him up." She won't take her eyes off mine. "We're fixing a gap in the evidence. You know he did it."

"Don't ask me to do this." I shoot a quick glance at Amy standing in the doorway of the kitchen. Her eyes are begging me. Her chin crinkles in a prelude to tears. She turns and disappears into the kitchen.

"You have to," Mom says. "It's the right thing to do."

"Don't do anything." I try to think up an alternative plan, but the look on Mom's face is breaking my heart. I can't do what they want, nor can I let them down.

"I'll bring it to you as soon as I can," she says. "Where are you stationed in this grand plan?"

"At the corner of Shore and Cottage."

As if she's seen a ray of sunshine, she smiles and bolts for the kitchen.

Isaiah stands by the front door and waves to me with a hurry-up gesture. The crowd is milling about on Main Street.

With my insides roiling like the Atlantic outside, I stride out front and raise my hand. "C'mon people! You know your assignments. Let's get moving."

# CHAPTER 48

## CHRISTINE, THE BAKER

SCOTTY DIDN'T LOOK CONVINCED MY plan would work, which makes me worry about Amy the whole time I make the trek to my assigned "station." The rain slows to almost nothing, but a thick mist still rolls between buildings as if someone set up fog machines in the alleys. Sunlight tries hard to break through heavy spiteful clouds.

Three people are standing at the corner when I reach my spot: Rick, Boo-Boo, and that big Indian, Miguel.

I'd like to know who thought it would be funny to pair me up with Boo-Boo. If it was Scotty, I'll kill him.

Ours is a strategic corner. There are three roads leading into town. We're situated at the middle one as the first line of defense. We're supposed to stop incoming traffic and hand out flyers. I look at my thin stack for the first time. A bold headline proclaims our excuse for stopping people: HOW TO IDENTIFY A DRUG DEALER. It lists how dealers act, how they interact with passersby, how to spot where they keep their stash, and what to do once you think you've spotted one. The first thing it recommends is calling the local police. The second is making a recording if you can do it surreptitiously. Below that is information on how to handle a family member who may be addicted to opioids or meth amphetamines. Several treatment programs are listed.

"Good morning, Christine," Boo-Boo says.

I walk straight up to her. "Stay away from Scotty."

Rick pushes his shoulder between us. "We have a job to do. Let's keep focused."

Boo-Boo lifts her chin, turns on her heel, and walks up the sidewalk as if she has the moral high ground. I want to jump her and beat the crap out of her. Who is she to act superior? I sniff the air for a trace of alcohol, there isn't any. Not surprising since her problems always involved needles.

Then something occurs to me. I ask Rick, "You scuba dive, right?"

"I have."

"Do you have all the masks, tanks and whatnot?"

"No, I rent. Why?"

"I need something plucked off the ocean floor."

"Lyn's husband, Norman, is the only guy in town with gear and a boat." He smirks. "But you're not going to ask him."

Ignoring his nasty joke, I ask, "Anyone in Kennebunkport or York have that stuff?"

"Nearest outfitters are in Portsmouth or Portland." Rick shrugs. "What're you up to that you need diving gear?"

"I think Al Devino gave someone cement flippers for a swimming lesson out past the breakwater."

"No, really. What are you up to?"

A car rolls through the fog. Miguel steps into the road with a reflective stop sign and an open palm. He cuts an imposing figure—if they see him through the soup before they run him down. But they see him. They stop.

Rick runs to the door of a white Toyota with a flyer. He looks back at me and gestures as the window rolls down. Realizing why Rick is waving—I'm supposed to live-stream the encounters—I whip out the Sabel phone and start.

It's Bud and Maureen Taggart, coming back from their grandson's bar mitzvah in Boston. Rick gives them the flyer, they go on about what a great mayor he is for stopping crime, then they talk about the storm, then the cleanup process, then … I drift away. Boring.

Boo-Boo comes back and takes over the video duties. The plan is we deliver these public service flyers and live-stream until we find a car full of suspicious characters. The video will prevent them from doing anything violent or crazy, but we'll get their faces, car type, and license plates on record. Deeper in town, Scotty and his officers are stationed at various choke points. They'll handle the interrogation once we identify the bad guys.

What's weighing on my mind is getting a diver who can find that big box. Just my luck it would be Norman Avery. With shaky fingers, I dial Lyn.

She picks up and I state my case. "I need Norman to retrieve something just outside the breakwater."

"So call him and ask him."

"Last time I did that, he told me I had to sleep with him."

"Oh, Christine, every saint has a past, and every sinner has a future."

That actually made sense and sounded clever, not twisted. I look at the phone to make sure I dialed Lyn Avery. Then I reply, "What?"

"Oscar Wilde," she replies. "Anyway, Norman claims you're the one making passes at him."

He probably didn't bother to tell her he grabbed my ass, but that was back when I had one to grab. Maybe I shouldn't worry—it's been a long time. I'll bet his sex drive slowed as much as his driving. I ask Lyn, "Will you just ask him for me?"

"My shoulder's just bruised, by the way."

"Oh. How's your shoulder?" I still have to ask even after I've been called out. Smalltown etiquette. "So. Can you ask him for me?"

She turns from the phone but not by much. "Norm, Christine needs you to do her a favor."

He must be inches away because I hear him answer, "Fuck her."

"Oh, just do it. She needs a man to go down—"

"No way," he says.

There's a silence where they must be exchanging scandalous glances because the next sound I hear is a slap.

"Not like that," Lyn says. "She needs a diver."

"OK fine. When?"

"Now," I tell her.

She relays it. Norm answers, "Can't, surf's too high. It'll be a few hours yet. I'll let her know."

I thank her and relax a little. If I can't get there, neither can anyone else.

Another car pulls up to Miguel's outstretched hand. Boo-Boo and Rick are chatting on the sidewalk.

Stepping up, I knock on the window of the blue Mazda and see two goon-looking guys inside eyeballing me. The window comes down.

"Whatcha want, lady?" the driver asks.

I hand him a flyer. "With all the summer tourists pouring into town, we need everyone to help ensure no drug dealers sneak in with them."

He looks it over, tosses it to his co-pilot who crunches it into a ball. "What are you, the fucking Stasi?"

"We're concerned citizens."

He shoves his door into me as he gets out, smacking my knees hard. I bounce back a step without falling over.

Leaning into my face, he says, "You think I look like one of them? Huh? Izzat what this is all about? You calling me a fucking drug dealer?"

Out of nowhere, Boo-Boo flies around my shoulder, and shoves both hands into the guy. He loses his balance and falls back against his car. His hands flail for something to grab, finds nothing, and slumps to an awkward seated position on the ground. His face bunches up with anger.

From the passenger side, Goon Two leaps out to race around the front of the car. He gets as far as the Indian's arm, at which point he finds himself flying through the air like a rag doll. He lands and skitters down the pavement for ten yards, his T-shirt and jeans shredded like a victim in a motorcycle accident.

Goon One jumps to his feet and lunges for me as Boo-Boo shoves him back a second time.

"Keep your hands off her!" she yells at him. "Get out of here—and take Al Devino with you! We don't want your kind."

He reaches inside his leather jacket.

Miguel has a pistol pressed to his temple before Goon One can pull his pistol out. Miguel disarms him as he says, "You don't want to get into a gunfight with an Army Ranger."

Goon Two is on his feet, wiping blood and dirt from his face when he sees what Miguel's doing. He reaches in his jacket.

Miguel kicks Goon One in the side of his knee so hard the man crumples, grabbing it with both hands. Before he hits the ground, Miguel has already spun and leveled his pistol at Goon Two.

The man wisely raises his hands, palms out. "Hey, take it easy, Geronimo. This is a public street, and we was just passing through. No need to get all hostile. Ain't that right Joey?" He looks to his companion, who is testing weight on his bad knee and deciding it's not good. "We was just heading down to Mom's Bakery for some blueberry muffins. No harm in that. We'll be on our way."

Miguel gestures to the blue Mazda with his free hand. Both goons fall in their seats while trying to kill us with their eyes. Miguel's gaze looks closer to bored than frightened.

Before they get their seatbelts on, Miguel reaches through the driver's window to the passenger, grabs Goon Two by the jacket, and yanks him across the interior until his head is sticking out the driver's window. With the man's expression turned to abject fear, Miguel says, "For your personal growth and development, Geronimo was Bedonkohe, what you illegal aliens call Apache. I'm Diné, very different. It's like me calling you Sun Tzu—it just doesn't fit."

The man bleats, "OK."

Miguel lets him go and the two squirm their way back into their seats. As soon as they drive off, he texts the group a picture of the car and a note that reads, "Two heading down Borne Lane."

Scotty replies, "Thanks, we'll get them."

We don't need this many people here. I decide to back away and head for Town Harbor. If the storm surge is down, I can check out the seas beyond the breakwater. Maybe I can light a fire under Norman and get him moving.

Boo-Boo stands in my way with the expectant look of a child waiting to be awarded a blue ribbon. I give her a cursory hug and the accolades she's expecting. "Thanks, Boo-Boo. I appreciate the help."

Feeling slimed, I turn and walk into the fog.

# CHAPTER 49

## ISAIAH, THE ADVISOR

MISTAKE ISLAND, MAINE LEADS SAN Francisco as the foggiest place on Earth. We're just down the coast from there. The rain appears to be suspended in midair. Visibility is no more than fifty yards, only ten of those with any clarity. Reading license plates is going to be harder than we thought. At least the sky is brightening to a lighter gray. I can make out faces and expressions without a flashlight.

The others are arriving one at a time. Pat Armstrong, a woman about my grandmother's age, is first. Her spiked hair and black leather jacket make her look like she just left a Ramones concert. By her thigh, she casually dangles a sawed-off shotgun.

"Pat, thanks for coming," I say, "but we don't want armed civilians. If you have a weapon, you're likely to use it unnecessarily. I'd appreciate it if you left it under the awning over there."

Instead of answering, she whips out a leather strap, snaps a quick-release buckle to the barrel, and the other end to the butt. She shoulders the rig. Now her shotgun is on her back with the strap across her chest like a bandolier.

"OK, absolutely last resort," I say. When she nods, I continue, "You've got your phone?"

She holds it up and says, "Power of the live-stream ain't shit compared to a 12 gauge."

"Police have qualified immunity, which lets them shoot people without getting into the legal problems you and I would have. Let's leave it to them."

We're standing in the largest intersection in this small town. All four corners are commercial properties. A seafood takeout stand called Brine and Bone sits on one corner; a large and well-kept motel hides behind a parking lot on another. The other two are office buildings made to look like modern versions of New England farmhouses. One hosts an accounting firm and other services. The other has Dr. Orellana listed at the top of other small businesses. Everything's painted soft blue with white trim and surrounded by neatly edged grass and well-clipped trees.

Kubari Eady strides out of the mist. He says, "Hey, brotha. Refreshing to see you here. Can't believe I answered the mayor's call since I was closing the bar just four hours ago."

We give dap and I answer, "Good to see you, too. Especially since you're one of the community's anchors."

That answer makes him beam with pride. Then he glances over my shoulder with a concerned expression. "Pat, is that your 12 gauge?"

She gives him a wry smile.

Chief Jacobsen appears next. He extends a hand to Kubari. Instead of shaking, Kubari squares off, a glare on his face. "What the hell is this about? Am I your token in a photo op?"

Chief shakes his head, a little confused. "No, Kubari. Nothing like—"

"What, you think we're friends now, like you can conscript me into a police action? Think I'm gonna watch your six at this here checkpoint? We got some unfinished business, muthafucka."

The chief's demeanor responds to Kubari's challenge in kind. He straightens up, clenches his jaw, and tenses every muscle. "I apologized, Kubari. I meant it. If you can't accept that, I'm not going to grovel. But I had nothing to do with the assignments."

"I thought this was a community event," Kubari says. He stabs the air with a dagger-like index finger. "I'm down for the community. But I'll be damned if I'm going to let you drag me into working by your side to make it look like I support you."

The two glare at each other.

"I made the assignments," I tell them.

Chief Jacobsen steps back, his gaze rolling to the heavens.

Kubari looks at me as if I told him I'd gone vegan. "You what?" he asks. Now his expression telegraphs his new assessment of me: somewhere between backstabber and Uncle Tom.

"The way the plan works," I say, "this is going to be the most dangerous location. I chose people for courage, not compatibility."

Kubari and Chief both turn to Pat, who has her back to us. On paper, you'd think she aged out of dangerous encounters, but the shotgun tells a different story. The big, burly men sniff and hoist their shoulders. I can almost hear their thoughts. *Courage? Sure, I'm as tough as Pat Armstrong. I can hang.*

Pat doesn't bother to look at us, her smirk visible from the side.

Our first car approaches, its headlights spearing the eerie gloom despite the rising daylight. I nod at Pat to get her camera out. I step into the path of a white Toyota with my hand raised. They stop and lower the window. I start to question them, but Chief Jacobsen puts a hand on my shoulder and pulls me back.

"Good morning, Bud," he says to the driver. "How was your grandson's bar mitzvah?"

"Didn't understand a word of it, but what a great party!"

They chat a little and he waves them on. Chief turns to me and says, "Bud and Maureen Taggart."

I feel the smalltown charm. Everyone knows each other, regardless of background or age. In my anonymous city, I rarely see the same face twice, much less someone I know by name.

Chief gets a text and strides away. A minute later, he calls from the sidewalk, "Did you assign my mom and Boo-Boo to work together?"

I think it's best not to answer that.

Another vehicle approaches. Judging by the grill, it's the black Explorer that went peacefully through Vanessa's checkpoint. I hail them.

With the headlights, the glow from the sky above, and the heavy mist, I can't see anything through the windshield. I track around to the driver's side.

The window comes down. A slick guy sticks his face out. "Well, looky what we have here—another fucking checkpoint. What is this, Communist China?"

"Due to the storm," I say, "several roads are blocked, and others are dangerous. Where're you headed?"

"Mom's Bakery."

"Save you the trouble, it's closed this morning. You can turn around here."

His face twists and contorts as he thinks up a good reason to go around me. He didn't do his homework and can't think of another establishment in Town Harbor. His passenger fidgets with a long gun propped at his side. His eyes check out the hulking forms in the fog behind me.

"Where else can I get a blueberry muffin?" the driver asks.

I point behind him. "Danny's Diner, out by 95."

"You seen my old friend Scotty Jacobsen lately?" he asks.

"Who's asking?"

"Zat him over there?" He points at Chief's silhouette.

Chief steps up to the door. He scoffs, "Old friend? Never met you."

The driver nods slowly while his passenger pulls his phone.

To whoever's on the other end, the passenger says, "Hey, boss. Yeah, found him. Corner of Cottage and Shore."

"Danny's is going to run out of muffins," I tell the driver. "Turn this thing around and head on back across Route 1 and take Berwick Road. Danny's is a mile and a half from there. Can't miss it."

Without a better excuse at the ready, he backs up and turns around in the intersection. He gets aimed toward Route 1 when another car comes through the haze. This one looks like the blue Mazda Mayor Rick live-streamed giving Christine a hard time. I step into the street.

The muffin-seekers in the Explorer haven't left the area yet. After turning around, they pull to a parking strip and stop fifty yards uphill. Pat strides toward their car, stops five yards behind it, plants her feet shoulder-width apart, and lets her hands hang loose by her side. The black Explorer sits there a moment before the brake lights go out, telling me they've put it in park. They're not going to Danny's.

The tough guys in front of me roll to a stop but don't roll down the window. Standing two feet from the front bumper, I can't see through the windshield for the glare.

Chief walks up, raps a knuckle on the Mazda's glass. Kubari takes up a position two feet behind him on his right, live-streaming from his phone.

Up the road a couple buildings, the muffin-seekers hop out of the Explorer and start marching our way. Pat unclips her rig and swings the shotgun around in one smooth and impressive motion. She racks a shell into the firing chamber. Instantly, I recognize the familiar sound of a Mossberg 590, the combat shotgun favored by the US Marine Corps. The goons in front of her freeze and slowly raise their hands.

While I take in that scenario, Kubari drops his phone and flies at Chief Jacobsen. Wrapping his arms around Chief's shoulders, he drives the man to the ground sideways. They land near the front tire.

Three rapid gunshots erupt from inside the car, blowing holes in the driver's side window.

I draw my weapon and assess visible threats. Adrenaline shoots through my veins like a jolt of electricity. The Mazda's shiny windshield obscures my view of the car's occupants. I fire at their windshield where I know my bullet will take out the mirror, not a person. A warning shot. My round hits the mirror mount, shredding a basketball-sized piece of glass with it. Two shocked faces lean together to look through it. The gunman knows he can't bring his weapon around before I can take him out. Silence follows.

Chief and Kubari scramble to their feet. Both have pistols aimed at the interior. Chief shouts, "HANDS! HANDS WHERE I CAN SEE THEM! NOW!"

The two comply. In a few seconds, both men are face down on the pavement, cuffed.

The first two goons rush for their black Explorer and drive away despite Pat firing a warning shot over their heads.

While Chief reads the perps their rights, Kubari comes over. He's shaking, the side effect of an adrenaline overload.

"That was spectacular," I tell him and slap his back.

"Been in some scrapes at the bar," he says. "Never been in a gunfight before."

"How did you know?"

"About the gun?" He shakes his head. "I saw a shadow against the headlight glare in front. The passenger's arm extended across the console and that weren't right. I couldn't tell what it was for sure, but the way he moved, I figured, gotta be a gun. After that, I guess I moved on instinct."

With his prisoners secured, Chief walks up. In a shaky voice, he says, "Thank you, Kubari. I appreciate your help. You put yourself at risk, and it's not that I don't appreciate you saving my ass, but next time, don't do it. These risks are my job, not yours."

"Fuck you, Scott," Kubari says with a laugh. "You shoulda just stopped at 'thank you.'"

"Yeah. OK. So. Thank you." Chief looks up the street, then down the street, then at Kubari. "You saved my life."

"Against my better judgement." Kubari bursts out laughing and punches Chief's shoulder. Three seconds later, Chief lets out a laugh of his own.

Long minutes pass and no new cars come our way. For safety's sake, our outer checkpoints have been warning the locals and tourists to take alternate routes to Town Harbor. Watching the goons sitting cross-legged on a patch of wet grass, I wonder what they were trying to accomplish. We thought they were coming to claim the town as their territory. But they tried to kill the Police Chief. Why such an aggressive move? That would bring down every police department in the state on them.

Checking out the Mazda, I see the bullet holes in the driver's side window are low, just above the metal of the door. The shooter aimed low. From his passenger seat, he wouldn't have the angle to see Chief's face. But a slightly higher shot would hit center mass, the most effective shot. I look over at Chief. He's wearing standard police body armor: thick, heavy, and noticeable. Walking around to the passenger side of the car, I look through the window. It was harder to aim lower than higher. He knew Chief was wearing body armor. He wasn't trying to kill the man.

I realize what's going on.

# CHAPTER 50

## SCOTT, THE POLICE CHIEF

I REALLY DO WANT KUBARI to be more careful because I'm wearing body armor and he isn't. It would be terrible if a civilian were injured protecting an officer. It's supposed to be the other way around. I'll have to choose a better time to tell him. Kathy and another officer take my suspects to the station. Attempted murder of a cop is a felony, so they'll call the county and have them taken up there. My other squad car reports no sign of the muffin-seekers.

Kubari, Pat, and I stand waiting in the intersection. We debated whether Al Devino went home after losing two men or stuck around. Isaiah comes over and sets us straight with the reality of the situation. Odds are Devino is not far away, waiting for us to lower our guard. There are too many of his people unaccounted for. It's not a matter of if he will come, but when and from where.

Footsteps come toward us a few seconds before Mom's form emerges from the fog. With a toss of her head, she summons me to the sidewalk.

"Why aren't you at your checkpoint?" I ask.

"They don't need me. Listen." She moves in close and takes my hand. "This is Al's bottle of cyanide. When he gets here, plant it on him and take him in."

I feel the transfer of a plastic bottle from her hand to mine. She's not wearing gloves. And that means the only fingerprints on it will be hers and mine. I want to yell at her for making such a simple mistake. Anyone who's read a murder mystery knows that much. But what flows out of my mouth is different. "I can't do that, Mom."

"You have to, Scotty."

Against everything I believe in, I pocket the bottle without looking at it. I ask, "Why?"

"If you don't, he takes over Deeping. Instead of getting her SRC and a thousand jobs, we get meth addicts. Is that what you want?"

"Did Al do it?" I ask.

"Who else?"

We search each other's eyes. I see no deception, no second thoughts, no doubt in her mind. I've trusted her my whole life. She must know something she's not telling me. And that leads me back to my biggest fear. "Was Amy involved?"

"Hell no."

I don't believe her. My heart pounds hard inside my ribs and my blood runs to ice water. Distrusting your mother is not a good feeling.

I say, "Al Devino has never been known to use poison."

"He was never known to use a bio-cremation machine either. I have no idea how many people he's killed, but I doubt he's ever used the same method twice. If there's no MO, he's harder to trace. That makes poison the perfect cover for him—because it's working on you!"

Mom turns on her heel and heads down Shore Road.

In the opposite direction, I hear a car engine purring to a stop obscured somewhere in the fog. I jog back to my people and notice they have their ears cocked toward the sound.

I check my phone. None of the checkpoints reported new arrivals in the last thirty minutes. I'm starting to think Devino's men figured out how to pass themselves off as tourists and slip through. They may know about the few roundabout alleyways past our sentries. Or the sounds could be locals stopping to check on friends. I take a slow, deep breath.

Two car doors open and close to my left, their bangs echoing in the damp atmosphere. At a diagonal to that car, equally hidden in the mist, another engine cuts off.

A drone buzzes somewhere overhead.

When I look for it, Isaiah says, "It's ours. Thermal imaging."

Then he gets a call. After a few short responses on the phone, he tells me, "Someone on a roof with a clear line of sight over that way. I'll check it out. Stay frosty."

He trots off and disappears around the side of Dr. Orellana's office complex. Working his words over in my mind, I realize he was saying there's a potential sniper on the roof. It could be Michael Arnold, the building's owner, checking for roof damage. I consider telling Isaiah to use care, but he knows that.

Another pair of car doors open and close. These coming from a third direction.

Suddenly, I'm glad Pat brought her Mossberg Shockwave, the I-can't-believe-it's-legal short-barrel version of the full-sized Mossberg. My Glock 22 has the large magazine and I have two extra magazines. Kubari has a silver revolver tucked in his belt. Still, I'm feeling insecure.

"Where the hell you think you're going?" Pat asks into the cloud on her side of the road. She's looking at someone we can't see. When there's no answer, she racks a shell.

Still no answer. She takes three steps in that direction. Then three more. I can barely see her.

The silence around us ratchets up the nerves spasming in my muscles. There's someone out there. At least four, possibly more. I draw my weapon. When Kubari sees me, he does the same.

In the middle distance, I hear the hollow thunk of an aluminum ladder, the sound it makes when someone climbs the rungs on a long extension and rattles the frame. In my mind, I picture Isaiah climbing to the roof on a ladder he found in place. The next sound I hear is a ladder clanging flat on the ground. A grunt follows, as if someone has been punched. More blows and groans follow.

Kubari and I look at each other. Someone's in a desperate struggle on the roof of the doctor's office. We look at Pat. She's a shadow near the Brine and Bone, her Mossberg aimed up Cottage Lane.

Devino's plan becomes clear: divide and conquer. That gives me few options. Helping Isaiah would be the standard move, except that the ladder is on the ground and whoever is at the top has the high ground. If the mobster wins the fight, anyone coming up will die instantly. If Isaiah wins, we will have left Pat exposed for no reason. Splitting up only weakens our position.

I glance at Kubari again and nod toward Pat. If we keep close to her, we won't expose our flank. I'm leaving Isaiah on his own, which makes me feel like a heel, but he's the best trained of our bunch and the most likely to survive a fight.

We turn our backs to each other, watching as much terrain as possible, and walk sideways toward Pat.

Her Mossberg roars and she takes off running.

"DON'T FOLLOW THEM!" I yell.

Too late—her reverberating footfalls fade as she rounds the building. A second later, we hear a whump, then the distinct sound of duct tape peeling from a reel, twice, three times. And then nothing.

"Pat?" Kubari calls out with a shaky voice. "Pat?"

I touch his arm. He gets it. It's down to us now. He recenters his attention.

Our eyes sweep the fuzzy gray surrounding us. We see nothing but the dim shapes of trees and buildings.

"Got the sniper!" Isaiah's voice calls from the top of the office building.

"Does he know he lost his ladder?" Kubari asks quietly.

"He will soon enough."

We both glance in Isaiah's direction. Since we can't see him, he can't see us and the sniper rifle won't help cover us. We glance at each other, knowing our team of four is now down to two. We're breathing heavily as if we've been lifting weights. They make standoffs look so easy in the movies. I had no idea they're so bone-rattling terrifying.

Through the gray cotton-candy I see muzzle flash to my right before I hear the gunshot. The bullet whizzes by us like an angry bee. Moving sideways, I put myself between the shooter and Kubari just as the second flash appears. It hits me square in the vest. I fall backward into him.

"Whoa!" He catches me while I struggle for air after having the wind knocked out of me. "Scott, Scott! Talk to me."

"I'm good," I manage.

I fire back while he holds my shoulders. I can make out the dark hulk of the shooter as Kubari gets me to my feet. I feel him turn around and press his back to mine, half to prop me up and half to maximize our field of fire. He's trembling as much as I am. Taking my time, I line up the shot and squeeze.

The goon goes down with a loud yell that's a mix of surprise and pain.

Shouts erupt when the others hiding in the haze realize things just got real. A figure charges out of the mist straight ahead and slightly to my left. Aiming carefully, I fire another round and miss as he zigs. I realign. As I do, I see another figure charging in my peripheral vision.

Kubari fires at someone in a different direction. I've no time to analyze whether he hit his target or not.

I fire and my second opponent falls to the ground. This one is wounded, judging from the torrent of foul language spewing from him. He rolls to a seated position and raises his gun. At the same time, the man in my peripheral vision gets slammed by something moving too fast to see. He falls face-first. A large shadow lands on his back. My biggest problem is in front of me, wounded and aiming to take a shot. I reacquire him and put him down for good.

Kubari fires again. "Got him!"

A split second later, a gunshot rings out, amplified by the dense air. Kubari falls to the pavement clutching his leg. "Fuck!"

Another mobster runs toward me, this one with a yellow jacket that makes him easier to see. Leveling my sights, I hold my fire as the mysterious shadow who leapt on my peripheral assailant rises, hobbles a few steps, and sweeps the feet out from under the yellow jacket. When he hits the ground, the shadow leaps on him like a vampire on a victim.

From the ground, Kubari shouts, "Right back atcha, muthafucka!"

His revolver blasts out two quick shots. Nothing falls. No one cries out. I hear the clatter of spent cartridges clinking on the street. He's reloading. That makes him vulnerable.

I spin around and see a figure in the mist aiming at Kubari. I fire and see the figure fall and scream in pain. Kubari brings his revolver up, fires again, and then once more.

From an indistinct direction, I hear, "Fuck this, Donny, I'm outta here."

"Hold up," the voice who must be Donny responds. "I'm coming with you."

Their feet slapping on the pavement beats out a hasty retreat.

A third voice joins them. "Donny, Josh, wait!"

The bleat of a remote car lock is followed by two car doors creaking open. I make out the flashing brake lights and move my aim there in case it's a feint.

A dark figure runs from my left toward the car.

The vampire on the ground rises and lashes out at the indistinct form trying to join Donny and Josh. He goes down, and once more, the vampire rises on pained legs and lands on the man's back.

Tires spin on wet asphalt before catching and leaping forward. A second later, it's gone.

"Clear by my count," Pia Sabel's voice comes from the vampire.

"Ms. Sabel?" I ask.

"How's Kubari?" She rises and hops toward me on one foot, holding a broken cane.

Turning to my partner, I see a pained expression and his hands staunching the bleeding mid-thigh.

"Clean through," he says while grimacing. "But it burns. Holy Mother of God, it burns."

With a disappointed look at the cane, Ms. Sabel tosses it aside and makes a call. She gets Dr. Orellana on the line.

I tug at my double-stitched sleeve. After several attempts, I realize I can't rip anything off my uniform for a tourniquet. Watching my struggle while she describes Kubari's condition to the doctor, she puts the phone on speaker and hands it to me. She whips off her jacket, then her long sleeve top, leaving her in an athletic bra and leggings.

The woman is fit and has abs of steel. It's hard not to notice. I return my attention to Kubari.

She jabs her bad foot on the main fabric of her shirt, then rips the sleeve off. Dropping to her knees, she wraps the material around Kubari's leg, pulls it tight, and ties it off. Kubari groans. The whole time, she continues to report his condition over the phone.

In the distance I hear the ladder bang against the building and Isaiah's voice thanks someone. He rattles down. Within seconds, he and Miguel jog to us.

They help Kubari to stand, pushing their shoulders under his, and head for the doctor's office.

They stop five steps away. Kubari twists over his shoulder and says, "Thanks, Scott. That guy was about to take me out. You saved my life back there."

"We're even, buddy," I answer while making a finger pistol.

He laughs and grimaces. They get moving toward the office.

"Thank you," I say to Ms. Sabel. "You saved my life."

She grabs my arm and pulls herself to standing, leaning heavily on my shoulder.

"You had it under control. Just shortened the timeline for you is all." She points at the three bodies she jumped on. "I popped them with Sabel Darts. It delivers a minimal dose of Inland Taipan snake venom combined with a powerful sleep medication. The venom produces a flaccid paralysis that incapacitates the victim long enough for the sleep medication to knock them out. They'll be down for roughly four hours. It's a mostly-non-lethal weapon."

"Mostly?"

"Dosage is a problem, and some people have an allergic reaction. Sometimes people die. That's why it's not commercially available. We're working on that." She waves a hand at the bodies. "Given the circumstances, I don't really care if it proves fatal."

A car rolls slowly toward us, parting the clouds of fog. The driver's window comes down as Al Devino pulls even with us. He stops.

When his window comes down, he stares at me a beat before turning his gaze to Ms. Sabel. She's six feet over my right shoulder.

He scowls. "The fuck are you doing here? You was leaving town last I heard."

"And miss a chance to beat the crap out of you?" she says.

He sneers at me. "Planning to arrest me or something, Scotty?"

I sense Ms. Sabel tensing up like a storm the instant before a lightning bolt strikes.

"Not until one of your henchmen turns state's evidence." I step back and gesture down the road. "This is a public street. It's a free country. Go wherever you'd like."

# CHAPTER 51

## ISAIAH, THE ADVISOR

DRAWING FROM HIS MANY COMBAT tours, Miguel acts as medic and has Kubari stabilized by the time Dr. Orellana meets us in his clinic. I take an old-lady medical cane with three toes from the office and leave my friends to go in search of Pat Armstrong.

Pat gambled on what she thought best and got ambushed. The Devino gang expected Kubari, a civilian with no military background, to run. Instead, he stood by a cop who had done him wrong—twice. If I were giving out medals for this operation, he'd get the shiniest.

Pat lies duct-taped in the parking lot behind the Brine and Bistro. She also deserves a medal. It takes a bit of effort to cut her free. Before I can get the tape out of her hair, she writhes out of my reach with a feral look in her eye.

"The bastards took my Mossberg," she says with venom. She stomps away, heading for the nearest downed mobster. She kicks him and jogs to the next before finding her weapon. She kicks that guy repeatedly while swearing extensively.

I see Chief Jacobsen and Pia talking to someone in a stopped car and head out to join them.

Before I get far, I see Chief tell the driver it's a free country. He waves the car on. But Pia isn't having it. I don't hear all of what she says, but her volume increases as she speaks allowing me to hear the finish: "… you pencil-dick rapist!"

The driver shouts something back that I can't make out. I break into a run.

"You're a coward," Pia yells.

"You can't talk to me like that," Al Devino sneers back.

She smacks his face disrespectfully with the back of her hand. "Just because you wormed your way out of convictions on technicalities doesn't mean you aren't guilty. Russell Burnett, Diana Estey, Guy Carmel, Marylin Lehan—"

"You can't pin those murders on me," Al snaps. "They tried, but they got nothing. Nothing! Ya hear me?"

"I didn't say they were murders, Al." She leaves a silent beat. "Those are names from the missing persons list. You're dumber than Scott led me to believe."

"I got nothing to say to you."

"I have something to say to you," she counters. "I found the big, water-tight box."

"That's MINE!" he yells.

"Really? I doubt anything in it belongs to you. Prove to me you know what's in it. Give me a short inventory."

Al's eyes bounce between Pia and Chief.

"Fuck you!" Al shoves his door open, smacking Pia in the thigh as he leaps out.

She stumbles back a step. Chief grabs her arms and holds her upright. She bends at the waist, looking wounded.

Al slams the door behind him, facing them both. I take a few steps to the side to make sure Al knows I'm flanking him. He sees me.

"Someone needs to teach you a lesson!" Al yells. And then he makes a big mistake.

Twisting from his waist, he raises a backhand high above his shoulder and brings it across his body. Before it gains momentum, Pia rises from her crouch with her left arm rising into his arc, blocking his blow. At the same time, she uses her powerful legs to fire a right uppercut that slams the heel of her hand into the bottom of his jaw.

A properly executed uppercut requires the boxer to drive their weight off the back foot. In her case, it's her damaged ankle. The pain it causes her is written all over her face. When I move to step in, she waves me off.

Chief is too stunned to move. His mouth is open as wide as his eyes.

Al falls over and spiders backward until he can bounce up on his feet. Feeling his jaw, he flies right back at her with three quick steps.

Pia twists on her good foot like a gate. His blow glances off her shoulder. As his momentum pushes his body past hers, she hooks his foot with her bad one and sends him sprawling.

She hops on her good leg and grabs Chief's shoulder, then takes another hop backward and grabs the hood of the car for balance. She can't put weight on that bad foot anymore.

Al gets to his hands and knees.

Handing Pia the cane, I put my foot on his back. "Better off where you are, Al. Maybe you didn't read her bio, but she did some serious boxing a few years back—and you look like you ditched class."

Chief slaps a cuff on one of Al's wrists, drags it around his back where he pulls the other one and completes the set. "Al Devino, you're under arrest for attempted assault and battery. You have the—"

"What? She assaulted me!"

"Both times she reacted to your initiative. Got it right here on my body cam. I suggest you cop a plea. If you fight it in court, I'll have to submit the video as evidence." Chief hauls Al to his feet. "Then it'll be public record, and everyone will see you get laid out twice—by a girl."

He shoves Al to the sidewalk and makes him sit cross-legged on the ground.

Pia looks at the cane as if it were toxic fashion. She looks around, hoping an artistically carved walking stick might magically appear. When she realizes this is her only option, she tests her weight on it. I consider telling her I'll take her to the doctor, but that never went over well before.

Miguel comes through the mists, which have burned off a little. He crosses to us as the noise of an approaching chopper grows louder. When he's close, he says to Pia, "Seas are calmer now. Not ideal, but close enough."

She answers, "Be careful."

He tosses her a sloppy salute. Typical Army. But he keeps marching across the intersection to the parking lot of the motel. A huge blue-and-white helicopter with "Sabel" written across the side lands between the cars. Miguel climbs in and it takes off again.

I ask Pia, "Where's he going?"

She shoots a surreptitious look at Chief, letting me know she doesn't want him to know, and says, "He's a busy man."

While I contemplate what Miguel could be doing that we don't want Chief to know about, Deeping's top cop is looking in the passenger compartment.

Moving next to him, I ask, "Do we need a warrant to search it?"

"We need reasonable cause," he says. "Attacking Ms. Sabel like that leads me to believe he was high on drugs. If he is, he might need medical attention. For that, we'll need to know what he's high on. That gives me probable cause to see what's in the car."

"Works for me." From my view, the interior looks clean and tidy. There is nothing that didn't come from the factory in sight.

He shrugs. Reaching inside, he pulls the trunk release. He tracks around to the back of the car. While he does, he watches me. His attention gives me an uneasy feeling. I come around and join him.

The trunk is less tidy. A cardboard box lies in plain sight. Tucked behind it are an old sweatshirt and a greasy rag. On the left, a hard pistol case lies unlatched on both sides. Chief pulls nitrile gloves out of his jacket pocket, puts them on with a snap, and gingerly lifts the lid on the case. A Beretta M9 sits in the foam cutout. He waves his hand over it.

"It's still hot," he says. He motions for me to confirm it.

It's radiating heat when I put my hand an inch above the barrel. Putting it in the case trapped the heat inside. Something Al didn't think about after shooting at us.

Chief taps his body camera, a motion I take to mean he's turning it off. Then I notice a blue and white bottle in Chief's right hand as he reaches for the cardboard box. He stops, straightens up, and looks skyward.

After a pensive moment, he twists to face me. "You're tight with your family, right?"

"Yes."

"How far would you go to protect them? Would you break the law to clear them if you knew you could get away with it?"

I have a bad feeling about his question. Law enforcement is not my area of expertise. I'm not sure how to handle it. I answer, "I would do what's best for them. Sometimes that means hiring the best defense attorney or encouraging them to confess."

He looks around the area, turning left and right to see if anyone else is watching. "You're right, Isaiah. The truth always comes out."

His jaw flexes and his cheeks tighten. I wait patiently while he thinks some more.

Finally he says, "We'll have to ask the county for help finding the spent shells from that gun, but we'll get him on attempted murder. We have plenty of evidence to put him away for a long time."

Pia is standing behind us. When she speaks, she surprises us both. "I'll bet at least one of his guys turns against him. You'll have plenty."

Chief looks at me, then at Pia. He touches his chest in a move that I take to be him restarting his camera. Turning back to the cardboard box, he lifts a flap. A hundred plastic baggies filled with what looks like salt crystals with a bluish tint greet us. He mutters, "Crystal meth."

A moment of silence follows. Al Devino's confidence level was so high, he brought his wares with him.

"Wow," Chied says. He leans back and slams the trunk closed. "We have tons of evidence."

# CHAPTER 52

## CHRISTINE, THE BAKER

NORMAN AVERY STANDS IN HIS doorway with a leer on his face.

I roll my eyes. "Oh, for Christ's sake, Norman. I'm not giving you a blow job for this. Besides, you're too old to get it up without your little pills." I push him inside. "I'm in a hurry. Get moving."

He backs up. "Seas are too high yet."

"We need to be out there when it settles down—so move it."

He makes me wait while he gets his wetsuit and other gear loaded in his truck out back. He takes longer than a teenager going on a first date. I can't stop tapping my foot while I'm waiting.

I'm worried because I heard gunfire before I got very far from Scotty's checkpoint. I'm sure he's OK or someone would've called me.

What worries me more than his health is the look he gave me when I handed him the cyanide. Christ. My fingerprints are all over it now. Doesn't he realize if he doesn't plant it on Devino, I could take the fall for it? But I can't worry about that. I'm sure he'll do the right thing. No one wants to see Al run this town.

Now that the drama at the roadblocks is over, Sabel and Devino will be after the box. If Al's tied up, I'm sure one of his henchmen will move fast. Either one of them might be down at the Plant right now for all I know. And I left the pipe open. If one of them pulls that box out of the deep … I can't contemplate that. I'm going to win this race and get the jump on them for once.

Eventually, Norman's ready to go. We make it down to the dock and walk out to his 44-foot Grand Banks Express that cost more than my house. It's a sleek boat, nice and clean, and has *Aquaholic* painted across the stern. Norman made his money the old-fashioned way: his daddy left it to him. And he spent it on a boat. Why anyone would want to spend so much money on a hole in the water is beyond me. But I'm glad he did.

He drags his tanks and gear onboard while I go inside the cabin and wait next to the helm. When he finally casts off and putters out of the harbor, he watches the ocean beyond the breakwater.

"Seas are still three feet," he says as we round the south end of the long granite wall.

"You can dive in that, can't you?" I ask.

"I can go down. I can get your package. I can come back up. The problem is getting in the boat. See those waves slapping against the hull? Those waves weigh a ton, and they slam you against the ladder there, like to knock your teeth out or break an arm."

"Stop exaggerating."

"Look it up, Christine," he says. "Sea water is literally a ton, two thousand pounds, per cubic meter. That's what's hitting you in the back when you try to climb back onboard."

We round the end of the breakwater and head out to sea. Born out here, raised out here, and I still get seasick. If feels like we're on a broken rollercoaster, riding up one wave and down the next, tilting this way and that.

Our arc is taking us farther out to sea than I wanted. I ask, "Where the hell are you going? We want to be straight across from the Plant, as close to the breakwater as possible."

He laughs. "Tide's going out. The odd thing about our little granite wall is the currents it creates. You get a good strong current running north at about one knot when the tide comes in. Right now, that's going south. So, we're going to go up north a bit from where we want to end up. We'll use the currents to our advantage."

He lines the boat up, out far enough for safety, and drops anchor.

"Now we wait," he says. He crosses his legs and arms.

I can't wait. I'm itching to know what's down there. I don't want to be sitting here scratching my aging butt while Sabel or Devino are across town pulling the damn box out of a dumpster. As soon as I think that, I wonder if that's why her people were dumpster-diving all over town. No way. If a six-foot box was in any dumpster, those guys wouldn't have to get in the thing to see it. Besides, it could end up in a landfill. Phil was a screwup, but he wouldn't be that dumb. Would he?

"Had some good times, Christine." Norman looks me over. "You still got it, you know that?"

"Shut the fuck up, Norman. That was a long time ago. Our kids were little."

Nothing stops men. Not old age, not infirmity, not stupidity—they're always tilting at windmills.

"Yeah, but we had fun," he says.

"That was then. Say, did you ever tell Lyn about us?"

"Hell no. Taking that to my grave. And if you ever tell her, I'll call you a liar."

"Well, at least we're of the same mind on that topic." I cross my arms and lean back.

He's right about the good times. It felt good to be bad at the time, but looking back on it, I was behaving like an idiot. Trying to get away with shit. Lyn's sister gets laid up with a broken back from an accident, she goes down to Virginia to help out—and Norman and I … fricking idiots. The beginning of the end of my marriage. My beloved never knew who—but he knew.

An unseen helicopter flies overhead a mile or two away, deep in the fog. It's heading from the coast out to sea. The noise kills our conversation, leaving us in an awkward silence. I go out on the back deck and look at the waves. They seem smaller now. I hope they're smaller. I need to get this operation underway.

Norman joins me at the stern and puts an arm around me in a familiar way. I find myself nuzzling into him. It feels good to be held. Strange as that is at my age. It doesn't get me in the mood for sex, it just feels nice. He doesn't push it, which helps. Instead, he finds a topic he likes to talk about: himself. He prattles on while I listen for the sound of other boats nearby. Nothing until another helicopter goes overhead. This time it's going from sea toward land.

He goes back inside and asks if I'd like a water. I don't. Then I hear him say, "Holy aircraft carriers."

Marching back in, I find him staring at a radar screen. "What is it?"

He points. "Thing that big's gotta be the *Numina*. I heard she was up this way."

"What are you talking about?"

"Ever heard of the Sabel Yacht Corporation? They rent yachts to the ultra-rich. Couple million bucks a week. They've got six or eight of the damn things. This one's an Explorer—four hundred feet long and then some. The tender is bigger than the skiff you're standing on. They take it around the Mediterranean one month, and down to Antarctica the next. Give you one guess who owns it."

I'm having a heart attack. That bitch is a step ahead of me again. I don't know what that damn yacht's doing out there, but I know she's up to something.

I push Norman. "Get your suit on. You've got to get down there and get that box for me."

He looks at me as if I'd turned into a cockroach.

"There's only two of us," Norman says. "I get it to the surface, and we'll have to pull it aboard by hand. You said this thing is six feet by five feet. That means one wave hits it and the thing goes from weighing whatever it weighs now—to 8,000 pounds. It could crack the hull."

"OK, I get it. Can you at least go down there and see if it's there?"

He stares at me like I'd gone stark raving mad. "It's murky as hell after a storm. All the sediments stirred up and—"

"Can you just do it and spare me the dramatics?" I plead with big eyes.

He huffs and stomps around the deck. Then he raises the anchor and moves us close enough to see the Plant through the slowly clearing haze. Still puffing and making I'm-pissed-at-you noises, he pulls on his wetsuit, flippers and gear. He gives me instructions for every contingency from him dying down there to the Swiss Navy declaring war on Maine. Finally, he moves to the wooden diving deck attached to the stern and gets in the water.

He's right about the murkiness. He disappears so quickly, the water may as well be ink. I realize how far he's going for me and appreciate him. He's not such a bad guy, I'm just impatient.

And for good reason. There's a lot at stake.

After another ten minutes, that chopper flies out from the coast toward the open seas again. I can't imagine where they're going. It doesn't seem like a search pattern. Deeping isn't on the map for heli-tours. Besides, there's little to see in this soup.

Waiting alone for an undetermined amount of time is nerve-racking. I pace around the deck for what feels like hours but is probably another fifteen minutes. While I'm biting my thumbnail, I hear the radio squawking like a wounded duck. It occurs to me that someone said *Aquaholic* in that noise.

I go back to the cabin and pick up the microphone thing. I try to remember what Norman said about using it. I should've paid attention. I push the button. "This is the *Aquaholic*."

"Ah, very good," a voice with an English accent says. "Would you have Christine Jacobsen aboard?"

"This is she." I forgot to push the button. I push it. "This is she."

"This is Captain Chamberlain of the *Numina*. Pia Sabel requests that you join us. I shall send a tender for you shortly."

*Requests* I join her? Sending a tender makes it more of a demand. I look at the waves. They're getting smaller. That's a good thing. Maybe Norman can bring it up and we can ignore Sabel's *request*.

But then, Sabel has a thousand high-paying jobs we need. Damn it.

"I'm sorry, could you repeat that?" I say without pushing the button. I push it, then repeat myself.

He repeats himself while I think up a good excuse. I don't have one. For some reason, it feels like I'm being summoned to the principal's office in grade school. My stomach fills with empty air like a popover.

"My captain says he needs a few minutes. Let me get back to you." I put the microphone back and turn the volume down.

I walk to the stern and scan the surface. Dark green waves and a rolling deck makes me want to toss my breakfast into the mix. I sit on a bench seat and close my eyes for what seems like forever.

On the bridge, Captain Chamberlain repeats his *request*. In the distance, I hear the sound of a powerful launch.

Norman shouts and waves to me from fifty yards away. He's holding something up and waving it. I can't tell what it is. He gives up and swims back to the boat. Climbing up the ladder, he plops down on the deck and pulls his mask off. With alarm at the sound of the launch, he twists to his right. "What the hell is that?"

A boat appears in the mist. It's bigger, sleeker, and shinier than the *Aquaholic*. It slows and makes an arc toward us.

"The *Numina's* tender," I tell him. "Pia Sabel has requested my attendance. Apparently, I don't have a say in the matter. What did you find?"

"That was the yellow rope. It's been sliced clean off."

# CHAPTER 53

## ISAIAH, THE ADVISOR

AMBULANCES AND OFFICERS ARRIVE TO deal with the mobsters Chief Jacobsen and Kubari put down. The fog that hasn't burned off vibrates with flashing red and blue emergency lights. While Pat keeps an eye on Devino, Pia tells Chief Jacobsen she's bringing a chopper in to pick up all three of us. Miguel is waiting on the *Numina* with Phil's big dry box.

She says, "Your mother appears to be out at sea in a boat. Do you know what she's doing?"

Chief shakes his head. "No idea. She's been acting strange all week."

He heads over to his officers, giving them specific instructions on procedure and process before he leaves.

Pia looks at her cane with disappointment. "Did they have any others? I look like someone's grandmother."

I shake my head, no. She grimaces and makes her way to Devino.

Leaning against the trunk of Al's car, I start rolling Kitty's words over in my head. As I do, Vanessa and Kitty walk up the narrow asphalt sidewalk.

"You're alright?" Vanessa asks as they come near enough.

"Unscratched." I wave my arm at the emergency vehicles. "Can't say the same for the bad guys."

She looks me over with an uncertain appraisal. My casual assessment of a gunfight takes her a moment to process. We come from entirely different worlds. Once she digests that concept, she tugs the reluctant Kitty into a closer position.

Vanessa says, "I went back to the house and found her right where we left her. She started spouting some of that Greek stuff again. Kitty, tell him what you told me."

"Let me go home; prevent me not," Kitty says. "'twere best that thou shouldst bear thy burden and I mine."

"Tiresias, again." I stare at her as an inchoate idea forms in my head. That's something she said the first time I saw her. The play comes back to me in pieces. I played Creon, but some of the other lines are still embedded in my head. I remember the answer. I recite, "For shame! no true-born Theban patriot would thus withhold the word of prophecy."

Kitty cackles in that less-than-charming way she has.

Our first meeting comes back to me. She said several things that sounded familiar yet off a notch. She's adapting the works to make a point. But the point is confused. While I'd love to think someone with her cognitive problems might have moments of brilliance, that she might be a savant, the reality is different. There are points in her quotes, but who each refers to and who's point of view she's using are scrambled. To unravel her thoughts, the first thing I need to uncover is who the players represent in the modern world.

I tell Vanessa, "The lines we just played out are an exchange between the blind prophet Tiresias and King Oedipus. The king consults Tiresias to understand why the gods have plagued Thebes." Turning to Kitty, I ask, "What is the plague on Deeping?"

"I say thou art the murderer of the man whose murderer thou pursuest." Kitty waits for me to respond.

I don't remember my lines. All I recall is a testy exchange between prophet and king. "Who was murdered? You mean Phil?"

She looks exasperated as if I'm an idiot.

"But I didn't murder him," I say, thinking out loud. "Do you know who did?"

Kitty tosses up her hands and turns away. Before she gets a step, Vanessa reaches out and grabs her elbow. "You can't keep walking away, Kitty. We're trying to figure it out. Be patient."

Kitty snaps back to face me. "See'st not in what misery thou art fallen ..."

The line comes back to me and I finish it. "Nor where thou dwellest nor with whom for mate."

She nods a little more enthusiastically. "Dost know thy lineage? Nay, thou know'st it not, and all unwitting art a double foe."

Vanessa says, "Isn't that what she said to Scott when he came to the house last night?"

"Yes," I answer as my brain dredges up a few other things she said. At the dumpster, she quoted Tecmessa from *Ajax. To look on self-wrought woes, when no other had a hand therein—this plays sharp pangs in the soul.* That has to be from the murderer's point of view. Who is the killer? Why quote *Ajax* instead of continuing with Oedipus? Because in *Oedipus Rex*, the king himself was the killer, but in Phil's case, someone other than the king is the killer.

"Phil had Scott's birth certificate," I say. Kitty nods. "Did you see it?"

A sour face pulls down over her like a curtain. Slowly she nods.

"And that is the burden you keep? And if you tell me, it'll be my burden?"

She nods again.

"What was Oedipus about?" Vanessa asks. "Other than sleeping with his mother."

"Free will versus fate. Had Oedipus listened to Tiresias, he could've avoided half his troubles, but he was too proud and unyielding to believe the prophet. That led him to fulfill the prophecy of the oracle." I try to remember the play. "To end a plague, Oedipus must find out who killed King Laius, the previous King of Thebes. Tiresias tells Oedipus that he is the man who killed Laius. Which turns out to be true because …" Both women lean toward me as my voice trails off. It's beginning to make sense. "Because Oedipus was adopted. As a young man, he left his adopted parents and went in search of his fortune. He ran afoul of some rich guy and killed him. The rich guy turned out to be his biological father, Laius."

Kitty nods enthusiastically. Vanessa doesn't get it yet.

I ask Kitty, "Who is King Oedipus?" When she doesn't answer, I prompt her. "Is it Scott?"

Kitty's chin crinkles, her lips tremble, and she tears up as she nods. Vanessa hands her a tissue while keeping her gaze on me.

"And all unwitting art a double foe," I repeat. "Meaning everything happened to cover it up, thereby doubling the problem?"

Kitty nods and sniffles into the tissue. She looks back and forth between us, letting me know she's already told me everything, I just haven't untangled it yet. Her myriad quotes swirl in my head.

Then it hits me like the waves booming and crashing against the breakwater. Everything Kitty said from the beginning comes into focus. I know what she's telling me. Kitty was right: now that I know, it is my burden.

The noise of a helicopter pounds an incessant beat as it closes in on us.

Pia and Scott march toward us. She points to the motel's parking lot and veers that way.

I'm still the new guy, so I can dump this one on Pia. It dawns on me why she introduces me as her advisor. She doesn't want me handling delicate matters like this directly; she wants my advice on how she should handle it. In this case, I don't have a problem with that.

"Thank you, Kitty." I squeeze her hand. "And thank you, Vanessa. I really appreciate the way you helped me."

"I want to see you succeed," she says. She gives me a hug, and after looking both ways to see who's watching us, a kiss.

When we come up for air, she says, "You know what my favorite Zora Neale Hurston quote is? *Love is like the sea. It takes its shape from the shore it meets and it's different with every shore.*" She squeezes me. "I'm here all summer."

I can't stop the smile spreading across my face. I'll get back here at some point. Some point soon. I touch her lips before trotting into the area being cleared by the chopper's rotor wash. My eyes squeeze to slits.

Under the roar of the rotor wash, I tug Pia close and explain what Kitty has been telling us all along.

# CHAPTER 54

## CHRISTINE, THE BAKER

APPROACHING AT AN ANGLE THROUGH belts of dense fog, the *Numina's* dark silhouette rises before me like a dormant volcano about to erupt. My fear of the principal's office skyrockets into intense anxiety. I feel sick to my stomach and am having palpitations.

Norman and the *Aquaholic* are nowhere to be seen.

The tender swings around and comes straight at the back of the ship. As we draw near, half the *Numina's* transom wall rises on a hinge, opening her internal dock to us. High overhead, a helicopter perches on the stern. The launch glides inside.

In his perfectly crisp Sabel Yachts uniform, the coxswain leads me to the gunwales and helps me up. Another man in uniform waits on the *Numina's* walkway. He extends a hand. The seas are calmer but both ships still bob and sway. With their help, I make it to the big ship's deck without a clumsy fall.

I grab a handrail for balance and glance around the cavernous internal dock. A large submarine that looks like a glass sausage rests on davits on one side near several other boats and jet skis. The submarine has six captain's chairs inside. Robotic claws and baskets festoon the outside. Water drips from her sides.

Now I know how Sabel beat me to Phil's dry box in such a rough sea—she went under it.

Damn. This accelerates my anxiety. She's way ahead of me. And that's bad. Really bad.

The steward leads me upstairs to a sunbathing deck with a pool and spa. He keeps going up another level to an interior ball room as big as the Deeping Community Center. Holy Christ in heaven, we need to tax the rich. Marching through without stopping, we come to more stairs. This boat never ends. At the top of another set, I get a glimpse of the outside. The *Aquaholic* is still half a mile east of the *Numina's* bow. My guide opens a door and points inside.

It's a library with books lining shelves filling every square inch between oversized portals. In the center, Pia Sabel stands in her signature athleisure outfit and sporting a three-toed cane meant for octogenarians. I feel bad for her; even I wouldn't be caught dead with that stick. When she sees me staring, she moves it behind her leg.

Scotty, Isaiah, Miguel, and a woman in a business suit stand next to her, watching a throng of stewards as they wipe down the large yellow dry box resting on two coffee tables in the center of the room.

"They found it, Mom," Scotty says with excitement.

Sabel watches me like a cat toying with a mouse under its paw.

"Good news," I say weakly. I try to figure who the new woman is.

"Allow me to introduce Special Agent Kathy Menezes," Sabel says as if reading my mind. "Agent Menezes is with the FBI's Art Crime Team."

"You think Vinny had the Gardner Museum paintings?" I ask. I greet the agent with a nod, and she nods back.

Sabel and her bodyguards shrug in unison. One of them says, "We'll see."

The stewards step back and Menezes steps forward, feeling the rubber seals with her fingers. After joining a video call of experts on her phone, she aims her camera at the proceedings. Her online experts make observations and argue until she silences them. She gestures to the stewards, and they unlatch the box, then wipe the loosened seams down again. She inspects their work. With an anxious face, she asks them to lift it an inch. She doesn't want one drop of seawater to reach whatever might be inside. They make the move and wipe it down again. Then another inch and another wipe down. They repeat this painstaking procedure until the entire top is several inches above the box. Inside, we can see a large and dark canvas.

Ms. Menezes tells them to rip off the Band-Aid. They quickly pull it up and set it to one side so that any drips will be propelled away from the painting. They set the lid on edge.

Inside is an incredibly beautiful painting with bright white waves on the left crashing into a small sailboat that fades into darkness on the right. I don't know much about paintings, but anyone would recognize this masterpiece: *The Storm on the Sea of Galilee* by Rembrandt. Jesus chills in the stern while his twelve apostles struggle and fret. It's a stunning work of art.

It reflects my life over the last few days. Like the apostles, I've been running around in a frenzy working hard to save everyone's future from the storm. Meanwhile, Jesus sets an example for us to remain calm and accept our fate. I glance at Sabel. Is that who she thinks she is in her little drama? The sanctimonious bitch doesn't have a care in the world because she owns it all. She doesn't know what it's like to bail for all your worth to keep the ship from sinking.

"It's ruined!" Ms. Menezes cries.

She rushes to it and examines it, holding her phone above the surface so her colleagues can see it. The phone conversation is a mix of joy and despair. They've recovered the works stolen over thirty years ago, but the thieves treated them badly. The painting has stains, blood, and appears to have been rolled up like a carpet at some point. At least the inside of the box is dry.

As she agonizes over the canvas, the stewards set up a new box next to it. With her permission, they test the canvas's sides to see if it's stuck to the edges or anything beneath it. Satisfied it's free, they lift the canvas gingerly and move it to the next box, covering the top and bottom with a special material.

In Vinny's dry box, a layer of butcher paper separates the top painting from the one below. The next painting shows three people practicing music. Again, the agents and experts react with joy and despair. The painting of the musicians and several others are revealed. One by one, they are extracted and moved. Finally, the stewards reach the bottom of the pile.

Sabel helps herself to a peek beneath the last layer of butcher paper. The rich always assume they're in charge. She turns to Special Agent

Menezes and says, "That's it."

After thanking our hostess, the FBI agent supervises the stewards as they carry the new box out of the room. Someone mentions helicopter "number two" waiting for them on the foredeck. Apparently, the *Numina* has two helipads. Of course it does.

"So you get the $10 million reward?" I ask Sabel with a sharp voice. "Isn't that nice."

"It'll go toward a college fund for children in Deeping's foster care system," she answers. "I'll match it."

That cuts me off at the knees. My gaze sweeps the room, trying to land as far from her as possible. After a moment of thought, I realize what package is waiting under that butcher paper. My mounting fears are not so irrational after all. I have definitely been dragged to the Principal's office.

The good news is, Al Devino doesn't have that package. The bad news is, Sabel does. What she chooses to do with it could be the end of Deeping as I know it.

Not only is Sabel ahead of me—she has me cornered. She knows exactly what she's doing. I can see it in her ray-gun gaze. Suddenly, I can't breathe. I try the 4-7-8 technique for panic attacks. As quietly as possible, I inhale for four counts, hold it for seven, and exhale for eight. It doesn't help that Sabel's gray-green eyes stab through me like bayonets.

Sabel faces Scotty. "The last package is for you."

He looks around at the rest of us, confused and uncertain.

I consider options. Sabel carries a pistol tucked beneath her jacket. I could grab that. But I wouldn't know what to do with a gun. The way my hands are shaking, I'd most likely blow a hole in my foot. Besides, she's a big strong girl, thirty years younger than me. She'd break my arm.

I continue my 4-7-8s.

Miguel and Isaiah stand perfectly still. Not an ounce of curiosity on their faces. They figured out what's in there. No one opened the box before this little ceremony of hers, so they shouldn't know. But somehow the three of them pieced it together. I can tell by their silence.

"Would you like to know why Phil Jacobsen died?" she asks Scotty.

I should run to the door and jump overboard. Except the exterior doors are on the other side of Sabel's bodyguards.

Scotty says, "I don't understand. Al did it, right? Because Uncle Phil stole the paintings from Vinny."

Sabel shakes her head slowly, never taking those gray-green eyes off me. She peels back the last bit of paper and pulls something from beneath it.

A manila envelope.

With a solemn flourish, she hands it to Scotty. He's baffled, watching her as if to ask why she would hand him something from the Gardner heist.

"This is yours," she says and directs his attention to the label on it with a glance.

When he reads it, he looks at me with even greater bewilderment.

"In the world of foster care and adoption agencies," Sabel says, "the abbreviation for 'adopted child' is 'A-d-C-I.'"

Scotty tilts his head and looks her over with a quizzical frown. "The letters Uncle Phil wrote on the bench?"

"Exactly. He wrote, *Secret AdCI*. A secret adoption. It's anyone's guess what else he hoped to write, but I believe he was trying to point us to this package."

"But where … I don't understand. How did he get it?"

"He stole what he knew was the cache of Gardner paintings from ailing Vinny. He'd planned to get out of town and clear of Al before claiming the reward. When he finally opened it, he found this package among the art works. This package is how Vinny kept your mother in check and stopped her from telling the authorities about those priceless paintings. She kept his secret because he had hers. When Phil found it, he was livid that it had been kept secret at all. That's what he was raging about on the street with Kitty the afternoon before he was killed. He called your mother and screamed at her. He was angry she'd never told you."

Scotty looks at me, still uncertain what's going on. He faces Sabel and asks, "Told me what?"

"About your parents," she says quietly.

# CHAPTER 55

## CHRISTINE, THE BAKER

MY ANGER RISES AS BITTER bile in the back of my throat. Who does Sabel think she is to drop this on my son? These are delicate family matters, not some parlor game.

Scotty pulls the papers out of the envelope and stares at them. He begins skimming through each page of bureaucratic gobbledygook, trying to figure out which forms are important. I can tell when he gets to the certificate of live birth because he stares at it for a long time with his mouth open. Then, slowly, and with growing anger, he turns to me. He's too upset to speak.

Finally, he finds his voice. "Mom, you told Boo-Boo her baby was stillborn."

I have no answer.

"Christine Jacobsen wears a size 8 shoe," Sabel says. "They fit neatly in a men's size 12 shrimper boot, the same size as the shoe prints at the crime scene."

"What's that supposed to mean?" I ask.

"Remember the bootprints in Phil's front room?" Sabel asks Scotty. When he nods, she says, "They have the same tread as the men's shrimper boots your mother was wearing as overshoes when I found her poking around the Plant last night. She searched Phil's house for this package."

"Everyone has a pair of shrimper boots," Scotty says. "Best thing at the end of winter when the town is all slush and mud."

"The morning I found your uncle's body," she continues, "you told me to wait in her bakery. While I was there, I dripped sweat on her nice clean floors. I mopped it up and put the mop away in the back room. There was a bottle on the top shelf that had a warning label on it. It stuck out in my mind because most baking ingredients don't need warning labels. One hopes. Unfortunately, I didn't act on my suspicion at the time.

"When I had a moment later, I looked up what cyanide looks like. The most common type is the industrial, which we found at the Plant. The next most common is the smaller types often used by entomologists, farmers, and others. The latter comes in a blue-and-white bottle about the size of an aspirin bottle. That's what I saw in your mother's kitchen the morning of the murder. After I found what the smaller bottles looked like, I went back to get it—but it was gone. My team and I checked the dumpsters all over town and didn't find it. That told me it was still in her bakery, but better hidden. After that, we made sure she knew we were checking the dumpsters to keep her from throwing it away."

Isaiah's expression changes to *so-that's-what-the-dumpsters-were-all-about*.

"That's impossible," Scotty says. "She would never keep a powdered poison next to the baking powder. That would be dangerous."

I want to say *thank you for sticking up for me,* but Sabel goes on before I can get the words out.

"Isaiah spent hours working with Kitty Robinson to unravel her strange quotes. I haven't looked at that package, but thanks to his diligent work, we discovered she was invoking *Oedipus Rex,* the Greek tragedy of an adopted man who unwittingly kills his biological father and marries his biological mother. Once Isaiah figured that out, he pulled the pieces of your heritage together. I haven't looked at it yet, but I'll bet your birth certificate lists your father as Mike Davis and your mother as Jennifer Vitelli, commonly known as Boo-Boo."

Scotty's gaze drops to the papers in his hand. His head shakes back and forth in denial.

No one speaks.

After a full minute, Scotty makes a sound that is not a word. It's more like a syllable of anguish. He takes another gulp of air and pulls himself together.

"No," he says. "Boo-Boo had a stillborn. Mom was with her. This must be wrong." Tears fill Scotty's eyes when he finally looks to me for an explanation.

I say the only thing that comes to mind. "I told you not to date her."

Bottom lip quivering, his mouth opens and shuts without any words coming out.

Isaiah holds a phone up and points to it. Sabel looks to him and nods. Her bodyguard turns off the mute and Sabel says, "Bill Koller, are you still there?"

"Yes, ma'am!" an enthusiastic and familiar voice comes through.

"Thank you for your patience while we worked through a few things on our end. I'm calling because I understand we have a mutual admiration of Del Porto Extra Añejo."

"You're a woman of fine taste," Bill says.

"Could you repeat what you told me earlier: to whom in Deeping, Maine were those great bottles of tequila shipped?"

"I sent one to Kubari Eady. He's a helluva good man and makes the best pork this side of Bora Bora. And the other one went to the amazing Christine Jacobsen. She knows how to show a stranger a good time, I can tell you. She's a fine lady with a golden touch when it comes to baking. Have you tried her brioche?"

"I have, and I couldn't agree more," Sabel says. Isaiah takes the phone off speaker and steps away to finish up with Bill.

Scotty is staring at me while everything he believed in crashes around him.

Sabel turns to me. "I predicted the evidence would mount and the guilty would confess."

Confess?

Fuck that.

I bolt past her, kicking that stupid cane out of her hand as I run by. Instead of chasing me, her trusted bodyguards rush to her aid as she falls on the floor. Tearing through the room, I exit through a different door from where I came in. It's a dining room fit for the Queen of England. At the far end, I find a bar and a spiral staircase. Taking the steps two at a time, which kills my antique ankles, I make it to the ballroom I'd seen earlier. I think the exit I need is on the far left.

I don't hear anyone running after me. Maybe they're taking a shortcut.

It's not the same stairs I came up, this is a grand stairway to another reception room. But it's closer to the water, so I'm going in the right direction. Racing to the side, I look overboard. Two more decks below, Norman's *Aquaholic* is tied to a waterline walkway. I don't see him.

Cupping my hands, I call out and see movement in his cabin. He steps out and looks around. I call out again. He looks up, smiles, and waves. I yell, "Untie the boat! I need to leave fast!"

He looks surprised. I don't care. I look around but there are no stairs on this deck. I run back inside and see an elevator. Next to the elevator is a narrow stairway. I take that, sliding my hands down the gold banisters as I jump the steps. My ankle turns on the landing, pain shrieks through my body. I sprawl on the polished floor wanting to cry.

No. I don't have time. If Pia Sabel can walk it off, so can I. I get up and see stairs leading down another level. They have grip strips on them, so I must be close to the water. My ankle stings like a viper's biting it on each step. Limping along the handrail on the side, I make it to the stairs. They lead down to a scuba gear room. An open door leads outside. From there, it's a short hobble to Norman's boat.

Too shocked to move as I fall aboard, Norman gapes at me like a moron.

I shout, "Go! Go! Go!"

# CHAPTER 56

## SCOTT, THE POLICE CHIEF

WHY WOULD MOM RUN LIKE that? I feel like an earthquake survivor who was watching TV in his apartment one minute and crushed in a pancaked building breathing concrete dust the next. The voices around me are muddled and indistinct. Shaking my head to clear it, I'm still stunned, staring into the middle distance like a fool as Isaiah and Miguel pick Ms. Sabel off the floor. Isaiah starts to run after Mom, but Ms. Sabel grabs his arm. As if I'm underwater, I hear her ask the obvious question, *Where will she go?*

Ms. Sabel's ray-gun gaze swings my way, and she speaks words I don't hear. I'm still processing everything she said in the last few minutes, but none of it makes sense. I interrupt her to ask, "Why did Uncle Phil die?"

"Your mom thought he was going to expose her secret." She has a patient, caring look on her face. Knowing I'm in denial, she explains, "Your mom kept Vinny Devino out of Deeping by threatening to expose his possession of the Gardner paintings. At the same time, Vinny knew Ms. Vitelli had given birth to a healthy baby—you—and that Christine lied to her about it being stillborn. He stole the adoption papers as collateral to make sure your mom never told anyone about the paintings. For years they had a stalemate. When Phil stole the paintings, he went through them and found the pilfered adoption papers. Once he understood what they meant, he lost it."

She turns to Isaiah and waves a hand for him to continue.

He says, "The first thing Kitty said to us was a quote from *Oedipus*

*Rex*, 'Alas, how terrible knowing the truth can be when there is no help in the truth.'"

He moves closer, and in a compassionate voice, continues, "After seeing the birth certificate, Phil started ranting wildly. Kitty tried to calm him down. Later, when Kitty met me at the dumpster, she told me about it by quoting from *Ajax*: 'Alas, he darted forward through the door, and began ranting to some creature of his brain,—now against Devino, now against Vitelli, finally against Jacobsen ...' When we met Leslie Dingwall from your adoption agency, she told us the vandalism of your records was part of a mob war. It wasn't exactly a mob war; it was Vinny getting evidence against Christine Jacobsen. Discovering that blackmail evidence had existed for years enraged Phil. He called your mom, let her know what he thought of her deception, and insisted she tell everyone the truth. Phil threatened to expose the story if she didn't come clean.

"Since you'd taken up with Ms. Vitelli, your mom decided everything had to be buried. As we all know, the truth is an immovable object. Your mom also understood this, and the mounting pressure of Phil's threat drove her anxieties through the roof. While anger was accelerating her anxiety, Phil cooled off. He realized he should hide everything and think about how to handle it the next day."

I find myself on the defensive. "You can't rely on Crazy Kitty as a witness."

"Rick told us about his doorbell video," Miguel says. "How did your mom explain walking past his house in the direction of Harbor Park at that hour?"

Instantly, I feel like a fool. Rick's house is not on the way to Jana Siverling's. It's two blocks off the path. Was she sleepwalking? Maybe. But she grew up here and would know her way blindfolded. There was no casserole dish in that bag Mom was carrying—it was an oddly shaped bottle of tequila.

"The physical evidence is strong," Ms. Sabel says. "Did your mom give you a bottle of cyanide?"

"Yes, but she bought it."

Without saying a word, her eyes burn through me. She doesn't believe it.

I pull the bottle out of my pocket and look at it. Flour is trapped between the piping grooves on the cap. Flour gets on everything. She had this at the bakery, but that doesn't prove anything. She could've bought it yesterday and gotten flour on it this morning.

"Think about Kitty's statements," Isaiah says in a soft, sympathetic voice. "She said, 'Nay, thou art thine own plague,' and told your mother, 'Thou art the accursed defiler of this land.' And when you came to the house in the storm, 'Dost know thy lineage? Nay, thou know'st it not. And all unwitting art a double foe.' That last bit means killing Phil was a double problem for Christine because—unbeknownst to her—he had already changed his mind about exposing everything. He'd gone to great lengths to hide the dry box. If she hadn't killed him, there would've been no investigation and they would've worked out the best way to handle it."

"Still," I say, clinging to the last threads of hope, "there's no proof."

Ms. Sabel says, "When I brought the bottle of Del Porto to your mother's house, it wasn't just for shock value, although I'm sure you noticed how she turned white. I did it to see how she handled the odd shape. When you pick the bottle up by the neck, it's back-heavy and unwieldy, especially when full. She wanted us to believe she'd never seen it before, yet she knew the bottle's characteristics. She slid her fingers underneath where she could get a better handle on the weight. Tell your fingerprint people to check the bottom and there's a good chance you'll find your mother's."

The report on the bottle mentioned Uncle Phil's prints on the neck. It didn't mention the bottom. They probably didn't check it.

Everything blurs again. My knees are weak. I think Miguel is going for a glass of water. Ms. Sabel is giving orders to a pilot to ready the helicopter. He says it'll take a few minutes.

I sense my phone at my ear. I've called Boo-Boo. When she answers, I blurt out, "Mom lied. Christine lied to you. You didn't have a stillborn, you had a baby. Me. I'm your son. You're my birth mother. She adopted me knowing damn well I was your son. Boo-Boo, I …"

I stop talking because using her nickname suddenly feels wrong. Everything feels wrong. There is silence on the other end of the phone.

I have a strange sensation of Isaiah pushing a chair up behind me and me falling into it. Miguel might be handing me a glass of water, I'm not sure. Ms. Sabel is pulling her advisors back, giving me privacy.

"Is this some kind of joke?" Boo-Boo asks.

"I wish," I say with an exasperated exhale. "I have the birth certificate. Mike Davis is listed as my father. I killed my father."

Picking up the birth certificate in front of me, I click a photo and send it to her.

When she gets it, she screams, then cries, then asks, "You're not going to tell anyone, are you?"

"It's the truth," I answer. "People always find—"

"Burn the papers. Pretend this didn't happen. We can't go on … Oh, Scotty, I couldn't live in this town if anyone found out. You have to destroy the papers. You have to—"

"The truth always comes out."

"Who did you tell?" She's screaming now.

"I didn't tell anyone. But people know. The Sabel people are here, there was an FBI agent—"

An anguished shriek blows through the phone. She screams, "I'm going to kill her. I'm going to fucking kill Christine."

The connection goes dead. I dial back but go straight to voicemail.

When I look up, my hostess is looking at me with sadness written all over her face. Ms. Sabel says, "Sorry, we heard that last part. Understandable how she would feel that way, but we should go. People in situations like that act in unpredictable ways."

I follow them through a maze of stairways and rooms and out to a landing pad on the stern. We climb aboard and don headsets.

Ms. Sabel says, "Your top priority is to find Christine."

Those words leave a tremendous weight on my shoulders. She didn't say, *your mom*; she didn't say, *arrest*; she didn't say, *protect her from your birth mother*. As an adopted child, she knows the feelings involved are tangled and torn. Loyalties are upside down.

We lift off over the shrouded Atlantic coast, the rotor wash pushing clouds in radiating circles from the ship until we reach altitude. It's a short ride, not long enough to get clarity about how I should resolve this.

Ms. Sabel's right, though. I need to find Mom.

What was she thinking? That she could keep the records secret forever? The break-in at the agency happened long before I was old enough to request my records. Since Vinny had them, she knew where they were. And she knew who was listed on them. Which means, she could've told me ten years ago, long before I started dating Boo-Boo … Jennifer. Ms. Vitelli. My birth mother. None of those labels fit. What do I call her, Mom? Something else? I close my eyes.

I don't know who *mother* is.

I do know who mothered me. Christine Jacobsen. Everything she did in life was to make the world a better place for Amy and me. She joined the Deeping Board of Education to make our schools better. She ran for mayor to make it a town we would want to come home to after college.

I can smell her baking now. Mom always smells of fresh baked goods: tangy sourdough, rich blueberry muffins, delicate brioche, eggy popovers, salty olive bread. Chocolate chip cookies. A memory plays in my head like a movie: Mom holds my hand while the popover's heat burns my fingers, she shows me how to stuff a dollop of butter inside, following it quickly with a knife blade slathered in jam. Everything melts together, and I take a bite. The scents and flavors explode in my mouth. Joy and excitement at discovering something new overwhelms me. I look up at her, thankful that she knows how to make me smile. She's beaming with pride. She loved me in that moment. And I loved her.

It wasn't just that one moment. It was the swings in the park where she loved to push me. It was the baseball games she never missed. It was the homework she helped me master, the broken heart she helped me mend in high school. It was the reading time that came at bedtime. She read to Amy and me separately, each getting our own story and our own time snuggled with Mom. When I heard her finish with Amy, and they said goodnight, my heart would race with excitement. It was my turn. I was older with a bedtime a whole twenty minutes later than Amy's. She read Robert Louis Stevenson with accents and dramatic interpretations. When Mom saw how I loved *Treasure Island*, she found *Kidnapped* and *Black Arrow*. Next, she introduced me to Rudyard Kipling's *Kim*. Then Jules Verne and Edgar Rice Burroughs.

It wasn't just the good times either. It was how she laughed and got me an ice cream after my suspension for punching Davy Jones. It was when she brought me ice packs and chocolate bars after a jealous senior kicked my ass for asking out his girlfriend. Whenever I was angry, beaten, humiliated, she was there.

Those were the most beautiful moments in my life. She spent those hours with me because she really did love me.

Now that I think about it, if she really killed Uncle Phil, I know why: because she loves me.

Obviously, too much.

As misguided as her actions were, as ill-conceived and madness-driven, she was trying to protect me. She was doing what she always did—clearing a path for me that I might thrive.

What would Jennifer Vitelli have done had she been given the chance? She gave birth to me when she was sixteen. Single. Tenth grade. Would she have struggled with drugs and alcohol if she had me to raise? I know the statistical answer: yes. Most of our calls for domestic abuse involve one or more adults with unplanned children, no higher education, little money, and lots of self-medication. But Boo-Boo would've done things differently, right? Had she known her baby was healthy, she would've kept me and provided for me and gone to college and gotten a good job. Maybe she would've married a nice man who would adopt me. Not a man who ran drugs for Devino, but someone else with a real job.

Sure. That could've happened.

But it didn't.

What am I going to do about Christine Jacobsen, the criminal? She handed me the cyanide. Bill Koller sent her a bottle of Del Porto and she never mentioned it. When confronted by Ms. Sabel, she ran.

She thought I would plant the evidence on Al Devino. No critical thinking involved. I did *not* like that. It went against everything Mom ever taught me. I chose not to do it. Did I make the right choice? If she had given me reasons why, would I have made a different decision? Would I have broken the law to save my mother?

The chopper door is standing open. We're on the ground. Isaiah has just tapped my knee to break my meditation.

I climb out and find the three of them standing in a circle. Miguel and Isaiah say nothing. Ms. Sabel says, "How can we best support you?"

The words come out of my mouth without a clear thought. "Go to Boo-Boo's house, make sure she's there and get her calmed down. I'll find Mom and … and."

I walk away from them. I have no idea how to finish that last sentence.

Striding across Harbor Park where we landed, I march up Main Street. My body is going to Mom's Bakery. My mind is going to Hell.

# CHAPTER 57

## ISAIAH, THE ADVISOR

As we track through the *Numina's* endless interior heading to the chopper, Chief Jacobsen appears to be in a trance. He's slow to respond and follows Miguel like a child, eyes downcast. I can't blame him. We dumped a lot on him all at once. We get in and I hand him a headset that he stares at for a long time before putting it on. The rotors stir clouds of fog around us as we lift into the sky. He says nothing the whole way.

Chief's story reminds me of how lucky I have been. Two loving parents, still married, aging well, and respected in their fields. A sister who makes me proud and is equally proud of me. My home is filled with love.

Scott Jacobsen had a different family, equally loving and close—and a meteor just crashed into it.

When we land, everyone gets out except the Chief. He sits for a long time, staring straight ahead. When I tap his knee, he blows out a big breath, shakes his head, and hops down. We're standing in a semicircle, waiting for him. Ms. Sabel says, "How can we best support you?"

He mumbles about checking on Ms. Vitelli, but I can barely hear him over the engines. He turns and walks away.

When he turns a corner, Miguel gives us a nod and follows the Chief out of concern for his mental health. Pia and I head up the street in a different direction, to Ms. Vitelli's house. I'm beginning to understand how they think. I feel included in the telepathy Pia shares with her people.

We walk the first block in silence. Her limp has gotten noticeably worse since the fight with Devino. She ignored the pain in the heat of conflict and now she's paying for it.

"I'm worried about Ms. Vitelli," Pia says. "The desperation in her voice struck a nerve in me. She'll need help coping with all this."

"Do you think she's a danger to Christine?"

"Christine stole her baby thirty years ago. She's been betrayed, lied to, not to mention publicly humiliated. She's a victim and they either collapse or explode."

We pass another two houses quietly. I ask, "How was your experience with adoption?"

"You mean family acceptance? The Sabel family treats me like I have a contagious disease. Alan Sabel has a surviving brother and a sister, my aunt and uncle. They both have children. I pay their bills, private school tuition, provide care for Grampa Sabel's Parkinson's, in-home care, all that. They send cards of appreciation and gift baskets of artisanal jams. But none of them has ever invited me for Thanksgiving. When Dad was killed, they sent an attorney to examine his will. They wanted to contest it."

"That's rude."

"I don't waste time thinking about them." She looks at me sideways as we walk. "What about your family? Close?"

"So close, my Dad's trying to talk me into med school."

"I didn't realize that was something you wanted to pursue."

"I'm not sure it is. It's a respected profession and there's no denying the money's good."

"Is that what motivates you, the money?" she asks.

"Money's a factor, can't deny that." I think about it for a moment. "To be honest, I prefer the heroic nature of our work at Sabel Security."

We arrive at Ms. Vitelli's house. No one answers the bell we hear chiming inside. We knock anyway. Pia points to the gap between the door and the jamb where we can see an inside deadbolt latched.

"She could have gone to Chief's house," I say.

"Possible," Pia answers. "Or, she might've gone to confront Christine. But if she's here, she might be in a dark place and need a friend."

We track around the side to the kitchen door. It's unlocked.

Before we open it, Pia glances at me. I'm dialed in now. I know what she's thinking: *A woman's voice will be less threatening.*

When I nod, she swings the door open and calls out, "Ms. Vitelli, are you home? I'm here to listen to anything you want to tell me."

Silence.

We proceed inside cautiously. Instinctively, I glance around the neighborhood behind us. In this all-white community, a black man sliding in the back door might be mistaken for a criminal act. And some people might get trigger-happy. I don't see any pulled-back curtains or any questioning faces in windows. I close the door behind me.

Pia points me toward an opening to the living room on one end of the kitchen while she heads in the opposite direction through the dining nook. She repeats her call.

Still no answer.

The living room has a sagging couch and loveseat covered with worn-out throw blankets. The carpet is in dire need of a scrubbing. The coffee table is a plank on cinderblocks. A small TV rests on a stack of blocks in front of the window. Half a bottle of Jack Daniels sits next to a tumbler with a puddle of whiskey left in the bottom. Pia calls out again.

Exiting the living room, I find the front door to the left. A tiny foyer-space with a coatrack on the wall holds two coats and a plaid muffler. All dry and cold. A staircase to the right leads up.

The worn treads creak all the way, so I don't have to announce myself. A short hallway offers three doors. The closest one is a sewing room with a prominent machine in the middle. Bolts of cloth and scraps of material litter the otherwise empty room. A pad of paper lies on the floor next to a ballpoint pen. In large letters ground in deep, then crossed out, are unfinished sentences, "Fuck you, Christine! You had no fucking right" followed by another line that reads, "Dearest Scotty, I never wanted." There are more words scratched out so deeply they're illegible. Messages started and stopped in agony.

Across the hall is a bedroom, the door stands wide open. As I start for it, something about the third door catches my eye.

It's open four inches revealing the crest of a toe lying sideways on the tile floor.

Pushing the door an inch more shows me all I need to see. I know who it is and what it means. My stomach sinks and I let out a breath. An unnaturally gray foot, toenails painted red, black sweatpants, and everything too still. I call out over my shoulder, "Pia, I found her."

The door sticks at her knee. I gently lift her leg and get the door open. Boo-Boo Vitelli lies with her head stuck between the tub and toilet, her legs splayed out across the floor, one arm is stretched out, still tied off with a thin belt above the elbow. The other awkwardly held aloft by the toilet bowl. A needle, spoon, and matches are scattered where they fell beneath the sink.

I check her pulse. Nothing.

Pia's cane stomps up the stairs slowly. I can't wait for her to get here. It's too depressing to witness alone. A sense of relief comes to me when she sighs over my right shoulder. She opens the medicine cabinet and paws around. She asks, "Narcan anywhere?"

"Too late," I respond.

We stand still a moment in reverence for the dead. Pia puts a hand on my shoulder and squeezes. A glance her way reveals tears forming in her eyes.

"I'll call it in," Pia says, her voice cracking. "Find Scott at once and tell him. I don't want him to find out by hearing the ambulance dispatch."

# CHAPTER 58

## SCOTT, THE POLICE CHIEF

A SIGN IN THE WINDOW of Mom's Bakery says opening has been delayed by the storm. Amy comes out of the back when I bang on the glass. Seeing me, she unlocks the door and lets me in.

"Is Mom here?" I ask.

"What happened?" she asks. "She's in back crying. She said Pia Sabel's accused her of awful things. Scotty, what's going on?"

"Give me a few minutes alone with her."

Gently moving Amy aside, I make my way through to find Mom sitting at her desk with an icepack on her ankle. She's pale and drawn, tracks of dried tears stain her cheeks. Crunched tissues are piled on her desk.

"M-Mom …" I stammer, "tell me something. Anything. Tell me the evidence is wrong. Tell me what I'm missing."

"Who do you want to believe?" Her pleading face turns up to me. "Your mother, or some random billionaire who shows up unannounced?"

"You invited her." I cross my arms and lean against the edge of her desk. "Why didn't you tell me about the bottle of Del Porto?"

"I never looked at the name." Her eyes rise to the ceiling as if remembering something. "It was just a pretty bottle Bill Koller sent me after we had … when he left."

"The poison you gave me at the checkpoint, Mom. Where did you get it?"

"Does it matter?" She adjusts her icepack, keeping her focus on wrapping it around her leg. "You can get it anywhere. I bought it online."

"Mom, remember when I was a kid and you told me lying was a terrible thing? That the truth is the truth, but a lie always trips you up?"

I pause waiting for her gaze to come back to me. It doesn't. And that breaks my heart.

I ask her, "You expect me to believe you found it online and had it shipped overnight? You handed it to me this morning before any deliveries were made."

Her eyes narrow and scowl at me. "What are you saying, Scotty?" Her voice rises in volume. "You believe Sabel? Do you think I could do a thing like that?"

"Remember when I got interested in bugs?" My volume cranks up to match hers. I point at my insect collection just a few feet away. "You made a kill jar to catch those bugs. What kind of poison did you use? And what did you tell me about it?" She keeps her eyes on the framed collection and doesn't answer. "You told me it was so deadly that you would mix it for safety's sake. Where did you get it all those years ago? Mom, everything points to you. Tell me I'm wrong."

"We can still blame Al," she says. She grabs my arm and gives it a desperate squeeze. "You can plant it in his car. Say you found it there. Put his fingerprints on it."

"Why would I do that? Why would I even need—"

I sense Amy pushing the door open from the main room. When I turn to face her, she steps in.

"What are you two yelling about?" she asks.

Mom's gaze drops to the floor.

"Pia Sabel saw this bottle," I say as I pull the cyanide out of my pocket, "on Mom's ingredients shelf the day of Uncle Phil's murder."

Amy falls back against the door jamb. She blurts out, "Because I did it! I killed Uncle Phil."

My world falls apart again. I look at Mom, but she won't look up.

She's been covering for Amy this whole time? That would explain everything. Mom would do anything for either of us. She would frame Al Devino in an instant. Nothing is out of the question for her if it means saving one of us.

"Why?" I ask Amy.

"I made some videos back in—"

"I know about that," I say to spare her the indignity of divulging the details. "Isaiah sketched out the specifics for me."

Amy takes a minute, fretting her fingers and trembling. "He blackmailed Siobahn Allen and I lost it. I got drunk and, well, to be honest, I don't know what happened from there. I have scraps of memories, that's all."

Something bothers me about Amy's confession. If Isaiah told me about the video connection, he told Ms. Sabel as well. He never accused Amy and didn't mention it as motive earlier when we were on the ship. That means both Isaiah and Ms. Sabel knew Amy had motive. Yet they accused Mom directly and never mentioned Amy.

I look at Mom. She's still downcast, saying nothing.

Turning back to Amy, I ask her, "Are your fingerprints on the bottom of the Del Porto bottle?"

"No, why would they be?"

Mom's gaze rises to the ceiling. She knows why I'm asking.

"Where did you get the tequila?" I ask.

"It was here, at the bakery," she answers.

"I've been in this bakery every day for the last decade and never saw a bottle of tequila. Mom doesn't allow alcohol in here."

"Then … I probably brought it from the house," Amy's on the verge of tears.

"Where did you get the bottle of cyanide?" I snap.

"I don't know. It was here, on the kneading table with the tequila."

"Why would deadly poison be sitting on the kneading table?" I ask with a bite.

"I … I don't know."

"Where did the cyanide come from?" I ask.

"It came from Al's house!" she shouts. "Mom saw it there."

"Did you drive up to Al's house the night of the murder?" I've risen to a shout as well. "Find a bottle of cyanide? Drive back here, poison Uncle Phil, then drive it back to Al's? All while black-out drunk?"

Amy stutters without forming a word.

"Where did it come from, Amy?"

"York County Community College," Mom says. "For twenty years I've known where Paul Thompson keeps his. He's the one who showed me how to use it for your bug collection." She gives us a long, tired sigh. "I did it. Not Amy. I made that part up about seeing it at Al's. That was a mistake. I thought I could get back there and plant the bottle but you moved too fast for me. And that's why the search warrant turned up nothing. The tequila I kept hidden in my bedroom in case Bill Koller came back. After Phil and I argued about telling you the truth, I tried to get him to meet me, he kept saying no until I told him I had this fancy tequila. You know he's a sucker for good booze. I told him I wanted to make peace with my brother. The whole time I was thinking it was the only way to keep your birth-mom a secret. Sooner or later, he'd blab. He'd get mad at me some day, get drunk, and tell everyone. I couldn't let that happen. God, I feel so sick about it."

I recall Ms. Sabel saying she'd pile up evidence until the killer confessed.

Mom buries her face in her hands. After a beat, she looks up at Amy and says, "You came in that night just as I was going to meet Phil. I scrambled to hide in the storeroom but left everything on the kneading table. That's where you saw it. I'm sorry, Amy. It was cowardly of me to let you think you did it."

Amy and I share a look of disbelief. I reach out and take Mom's hand, the same warm, caring hand that held mine every time I crossed a road, when I was sick, when I was scared.

"I'm sorry, Scotty." She looks up at me with watery eyes. "I'm so sorry. I told you about being adopted as soon as you were old enough to understand. I intended to tell you about Boo-Boo." She shakes her head. "But she kept getting into drugs and I kept sending her off to rehab. I didn't want you to think you had those genes. I thought if you found out about Boo-Boo, she'd drag you down with her. I couldn't let that happen. Besides. I wanted to be your mom—your only mom. I thought it would be better if you had a story like Amy's. Oh, Scotty. I wanted the best for you. But Boo-Boo makes such terrible choices. I didn't want you to fall into that pit."

After another silent moment, Mom says, "I'm sorry for Crazy Kitty too. She came here after Phil told her why he was so mad. I told her if she told anyone, I'd kill her. I scared the hell out of her. That's why she's been spouting Greek riddles."

Looking at Amy, she adds, "You bought all that crap Vinny peddled about your mom being a whore, but it wasn't true. Your mom was the daughter of a sanctimonious Holy Roller, like I told you. Lives in Boston now, has three kids. Go find her, Amy. I'm sure she's a nice person."

We remain motionless in silence for a long time. Whole minutes pass.

A thousand ideas go through my mind. Ms. Sabel never said what I should do. She never told me to arrest the only person I've ever considered my mother. She knew this would be hard. Isaiah knows who killed Phil. Miguel knows, but what would they do about it? She told the president she'd be in Monaco by morning. Her whole crew will leave town in a matter of hours. At this point, it would be a miracle if they picked Deeping for the SRC, so they'll never come back. I can still plant the damn bottle on Al. I could drive up to Al's house and plant it there. Then call the locals and tell them we had a new tip. Let them find it.

But that's the same thing I almost did to Kubari. It's not the right thing to do.

Neither is sending your mom to jail for murder.

I sense Mom's hand on top of mine. She says, "I know what you're thinking. Don't do it. The truth always comes out. I can't let you sacrifice your future for me. I'm guilty of killing my brother, I'm ready to pay for my sin."

That's Mom, protecting me. And worse, she's right. Which leaves me no option.

With my gut twisted up in knots, I tell her, "Mom, you are under arrest for the murder of Phil Jacobsen. You have the right to—"

A frantic banging on the glass interrupts us.

Amy and I go to the main room.

It's Isaiah. He came in person.

Instantly, I know why he's here. If it was anything else, he would've called.

# CHAPTER 59

## SCOTT, THE POLICE CHIEF

ISAIAH LEADS THE WAY TO Boo-Boo's house a few steps ahead of me. He bounds up the stoop and holds the door open. I can see people inside. As I make the top step, two of my officers, Ms. Sabel, and Dr. Orellana form an aisle for me. No one speaks as I squeeze between them.

I can barely move, I can't breathe, I can't think. I climb the steps to the second floor on autopilot.

A gurney waits in the hall outside the bathroom. Inside, two techs wrestle with a sheet under Boo-Boo's body. When they notice me, they stop what they're doing. They hold her suspended just off the floor while they stare at me with open mouths. They don't know what to say.

I observe her for a moment. Her lifeless face, so loving and happy just yesterday, stares blankly skyward, her earthly vessel now devoid of her soul.

"It's OK," I say quietly. "Let me help."

I take hold of the sheet near her feet and the three of us bend her around the cramped space and out to the gurney. We place her on it gently. I find myself staring at someone who looks nothing like the woman I've known for years. My eyes squeeze shut involuntarily.

One of the techs twists around me and straps down her legs. The other secures her torso. I back out and trudge down the stairs while they finish.

Ms. Sabel tugs Dr. Orellana's sleeve and they move to the living room to give me space.

Numbed from head to toe, I feel no emotion at all. I expected to feel something. She was my mother. And my lover—a fact I don't want to ever think about again. Now, minutes after learning the truth, she's gone. No goodbye, no note, no last hug, no reconciliation. In the end, the abyss she struggled to climb out of reclaimed her.

The techs bring the gurney down the stairs with my officers assisting. I stand in the living room entrance, watching as scattered thoughts flit through my mind.

Isaiah stands next to me and puts his arm around me. He says, "Everyone thinks soldiers are tough as hell. We are when we need to be. It's the next day that hurts. I've seen a lot of strong men bottle it up for too long. Sometimes they collapse into drugs, sometimes they become suicidal. But the strong ones, they let it out. Go ahead, Chief, let it out. I've got you."

Held up by a man I hardly know, I feel it erupting from the center of my chest, hot and hollow. My chest heaves and hot tears flow but no sound comes out of me. I feel my weight shift against him like I'm leaning against a rock. A few seconds later, I hear sobs.

I sense Amy's presence on the other side of me. She rests her cheek on my shoulder and rubs my back like Mom used to.

A sense of loss drives my pain. Both mothers have been taken from me within minutes of each other. Cast adrift, I no longer have a connection to either my genetic history or my loving childhood. For the first time in my life, I feel orphaned. Christine tried to protect me from this.

Now I see how Crazy Kitty's ranting makes sense: *Alas, how terrible knowing the truth can be when there is no help in the truth.* There is a certain peace in knowing the ancient Greeks struggled with the same problems twenty-five hundred years ago. My sobs slow. My tears drain.

No matter what Isaiah says about letting it out, I'm still Police Chief. I straighten up and take a deep breath. Isaiah senses my change and lets go.

As they wheel the stretcher past me, I wonder: am I like her, destined to suffer the same fate? Or my father for that matter? My DNA came from them, am I given to the same failures of reason? Will I struggle with drugs one day? Make bad decisions? Or did Christine nurture me in the right direction?

Cheryl Walton, the county coroner, enters and the machinery of state takes charge. They wheel the body out and close the door behind them.

I feel Pia Sabel's gaze on my back. She knew Mom was the killer from the beginning. She didn't know about Boo-Boo, but she knew something tragic drove Mom to madness. That's why she dug into those personal questions like a therapist. She let me know I was not alone. She's been trying to tell me adoption is not what defines me.

Ms. Sabel moves next to me, and says, "We can wallow in what could've been or revel in what can be."

"I suspect that wisdom comes from your well of experience," I answer. "Don't worry about me. It won't be easy, but I'll get through it."

"It was our fate to be adopted," she says. "Don't think of that as abandonment. It just makes us different from others. If you believe in the brotherhood of humankind, we are called to reach across our differences and love one another."

"Treat others the way we want to be treated?" A silence beats between us as I figure out what she's talking about. Kubari is different, it was easier to suspect him than someone close to me.

I say, "Thanks for handling this gently."

She nods thoughtfully before changing the subject. "What did you decide to do about your mom?"

It takes me a moment to sort out that she means my adopted mother and another moment to realize she half-expected me to take the dishonest route. "She made a full confession and I arrested her."

"Probably for the best."

"I have to admit, I was tempted to frame Al Devino for it."

"I know," she says. "We were prepared to back you up either way."

Surprised, I face her. "Why?"

"Remember when we talked about those dark and lonely periods? This could trigger that kind of reaction. I didn't want you sliding into that oblivion. Framing Al Devino would be a better alternative."

She puts an arm around me. It feels good.

I ask, "Would you have thought less of me if I'd let her go?"

"Yes," she says, "but with full empathy."

She never backs away from an honest answer. I find that admirable.

But I don't know what else to say. I really need to be alone.

"I'll pay for her defense attorney," she says as she steps away. "Whatever madness possessed her in the moment was temporary compared to how much love she provided for you and Amy."

# CHAPTER 60

## ISAIAH, THE ADVISOR

I FEEL LIKE THE ODD man out. Pia stepped in to console Chief Jacobsen, which forced me to the side. Then Amy came in to commiserate in the foyer for a moment. And now Lyn Avery bursts through the door. She's one step ahead of Rick Tara.

Before Lyn can speak, Rick steps around her and says, "She was a wonderful woman, Scott."

Behind me I sense Pia pulling Miguel and nodding for me to join them. She says, "Isaiah, you've proved to be a tremendous addition to the team. I've learned to count on you with confidence. Thank you for doing such a great job under pressure. My most trusted advisors, like Miguel, form something of a hive-mind that works on intuition. You fit right in. We couldn't have solved this mystery without you."

Pride lifts me an inch. It also gives me a boldness that might backfire. "Thank you, I appreciate that. There's one question though. Twenty-four hours ago, when we visited the adoption agency, you told me I had all the information I needed to figure out who killed Phil Jacobsen. But I didn't. You didn't tell me you had seen the cyanide on Christine's shelf."

Behind her, Miguel represses a laugh and turns away.

A sly smile grows across Pia's face. It's the same expression she had in that post-World Cup interview I watched. She says, "To stay on top, you have to keep a few tricks up your sleeve."

"Why?" I ask with more heat than intended.

"It's that age old question about free will versus fate," she shrugs. "In *Oedipus Rex,* Tiresias broke down and told the king what he wanted to know. But Oedipus rejected the facts, sealing his fate. Since that didn't work, I used a different tactic. I led Scott to the facts. If I accused your mother of murder, you'd stop at nothing to prove me wrong. Scott had to discover the truth for himself."

"I thought you didn't study Greek tragedies."

"Research," she grins. "That's what I do when everyone else is sleeping."

Dr. Orellana comes out of the other room and stands to Pia's side, his gaze on her swollen ankle.

Ignoring him, she reaches for Miguel, tugs him back, and says, "Now that this is done, we need to get moving. I promised President Williams I'd be in Monaco tonight to start Operation Chaac. Tania is already there doing surveillance. And I still have to meet with Ursula and Christine for the rescheduled EU meetings. Meaning, we have a heavy schedule. Isaiah, you've been briefed on Operation Chaac, so—"

"Sit down," Dr. Orellana tells Pia. "I want to look at that ankle."

"It's fine," she says, glancing over her shoulder at the shorter man. "I've walked off worse."

"Where did you get your medical degree?" he asks with a snarl. "Sit down and give me your ankle."

"No, really, it's—"

"Science is why we live twice as long today as we did a hundred years ago. Sit. Down!"

Pia falls back into the loveseat with wide eyes. He picks up her ankle, sending her over backwards onto her elbows. He pushes up the fabric of her leggings and pulls off her trainers, ankle brace, and socks. He frowns.

"You've been walking around on this for the last few days?" the doctor asks.

"It's no big deal. I've had—"

The doctor pushes a finger into one side of her ankle. "Does this hurt?"

"Jesus." She winces with more pain than she wants to let on. "A little."

"And this?" He pokes the opposite side.

"Ow! Shit."

He drops her foot. "You have multiple fractures. You need surgery and recovery before you put another ounce of weight on that foot."

"I don't have time for surgery. It'll be fine."

"The bones will fuse into a lump. The ankle will lose all movement. In a few years—long before your time—you'll need a walker 24/7."

Pia's face drains. She gulps. "A what?"

Dr. Orellana says slowly, "Walker."

Pia looks to Miguel then me as if we might have a better diagnosis. We both shrug while suppressing *I told you so.*

The doctor says, "It looks as if you've been ignoring it too long. I can't tell without an x-ray, but I'd say you've pulverized the already broken bones and possibly broken new ones."

"Huh. Well. How long does surgery take?"

"You'll be on crutches for a couple weeks, then—"

"I don't have time for that."

"W-A-L-K-E-R."

"OK, fine!" She crosses her arms across her chest. "Can I get the surgery this afternoon?"

Dr. Orellana looks like she slapped him. "Today? Impossible. There's scheduling and I have no idea—"

"I need to be in Monaco by tonight."

"Well, you're not going to be in Monaco tonight. They don't have the surgeons for this." He pinches his chin. "I interned with a specialist in Boston. I'll ask her."

"I have my own specialists," she says.

"Have them meet you at Mass General." He steps back and makes a call.

Pia looks at Miguel and me. She rolls her eyes. "Get me out of this."

Miguel speaks for both of us. "You broke your ankle."

"Shit." She scowls. "How the hell … doesn't matter. I'll deal with it. Two weeks? I don't have two weeks."

"Two weeks for the surgical recovery," Doc says over his phone. "You won't walk for eight weeks, minimum. You won't be 100 percent for three months."

He may as well have hit her with a baseball bat. Her stunned eyes close tightly. She taps her lips while thinking. After working with her for two days, I'm getting to know her expressions. She's working her way through dealing with the reality and now needs to make adjustments to her schedule.

While she thinks, Miguel shoulder bumps me. "Welcome to the club."

"To be honest, Miguel," I say even though part of me thinks I shouldn't confide this in him, "I have an interview at Johns Hopkins for med school. I'm not sure—"

He grins. "Today is payday and that means bonus time. Check your banking app."

Staring at him and his I've-got-a-secret grin, I pull up my bank balance. It displays a number that could pay for all four years of med school in advance. There's a message attached to the deposit that reads, "The heroic nature of our work also pays well—Pia." I look up at Miguel with a thousand questions.

His grin gets a notch bigger. "She's hard to work with—in case you haven't noticed. Gets us into dangerous situations without a plan for getting out, expects us to pick up in the middle of the night and follow her into the bowels of hell, thinks we can read her mind while not telling us what's on it. But there's an upside. I've already set up an education fund for my niece and nephew that pays for private school and college. My anonymous scholarship is putting three reservation kids through school as well. But what I love most"—he leans to my ear—"is getting on the elevator in my all-white-doctors-lawyers-and-celebrities building when it's packed full and putting in my key for the penthouse."

Uh huh. Penthouse. Or med school. Tough decision.

Pia snaps her fingers like she just remembered something. Reading her mind, I figure she has everything prioritized and she's ready to start fixing her schedule.

"Hey, Mayor Rick," she says. "I need to speak to you and Lyn."

When they march over, she says, "Rick, my executive planning committee picked Deeping as the location for the SRC two weeks ago. I held up the announcement until I had a chance to see the town up close—"

"You what?" Rick asks while gasping for air.

"I wanted to get a look at the town and the people before rolling forward. I intended to ask the citizens if they want to be associated with me. Events took us in a different direction. So now, I need you to convene a town hall and ask everyone if they want the changes that come with the Sabel Research Center. Twice as many people, higher real estate values—which leads to higher property taxes. Roads torn up for new infrastructure, new schools built, congestion, longer lines, things like that. Progress is messy."

"Well," Rick looks around, "Christine had that all worked out and she—"

"Is no longer mayor," Pia finishes for him.

Lyn steps back as if she'd just heard blasphemy.

"Right." Rick straightens up. A new, more confident look crosses his face. "Lyn, I'm going to need your help."

The two of them walk away, planning their meeting.

"Miguel," Pia says. "You've met Ursula von der Leyen, President of the European Union, right?" When he nods, she asks, "And Christine Legarde, President of the European Central Bank?" He shakes his head, no. "Don't worry, she'll love you. I need you to charm them both. They're still butt-hurt about the satellite deal. They think we stole that contract from Eutelsat. Yeah. Well, we did. Smooth it over. We can open an office in Germany or France if we have to. Give them something."

Her gray-green eyes turn to me like ray guns.

This is the moment of truth: Where do I fit in? The question I've been asking since Jacob Stearne conscripted me into Pia Sabel's inner circle. What's my career path at Sabel Security? More dumpster diving? Interpreting the ramblings of unhoused people? Chasing clues in some obscure town for reasons I still don't understand? I'm really close to telling her not to include me in what she's going to say next. If I am as smart as I think I am, I'll ignore the hazardous-duty bonuses and text Dad to set up that interview at Johns Hopkins. Sure, a tedious mundane life, but an OK income and less danger.

"Isaiah," Pia says and grabs my hand, "If you accept, I have a mission for you. I need you to take my place in Monaco. As you know, this is a special mission for President Williams. You will communicate directly and exclusively with him. You know the stakes. You know what Deng

Zhipeng and his faction are capable of: torture, dismemberment, murder. If you do have to eliminate imminent threats, take any initiative you see fit. There's no such thing as a license to kill, but we have something better: lawyers. I'm not going to order you to do this because it's far too dangerous. I'm asking you as a personal favor. Will you take it?"

She's speaking my language: danger, intrigue, presidents, and noble causes. I consider my choice carefully: med school or heroic work.

I can't stop my grin from growing as I give her a crisp Marine salute and say, "All in, ma'am."

# CHAPTER 61

## SCOTT, THE POLICE CHIEF

MOM. WHY? I STILL CAN'T believe it.

I leave the remnants of my takeout dinner from Brine and Bone in my kitchen nook and answer the door. Amy gives me a hug as soon as it's halfway open.

"Mayor Rick said you weren't answering your phone," she says. "Why didn't you come to the town hall?"

"What did they decide?"

"Nearly unanimous in favor. They're ready to rename the town to Sabelville or Sabel City, whatever she wants. They all went to Eady's to celebrate. They think they've won the lottery."

"Nearly unanimous?"

"You know the nay-sayers: Bud Blaine, Stacey Hartley, Jenni Cornell."

"Yep, they say no to everything before they hear what it is. Bud once told me, 'Change is bad.'"

She laughs. I track back to the kitchen and stare at the Styrofoam box.

Amy follows me in and nods at my barely eaten sandwich. "Not hungry?"

"I've had one too many lobster rolls."

She gasps at my sacrilegious statement. No one in the history of Maine has ever said that. She puts a hand on my shoulder. "I know it's tough, Scotty. We'll get through this. I'm going to take over the bakery and run it while Mom's gone."

"I'm not getting through anything. I'm leaving. Tonight."

"You can't!" She tugs my arm. "I need help with my kids. You can't just run away."

"It's all about you?" I snap.

She looks hurt. I feel bad about my tone of voice and apologize with a remorseful sideways glance. We sit at the table in adjoining chairs pulled out to face each other.

She says, "I'm sorry. I mean, you have a job here. The town needs you. Where would you go?"

"Anywhere. Charleston, Miami, maybe out west. Somewhere far away where they've never heard of me. I can't stay here. Not with everyone looking at me like … I can't stay here."

She doesn't say anything. Her eyes search mine until I look away.

"There's nothing for me here," I say. "I'm alone and—"

"You have me. I'm your sister."

"Are you?" The question comes out before I can stop it. Like a javelin, its sharp and painful point leaves her wounded. "I'm sorry. I didn't mean that. You know I would never mean that. I'm just … it's been a tough day."

"You're my real brother." She strokes my arm again. "You're not the only one in mourning. I lost Mom too, you know. You're all I have now. And I need you. Please stay."

Except for a few years in high school, we were always close. I feel her plea in my heart.

I put my hand on hers. "Come with me, Amy. With Mom's recipes, you could open a bakery anywhere. How does Carmel, California sound?"

I get up and march up the stairs toward my bedroom. Pulling a suitcase from the hall closet, I lay it on my bed with a sad sigh. She follows me and leans against the jamb, playing with her phone.

I'll need five days' worth of clothes. If I can't find a police department that wants me by then, I'll come back, do some laundry, and go back out. I toss in the socks and underwear, then pull some dress shirts and business casual slacks. It's not big city fashion, but it's all I've got. They probably don't wear flannel long sleeves in Miami. Staring at my extra uniforms, I wonder if they would be appropriate. I haven't resigned yet. Would wearing my uniform be a good thing or a bad thing? Bad, I decide. Since I'm applying in person and I'd be far outside my jurisdiction, I'd look like I was impersonating one of theirs. No, better to show up looking like I was on vacation and thought their department looked like a nice place. That way I won't seem desperate.

"Scotty?" Amy stands at my dresser, holding a policeman's hat from my childhood. "Is this from fourth grade?"

I pull it from her hand. "Leave that alone."

"It's from the school play, right? You played the cop." She stops herself from laughing. "You still have that?"

"Yes." I set it back in its sacred place. "It was a pivotal day in my life. That's when I decided ..."

I stop talking and brush the dust off the brim.

She picks up my Little League trophy. "Player of the year? I didn't know they voted you—"

"They give those to everyone." I take it from her and put it back down where it belongs.

"No, they don't. The other kids got benchwarmer awards the size of your finger."

That was a good year for me. Mom stood in the stands cheering so loud the other parents had to tell her to quit bragging. We did well only because the league threw Deeping in with rural Oxford County that year. Beating the hicks from the sticks was no big deal. But it sure was fun. Come to think of it, Mom forced the league to gerrymander us in there. There wasn't anything she wouldn't do for us.

"Do you think Teresa or Thomas should play Little League?" Amy's question stirs me from my revelry.

"It's all about soccer these days," I say.

I find my black dress shoes in the back of the closet. I'll need to polish them. Should I wear my cop shoes with the two-inch-thick solid rubber soles? In an interview, they would send the message: *I'm one of you.*

Amy picks up a framed photo of the two of us at her college graduation. As she does, she sees the picture right behind it: the two of us at her high school graduation. And behind that, graduation from eighth grade. Next to it, the two of us at her wedding. Behind that, Amy and her date leaving for Prom. She turns to me with a warm, loving face.

I feel myself flush with embarrassment. "Yeah, so what? I'm sentimental. OK? Don't make a big deal out of it."

My phone vibrates with a text from Isaiah. It reads, "I didn't get a chance to say goodbye. If you've never read the *Oedipus Cycle*, the three plays about the man and his children, he blamed himself for his tragedy and wandered the countryside in shame. Everyone else knew it wasn't his fault. In *Oedipus at Colonus*, the new king of Thebes begged him to return. Don't be Oedipus. Don't blame yourself. Everything you did was honorable. It was a privilege to work with you. You're a good man, Chief. Stay strong—and if you ever feel less than strong, call me."

Amy pulls my screen so she can read it. I let her have the phone and grab the cop shoes.

"See?" she says. "Isaiah agrees with me."

"He's just doing damage control for his boss. Notice she didn't send the text?"

My phone dings in Amy's hand. She looks at me. "Oh, really? Guess what?"

"I don't care." I toss the extra shoes in my suitcase and think about toiletries.

Amy shoves the phone in front of me.

Ms. Sabel texted, "When my father was murdered, I suffered from a deep depression. I couldn't let it show because thousands of employees needed me to carry on. I know how tough it is to get through such a loss. We're not so different, Scott. I've been there. The anesthesiologist is waiting for me to stop texting, but as soon as I'm out of surgery and clear headed, I'm going to call you. We'll talk it through. No bullshit, no psychology, just two people who've lived through blessings and tragedies. Don't ignore my call or I'll come up there in person."

I push Amy's hand away. "OK, so they conspired to make me feel better. So what?"

Despite my bitterness, I feel Ms. Sabel's text. She and I have a connection through the broader family of adopted kids. My story didn't leave me with a yacht the size of the *Titanic*, but the one thing I learned from her is that money can't heal a shattered soul. Healing comes from friends and family.

That thought makes me appreciate Amy even more. I turn to her. "Come with me. Alaska, Hawaii, somewhere far from here. We'll start over. We'll make new friends, make a clean start."

She thinks about it and chokes back tears. "What if I agree with Bud? Change is bad?"

We escape tears with a weak laugh. I say, "Yeah. What was I thinking?"

Someone pounds on the door downstairs. Kubari Eady's voice booms through the wood. "Open up, Scott. I gotta talk to you."

His tone is not friendly. I'm a bit shaken since we worked so well together against Devino. Now that our common enemy is defeated, has he gone back to treating me like an adversary? I apologized. I haven't had time to take Ms. Sabel's advice and invite him over for dinner. One thing I know: I can't leave town without working this out with him.

I make my way downstairs and yank the door open. A mass of people stand behind Kubari: Rick Tara, Mike Culpepper, Kathy Butler, Lyn Avery, Mike Tenenbaum, and Cheryl Walton are the ones I can see. More cover my walkway, lawn, and spill into the street. Every damn one of them has their phone lit up and held aloft. Kubari holds a giant covered chafing dish in his hands while balancing on crutches.

Rick puffs out his chest and says, "Scott Jacobsen, years ago, the town of Deeping adopted you as our Police Chief. Now, we ask you to adopt us as your family."

Over his heavy stainless-steel chafer, Kubari says, "Don't you dare say no, muthafucka. I just got you trained to be the best cop north of Miami. You can't walk out and make me go through all that shit again with some other dude."

He thrusts the chafer into my chest hard enough to send me back a step. The smell of pork ribs wafts up from it. He does make the best ribs I've ever tasted. Kubari keeps pushing me back. I end up stepping to the side as the entire population of Deeping streams into my living room. Someone has a stack of paper plates, another person is carrying napkins with Eady's logo on them. Others are carrying bottles of various liquors.

Somehow Crazy Kitty and Tom Baird slide by me. That's not going to end well.

"Come on now," Kubari says. "I didn't save your scrawny ass so I could go hungry at dinner time. Put that thing down and let's eat. That is, if my home-cooked ribs are good enough for you."

"You know, Kubari," I say with a grin spreading across my face. "I am SO sick of lobster."

**THE END**

# THANK YOU!

Thank you for choosing my book. As an independent writer, I live and die on word-of-mouth referrals and book reviews. If you liked this book, please tell everyone you know and leave reviews all over the place. I will be eternally grateful. If you didn't like this book, let's just keep that between us, OK?

If you can't get enough of Pia and her *advisors**, checkout the series at SeeleyJames.com/books. While you're there, join my newsletter to get discounts, drawings, news, outtakes, and more about the Sabel Agents club on Facebook! Every week or so (sometimes I'm lazy), I'll let you know about the book in progress, personal triumphs & tragedies, what I'm reading and other fun stuff.

I love hearing from fans. Don't hesitate to email or message me on Facebook to let me know what you think.

*I like you already.

## NOW THAT YOU'VE READ THIS BOOK, WHICH ONE SHOULD YOU READ NEXT?
## HTTPS://SEELEYJAMES.COM/BOOKS

# TRUTH IN FICTION

As an avid reader of fiction, I'm often curious about the facts, physics, and philosophies of the books I read. In this book, I've written about some deeply personal, and sometimes painful, topics. Because some scenes were derived from firsthand experiences and others from research, I feel you deserve a peek at the extensive notes I've taken during the planning process for this book. To address and preempt commonly asked questions:

1) **Do adopted children and parents really face challenges of acceptance?** Many do, some do not. The kernel for this story was based on many conversations in my life. One all-too-common encounter took place between my uncle, his second wife, and me. My uncle and his first wife had adopted and raised two wonderful children. When his wife died, he later remarried a woman who had children of her own. Since I have one adopted and two biological children, she asked me to tell my uncle how much more of a connection parents have to their "real children." It was something I'd heard from other parents many times. I always find it untrue and deeply offensive. I told my uncle, "I feel the exact same connection to all three of my children. Unfortunately, many around me do not support her with the same love and affection they shower on my biological children."

2) **Do adopted children really face mental health challenges?** Don't we all? Being adopted is inherently a more difficult reality, regardless of the reason behind the adoption. Every family is different, and most have happy lives. But many deal with issues of abandonment and rejection. I have personally seen several adopted children struggle with and overcome serious mental health crises. I've also seen the people around them react in unpredictable ways; some without compassion and others with remarkable empathy. A few of my family members have been eager to help, others have

helped when asked, and still others have been painfully disengaged. I've also known many adopted children who have had no problems whatsoever. No matter what, all adopted families will benefit from your unconditional love and support.

3) **Are those examples of institutionalized racism true?** Sadly, the book touches on just a few of many, many instances. While doing my research, I quickly found hundreds of examples where African Americans were denied the benefits of programs their own taxes helped fund. The biggest problem I faced was selecting which of the many examples should be included. Early in the writing process, I had to choose the direction of the mystery. I decided to leave the hard facts to great non-fiction writers like Ta-Nehisi Coats, Brittney C. Cooper, Jennifer E. Cobbina, and James Baldwin, to name a few. If the topic interests or frightens you, I recommend you read about the facts and find a way to help reverse injustices both historic and ongoing.

4) **Are those quotes from Sophocles and Aeschylus real?** Yes! I've taken the liberty of adjusting a word or two here and there for story clarity, but they're largely direct quotes. I used the Jebb translation of 1904, as Isaiah notes in the story, because its affected Elizabethan English is better at obscuring the clues. There are more accessible translations using modern English, but that takes the fun out of keeping you guessing. (Yes, I love torturing readers. Ha!) I've read several versions of the Greek tragedies though I've never had any formal training in them. If you have, and you think I've completely screwed it up and have it all wrong, please keep it to yourself. My ignorance is bliss right now so don't harsh my mellow.

5) **Is this town of Deeping a real place?** Yes! Probably. OK … no. First, the name *Deeping, Maine* is an homage to Agatha Christie who often poked fun at the many oddly named towns in Britain. One of her settings she named *Much Deeping*. I found that hilarious. Some elements for my fictional town were drawn from the real town of Ogunquit, Maine. In the 1980s, before it was gentrified, I lived in Annapolis, Maryland and always loved the location, so I based Main

Street on that town. When I lived there, there was a bakery that had the most amazing brioche I've ever tasted.

Still not sure how much of this story you believe? You're not alone. So, check out my OneNote file for this book where I stashed some of my research https://seeleyjames.com/rembrandt-notes. Not all the research made it into the book and some research I forgot to drag into the folder, but there's plenty to chew on.

Thanks for getting this far, you're now my favorite reader!

# ACKNOWLEDGMENTS

My heartfelt thanks to the people who, without hesitation or concern for bodily injury, gave their time and attention to make *The Rembrandt Decision* the greatest book ever written by a human. (That's my opinion, and I'm sticking with it.) Without the insightful contributions of these few selfless, hardworking readers, editors, and writers, the story would teeter on the verge of putting you to sleep better than a Sabel Dart. I am forever in debt to these brave souls:

- **Extraordinary Editor and Idea man:** Lance Charnes, author of the highly acclaimed *Doha 12, SOUTH,* not to mention the DeWitt Agency series: *THE COLLLECTION, STEALING GHOSTS, CHASING CLAY* and, if you like ass-kicking heroines: *ZRADA and ENGAÑO.* I highly recommend his exciting novels, visit http://wombatgroup.com. With his contribution on nearly every scene, this book is a more powerful story.

- **Medical Advisor and Character Diviner:** Dr. Louis Kirby, famed neurologist and author of *SHADOW OF EDEN.* http://louiskirby.com His analysis ratcheted up the tension, and now the bad guy is badder, the good guys are gooder, and the story more engrossing.

- **Amazing Editor and Character Arc Speicalist:** Mary Maddox, horror and dark fantasy novelist, and author of the *DAEMON WORLD* series and the fantastic thrillers: *DARK ROOM* and *HOMETOWN BOYS.* http://marymaddox.com. Her analysis made each character more real and engaging. And also exposed a clue that gave away the ending!

- **Comedian and Brilliant Idea Man:** Kubari Eady, whose comedy act is sure to move from Zoom to Netflix any day now. Yes, he leant his name to the bar owner. Kubari's ideas helped change Isaiah from just another sidekick to the character you just found fascinating. You can find Kubari at http://comedywithkubari.com Catch his act!

- **Modern Culture Editor:** Amelia Montooth is a social media strategist for Crooked Media who has previously worked for political campaigns and important non-profits. She kept me honest about police statistics, racism, and social sensitivities. Without her help, Scott wouldn't have had a learning curve (aka character arc).

**My additional thanks to the beta readers** who aided and abetted my endeavors. No amount of proofreading, professional or amateur, can match their diligence in finding the niggling little malapropisms, mondegreens, spoonerisms, homophones, and actual typos: Rick Tara, Michael Davis, Fritzi Redgrave, Eleanor Anderson, and Serena Montague. But don't blame them for my bad grammar. That's all mine.

**Above and beyond the usual acknowledgements, I'd like to thank the many fans who leant their names** (and some family members, frenemies, and neighbors) to the character list in this book. When I wrote my first novel, I asked my fans if anyone would like to have a character named after them. Five people said yes (only one, Miguel Rodriguez, stuck around for all fourteen books). When I started writing this one, I thought I should try that again and posted a call for character names on Facebook. Thirty-eight fans signed up so quickly, I had to take down the post or I might've had five hundred. In addition to those, Phil Jacobsen won a drawing for the naming rights to the central family. You can thank him for the dead guy (he chose that role for himself!), the baker, the police chief, and the sister. May his family forgive him. Also, Jose Orellana, a long-suffering fan, won the second drawing to name the town's doctor. He chose to name Doc in memory of his father, also named Jose Orellana.

**Here is the full list (in no particular order) of the wonderful fans who willing sacrificed their dignity for the characters in this novel**, if you see them in public, please pat them on the back and tell them it'll all be OK eventually: Christine Jacobsen, Amy Jacobsen, Scott Jacobsen, Phil Jacobsen, Bill Koller, Jose Orellana, Kitty Robinson, Craig Balch, Mike Culpepper, Jana Siverling, Julie Stafford, Mike Tenenbaum, Joanne Ranzell, Diane McGar, Cheryl Walton, Rick Tara, Stacey Hartley, Lyn Avery, Jill Williams, Mike & Nikki Larson, Nancy Shepherd, Debra Freeto, Pat Armstrong, Bud Blaine, Karen Smith, Jenni Cornell, Mary Arnold, Leslie Dingwall, Michael Arnold, Eleanor Andersen, LeeAnn Pratt, Olivia Marie Benton, Madeline Grace Benton, Tim Dunn, Chrisana Droigk, Joy Cobb, Ruth Jackson, Tom Baird, Kathy Butler, Kathy Menezes, Siobahn Allen, Paul Thompson, Bud & Maureen Taggart.

# SEE THE SEELEY JAMES COLLECTION

International intrigue, neo-Nazis, corruption, and justice for the underdogs. Join the millions of fans who think of Pia Sabel and Jacob Stearne as old friends and give the series a full five stars.

## VISIT SEELEYJAMES.COM/BOOKS

### FOR COUPONS, PRIZES, MUGS, T-SHIRTS!

# ABOUT THE AUTHOR

His near-death experiences range from talking a jealous husband into putting the gun down to spinning out on an icy freeway in heavy traffic without touching anything. His resume ranges from washing dishes to global technology management. His personal life stretches from homeless at 17, adopting a 3-year-old at 19, getting married at 37, fathering his last child at 43, hiking the Grand Canyon Rim-to-Rim several times a year, and taking the occasional nap.

His writing career ranges from humble beginnings with short stories in The Battered Suitcase, to being awarded a Medallion from the Book Readers Appreciation Group. Seeley is best known for his Sabel Security series of thrillers featuring athlete and heiress Pia Sabel and her bodyguard, unhinged veteran Jacob Stearne. One of them kicks ass and the other talks to the wrong god.

His love of creativity began at an early age, growing up at Frank Lloyd Wright's School of Architecture in Arizona and Wisconsin. He carried his imagination first into a successful career in sales and marketing, and then to his real love: fiction.

For more books featuring Pia Sabel and Jacob Stearne, visit: SeeleyJames.com/books. Also, check the sales and discounts page for special offers: SeeleyJames.com/sale.

facebook.com/seeleyjamesauthor

instagram.com/seeleyjamesauth

bookbub.com/authors/seeley-james